Everything She Wanted

ROSEY KAUR HWANG

SUGAR SHACK BOOKS
CHARLOTTETOWN

Everything She Wanted.

Sugar Shack Books is an imprint of Pownal Street Press. Requests for permission to make copies of any part of the work should be emailed to permissions at hello@pownalstreetpress.com. Our books may be purchased for promotional, educational, or business use. Please contact your local bookseller or Pownal Street Press to purchase.

pownalstreetpress.com • @sugarshackbooks

Cataloguing data available from Library Archives Canada:
ISBN 978-1-997918-14-1 • eBook ISBN 978-1-997918-15-8

Edited by Mo Duffy. Copyedited by Alison Strumberger. Proofread by Lara Hyde. Cover design by Erin Craig. Book design by Jordan Beaulieu. The text was set in Baskerville.

Pownal Street Press gratefully acknowledges Mi'kma'ki, the ancestral and unceded territory of the Mi'kmaq First Nation on whose land our office is located.

Printed and bound in Canada.

1 2 3 4 5 26 27 28 29 30

For the women who never had a choice and the women who now do:
You deserve everything you've ever wanted.

&

For you, Mom, reading this from heaven.

PROLOGUE: NISHA 2.0

Here, I can be anyone. I can be her.

The woman I fantasize about. The one who has it all together, a model of pure class and sophistication.

Confident.

Empowered.

Unattached.

Beautiful.

Free.

I carefully apply red lipstick, press my lips together, and stand back to take in my reflection in the ladies' room mirror while the women around me do the same. We're all priming and posing for an invisible audience while elevating into a cloud of floral perfume. Elegant chairs and the floor-length mirror make it feel like I'm in a high-end hotel, not a bar.

As I take in my reflection, I almost can't believe it's me. My long-sleeved black dress is short and tight, hugging my curves. It hung in the back of my closet for far too long, hidden behind my sarees and lehengas, but I can finally wear it here, where I don't have to worry about prying eyes judging me. I added some highlights to my long, dark brown hair just a few days ago, and I feel lighter, too. Like a new version of me.

I can be her so effortlessly when my old tethers are gone. When I don't need to remember my past or my many flaws, and no one is here to remind me of them. Still, my stomach flutters as I step into this new reality in this new city.

I leave the bathroom and make my way back to the bar. Heads turn and I welcome the gazes, though I'm not sure if they're meant for me or the woman behind me. For a moment, I let myself pretend I'm interesting. I rarely get to be in the spotlight—for most of my life, I've tried to stay out of it, but not tonight.

"Nisha, there you are." Rachel hands me a drink and I take in the soft brown waves that frame her stunning face. She is Japanese American, and striking without even trying. Her emerald eyes light up as we clink glasses, and I take a sip, gin and citrus notes hitting me in equal measure. I hold the cool liquid in my mouth for a moment, savouring the rich taste.

I still can't believe that Rachel offered to let me move into her swanky condo at a steeply discounted rate, making my relocation so much easier. Even though we've only seen each other sporadically since we first met during my semester off in Mexico, we easily picked up where we left off. While I told my family I was doing research for university, what I was really doing was escaping all the drama. It was one of the rare moments I let loose without worrying about the repercussions. This time we aren't doing tequila shots with strangers, but it's just as fun being here with her.

"This place is amazing," I say as I gaze around the room. Yellow, pink, and purple vertical LEDs hang from the ceiling, and candles line the bar creating a cozy, stylish ambiance. The bar is fully stocked and backlit with a dark red glow. The DJ plays an eclectic blend of electronica, accompanied by live trumpet. Everything about the bar screams chic. I love it. Sure, there are great places in Toronto, but everything is fresh here in Vancouver. Intriguing places instead of the same old bars frequented by the same old people.

"It's great, right?"

"Such a vibe," I say as I continue to admire the surroundings.

"Let's take a selfie." Rachel pulls out her phone and I put on a genuine smile. Something I'm not used to doing. She takes a few photos at different angles, and we swipe through the shots, trying to find the best one.

The bartender comes up to us. "Rachel, we lined up some of our best mocktails for you to try over in that booth." He points past the end of the bar. "And a meet-and-greet with the chef."

I had forgotten that while this was a night out for me, for Rachel it was work. She had amassed a huge online following, and clients often hired her to share information about Vancouver bars and restaurants.

"Thanks, I'll be right over."

He nods and goes back to serving the other customers.

"Join me?" She gives me an encouraging look.

"Is it okay if I just hang out here for a bit?" I'm still a little nervous about being online too much, always worried someone I know will see me.

"Are you sure?" She hesitates, not wanting to leave me alone on our first night out together as not only good friends but also roommates.

"I'm fine. Go. I'm going to enjoy the ambience." I sit back on a barstool and shoo her away. She is already doing so much for me. I don't want her to feel like she has to babysit me, too.

"Okay, if you're sure." She squeezes my arm and walks over to the booth. She glances back and says, "I may need you later."

"Got it." I agreed to pose in a few photos to help her make it look like this was the place to be. Luckily, she'll let me curate which ones to post.

I breathe in the atmosphere and scan the room. A few girlfriends chat away at a table without a care in the world. There is a couple I presume are on a first date, given the way they look at each other. So many people just stand around and sway to the music, fancy colourful drinks in hand.

Usually, I'm self-conscious sitting alone anywhere and will instinctively reach for my phone, but this time, I relax.

I sit for a while, taking it all in, when I feel eyes on me. I glance around the room, and that's when I see him casually looking my way. Cool with a hint of something I can't put my finger on. Self-assurance, maybe?

He looks grounded and unbothered, like he doesn't have anything to prove to anyone. He knows who he is.

At first, I think I'm imagining it, but then our eyes meet and he smiles. I quickly turn away to take another sip of my drink, but find my glass almost empty. I sit there awkwardly but try to act casual. When I glimpse him moving closer from the corner of my eye, my heart races.

Dressing up like someone special is one thing, but acting like that empowered version of me is a whole other thing.

"Can I get you a drink?" He stares at my glass and gives me a breathtaking smile as he leans on the bar next to me. He's hot as hell, and I freeze. I can't glance away from his piercing blue eyes, and I stare for longer than is socially acceptable.

I catch myself shifting uncomfortably while trying to look like the picture of elegance, and I turn toward the bar as he takes the stool next to me. I catch a whiff of his cologne as he sits down, and the scent is intoxicating: musky, with notes of dark pine and sandalwood, like a forbidden forest. He smells like a delicious mistake I want to make.

"I, um, sure." *Act like her.* I criticize myself silently. It isn't every day you get to reinvent yourself.

The bartender materializes as if on cue.

"What can I get you?"

The beautiful stranger gestures for me to speak first.

"A gin and tonic, please."

"I'll have the same."

He turns to face me, and I take in more of him. He's striking—the sharp lines of his jaw frame his symmetrical face. His hair is a soft golden blonde, but his eyebrows and lashes are darker, adding intriguing dimension. His skin is smooth and radiant, like I'm staring at a face online with a filter. Sun-kissed like he just got back from a tropical vacation, with a hint of stubble forming. It's a face that belongs on the cover of *GQ* and not seated beside me. A slight smirk plays on his lips—he knows the effect of his presence.

"You're new here."

A statement, not a question.

"Yes, I guess I am," I start. "I haven't been here before." I stop there, not wanting to let on I'm still new to this city, to this life, to this me.

He oozes a confidence and luxury that can't be faked. I catch sight of his Omega Seamaster watch and look down with what I hope is a casual glance, taking in his tailored pants and immaculate shoes. It's his presence and deep gaze that reel me in most. He looks at me like he sees me, and a part of me wants him to. Not just Fantasy Nisha, but the real Nisha too.

"What lights you up these days?" He leans in and looks at me expectantly, like it's the most normal thing to ask.

"Oh." I look away and hesitate. "I'm not sure how to answer that." I don't like small talk, but jumping straight into something deeper? I'm not used to that either.

He smiles. "Let me try again. What are you working on that you're passionate about right now?"

"Well, I work at a tech start-up in marketing. I can't say too much, but we're working on some exciting things with AI." I make up a half-truth, not used to talking so openly to attractive strangers in bars. The city is sprinkled with hundreds of start-ups, so I know it isn't too unusual. I hope he won't ask me which one.

"Is that what you really want to be doing?" he asks.

"I'd love to be in investor relations. I've prepared so many pitch decks, it would be nice to present them." He nods encouragingly, and he makes me want to open up. "It's fun to see the impact right away of what you're creating."

He gives me a look I can't quite decipher, then asks, "If you could create anything, what would it be?"

I pause, thoughtfully. No one has ever asked me anything like this, and it's nice for a change. More than nice.

"Tech tools that support people, no matter what their background."

He shifts closer to me like he's thinking and wants to ask more, but he says nothing. He's taking whatever I'm willing to give him. Not pushing me or wanting more than I have the capacity to give.

"What about you?" I move the attention away from myself, unnerved by his direct questions.

"I'm an IT consultant. Short-term contracts with whoever needs me," he shares modestly, but I can tell by the way he's dressed that he commands big dollars.

The bartender comes by with our drinks. I lift my glass to his, faking confidence.

"Cheers."

"Cheers." He clinks his glass to mine and gives me a little wink that sends a shiver down my spine.

"So, what do you like to do for fun?" he asks.

Fun? Is that even part of my vocabulary anymore? My life is mostly working and trying to make my family happy—an impossible task.

"I love live music actually." I look over at the trumpet player, who's packing up after just finishing his set.

"Really? Me too." He glances down at his watch. "There's this new jazz place that opened near here with a late show this evening," he says, taking another sip of his drink.

"I was going to head there in a bit if you want to join me." I see a glint of something in his eyes, and my heart flutters. I smooth the napkin on the bar before putting my drink down. My pulse speeds up. I know I shouldn't be having this conversation—I'm here to focus on my work. I tell myself it's harmless.

What would Fantasy Nisha do? She would go for it.

"That sounds nice, actually."

What kind of guy are you going to attract dressed like that? Not a husband. My mom's voice leeches into my thoughts abruptly, threatening to ruin whatever this is.

I squash it down with another gulp of my drink. I won't let my old life and limitations take over now.

The bartender rushes over.

"Sorry to interrupt, but Rachel wants you for a few photos." He fidgets with his apron and gives me a tight-lipped smile.

"Oh, of course. Just give me a sec." I flash the bartender a reassuring smile.

"My friend is helping to promote this place. She helps local businesses with social media marketing." I look over at his gorgeous face.

"That's awesome. Good for her." He seems sincere in his praise, which is refreshing. Some people don't get it.

"Maybe I could meet you there in a bit?" I slide off the stool and gaze up at him, not sure what to do with myself.

"Sure. It's called Prohibition. Just over on Howe Street, about a five-minute drive from here." He gives me a look that makes me lightheaded with anticipation.

I walk away gracefully, swaying in a way that I hope is both alluring and aloof. My heart is racing, and it takes everything in me to play it cool.

* * *

The photos with Rachel take longer than expected, but there's still time to go to the jazz club, even though old me would never do anything like this.

Rachel offers to come with me, but I tell her I'll be fine. I know she's tired after a long day and night.

"Make sure to text me if you need an escape hatch," she calls out, as she leaves me waiting for my Uber.

"I will," I call back. I relish the security of having someone to rely on.

I step out of the car in front of Prohibition. I walk in, pay the cover, and gaze around the venue in awe. Low blue couches surround circular tables, and blue high-backed seats line the stone bar. Black drapes adorn the walls, and a vintage chandelier adds to the opulent feel. It has a clandestine vibe that makes me feel even more like Fantasy Nisha: sexy, illicit, dark, and daring.

The club is heaving with people, and I have no idea how I'm going to find mystery man again. I scan the crowd, starting with the bar, and after a while I finally spot him seated on a couch, looking like a daydream I couldn't even dare to let myself imagine. One spotless shoe rests on his knee, and he holds a glass of amber liquid while glancing down at his watch. He looks up and scans the room.

I almost don't want him to see me so I can just stay here and observe him from afar. No such luck. His eyes meet mine, and he gives me a little smile that sends a thrill through me. I gather up my courage and take slow steps toward him, even as my mind races with reasons I should leave. I promised myself I would never do casual, having it ingrained in me to 'find the one,' but maybe this could be something more. It probably couldn't hurt, since I'm approaching the big three zero and don't have any prospects on the horizon—a fact my family finds every opportunity to remind me of. Luckily, the few drinks I had earlier dull my senses enough to subdue my anxious thoughts.

He stands to greet me like an old-fashioned gentleman.

"You made it."

I'm mesmerized as I take in his eyes again, matching the blue all around me, and speckled with what looked like a scattering of stars from a distant universe.

"I'm glad you came." He gestures to the seat next to him, but there isn't much space, so when I sit, I'm pressed right up against him and the woman next to me. My already short dress shifts even higher, and I try not to pull it down self-consciously. He moves to face me and gives me more room. The jazz band is between sets, so we have a chance to talk.

He subtly looks me up and down as if he needs to drink me in. I take a moment to do the same and notice his shirt is unbuttoned at the top, the dark grey poplin contrasting with his slightly tanned skin and bright eyes. I want to run my fingers over the cool, crisp fabric.

I smile, acting more confident than I am.

He signals to the server, who takes my drink order.

"How were the photos?" he asks, and I like that he's curious.

"Fun and also not fun. Not my thing, you know." I try to figure out what to do with my hands and decide to rest one on my leg and the other on the seat between us, my fingertips skimming his thigh.

"What is your thing?"

Definitely not jazz clubs with strangers in the middle of the night is how I want to respond, but I don't.

"Mostly staying behind the camera and out of the spotlight," is what I say instead. "That's my thing." I know I'm supposed to pretend to be sultrier, but how he looks at me is disarming my defences.

"Could have fooled me," he says. "You totally give movie star vibes." Heat rushes through me at his compliment, even as I suspect he's used this line before.

The jazz band strikes up, so I don't have to respond, and it's nice to sit next to him and have a drink. It's been months since I've been on a date, with all the logistics of the move, and even longer since I had anyone look at me like that. I don't know if anyone ever has.

He leans in to whisper in my ear so I can hear him over the saxophone set that just started. "What do you like to take pictures of?" His voice reverberates in my ear, and I suppress a shiver.

"Beautiful things." I turn to him a little more but not too much, already realizing we're too close. "Coffee, books, sunsets." This time, I look into his eyes. I would love to take a picture of those eyes.

"What about people?" he asks, as if he's reading my thoughts.

"Sometimes. It's generally frowned upon to take pictures of beautiful people without their permission." I pause. "But I might make an exception." I stare at him, pretend to measure him up in a frame. He gives me a little smirk at my compliment.

He continues to ask me thoughtful questions in between enjoying the music. I answer truthfully and don't hold back like I usually do, but all too soon the set is over, and people are leaving.

"I have a lot of beautiful things at my place you might like to photograph." He looks at me intensely and I forget to breathe.

My hair falls on my face as I look away, and he reaches out and pulls it back, running his fingers along the length of it.

"What kinds of things?"

"Oh, you know, artifacts, paintings, things like that." His eyes drop to my mouth, and I know taking photos is not what he has in mind for us at all. "No sunsets though, but there will be a sunrise soon," he says as he arches a brow.

My heart beats out of control.

When the bill comes, I reach for my purse, but he taps his phone on the reader before I even get the chance.

"Thank you," I say as we get up.

"No problem."

He smiles at me and my legs wobble as we weave through the now empty tables.

We walk outside where the cool night air hits me, and I can feel the buzz of the alcohol begin to subside. This act, being here with him, is already way outside of my comfort zone, and the familiar insecurity and anxiety paws at me, looking for a foothold.

As he steps closer, I get a waft of his crisp pine scent with dark notes of smooth and smoky sandalwood. It ripples around me, tempting me and taking over my senses. A scent that I would love to have linger on my pillow. Desire stirs within me and mixes with my apprehension.

What if?

He takes my hand gently, and my heart hammers out of my chest.

I want to reinvent myself, but truthfully, I'm not sure if I'm ready for anything like this, as hypnotic as he is.

"So, my place?" He gazes at me expectantly. My heart rises to my throat and I can't meet his eyes. I pull my hand away from his too fast, and my feet move away from him without me even telling them to.

"I'm sorry, I can't." I take a few more steps away from him.

"Wait, I don't even know your name."

"Nisha," I say. I take in one last glimpse of ocean blue before I turn around and walk briskly away.

I look at my phone and see an Uber just a minute away, and before I know it, I'm jumping inside and away from him. I put my hand on my heart to help give myself a moment of calm. I feel flushed and foolish.

After the panic subsides, I realize I don't even know his name. I know nothing about him, not really. I tell myself that it doesn't matter. That he was attracted to *her*, not me, the woman I was so desperately pretending to be. My mind tells me it's for the best—but regret lodges itself in my stomach and I wonder if I'll ever see him again.

1. THE LIST

ONE YEAR LATER

Every almost thirty-something girl wants:

1. a Bollywood movie-esque love that feels as good #IRL as it looks on Instagram
2. a matcha latte, half sweet (because of calories, obviously)
3. dolla dolla bills because we like expensive things
4. real friends (you know those special ones that hold back your hair while you vomit into the toilet)
5. a LinkedIn-worthy career, like *Look at me, I'm killing it at adulting and now everyone back in Toronto is envious.*

Other people have resolutions, but I make lists because a to-do list is much easier to check off than a resolution. I mean, don't most resolutions fail by February, anyway? But a list I can constantly refer to and use to monitor my progress is just an incredible life hack.

"Nisha, extra-sweet matcha latte," the barista calls out.

I take my drink from the counter and settle back into my booth. Out the window, the clouds hide the sun and it's softly drizzling, making the morning even cozier.

I take out my fancy pen and hold it in position, ready to continue the list and reflect on my growth over the last year.

I'm making real progress on almost everything—besides the extra-sweet latte I'm sipping—who can make it through the day on half-sweet anyway? I cross 'half-sweet' off the list just as my phone rings.

Mom never calls this early. My heart beats frantically even before I hear her voice. I place my pen on the polished wooden coffee table, mentally preparing myself for the conversation.

"Mom, is everything okay?"

"You didn't call me back yesterday. Why even have a phone if you never pick up?"

"Sorry, I had to work late." I take a deep, calming breath.

"Work is more important than your mom?"

"No, of course not." Then another one.

I won't let her trigger me anymore. I have so much going for me now—even my mom must see that.

"Are you at work?"

"Not yet. Just getting coffee."

"You should make cha at home and bring it to work, like I did for your father."

I smile as I think about him and remember the soft cinnamon and cardamom fragrance that would drift into my room every morning when I was younger.

"I know, but it doesn't taste as good as yours," I say as she tuts at me. It's true. I can never get the blend of spices just right.

"Did they promote you yet?"

I dig my manicured nails into my palm before responding.

I'm positive my next promotion is right around the corner, and that's why I'm slogging it out every single day at one of the hottest start-ups in Vancouver, Evolve Tech Industries. They'll realize I'm an incredible asset to the marketing team and the company, and then I can finally have some savings instead of living paycheque to paycheque.

"Not yet, Mom. But I'm sure it will happen soon."

Silence greets me on the other end, and I quell the doubt rising in my gut.

I pick up my pen and add an arrow next to LinkedIn-worthy career to show this is a work in progress, even as my hand trembles.

"What about the wedding?"

"The wedding?" I echo. Confusion hovers on the line between us.

"Have you and Eshaan set a date for the wedding? Your Mama Ji was asking."

I sigh.

Eshaan and I aren't even engaged yet, and my mom is already pushing us to lock down a wedding date.

"We're going to wait until after the engagement. Then we'll decide." I tighten my jaw as I wait for her response.

The tightness subsides a little as I think about Eshaan, my soon-to-be fiancé, my Bollywood happily ever after, my incredible love story. He is a man that my family actually approves of, and they have extremely high standards. He checks all the boxes: good—meaning rich and reputable—family; great career in his family's successful business; owns his own place; drives a super nice car. The best part is that he's madly in love with me, and we're making it official soon with an epic engagement ceremony. I let my pen glide across the page with a bold checkmark.

"Wait? You know you're turning thirty this year. Preeti was already married five years and pregnant with Aman by then."

She just had to bring up Preeti, my perfect, amazing sister.

I lean back against the cushion, calling on support in any way I can.

"I know, Mom." I try to keep the resentment from my voice. I wish she could see how great I'm doing, how the puzzle pieces of my love life and career are finally falling into place.

"No husband, no kids, no house, no car...and at your age! What are people going to say?"

My shoulders tense and my throat goes dry as I try to ignore the blatant dig. Instead, I take a sip from my matcha latte, letting the extra-sweetness wash over my tongue and erase the bitterness lingering in my mouth. *It's too early for this.*

"Your father would have wanted you to be married by now." She clicks her tongue, and her disapproval sinks into my wounds, opening them up again.

"Mom, please." My shoulders slump and my breaths are shallow.

"Fine. I know you don't care what anyone thinks. Always thinking of yourself, not your family." With that, she abruptly hangs up.

I sit back in the booth, deflated. Instantly, my list and my progress look ridiculous. I'm a fool to think I have anything together when a single call from my mom puts me into a tailspin.

I'm turning thirty this year, but when I talk to my mom I'm sixteen again, incompetent and never good enough. It doesn't matter that I'm working at one of the most talked-about start-ups in the city and they wanted me so badly, they relocated me here.

I take the lid off my matcha latte and inhale the sweet scent of vanilla mixed with a touch of earthy green tea, letting it comfort me briefly. Then I pop the lid back on, stuff my notebook and pen back into my bag, and pull on my coat.

The coat. It's something Rachel and I bought together when I first moved here, when she suggested I upgrade my wardrobe to become the most successful version of me. It makes me smile every time I wear it. It's something Fantasy Nisha would wear—*she* has her shit together and isn't just making things up as she goes along.

I stand and look around the busy café, the office workers all dressed pristinely. I imagine a life where I belong, where I have a voice, where I can speak my mind. I worry that someone will see through my polished facade and discover the broken little girl pretending to be a sophisticated woman.

I step outside and the breeze grants me a brief reprieve from my tumultuous thoughts. The sidewalk is busy as people rush to their offices, and the streets are bumper to bumper. I usually love the hum of city life, but today I feel the chaos of it, and I wish for more calm.

I walk to the office on autopilot, drifting between my worries and fears, when I find myself staring at the back of someone who looks familiar, but I can't figure out why. It's something about his perfectly tailored suit. Before I glimpse his face, he walks through my office building's revolving door.

My heart races foolishly.

There's no way that's who I think it is.

I'm imagining things, like always.

I tug my coat around me even tighter, suddenly feeling cold despite the sun's warm rays peeking through the early morning clouds.

2. #WTF

I exit the elevators and turn toward my office, then, at the last second, I turn around, remembering to drop off my lunch in the kitchen. When I turn the corner, I see that a meeting is already happening in the boardroom. When I see him sitting next to the CEO and all the VPs, I nearly drop my latte.

I often wondered if I would recognize those piercing blue eyes in the daylight, but here they are. I remember him perfectly—the strong line of his jaw, his hair like radiant golden beams of light framing his flawless face, and the precision of his appearance, without even a hair out of place. His eyes meet mine. His gaze is thoughtful yet intense, and I catch a flicker of something. I abruptly pull my eyes away, even though all I want to do is stare. I try to walk casually instead of bolting, but my heel snags on the plush carpet and I almost tumble.

The night we met comes back in a blur, and I almost can't catch my breath. I immediately feel his presence, and it warms me. I want to burst into the meeting to talk to him again, even if just for a moment. I also want to hide away. Blood rushes to my cheeks at the thought of how he made me feel with just a few words.

I get to my office, slide the door closed, hang up my coat, pull on one of the blazers I keep at work, and put away my bag. Sunlight streams in through my window and lights up the bright white surface of my desk like Diwali diyas, overtaking the darkness and marking a new beginning. I would usually take a moment to embrace the beauty of this moment, but today I force myself to get to work. If I keep busy, I can ignore the emotions gathering like heavy rainclouds inside of me.

I sit at my desk and log in, but I can't focus on a single word as I look through my emails. Instead, my mind zeroes in on him.

What is he doing here?

Why would he show up now?

Why didn't he try to find me?

My palms are slick and my office seems stuffy around me as my thoughts spiral.

It all felt too unreal to be desirable to someone like him. Someone who was so effortlessly confident and charismatic, not to mention ridiculously hot. Someone who could have anyone, and now he probably had someone who wasn't me. I had someone, too, who wasn't him, and just the thought of Eshaan makes me feel guilty for being so thrown off by a guy I only met once casually in a bar.

Eshaan's a good fit for you, Nisha. The kind of guy your father would have approved of.

My mom's words resound in my head. She's right. Dad would have loved him.

Within a few weeks of dating, Eshaan told me he had never met anyone like me. At first, I was a little overwhelmed by his rapt attention, the over-the-top gifts (although I can't say I minded too much when it came to the Chanel handbag), and extravagant gestures, like the surprise birthday party her threw for me at the poshest West Vancouver venue last year. He invited all our friends to celebrate my birthday in a Great Gatsby-themed party—well, mostly his friends, but Rachel was there. Six months into our relationship, we started talking about marriage, and now we're planning our engagement party.

The thing is, I thought there would be fireworks when I finally met the one, but that's probably not even a thing. An unrealistic expectation after growing up watching too many Bollywood movies.

Eshaan checks all the boxes on the things that matter.

He's been wonderful with my family. He brought flowers for my mom and gifts for my nephew on his first visit to Toronto. Mom even started tearing up, and it's the first time I felt a sliver of approval from her. I could almost hear the sigh of relief when I found someone who met her expectations. He took us all out for dinner and didn't shy away when the next day, Mom unexpectedly invited everyone to meet him—even though it was a lot even for me, having all my extended family there, asking questions, and prying into our future. He held himself well through it all and was there for me when he sensed my discomfort. He even stood up for me when a family friend, after way too many drinks, brought up me dating my gay best friend, Sunny.

I didn't think you would ever find anyone. Not how you are.

I ruminate on my mom's words, along with memories they bring with them of the years of lackluster dates and endless nights spent swiping through dating profiles while trying to avoid my mom's matchmaking attempts.

I have someone amazing now. I breathe deeper to try to quell the familiar waves of unease when I think about my past.

Eshaan is the one for me. End of discussion.

I've moved on in a big way, and I have to step back into the shiny new reality I carefully curated over the past year. I continue to nudge away the unsettling feeling in my chest and return to what gets me through everything: work.

* * *

I'm diving deep into the fifth round of edits on a marketing plan for the upcoming relaunch of our website. The changes are minimal but still annoying to go through. The VP of Communications has written, "Add more details here," next to the key messages. I don't know exactly what she's referring to, so I'll take my best guess.

I've almost gotten my mind off Bar Guy. I don't know why he's here, but I know it won't have anything to do with me. I recall him mentioning that he worked in IT, and I only ever speak with the IT team about translating their product-specifications jargon into layperson's terms.

I wonder if he's just here for the meeting, or if he's here to stay. The office is big enough that I probably won't run into him anytime anyway, but still, my stomach flutters with nerves at the thought.

I'm so wrapped up in my thoughts that I almost don't hear the knock at my door.

"Nish." Jess, my work bestie and the office admin, slides the door open. Her shiny, dark brown bob settles perfectly on her shoulders and her light brown skin glows under the fluorescent lights. She's usually all smiles, but today her expertly shaped brows are pinched together and she's not her usual bubbly self. She must be stressed—she didn't even send me a silly GIF on our work chat this morning.

"I messaged you like five minutes ago."

"Sorry, I put my status on 'Do not disturb.' I really need to get this plan done."

"Yeah, it's just that Tom wants to see you stat."

"Oh, okay." I lock my computer and grab my notebook and pen. I saw Tom—my boss and the VP of Marketing, Investor Relations and AI Innovation—at our quarterly meeting last week, and we typically have minimal in-person interactions beyond that. My mind runs through everything I'm working on to see if there's anything I dropped the ball on, but I come up with nothing.

It's fine, I try to tell myself as my pulse beats rapidly in my ears.

I follow Jess down the hallway and out to reception where she sits back down at her desk, and I round the corner to Tom's office at the end of the hall. The door is only slightly open, so I knock hesitantly.

"Come in."

I poke my head in and he's at the window. Out of the corner of my eye, I see someone sitting in his guest chair, but I'm not sure who.

"Oh, Jess said you wanted to see me, but if this isn't a good time, I'll come back."

"This is perfect. Come in and take a seat." He gestures to the other guest chair as he walks back and sits behind his desk.

I move toward the chair, and my breath catches when two sea blue eyes land on me as I sit. Bar Guy. He gives me an easy smile and heat creeps up my neck.

What the fuck.

I force myself to take a breath, return a smile, and then turn to Tom, but it takes everything in me not to gawk.

"Nisha, I want you to meet Nick Tremblay. He's a consultant who will be joining us for a few months to oversee the launch of our latest AI product suite." Tom grins over at him. "Nick's worked with a lot of major players in the tech space and is making waves in the industry for being ahead of the AI curve."

Sounds like he's just as successful as I thought. Heck, maybe even more so, as Tom's praise is usually minimal at best. Or maybe it's that the accomplishments of men just don't go unnoticed.

Nick holds out his hand, and I stare at it like an idiot, but I quickly recover and put my hand in his.

My skin sizzles as our palms touch, and I wonder if he notices, but I only see a professional look in his eyes and not a hint of recognition. It stings, but I try my best to ignore it. That night was nothing, probably just a standard Saturday night for him, but for me, it was something else. Later, I can over-analyze. For now, I have to make it out of this meeting without embarrassing myself.

"So great to meet you, Nisha." His gaze lingers on me. "Tom's been telling me such good things about your work here."

"Thanks," I manage.

I take my hand away after what I deem is an appropriate amount of time and try to forget the feel of his skin on mine.

I turn to Tom, and the confusion on my face must show because he says, "You must be wondering why I called you in here."

"I'm curious," I answer.

"Should we fill her in, Nick?"

He gives a nod.

If he was hypnotic in the darkness, he's even more mesmerizing in the light of day. I know I need to focus. Instead, I'm calculating the distance between us. If I extended my arm just a little bit, my fingertips would caress his thigh just like they did at the jazz club.

I can't help but notice how his pressed powder-blue shirt perfectly fits his solid frame and complements his eyes.

Those eyes.

Framed by brows with an enviable arch. With his lower lip just slightly fuller than his top, his mouth looks soft, inviting, and sensual. A face made to tempt, tease, and distract, and it's doing all of that to me now.

Focus.

"You mentioned you wanted to expand your role here and help with Investor Relations."

I give a distracted nod while my heart thumps wildly.

"It just so happens that Nick's helped numerous tech companies raise millions of dollars in funding. With our busy schedules and most of the leadership team either away networking or pitching, this would be a great opportunity for you to get direct coaching from someone with a lot of experience in that area."

I smile, but inwardly I curse myself for my ambitions. I should have kept my fool mouth shut. I'm nearly hyperventilating just sitting in a room with him. I can't imagine having to work side-by-side with him.

"Nick can coach you on what investors are looking for, and you can help update the pitch decks and sales materials."

Grunt work. I suppress a sigh.

"Then from there, we'll see."

I feign enthusiasm. I don't need to be coached or to spend time making updates to existing materials. I want to be out there meeting investors and reeling them in.

"That sounds great," I lie as I plaster a smile on my face, not daring to look at Nick.

"Oh, and I know the IT team isn't the best at sharing product specs. He can also help with that. Nick's well-versed at taking tech terms and turning them into easy-to-digest information audiences can understand."

Tom looks at us both.

"So, for the next few months, you two will be spending a lot of time together."

Fucking hell.

I smile even as my heart leaps out of my chest. He looks at me with nothing but a professional demeanour. A wave of heaviness washes over me as it hits: He doesn't remember me.

My mind is having a hard time connecting Bar Guy to Nick Tremblay, even though they are the same in almost every way that I remember. The only difference was that for one fleeting moment, he was genuinely interested in me.

"Tom, thanks for this." I give him a grateful smile and stand up more abruptly than I mean to. "I better get back to it," I say, faking nonchalance.

"Right, you have that deadline. I won't keep you any longer."

I'm glad that I wore my new fitted white blazer and pencil skirt, and that I took care to apply a double coat of mascara this morning. Right now, they are the only things giving me confidence.

"It's lovely to meet you, Nick," I add in my most professional tone. I can pretend I don't remember him either. Pretending ranks first in my skill set.

"I'm looking forward to working together," he says sincerely. He gets up as I do, and I remember the last time he did that, too. *Such a gentleman.*

I try not to inhale the crisp yet slightly spicy scent of pine that clings to the air around him. A scent that takes me back to a night that should be nothing but an irrelevant memory.

I give them both a quick pressed-lip smile, grab my notebook, and do my best to walk out of the room at a normal pace.

I wanted to see him again, but not like this, and not now. Still, my heart doesn't get the memo, and a little rush shoots through me when I think about seeing him every day. The excitement sits next to the disappointment that he's forgotten me, though, and dulls it.

"Oh, and Nisha?"

I stop and turn back. Tom and Nick are both looking my way. "Nick will be in the vacant office next to yours, in case you need to find him."

"Gotcha."

Gotcha? I'm losing the ability to communicate articulately around him.

I turn and leave, passing Jess, who looks at me quizzically. I mouth, 'Talk later,' and rush into my office, sliding the door closed and leaning against it. My heart beats erratically.

I scoot around my desk and press speed dial on my phone.

"Rachel," I say, "it's him!" as soon as she picks up.

"Who?"

"The guy I met at that bar we went to when I first moved here."

"Where? How? I need details."

"He's going to be working with me for the next little while."

"Are you serious? That's a crazy synchronicity."

"I know, it's crazy, but he doesn't remember me." I fight the urge to pick at my fresh manicure.

"Um, that's hard to believe." She laughs. "Anyways, I'm just getting ready to teach at the studio. Let's chat more tonight."

"There's not much to talk about. I mean, it's just so random," I say with my insides vibrating.

"Right," she giggles. "That's why you're calling me from work."

"Exactly." I laugh too. "Have a good class."

The universe is obviously messing with me, but that doesn't mean I can't enjoy this a little bit.

3. UNPAID PERKS

The next day, I try my best to ignore the fact that Nick is in the office next to me. At least he's away for most of the morning in meetings with IT to get up to speed on everything, but still, I startle every time someone walks by. By some miracle, I manage to focus enough to get some work done before I head off to two back-to-back meetings.

As soon as I sit down at my desk, Nick walks by and slows outside my door.

"Hey, neighbour."

He's wearing a tight white polo shirt that hugs every muscle and contrasts with his slightly tanned yet fair skin. His hair swept to the side as if he just walked out of a photoshoot, not a meeting.

"Hey." He gives me a little smile.

That's all it takes—suddenly my heart's thumping and my thoughts are in torrents, like they'd sweep me up and toss me across the Pacific Ocean. I should let him walk by, but I don't.

"How's your first day so far?" I ask, barely looking up at him.

He leans against my door frame with his laptop casually at his side and his other hand in his pocket. He smiles at me, and I almost forget we're at work. "It's great. I love the vibe here, and everyone is so friendly."

"Good to hear. Let me know if I can help with anything."

I sound professional and not enamoured, and I'm grateful I'm holding it together.

"Maybe just a good coffee place?"

This time I look right at him. "For sure. There are a few great places nearby." I mentally start preparing a list to send him.

"Tomorrow morning, then?"

I wasn't expecting that, and my heartbeat quickens at the thought of being alone with him, even if it's only for coffee.

"Yes," I say without hesitation.

"Is nine a.m. good for you?"

"That's perfect. I'll see you then."

He leaves. I stare at my computer login screen and rest my hands on the keyboard, knowing I should at least pretend I'm working.

I'd always imagined we would bump into each other on a warm Saturday morning as I ran along the Seawall in Stanley Park. I would be wearing those stylish workout leggings with sexy see-through patches and a fitted jacket, my hair pulled up into a smooth ponytail that swayed as I ran. He'd be running toward me, a tight shirt over his strong chest, paired with fitted joggers accentuating his muscled thighs and, of course, sexy aviator shades. The ocean waves would lap next to us as the warm spring sun blazed overhead. He'd glance at me and then stop. *Nisha?* I'd stop, too. *Do I know you?* I'd reply breezily, as if I never gave him a second thought. *We met at a bar in Chinatown a week ago,* he'd say, catching his breath. *Oh right. Hi!* He'd run alongside me, and we'd pick up where we left off. He'd tell me he couldn't stop thinking of me and was losing his mind looking for me. I'd laugh and say, *I get that a lot.* He'd take me to lunch, and the conversation would flow until dinner. We'd go back to his place, but this time I wouldn't be afraid to take things further. Once he had a taste, he wouldn't just want me for a night, he'd want me for eternity.

But he doesn't even remember me.

Why would he? I mean, since he visited yesterday, the office was already thrumming with the news, everyone talking about the hot new consultant. He probably has women falling at his feet. Of course he wouldn't remember someone like me.

I wish he did.

The thought comes unbidden. I want to dissolve it. *Eternal Sunshine* him from my brain like in the movie.

It's better he doesn't remember, and it wouldn't matter if he did. I'm happy with Eshaan. Besides, he made his intentions clear that night. He didn't want to take me on a date, he only wanted to take me home.

"Um, hello?"

I smile as I look away from my screen and I turn to see Jess at my door. "Lunch?" she asks.

"Oh my gosh, yes. I need to get out of here.

"Gogi & Kimchi on Robson?"

"Perfect."

I grab my bag and follow her down the hallway. She winks at me as we walk by Nick's office and I try not to giggle.

The elevator doors bing open and we shuffle in, next to a few people I recognize from sales. I lean against the wall, staring up at the tiny screen displaying the weather and the headlines and not registering any of it.

"Tough morning?" asks Jess.

"Not really. Just a lot on my mind, I guess."

"Want to talk about it?" The elevator doors glide open and we step out.

I wait until we are out of earshot of others. "No, it's nothing."

She turns to face me and gently takes my elbow. "Are you sure?"

"Yes, I'm good. Really."

"Okay, you know I'm here, right?"

"I know." I hook her arm in mine as we step outside, and stroll to our favourite Korean restaurant. It's busy as usual, but we manage to grab a table and order the lunch special: beef galbi, spicy pork bulgogi, kimchi pancakes, and a selection of banchan.

"OMG, I can't believe the hot new consultant is in the office next to yours. I'm going to have to saunter by him slowly every time I come to see you."

"Oh, Nick. Yeah, he seems nice," I say casually.

"*Nice?* Lena was literally drooling when she saw him."

Lena is the events manager and on her third marriage.

"I think she drools over any remotely good-looking guy," I say, and we both laugh.

"Seriously, though, everyone in the office has been buzzing about him."

I shrug and take another bite. It's one thing for me to be enamoured with him, but to know that the entire office is too? It's way too much.

"I know you're all loved up, but for the rest of us, this is juicy, okay?" says Jess.

Our food arrives and I'm grateful for the disruption so I can think of something to say.

"Tom introduced us yesterday and we're going to be 'working closely together.'" I use air quotes over the last few words.

"What? You get to sit next to him and work with him? I'm so jealous."

"Perks of asking to take on more work at the same pay rate." I say as I take a bite of galbi. "After all, experience is invaluable on the fast-track to promotion. Who needs money?" I don't bother to hide the sarcasm in my voice.

"I would say that's faulty logic, but in this case, at least you get to work with him. Consider it part of your benefits package." She winks, and I roll my eyes.

She continues. "No fair that you get to spend your evenings and weekends with sexy Shaan and then your days with dreamy Nick and all I get are crappy dates with online creeps."

"What happened this time?" I relax, grateful for the change in subject.

"You don't even want to know. It's so cringe, but I'll tell you anyway." She smiles as she settles into her seat and regales me with her latest dating escapades. I do my best to listen, all the while trying desperately to suppress my thoughts of Nick, and the way he looked me up and down over jazz and gin and tonics.

4. UNFORGETTABLE

Nick holds the coffee shop door open for me, and my heart leaps a little. It doesn't feel forced, just a simple reflection of who he is: thoughtful and kind when no one is watching. Things with Eshaan sometimes feel like a display, like he's putting on a show for others. He plays the perfect attentive boyfriend when my family and friends are around but leaves me to do his own thing when they're not. Honestly, Eshaan has never made me feel like this. I hope that the way Nick is around me is something more than him just being polite. I step past him and linger for a second too long as I breathe in his warm sandalwood cologne. It reminds me of the wisps of incense my mom would burn every day after her morning prayers. I resist the urge to lean closer to him as we approach the counter.

"Extra-sweet matcha latte, right?" says the barista.

I smile. "That would be great."

"Is that all?"

"And whatever he's having."

The barista turns to Nick.

"An Americano, please."

I pull out my purse, but Nick beats me to it.

"My treat, as a thank-you for bringing me here."

I'd bring you anywhere.

"Thanks."

I've replayed the night we first met in my mind so many times, and each time, I envision a different ending. In the first scenario, I go home with him because #YOLO. In another, I give him my number. I've thought about what I would say and do if I ever saw him again, but now that it's really happening, all thoughts flee my mind, and instead I'm drawn in again by the light of his presence.

"Do you want to sit while we wait?" he asks.

"Sure." I walk toward the only available booth, the one from the other day, where Mom told me I'd better set a date for the wedding, and fast.

I put the feelings of inadequacy out of my mind and let myself enjoy the moment.

Nick slides in across from me. His pin-striped shirt is rolled up at the sleeves, exposing his tanned forearms. I force my gaze to his face.

"So, where were you before this?" I ask casually.

"I worked for a telecom corporation for a while. It was good, but this is more *interesting*."

He emphasizes *interesting* and looks at me with a smile playing on his lips, and I try to remain calm and unaffected—a near-impossible feat.

What did he mean by that?

"How about you? Have you been working here for a while?"

He rests his arm on the table, and I catch a glimpse of his watch, the same Omega Seamaster, then I quickly glance away.

"Just over a year. So not too long."

Right around the time we first met.

The barista calls out our order. "I'll get that," says Nick as he gets up.

I take a moment to tug a crease out of my white tank and smooth the front of my oversized black blazer—my daily armour. I pinned my hair in a messy bun this morning in an attempt to look like I'm not trying too hard, but the pin is already loosening. I take it out and let my long hair cascade down my back, then drape it over one shoulder and look over at Nick, who's walking back toward our table. I see him stop and stare for just a second. His lips part and his gaze smoulders, and just having him look at me sparks desire down to my core. I drag my eyes away, patting down my hair and playing with the simple gold chain around my neck. The one from my dad—it makes me feel closer to him every time I wear it.

"Your latte." His voice is soft, like we aren't in a crowded coffee shop, but somewhere more private.

He places the cup before me, and when I reach to grab it my fingers brush against his. My words become lost in my throat, but I manage to squeak out a thank you.

"Cheers," he says, and I flash back to the drinks we've had together before.

"To what exactly?" I ask, slowly regaining my voice and composure.

"To…fresh starts."

He bumps his paper cup to mine, and my heart pounds with hope.

Does he remember?

I shake off those thoughts as quickly as they came, because I'm not looking for a fresh start anymore, only a happy ending. And I already have one lined up. Just not with him.

5. ALL THAT GLITTERS

The rest of the week passes in a blur as I scramble to review the pitch materials, trying to bring myself up to speed before my meetings with Nick start next week. I don't want him to think I'm winging it—even though I am. It's all new to me, but I start thinking about the recommendations I can make so that I sound well-versed. I try to deny it, but I want to impress him. *So lame.*

When 5 p.m. hits, I'm happy to get out of here. I grab my things and notice Nick's still in his office. I stop at his door.

"Have a nice weekend."

He turns to look at me. "You, too. Up to anything exciting?"

I swear there's a glint in his eyes as he asks.

No more jazz bars with handsome strangers, if that's what you're wondering.

"Just a fashion show with my—" I catch myself before the word *boyfriend* can slip out "—friends."

"Oh, are you modelling?" he asks, looking intrigued.

"Um, no. I don't model," I stammer. *As if.*

"That's a shame." One corner of his mouth lifts in a smile, and I wonder if he's messing with me or if he's enjoying the effect he knows he has on me.

This is the part where I should ask about his plans, but I don't. I don't want to know. "Well, I'd better get going. See you Monday!"

"See you then," he says with what I swear is a smirk playing on his face.

I give him a small smile back and force my feet to move even though I could linger here all night.

See, I can be professional and pretend I don't remember him either—even though that face of his haunted my dreams for months after our first meeting.

I walk to the SkyTrain on autopilot and get excited for the evening. Eshaan invited me to a big fashion show that's featuring the latest designs from India, with many of the outfits only available at his parents' South Asian clothing store on Main Street. He manages their social media and has built quite a following as an influencer. He even convinced *me* to start a new Instagram account. I finally have a life to be proud of, from my dazzling boyfriend to my career, and I don't want to hide it anymore. I mean, Eshaan's perfect on paper and that's what matters. The other things I'm just overthinking. I don't exactly have the promotion I've been working so hard for, but no one needs to know *that*. Secretly, I want to show every judgmental asshole from my past how great I'm doing, so they'll feel bad about how they treated me. The thought comforts me as I walk home from the train station.

Rachel's out tonight promoting a new vegan sushi restaurant. I change into the saree Eshaan gave me and take my makeup from day to night.

I carefully apply my favourite red lipstick and my mind drifts to the first night I wore such a bold colour: The night I met Nick. I can still see his eyes meeting mine from across the bar. I replay every interaction we've had this week in my head. Seeing him again in the boardroom, the meeting in Tom's office, and then how he stopped at my office and asked me for coffee. I remember the way he looked at me at the coffee shop as he carried our drinks back to the table. The feel of his fingers brushing mine. Then the fact he thought I was modelling—did he think I was beautiful enough to?

I force my brain to focus on Eshaan and the life we're building together, pushing Nick to the edge of my mind. I've already given him far too much real estate. Eshaan is the safe, sensible choice. The one that already has my family's seal of approval. We're getting engaged and then married and one day we'll have a house and a family. And it's not just about us; we're forging new bonds between our families and continuing our culture, values, and traditions. The life I've dreamed of for so long is finally within my grasp.

When I arrive at the event, I stride through the hotel lobby and head for the grand ballroom, where I see other attendees milling about. Dread begins to form in my stomach. This is the part I hate the most. Milling about on my own making small talk with strangers until Eshaan makes time for me.

I look through the open doors into the dimly lit ballroom, with chairs laid out around the stage and runway. I'm standing awkwardly on my own as the crowd grows around me. I could grab a seat, even though no one is sitting, and browse my phone, or I could wander outside, grab a drink, and check out the silent auction.

I message Eshaan to let him know I'm here, and I hope he can get away and come see me. I know the drill: When we go to events together, he has to 'work the room,' meaning I can't expect him to stay with me. I get it, it's not like he goes to these things for fun, it's legit to market his parents' business, which I know one day he wants to take over. Still, I wish he would come see me right away to at least check if I'm comfortable. Most likely I won't see him until everything's over.

I decide on a drink and wander out of the room. This will take the edge off and help keep my anxiety at bay.

Rachel's voice plays in my head. *You need to deal with that anxiety and not just drink.* It's true, but for now, one drink won't hurt. I won't let myself think about how alcohol impacted my family growing up.

I stand in line behind a group of chatty twenty-somethings. One turns to look at me, looks away, and then looks at me again.

"Hey, I know you from Instagram."

The girls all whip their heads toward me. For a moment, I brim with pride. Did she hear the podcast I recently did about women in tech?

I smile at them.

My Instagram is mainly filled with fun photos of books, coffee, and flowers, but lately I've been sharing more about what matters to me: the talks I go to on women in the workplace and inclusion, the clean beauty brands I started using after my dad got sick with cancer.

"You're Eshaan's girlfriend, right?"

"Yes," I answer, hiding my disappointment. Of course, they weren't talking about my Instagram. They must have seen me on Shaan's. He has 10K followers, compared to my measly 500.

"Oh, he's dreamy," she says. "You're so lucky." They all nod in agreement. I sigh, irritated and embarrassed all at once. I can do this. Make small talk.

"Can we take a photo and tag you?" another one of them asks.

"Sure, I guess."

They swarm in like wasps, surrounding me and blasting their phones several times, and then they buzz away and click on their screens without even looking up.

"What's your handle?"

"YVRMarketingGal."

"YVR what? Actually, never mind. We'll just tag Eshaan."

I don't even have time to answer. When they reach the bar they all order the same fruity cocktail and then dash off without even a glance.

Was I like them at that age? I can't believe I would ever be that self-involved, but I guess no one thinks that about themself.

The bartender turns to me. "What can I get you?"

"Double gin and tonic, please."

My drink of choice. Not classy, but it does the trick. Sugary drinks make my stomach churn, and the anxiety does enough of that. He hands it to me with a flourish, and I swipe my card to pay.

I look up to see Eshaan beaming at me, and I rush over to him. He's wearing a silver kurta with a black scarf and looks like he just stepped out of a Bollywood movie. His inky-dark hair is slicked back, contrasting with his smooth, brown skin, making him look like a South Asian Ken doll. He has silver swirls of glitter around his eyes, like most of the models, for the glitter and glam theme they have tonight.

"Hey, babe." He wraps me in his arms and kisses me. A few people turn to look at us.

"I missed you." I lean into him.

"The saree looks so good on you."

He pulls back and looks me up and down. "You changed the blouse." Disapproval edges into his voice. He had chosen a modest blouse that just didn't go with it, so I swapped it for a cropped tank top instead.

He looks as if he wants to say more, but a guy comes rushing up to him. He's wearing a headset and a plain white T-shirt and jeans.

"We have a problem."

Eshaan turns away from me to face the guy. I linger at his side.

"One of the models is MIA."

"Fuck. The show starts in twenty. Do we have anyone else who can step in?"

"No, there's no one else. Unless we pull someone from out here." Headset Guy looks at me with an appraising gaze, and I slowly step away. There's no way I'm getting up there in front of all these people. I'm about to tell Shaan that I see a friend and I'm going to go say hi when he turns to me.

"Nish, what do you think? You can model one outfit for us, right?"

He says it in a way that makes me feel like I'd be rude to say no. Present a slide deck to a large audience, I can do. Walk a runway in front of them? Fuck no.

Having eyes on me when I didn't have the chance to meticulously prepare is my worst nightmare. Here are hundreds of people taking videos and photos and posting them, and I'd have no control over what someone might say about me. No, I won't let Eshaan push me into this, even though he's pushed me before to do what he needed instead of what I wanted. I try to gather my resolve.

"I, um."

My palms are slick, and the room is suddenly stifling. I just need to form one word to get out of this. I swallow as they both look at me expectantly, and I can't do it. I can't say no.

"Of course."

"Great. Follow me this way." Headset Guy races down the hallway. I shoot Eshaan a quick look that I hope conveys my agitation.

He leans in and gives me a peck. "You're the best, babe. You'll do great."

I smile even though my organs are twisting into knots. I down my drink, wishing I had time for another.

Headset Guy leads me backstage into a sea of high cheekbones, long limbs, and rail-thin arms, and I feel so self-conscious. I'm slim, but definitely not like these ladies. The bright lights, commotion, and cramped quarters raise my apprehension with every step. I look away from the glamorous models and instead focus on my breath. I make each step mindful. Headset Guy points to a makeshift change room that's just two sheets hung from the wall and points inside.

"Change into that outfit, and then Alyssa will do your hair and makeup."

I'm guessing Alyssa is the pink-haired woman with a lip ring, who's impatiently tapping her foot next to a table spread with more shades of makeup than I've ever seen in one place.

As he scutters away I step in, trying unsuccessfully to close the sheets around me. I give up and start undressing. The outfit is so stunning, I stop for a moment and just run my hands over it. It's silver with crystals everywhere. The top is cropped with short sleeves, and there's a tie with more crystals on the back, while the skirt is a mermaid-style lehenga. I'm grateful my tummy will be covered, as it's not concave like the other models'. I put on the skirt first and just manage to zip up the side. Then I try to put the top on, but it's way too tight and doesn't even close. Shame rises and flushes my cheeks.

Alyssa takes one look at me struggling and says, "I'll get the seamstress." She rushes away.

"Five minutes until showtime!" Headset Guy's voice breaks through the commotion, and the models start filing out behind the stage. My distress grows.

Alyssa rushes back with a lady I recognize from Eshaan's store.

"Auntie Ji."

"Hi, Nisha. Let me fix that."

Her reassurance relaxes me, and she deftly pulls apart the side seams, making more room on the bust.

"Take off your bra, and it should fit now." I do what she says, trying to hide how uncomfortable I am undressing in front of them.

It fits like a glove, but I don't have time to relish my relief as Alyssa leads me to the makeup chair and swipes off the makeup I spent so much time applying earlier. She then deftly paints my eyelids with pink, blue, and silver eyeshadow, followed by thick winged eyeliner and lashes so substantial I'd expect to see them on a drag queen.

She pauses as if she senses my anxiety. "We still have thirty minutes. You'll be the last one to go on stage."

I sink into the seat a little as she adds silver shimmer to my cheekbones. She places bindis not only on my forehead, but also all around my eyebrows and the sides of my eyes, with a large silver tikka leading into my hair. I notice that all the other models have similar bindi styles. If only I could pull off the look like they do. I can't believe I'm about to do this.

Alyssa puts hot pink lipstick on me and then stands back, satisfied. I notice massive crystal earrings on the table.

"Do I need to wear those?"

"What?" She's still looking at me with scrutiny but follows where I point my finger. "Yes, put them on."

My hands shake as I slide the earrings on.

Alyssa adds a final silver shimmer to my lips and then steps behind me and runs her hand through my voluminous hair.

"We're going to have to leave your hair like this."

I nod. The other models had their hair slicked and perfectly in place.

She sprays it down and is redoing the curls when Headset Guy comes rushes in.

"We need her out in five."

Alyssa just nods. She hairsprays me with what must be half the bottle and helps me up. The outfit is gorgeous, but it feels like it weighs twenty pounds. She places the net chunni over my arms.

"Do you know how to walk the runway?"

"Kind of."

"Sway your hips, keep your arms loose and give your best pouty face."

I walk a few steps back from her and try it, but the skirt is so tight, I find it hard to sway my hips. I do my best anyway, thinking back to when my sister and I would stay up late to watch the Victoria's Secret Fashion Show.

"No smile. Try slower, graceful steps."

I'm terrified I'll make a complete fool of myself. "Got it."

I try again, and she nods.

"That will do."

Fuck it. If I have to do this, I'm going to give it my all even if I feel like an imposter. I feel like that most of the time anyway.

The more I focus on who others need me to be, the easier my life is. Eshaan's ready to commit to me, my mom is pleased with me these days, and even Tom's giving me more responsibilities that are usually only reserved for leadership. With Eshaan, if I can be as low-maintenance as possible and not make a fuss, then things will continue to go smoothly. With my mom, if I stop going against the grain and questioning things like archaic cultural practices that make little sense to me, things will be better. At work, if I put in extra time and keep creating incredible results, they will notice. They'll have to.

Even modelling right now in this massive show is something my friends back home would have jumped at. A chance to shine and be seen, and in my case, in a positive way for once. Maybe it's time for me to step into the spotlight in all areas of my life instead of trying to stay in the shadows—to be the main character instead of a supporting cast member. This is something Fantasy Nisha would do. I've spent this whole year trying so hard to be her, and I know I need to keep it up until everything works out perfectly. I am already so close. Be who everyone else wants me to be. It is the secret to success—my success.

I swagger onto the runway in a way that I hope makes me look like a graceful, sexy model, and not a woman wearing an outfit a few sizes too small for her—a last-minute replacement who has no business being up here with these size-zero models.

Cheers erupt from the audience as I reach the far end and do a three-point turn, and it feels amazing. I really am Fantasy Nisha. I walk back lighter, holding my chin a little higher. I'm becoming so good at faking confidence and being someone I'm not—I'm even beginning to fool myself.

6. BOLLYWOOD IS CALLING

We settle in at a high-top table at the hotel's top-floor restaurant, and I take in the view of glittering skyline. We attracted quite a bit of attention when we walked in wearing our traditional outfits. I had been about to change back into my saree, but Eshaan insisted that I wear the silver mermaid dress out for a drink with some of the event sponsors and his cousin, Anjali, who's only in town for the weekend. It is probably worth thousands, so I'm being extra careful. Eshaan is deep in conversation with one of the sponsors. Anjali looks over at me with a sparkle in her eyes.

"You were amazing out there," she says, squeezing my arm.

"Really?"

She gives me a look that says, *Come on.* "Yes, really. That outfit fits you like a glove, and it was so refreshing to see a real-life model, not just the stick figures."

"Thanks, I think."

I liked Anjali from the first moment we met. She's extremely successful in her consulting business, travelling all over the world, hosting seminars, and speaking at conferences, while also finishing her MBA. I feel seen by her—she seems to understand me while the rest of Eshaan's family just don't get my ambitions.

The waitress takes our orders.

"Let's go freshen up and see if there are any hot guys here." She grins at me. "You can be my wing woman."

I turn over to see Eshaan still engrossed in conversation, so we slip away, weaving through the tables.

"Hey, Bollywood."

I stop and try to discern who said that and notice a table of three guys. Anjali has already stopped in front of them. I slide up next to her.

The guys are all wearing basketball jerseys and look like they must be in college.

"What my friend here was trying to say is, are you ladies like Bollywood movie stars?" His accent sounds American. He has tanned skin and a mop of dark curls.

Anjali answers for us. "I'm not, but she is." She gives me a naughty look while I gape at her.

What is she doing?

"A model and actor, actually. She just wrapped up a fashion show."

They all turn their eyes to look at me, astonished, and I want to laugh. The other two boys have short brown hair and look like brothers.

Curly Top speaks up again. "Chris here has no game, but maybe a picture with you could change that."

I hesitate and don't answer, but Anjali jumps right in.

"I think we can arrange that." She smiles at me like she's really enjoying this, and the boys look at me so earnestly that I relent. It's just a photo with some college kids.

"Really?" The boy I presume to be Chris lights up.

The waitress comes by just then. "Some more drinks?"

"We'll get another round and whatever they're having," Curly Top chimes in. "A thank-you for the photo op."

Anjali orders a martini, and since I'm ordering for Fantasy Nisha, I go with the same. We slide into the booth next to the boys.

"Where are you from?" Anjali asks as we wait for our drinks.

"Texas. We're just here for a tournament." I don't listen to the rest of the conversation, but I do admire how effortlessly Anjali makes small talk with just about anyone.

The waitress comes back with our drinks.

"Cheers!" We clink glasses, and I take a sip and let the gin soothe me.

"We have to get back to our promotional tour activities, so let's take that photo." She looks around appraisingly, trying to find a good background.

"Nisha, why don't you sit on the table, and guys, you can stand around her and hold up your drinks like you're toasting her."

I look at Anjali, imploringly. I don't know how I'm going to lift myself up there in this too-tight outfit.

"You two can give her a lift."

"No objections here," Chris says with a cheeky smile.

Chris and Curly Top gently place me on the table, and I stifle a giggle. Chris hands his phone to Anjali, who takes a few shots. I raise my martini glass in the air, and I'm sure we look like quite the sight: me in my sparkly Bollywood outfit and the boys in their basketball jerseys.

Chris and Curly Top help me back down, and I feel like a real-life princess. I give him my socials so he can tag me.

"Well," says Anjali, "we'd better get back to her other fans."

We make it to the bathroom and then both lose it, laughing. "What the fuck was that?"

"I couldn't resist, they just looked so smitten. Why not put a little smile on their faces."

"You're hilarious, you know that."

"That's why you love me."

"I do." I light up around Anjali. She's just so fun and genuine.

We freshen up and head back to the table. A warm glow settles in my stomach, and for a moment, I almost forget about Nick, even though he's been in the back of my mind all night.

* * *

On the ride back to Shaan's place, I'm so tired that I grab Shaan's arm and rest my head on his shoulder. He is swiping through his phone, reposting Stories from the night, when I feel him stiffen and pause. I open my eyes and see the photo Anjali took earlier this evening with the basketball guys.

"What the fuck is this?"

"Oh, some guys thought we were Bollywood movie stars, so Anjali and I just played along." I smile at the fun photo.

"And you thought this was a good idea?" His voice is harsh, and my body tenses.

"It was just a bit of fun." I keep my voice calm and let go of his arm.

He shakes his head. "What do you think people are going to think when they see this? You posing like this in photos with all these other guys?"

I take a deep breath. It was only one photo, but I don't say that. I know better than to speak up.

"It makes you look like a whore. You know that, right?"

The word cuts through my chest, and my body tingles with embarrassment. I can't even form a response, and my eyes prick with hot tears. I start to worry. Did his cousin set me up to look bad in front of Eshaan? Horrible things like this have happened to me before. I feel sick.

No, I can't believe she would do that. She's always been so kind to me. Shame sloshes around in my stomach.

"I just don't get why you always need attention." He continues with his voice low and full of spite. "It's actually kind of sad."

"I'm sorry, Shaan. I really am," I say, hoping to pacify him.

He shakes his head again. "Sometimes, I wonder why I put up with you."

My palms start to sweat. He can't mean that. He wouldn't break up with me over a photo, would he?

Before I know it, we're outside of his townhouse, and I follow him silently up the stairs. He unlocks the door, and we go inside. Worry and fear consume me with every step.

He throws the keys on the counter and turns around to look at me. He's still not happy. "Don't pull shit like that again."

I nod. I head into the washroom, close the door, stare at myself in the bathroom mirror. I will myself not to cry, but I can't stop myself, and the tears come rushing through. I start wiping away my makeup and my tears. I run the shower so he doesn't hear me, and I stay in there until I finally stop shaking. I carefully take off the expensive outfit and step outside the bathroom, placing it folded on his dresser while pulling out my PJs from the bottom drawer. Eshaan's already sound asleep, his breath even and slow, his fingers relaxed against the pillow, oblivious to the pain he caused me just moments ago. I let the tears fall, and I feel like a disgrace.

Shaan knows about the rumors people spread about me. I told him all about it, that I was pretending to date my childhood friend, Sunny, so his family wouldn't find out he was gay—but that people started saying I was using the relationship as a front to hook up with random guys. I was too busy with school and work to see anyone, but that didn't matter. No one believed me. He must know how much that word would impact me after everything I've been through. He knows he's only the second guy I have ever been with. The first was someone I thought I was in love with, and someone who I thought was serious about me. He spent months pursuing me, staying on the phone with me until 4 a.m., sending sweet texts when we weren't together, taking me on dates at the hottest spots—until I slept with him. After that, I never heard from him again. From then on, I was too cautious when it came to guys, something my friends back home would poke fun at me for—but I couldn't give people any more reasons to talk shit about me.

You're always making us look bad. Bringing shame to our family.

It's because of you that I can't even show my face.

My mom's voice lingers in my head, and as I lie down beside Eshaan, I find no comfort. I cover my eyes with my palms. I replay the incident in my head, thinking of how I could have done things differently—and avoided all of this.

7. HOT MESS

I push open the glass door and take the stairs up to the yoga studio. Rachel teaches here part-time, and I've been helping out in exchange for classes—a karma-based program that suits my budget just fine. Shaan wanted me to cancel and spend the day with him, playing the ring card as bait. He knows how much I want to go shopping for it, and he's probably trying to make up for going ballistic over a photo. Usually, I'd cave. But today feels different. I need space.

"Rach, I'm here." I put my bag behind the desk, but all I want to do is tuck myself away underneath it.

"I'll be right out," she calls back at me.

I log in to the computer and get ready to check in attendees.

Rachel walks over to me, and I get up to hug her. My heart hurts.

"Nish, what's wrong?" She takes one look at me and knows. She always knows.

She wraps her arms around me, and I want to burst into tears. I hold them back instead.

"Nothing. It was a late night," I choke out.

"Bullshit, something happened." She pulls back from our embrace, and her eyes search my face. "I can cancel the class, and we can go somewhere and talk."

"Rachel, no. You don't need to do that. I'm fine. We can talk later."

She eyes me up and down. I can see her deciding whether to trust the words I'm saying. Most of the time, I don't trust myself either. "Fine. Right after class, then. Let's go for coffee."

"Sounds like a plan." I smile halfheartedly.

Just then, a few women enter, and I head behind the desk while Rachel welcomes them. The room fills up, and I go through the motions of checking people in. I smile and nod along with the chatter without registering any of it until it's time for the breathwork class to begin.

I don't know exactly what it entails, but it sounds simple and like something I could manage more than yoga poses or Pilates today. We even get to lie down. As soon as we do, I realize I'm exhausted—more than exhausted. It's almost like my energy has completely seeped out of me. Somehow, I feel more held lying on the hardwood floor right now than I did last night in Eshaan's California king.

I listen to Rachel's soothing voice.

"In, in, out, out."

I can't keep pace, but relaxation still flows through my body. A gentle wave in the storm brewing within me.

"You may feel different sensations come up or different emotions, from fear to anger to sadness. Don't judge them or resist them."

I breathe.

"Let them come up…and then let them go."

All I feel is tired and something else I can't quite name. A heaviness. Maybe an emptiness.

I replay the fight with Eshaan last night in my head.

I just don't get why you always need attention. It's actually kind of sad.

I go rigid. Rage builds, replacing the calm. I'm an attention seeker for taking one picture? He's *always* surrounded by girls flirting with him, touching his arm, leaning in to whisper in his ear—all right in front of me. Even last night when Anjali and I returned to the table, Eshaan was sitting with some of the girls who took a picture with me earlier. One was sitting entirely too close. I stood back as anger blasted through my chest, but Anjali charged straight ahead, commanding the space, and they quickly got up and left. I gave him the grace of pretending not to notice, but he never lets me off the hook no matter how innocent.

Rachel's voice grounds me back in the present. I listen and tell myself to focus on the now. And that's what I do, or at least try to do, for the next hour.

"Great work, everyone. Now just breathe normally and give your body a stretch or shake if you need to."

This is exactly what I needed to clear my thoughts and get back into my body. The shame and anger are still there, but they're not as intense.

"Grab any props you need—maybe a pillow for your eyes, or a cushion to place under your knees—and lie down when you're ready. I'll ring a gentle chime to bring you back into this space."

My body is calmer, and I find my mind escaping to Nick. I see his eyes, meeting mine from across the boardroom and in an instant, I'm lost in the ocean blue, and I want to stay there.

I hear others around me stir.

Why would Nick pop into my life now? It feels like this universal test. But I can't afford to get caught up in it. I'll continue to be professional and focus on my goals, even if things with Eshaan aren't always easy.

* * *

Rachel and I are standing in front of the pastry case at our favourite café. The smell of freshly baked croissants is intoxicating. I only had a couple of drinks last night, but I barely slept and I'm ready to eat everything in sight.

"What do you feel like getting?" Rachel asks.

"Everything."

"That hungover, huh?"

"Just a little." I give her a small smile.

She looks over at me, concerned. "Want to tell me what's going on?"

I want to tell her everything, and I also want to pretend everything is fine. Rachel isn't like my other friends. She always tells me exactly what she thinks, whether I like it or not. I don't know if I could handle that right now, though.

I'm drained from everything. The striving at work to be perfect and get noticed. The engagement planning. The nights out with Eshaan that are more work appearances for him than actual dates.

After we order we make our way to a table near the window, I'm aware of a presence I could sense anywhere. I look over and see Nick sitting on the other side of the café. Our eyes meet, and he smiles at me. I smile back, and then I quickly avert my eyes as I glimpse his companion. I can tell she's gorgeous even from this distance. Insecurity brews inside me. I wish I had worn my sleek black leggings instead of the cotton ones I have on.

Rachel follows my gaze. "Who's that?"

"No one."

I look down at my food, and suddenly I don't want to eat.

"It's him, isn't it?"

"Who?"

"Bar Guy." She gives me a knowing look.

"Shhh."

The waiter comes by with our drinks. Rachel takes a bite of her croissant without making a mess. I don't know how she does it.

"She looks young," she continues.

"Who?" I ask coolly as I sip my drink, even though I know exactly who she means.

"Whoever he's with."

"I guess."

I don't want to think about it. I have spent so much time thinking about the night I met him. About how he made me feel. The reality is that he probably spends many nights talking up women, and I was just one of them. I feel hot with shame for thinking that I meant anything more than a fun night.

You'll never find anyone willing to put up with you.

I hear Shaan's voice echoing in my mind. He would tell me that no guy is really interested in me and they just want a quick hookup—and based on my track record he's probably right.

"Aren't you going to eat?" Rachel asks.

"Yes." I take a tiny bite of my macaroon, suddenly self-conscious, and although I don't look his way, I can't relax knowing he's only sitting a few tables away.

I see him get up, and I pray to the universe that he doesn't stop and say hello.

The universe ignores me.

He stops at our table with Ms. All Done Up On A Sunday Afternoon.

"Hey. I hope I'm not interrupting. I just wanted to say hi." He gives us his most charming smile, and I wish I could channel Fantasy Nisha in this moment. She would never go out in these leggings.

Rachel chimes in before I can answer. "Not at all." I resist kicking her under the table.

"I'm Rachel, and you are?"

"Nick. Nisha and I just started working together. This is my little sister, Lucy."

"Hey." She smiles, and I instantly see the resemblance. Relief courses through me.

"It's nice to meet you both." Rachel glares at me for my lack of conversation skills.

I notice that Lucy is holding a book close to her chest, and I know just which one it is.

"Is that *The Alchemist*?" I ask her.

She beams at me with her radiant smile. "Yes, it's my favourite. I've read it like a hundred times."

"Me too." I smile at her.

"This is like her third copy," Nick adds affectionately.

"You can never have enough books, am I right?" she says.

"Agreed," I say, relaxing. "Have you checked out Perfect Match Bookshop yet?" I'm so excited to meet another booklover that conversation flows effortlessly now.

"No, I haven't even heard of it."

"They just opened and specialize in romance books." I remember Nick is there, and immediately cringe. Why am I talking about this?

"Sounds amazing," she says.

No one seems to notice my embarrassment.

"Count me out for that one." Nick laughs while Lucy playfully shoves him in the stomach.

He checks his phone. "We'd better get going if we want to make the four o'clock ferry." He pauses before adding, "Lucy's taking design at UVic," he says with pride.

"I love it," Lucy says.

"It was nice to see you, Nisha, and to meet you, Rachel," Nick says, looking at us both. His eyes linger on mine for a beat too long.

"Great to meet you both, too," Lucy adds as they walk off.

"Thanks for stopping by," I say.

Thanks for stopping by? Why is it so hard to act cool around him?

His sister looks back and smiles at us on her way out.

"He seems nice." Rachel wiggles her eyebrows at me suggestively, like I don't have a boyfriend.

"He's a great colleague," I say without any emotion.

"Right." She sees through my lies but doesn't press me. "Are you going to fill me in on why you were so upset in class today?"

I explain, choosing details selectively. My whole life feels like an Instagram feed these days, and here I am, choosing which filter to apply. I want to be real, but not too much, like the natural filter that makes my skin a little smoother and my lips a little plumper than they actually are.

"Shaan didn't like the picture I posted with the basketball boys," I share.

"His jealousy is over the top." She can't hide her distaste. "Those guys weren't even touching you."

I don't know what level of jealousy is normal, never having been in a long-term relationship, but sometimes I don't feel like it's a bad thing—it makes me feel like I matter, and he's just being protective of me.

Rachel chews on her lip.

"I don't know how you put up with him," she continues.

"Put up with him?" I try to hide my irritation. It hurts to hear her speak to me this way. This is why I don't tell her stuff.

"Put up with him making you feel bad over nothing. I've seen his Stories. He's always posting photos with other girls." She shakes her head. "Such a double standard."

Anger and defensiveness flare in my chest. Yes, he posts photos with other girls, and yes it bothers me sometimes, but he's always out and about, and lots of people recognize him. That's it. Isn't it kind *of his job?*

"He needs to rein it in." She takes a sip of her latte. "Besides, if he's not going to give you the attention you deserve, then I'm sure *someone* else will." I know who she's thinking about.

"Just stop, Rach." I can't hide my irritation anymore.

"What?"

"We're getting engaged!" I blurt out, as if that ends all of this—because it kind of does.

"What? Nish you just met him."

"We've been together for almost a year, Rach. Besides, I'm turning thirty soon, which is basically like ancient to my mom. You know how traditional she is."

"Okay, but does she know about his over-the-top behaviour?"

I set my cappuccino cup down, wishing it were a gin and tonic. "I didn't realize you were such an expert in healthy relationships."

Rachel had been in an on-and-off-again relationship for years before she finally called it off, and now she's not seeing anyone.

Hurt flashes in her eyes, and I immediately regret my words.

"I'm sorry, Rach."

"It's fine. You're right. I'm not an expert, and obviously, the way you're dealing with things is working out really well for you." Her words land like a knife. "I should go." She gets up and leaves.

My fruit tart sits untouched, and my coffee's gone cold.

Rachel just doesn't get it. Her parents didn't question her when she told them she was quitting her lucrative job in corporate America to be a digital nomad and travel the world. They supported her when she ended her relationship. They encouraged her when she told them she wanted to settle in Vancouver. I couldn't even imagine having that kind of backing or the freedom to do whatever I wanted. I had to spend weeks convincing my mom to let me move here, and she only finally agreed, because my dad's sister, my Bhua Ji, lives nearby in South Surrey. She even wanted me to move in with my Bhua, or at least tell the rest of the family that's where I was staying, but I pushed back. I didn't want to lie to keep up appearances. I had done enough of that already.

I wasn't a teenager anymore, I could have just left, but at the risk of my mom not talking to me for months—at best—or at worst, disowning me like she threatened to do before. I couldn't be the cause of more pain for her. She had already been through so much with losing my dad.

Still, I wish she didn't scrutinize every little thing I did, especially because my dad isn't here to tell her to go easy on me. She hated how he would indulge me, whether it was allowing me to take up hip-hop dance or encouraging me when I mentioned I wanted to apply to universities and colleges outside the country. My eyes well up when I think that my dad's been gone for almost fifteen years. I can't help but think things would be easier if he were here. I wouldn't have to worry so much about getting it right, and maybe I could just let things flow instead of trying to hyper-control every aspect of my life.

I don't have that luxury, and it's fine, or at least, it's just how it is. I brush the tears away in the mostly empty dining area.

I want to get married, so why wait? It would make my family happy, and it's not like I'm looking for casual hook-ups. I only want the real thing, and I have it.

I take a sip of my cold cappuccino, barely tasting it. I wish Rachel could see things from my perspective. Even if I was single, hooking up with Nick, the guy hired to coach me, would be a major career-limiting move. I would never risk my shot at an epic career.

I obviously don't have anyone I can count on, except for Shaan. I grab my phone and dial him. It rings a few times before he picks up, out of breath. I can hear shouting in the background.

"What's up, babe?"

"Hey, do you still want to meet up for a bit?"

"Sure. I'm just finishing up a game of basketball with the guys. It's not too far from your place. I can stop by after for a bit."

"Okay. I'll order dinner."

He's the one I can count on no matter what. He's right: My friends don't get me the way he does. He accepts all the parts of me, even the ones I try to hide.

I'm grateful that I didn't do something stupid a year ago, the night I met Nick. It would have been fun, maybe, but meaningless—and I want so much more than that.

I want what Shaan is serving, and all I have to do is accept it. The bad with the good, and I will.

A new resolve takes hold.

Rachel doesn't want to settle and is waiting to meet 'the one.' In the meantime, she turns down anyone that isn't that in her quest.

I'm not settling, though. I found the one, and I won't let anyone or anything ruin what we have.

8. KILL ME NOW

I want to get to work early to prepare for my first meeting with Nick, but I sleep in and barely make it on time. I put my things away and log in quickly, pulling up the presentation I've been updating since last week, and I have it at the ready when Jess walks in.

"I can't believe you didn't tell me." She leans against the wall, looking at me with awe.

"What?" I say, turning back to my screen to double-check everything.

"That you were modelling in the fashion show."

I push away from my desk as I turn back to look at her. "Oh, that was just a last-minute thing," I say as if it's the most common thing in the world.

"And who are these hot guys in your Stories? I need all the details," she says, staring at her phone, not noticing Nick as he appears at my open door. I wish I could signal her to shut up.

Jess continues. "Like, they are *so* hot."

I want to die.

"Hey, Nick. Come on in," I say instead.

Jess looks around.

"Hi, Nick. Didn't know you were there." She smiles sweetly at him.

"Oh, sorry to interrupt. Nisha and I have a meeting, but I can come back." He's being professional, but a smirk plays at the corner of his mouth.

"Oh, that's okay. Nisha can fill me in on her wild weekend later."

I'm going to kill her.

"But I mean, you just have to look at this, isn't she so gorgeous?" She shoves her phone in his face.

I could murder her.

His smirk deepens into a smile. "That's a great photo," he says kindly.

"We'll see you later, Jess," I somehow manage to say without strangling her.

She finally gets the hint and leaves.

"Please, sit," I manage, even as my face burns.

I try to calm my nerves as I pull out a notebook and pen.

"How was the rest of your Sunday?" he asks.

All my careful planning to remain unaffected by his presence goes out the window, and after Jess going on and on about guys, I just want to hide under my desk for the rest of the day.

I pause for too long. "It was good, thanks. Just relaxed and got ready for the week." I leave out the fight with Rachel and dinner with Eshaan.

"What about you?"

"Same."

I doubt his evenings are anything like mine.

"Your sister is so sweet."

He smiles, and the whole room lights up. "She is."

"You seem close." I think about my own relationship with my sister, which is strained at best. She's always been the golden child, and I'm the screwed-up one.

"We are, especially after my dad left."

His vulnerability surprises me, and I roll my chair closer.

"I'm sorry." I glimpse a sadness I haven't seen before in his eyes.

"It's okay. It was a long time ago. I was only sixteen."

I give him a reassuring smile, and he continues.

"It was tough for a while, but things are so much better now…now that I'm old enough to take care of my mom and Lucy."

I know exactly what he means. In Toronto, I lived with my mom, even though most of my friends had long since moved out, so I could help pay the bills and the mortgage, making things easier on her. Preeti made me feel guilty for leaving her on her own for this job, and I almost didn't move here, but Rachel convinced me that going for my dreams would help us both in the long run.

I swallow the lump in my throat as I see him in a new light, the man behind the fancy clothes and put-together appearance. I resist the urge to place my hand on his.

"I lost my dad at the same age." I don't know why I'm telling him. I usually never share the intimate details of my life with anyone.

He shifts closer.

"That must have been so unimaginably hard." The kindness in his eyes dissolves some of the armour I wear into the office every day.

"It was." I take a deep breath and will myself to tuck my emotions away, like I always do. "You learn to deal, but the grief doesn't really go away."

He gazes at me with compassion and understanding that unlock some of the parts of me I keep hidden away.

"It's okay to still be sad."

I nod as warmth radiates from the centre of my heart outwards. The calls and check-ins were rampant at first but dwindled down within a few months. Now, years later, I barely mention it, except to Rachel, Sunny—my childhood best friend—and sometimes Eshaan. Most people think I should be over it by now.

"Thank you."

I turn to the screen, not trusting myself to continue this conversation without crying.

"I made some changes to the pitch deck that I'd like to show you. I mean, I know you're the expert, but I'd love to run these by you."

"Of course."

I turn my screen to him, and just like that, our conversation is back on track.

"Instead of walking me through it, why don't you pitch me like you would an investor?" he says.

My heart starts hammering and I freeze. I'm normally good at presenting, but even though we've only known each other for the equivalent of barely a few hours if I add them up, his opinion matters to me.

He senses my trepidation and gives me a reassuring smile. "Think of it as a trial run. It will give me a better idea of what we need to shift, if anything."

His words help relax the knot in my chest. Pretend. It's what I've done since coming here, and what I can do now. I put Fantasy Nisha to work.

I imagine putting on my facade. He's just an investor, not this captivating creature sent to me by a cruel universe that loves toying with me. I stand, even though I don't have to. *You can do hard things.* Rachel's voice resonates in my head, and I wish I could shake off the guilt I feel at hurting her with my harsh words.

I launch into my pitch, using the slides as jumping-off points and filling in the blanks with details I know investors would be interested in.

Nick's face betrays nothing, so I have no idea if what I'm saying is landing, but he nods and smiles encouragingly from time to time, so I keep talking.

When I'm finished, I sit down and try to remain composed, even though I'm dying to hear his thoughts. My need for approval laces every interaction, even this one.

"Nisha, wow. That was incredible." He genuinely looks impressed. "You've never pitched before?"

"I've never had the chance," I say honestly.

"I'm sure we can change that." He gives me his stunning smile and manages to make a tiny part of me believe that I might be good at this.

"I only have one minor suggestion, but everything else you already have covered," he says, sitting up in his chair.

Breathe. "What's that?" I say casually.

"Let's move the sales numbers up to show them this is a proven concept and it's already generating money, so that they can expect a quick ROI."

"Yes. I'll make that change now."

I move up that slide as he glances at his watch.

"I have to run to my next meeting, but I'm excited about working together."

I find myself puffing up at his words. I turn to him.

"Me too."

I'm excited about every moment I get to spend with you.

9. I CAN'T EVEN

I sink into the leather sectional and stare up at the vaulted ceilings, resting my feet in Eshaan's lap as he flicks through Netflix.

"What do you want to watch?"

"Anything is fine," I reply. With work being so busy, I barely have time to watch TV. All I'm looking forward to tonight is a drama-free evening together, especially after everything.

The doorbell rings, and I slide my feet off his lap as Shaan says, "Finally, dinner," and gets up. I wanted to just eat the aloo parathas Eshaan's mom made, but he insisted we order Thai. I glance at the clock in the kitchen. It's almost 8 p.m. I should let Rachel know I'll be home late, especially since I borrowed her car this morning to get to work on time. My phone died on the drive over here, so I grab Eshaan's from the coffee table to send her a quick text.

I unlock his phone, and Instagram notifications flood his screen. That's not unusual, and I'm about to swipe them closed when I notice a string of DMs from his ex, Sonia.

Why is she messaging him?

My skin prickles.

The front door closes and Eshaan's steps thud on the hardwood as he comes up the stairs, but I can't stop myself from opening up the DM chat, my pulse pounding in my ears.

Is this where I pretend I don't miss you?

Careful. We both know how things turned out last time 😏

Turned out pretty 🔥🔥🔥

Eshaan places our dinner on the dining room table and saunters over to the couch. "Let's eat."

I stare at the messages as he grabs his phone. "What are you doing with my phone?"

"My phone's dead. I was just going to message Rachel and tell her I'll be home late when your messages with Sonia popped up." I can't hide the edge in my voice.

I bring a cushion close to my chest as he looks at me, then away.

"She won't stop messaging me."

"Right." I shake my head and shift in my seat. "Looks like you're messaging her back."

He takes a step away from me.

"Have you seen her since you broke up?" I glare up at him, accusation in every word.

"What? You're being ridiculous," he replies as he goes back to the food on the table and starts unpacking it.

"You know how hard I've been working for our future and how busy I've been." I pause. Guilt floods my system for a moment before the anger flares up again.

"Yet somehow you found time to flirt with your ex." My words are barely more than a whisper, but he freezes. I've never spoken back like this, but cheating is something even I won't put up with.

He stares at me, his lips pressed into a thin line, and slams a container of curry into the wall. I flinch as the red sauce streaks down the wall and puddles on the hardwood, but I can't bring myself to look away.

"Un-fucking-believable." He comes toward me. My heart crawls up to my throat, and I inch back on the couch, hoping to disappear into the cushions.

"After everything I've done for you, that my parents have done for you, you say shit like this?" He holds me with his gaze. "Says a lot about you, doesn't it? How insecure and disrespectful you are."

I look at the floor, trying to hide how rattled I am.

The front door slams, and Dev walks into the room. His best friend and roommate. Usually I can't stand the guy, but right now I am grateful he's here.

"What the heck is going on? I could hear you from the street." His hazel-brown eyes narrow in on me, like of course I'm the cause of this. He stares at me a moment longer with distaste before turning to Eshaan.

I grab my purse and push past him.

"It's none of your business," I say quietly, summoning some strength.

I get in the car and force myself to start driving, and it's only when I'm a few blocks away that I park on a side street to regroup.

Maybe Rachel's right. Things are moving too fast and I'm not sure I'm ready for all this. Maybe the texts were nothing, but how he reacted wasn't okay.

I pull out my phone and scroll through my call history, finding my mom. I could explain to her that we just need to slow down, to delay the engagement for now and maybe do a simpler ceremony later. Everything is so over the top with the hall, outfits, decorations, and a guest list of hundreds. Do we really need all that to show our love and commitment?

I should have pushed back sooner on all of this, but now all my family back home know about us, and his enormous family here does too. My lip quivers as I think about breaking up. It would be so hard to move on from, especially since it wouldn't just be a breakup—it'd be a broken engagement. I'd forever be marked as damaged goods, and this would mar my reputation worse than anything that happened with Sunny.

I want to call, but I pause—it's close to 11 p.m. in Toronto. If I woke her, she wouldn't be able to sleep after. I know how much she worries about me. My finger hovers over the call button when a message from Eshaan comes through.

Babe, I'm sorry. I shouldn't have gone off like that.

Come back please. Let's talk about this.

I hold the phone in my hand, reading and re-reading the message, when two more pop up.

I only get like this when I really care, and you know how much I love you.
You're the love of my life...

I sink back into my seat and let out a slow breath.

I'm being irrational, and I'm probably not thinking straight. Everyone's always told me I'm too emotional and reactive. That's all this is—me worrying over nothing.

My phone flashes with more texts, but I turn my phone on silent and throw it on the passenger seat.

I'll let *him* squirm a little for a change.

* * *

It's after five and the office is quiet. I decided to stay late so I wouldn't have to deal with the rush-hour commute, but truthfully, I want to hide out in the office for as long as possible. I don't want to face anything. Not that Shaan would be waiting for me, but still, work feels like my escape, and I need it after last night.

I leave my office and head to the kitchen to get a glass of cold water. My mind drifts back to everything that happened. I remember feeling small, insignificant, and stupid. The anger, guilt, and shame all mix inside of me, a formulation I'm deeply familiar with. Then something new: fear. Last night was nothing if not a sign to hit pause.

When my glass is filled to the brim, I turn off the tap and, still lost in my thoughts, turn around straight into Nick. The cup slips out of my grasp and shatters on the ground.

"Oh my gosh, I'm sorry." I look at the shards sprinkled on the kitchen floor and reach down to pick up the biggest pieces. "Fuck," escapes my mouth as I cut myself.

Nick bends down and pulls me up by the shoulders. It's so comforting, I want to step into his embrace. "Let me," he says softly. He gives my shoulders a squeeze before letting go.

He steps over the glass and grabs a paper towel from the counter, wrapping my palm gently. I should feel pain, but all I can sense is the way his hands feel on mine.

"Thanks," I say with a small smile.

"I'll clean up the rest." I nod and watch him as he cleans up my mess.

"How's your hand?" he asks when he's finished.

"Better now."

He holds my gaze, and I can see a furrow forming between his brows. "Everything okay?"

He gives me a look that penetrates my well-constructed barriers, and it's like he sees everything: the anger, sadness, and exhaustion. I just hope he can't sense the guilt and shame, too.

"Just tired. It's been a long day." I play it off. I always do. "I have a marketing plan I need to finish and send off for tomorrow." The plan was for him, his project.

"If you need more time—"

"No, not at all. I just wanted to double-check it to make sure I got everything."

"I'm sure it will be great. I already love how detailed you are from what I've seen." He gives me an encouraging nod, and I feel energized.

"I should wrap things up," I share, not knowing what else to say.

He looks at me with a thought forming on his face. "Unless you want me to have a quick look now, and that way you don't have to worry about at least one approval?"

"Actually, that would be great." I am in no rush to leave and face reality.

"How about I order some dinner and meet you in the boardroom?"

"Oh, no, you don't have to do that."

"It's the least I can do for making you work late. Vietnamese okay?"

"It's perfect."

I walk back to my office with a lighter heart and softer step. I've been holding so much tension throughout the day. The cut on my hand is now pulsing, and I discard the paper towel and find some small bandages hidden away in my bottom drawer. Next, I look over my plan several times, nervous that his eyes will be on it in moments. My heart starts beating rapidly. I can't show him this! What if he thinks it's too basic, or he doesn't like the new elements I took the initiative to add?

My mind starts racing with excuses to get out of showing him the plan when my computer pings with a notification.

Running downstairs to grab dinner. I'll meet you in the boardroom.

It would be childish of me to run off now, especially since he went to so much trouble.

I steal one final glance at my plan, unplug my laptop, and make my way to the boardroom. The floor is all but empty now, except for a few other consultants working late, and the cleaner. I smile at her as she ducks into the washroom with her cart.

I walk by the empty offices, stealing glances inside. I always love to see how people decorate their desks, if at all. Do they feel like this is a temporary blip on their resume, or are they here to stay? I especially love seeing pictures of kids and pets. My heart pangs with longing that's quietly been there for as long as I can remember, wondering if I'll ever have that.

Things have been going great with Eshaan, but lately it just feels like we argue more than ever. I have to believe it will work out, as he's the only happily-ever-after on the radar after years of nothing. I couldn't let him go because of a fight or two, could I? I know he messaged his ex, but I didn't see anything that suggested more than that, and my chest pangs with remorse about jumping to conclusions. Maybe I could have avoided his crazy outburst. I can't help but feel it's my fault for pushing him to act like that.

My phone vibrates. I pull it out and glance at the latest text from Eshaan.

You're killing me babe. What can I do to make it up to you?

The ache in my chest softens. I've kept him waiting enough. I promise myself I'll respond later.

I walk into the boardroom and head to the front of the room to connect my laptop to the big screen, but honestly, I'm not sure exactly how to set it all up. I look helplessly at all the cords and the projector.

"Hey."

Nick walks in with way too much food.

"That smells amazing."

"I made it myself." He gives me a wink that makes my toes curl.

"Confession, I don't know how to hook my laptop up to any of this." I hold up the cables. There were other things that I would never confess to him, no matter how much I might want to.

"Don't worry, let's eat first." He hands me my lemongrass chicken vermicelli bowl, along with chopsticks, a fork, and napkins, and sits next to me.

I assumed he would sit across from me, so the proximity is unnerving, especially with the vast table.

My mind flashes unbidden to other things we could be doing on it right now. I use my fork to mix together the sprouts, noodles and chicken to distract myself.

"This is one of the biggest boardroom tables I've ever seen," he says as if he's anticipating my every desire.

I take a small bite to get my mind back on safer ground. "This is so good."

"It's amazing, right? It's just this little hole in the wall, but they have the best food."

"Those places usually do." I force myself not to shovel the food into my mouth and hope I won't end up with a carrot stuck in my teeth or sauce on my face. He doesn't seem to notice my inner struggle and eats as if we have all the time in the world, as if we are in an intimate restaurant and not under fluorescent tubes in a boardroom.

We sit like that for a while, this easy back and forth, and I almost forget we're supposed to be talking about work.

"Do you like working here?" he asks between mouthfuls.

"Yes." I pause while I try to think of what to say next.

"Yes, but…?"

I know better than to air my grievances.

"It's nothing."

"It's not nothing." He sees through me, and it's disarming.

"It's just that, when you first start somewhere, they seem to notice what you're contributing, and over time, it's harder to get your work noticed. That extra time and effort without any recognition can be so deflating. I mean, I'm grateful. It's such a great opportunity."

I feel vulnerable, wanting to stuff the words back in my mouth.

"I get it."

I exhale, not realizing I'd been holding my breath, waiting for his response.

"It's one of the reasons I became a consultant—people see your value when you're only there for a short time. You get to impress people and then leave."

I almost want to laugh. He seems to wow everyone in the office just by showing up. Gorgeous, not a minority, and a man. I wish for a moment it was that easy for me.

"There's something you're not telling me," he probes.

There's a lot I'm not telling him.

I want to change the subject, as I know it doesn't bode well when I speak up, but I find myself babbling on for some reason.

"I just feel like it's harder when you're a woman. You have to work so hard even to get noticed."

I expect him to balk or steer the discussion elsewhere, but he doesn't.

"It must be so tough. I'm sorry you have to go through that," he says earnestly.

"I mean, things are changing and going in the right direction, I hope. We're just not there yet."

"Let me know how I can help." He gives me a soft smile that feels like it's reserved just for me.

"I'm not even sure, but offering to look at my plan, that's a lot."

"Let's see it." He starts clearing away our containers, and I try to help. "Let me."

I'm not used to this, and I feel this weird discomfort. Since I was seven years old, I've been picking up after the men in my home.

When he sits down again, he angles his chair toward me, and I find myself doing the same. He's a forcefield; I'm a helpless magnet. I want to reach out and run my fingers up and down his solid bicep, but I sit on my hand instead.

He leans in closer as he brings his thumb to my cheek and grazes it softly. "You have something right here."

My breath hitches, and I lose myself in his sparkling eyes before breathing out a barely audible, "Oh."

He pulls his thumb slowly away.

I release my hand and bring a napkin to the exact spot he touched, but when I look down, there's nothing there.

"Got it." He licks his lips slowly as his eyes meet mine. They look like the most decadent dessert I want to bite into.

A low noise comes from outside the room, and my head snaps to the glass walls surrounding us, but I see nothing. My heart rate jumps like I'm on the elliptical at the gym, and I remind myself where I am.

At work.

With a guy I work with.

His eyes track my movements, but he's unperturbed by the possibility of being seen. To him, that was probably an innocent gesture, but to me, it felt like a naughty one that I want more of.

"I'm not sure how to connect this to the big screen." I gesture to the projector to get things back on track.

He sits up and glances at my screen.

"Don't worry about it. It's getting late. Do you mind if I look on your laptop?" His voice is all professional and calm, like he didn't just electrify my every nerve ending with a swipe of his thumb.

"Sure." I slide it over to him. I try my best not to stand up and pace as he reads through it. I pretend to peruse my notebook like it has the answers to all of life's questions within its pages.

Then, of course, I remember the SMS chat with Jess, and I'm praying I didn't leave that conversation open, where she made too many inappropriate comments about him, among other things.

"Is it okay if I add some comments?"

"Of course," I say like I'm not freaking out.

I glance over his shoulder, cringing inwardly and second-guessing every little thing I wrote.

He spends more time on it than I thought he would, and immediately, a sinking feeling makes its way into my gut. It's probably horrible and he doesn't know how to tell me how much it sucks. Here I am talking about getting noticed and how hard it is as a woman, but truthfully maybe it's just because my work is crap.

You're so high on yourself, is what Eshaan would say to me. *Who do you think you are?*

Flashes of memories I've tried to ignore start assaulting me, and when I think I can't take it anymore, he turns to face me, our knees just a hair apart.

"That's so incredible. I read it over three times, because I haven't seen a plan that thorough before. You came up with marketing options I never even thought of."

"Really?" Relief washes over me, and then a wave of exhaustion too. He likes something I created.

"I added a few details about the audience that you wouldn't have known, but other than that, that's it."

"Thank you. I appreciate your feedback and dinner and everything." My body sags with relief.

Just then, the bottom tab on my screen lights up with a string of messages from Jess.

Are you still at work?

You better not be.

Unless it's with hot AF Nick 🔥

That's all I read before I abruptly reach over and close the screen, realizing too late that my arm is over his and my chest is nearly grazing his elbow. I pull back too fast and get up.

He slowly slides the laptop back over to me, and I don't hazard a glance at him.

"I should get home." I stack my things, then get up and move away from the table. In my rush to get away, I drop my hardcopy of the plan on the floor. He reaches down to help me, and his fingers brush mine while a smile dances on his lips.

"Where do you live?"

"Just over on Cambie Street. It's about fifteen minutes away by SkyTrain."

"I'll walk with you to the station."

I don't know why he's offering, but I don't care as long as I get another moment with him, even as my embarrassment lingers in the air.

"Okay, sure." I take a calm, steadying breath. "Let me just grab my things, and I'll meet you at the elevators." I give him a quick look and see one corner of his mouth still lifted in a smirk he's trying and failing to suppress.

Jess. Seriously.

I hurry back to my office to grab my things, feeling better than I've felt in a long time.

He's waiting by the elevator doors, striking in his bomber jacket, and a tiny thrill shoots through me at having just a little more time with him. So many of the office ladies would be jealous right now, and I almost wish someone were here to see us. I'm grateful I took extra care choosing my armour today: beige high-waisted pants cinched at the waist with a belt and a tight pastel pink long-sleeved shirt. I wonder if he noticed.

We walk into the elevator and out the front door, where it's dark and softly raining. It's so romantic. Thanks, universe. As we walk toward the station I steal a glance at his profile. Calm, assured, confident, and just being next to him, I feel a little better, too.

"Where do you live?" I think to ask.

"Not too far from here in Coal Harbour."

That's only a few blocks away. "Oh, but that's so close. You don't need to walk me to the station."

"I don't mind. I could use the fresh air."

Because I don't want him to go, I let my objections hang in the air unsaid, evaporating like mist on the sidewalk after summer rain.

His fingers sweep across mine accidentally, and I fight the temptation to grab hold of them.

Dinner, high praise, being walked to the SkyTrain—is this guy for real?

We reach the station all too quickly, and I pause at the top of the staircase.

"I'll walk you down."

Such a gentleman.

We reach the platform as he turns to me. "I meant what I said before." He looks at me with that sea of blue, standing close enough that I can take a deep inhale of his delicious scent and imagine myself wrapped in it.

"What's that?"

"Let me know how I can support you."

You're doing so much already.

I nod and thank him again.

I float the rest of the way home. My mind knows it's just a colleague being nice, and that there's nothing more to it. But deep down, my heart wishes for something more. So much more.

10. PROGRESS

Another week rushes by in a flurry of meetings, marketing plans, pitch decks, emails, and late nights to get through it all, and I find myself loving every moment even more now. Nick is so easy to talk to, and I look forward to every interaction with him, from our meetings every other day to his impromptu visits to share the latest tech news. I know it's all business, but my delusional heart hopes that he craves seeing me as much as I crave seeing him. After this morning, I almost believe he might. He left an extra-sweet matcha latte on my desk with a Post-it that said: "Just the way you like it :) –Nick." I read it several times like a lovesick teenager before tucking it away inside my filing cabinet.

It's nearly 5 p.m. when Tom and Nick appear at my door.

Tom walks in and Nick lingers behind him. "Great, you're still here," he says. "I have something I'd like to run by you."

"Hi Tom. Yes, sure. Come in," I say, even though he's already standing right in front of my desk.

"I know it's early days, but Nick shared that you're doing an incredible job with the pitch decks, and that you've even walked him through your presentation."

Nick smiles at me over Tom's shoulder.

"So next week, there's a conference in Minneapolis. The leadership team will already be away at conferences in New Orleans and Denver, so we can't be there. If you're willing, we could have you step in."

My heart leaps. This is the chance I've been waiting for. "Yes, I'd love to." I try not to sound too enthused, but I'm thrilled.

"Great. It's a long shot as these investors have turned us down before, but we'll try to set things up again. At the very least, both of you can network and make connections."

"Both of us?" I ask.

"You and Nick. You can tag-team it."

I rub my hands up and down my arms to hide my discomfort and anticipation at us being away overnight together.

It's fine. Nothing's going to happen.

"Sounds great."

"It's next week, so clear your Wednesday to Friday."

"Will do," I say, somehow without shaking.

Tom leaves us alone, and I get up and walk toward Nick, but don't get too close.

"Thank you."

"For what?" he says nonchalantly. "I didn't do anything." He pauses and then adds, "It was all you."

My eyes follow him as he heads back to his office and my heart floods with happiness.

11. THE WEDDING & THE HACKER

"I have to leave." I pull Eshaan aside as soon as I get the call from work.

"What? Right now?"

"Yes. It's work. There's an emergency."

We're standing just inside the doors to the reception hall at his cousin's wedding, next to a flowery sign that says "Welcome to Gurdeep & Rani's Reception" in sweeping calligraphy. The lights are dim, soft Hindi music is flowing out the open doors, and guests are milling about everywhere. I catch a glimpse of the bridesmaids in varying shades of green lehengas, posing against a yellow satiny photo backdrop with golden butterflies hanging from the ceiling above them. The whole place looks like an enchanted forest and they're the glittery fairies.

"Are you fucking kidding me? It's Saturday." He rolls his eyes at me, exasperated.

I'm the misfit fairy who should have taken this weekend off-call, but I didn't.

"There was a data breach, okay? That's all I know." I give his arm a squeeze trying to get him to understand.

"Nish, you don't even work in IT, why do you need to be there?"

"I have to get messages ready for employees, stakeholders, and if it comes to it, the media."

"Can't they get someone else to do that?" He shakes his head and looks up at the ceiling. "Fuck, they're probably not going to even pay you for this."

"It's my responsibility," I share quietly.

"Quit. Just quit," he challenges me.

I dig my heels into the soft, plush carpet and look away. My eyes land on the floating LED candles next to the table beside the guest book.

I place a hand on the wall to steady myself before answering. "I can't."

Sometimes Shaan acts as if I work at the local diner, rather than in a coveted position at Evolve Tech, one of the hottest new start-ups creating a massive buzz throughout the entire industry.

"You're going to miss everything. I mean, the speeches haven't even started yet." His arrogance is baffling, but I stuff down the feelings boiling within me, like I always do.

Although most of his cousins have careers and work full time, they also have cars and houses paid for by their parents and still argue over who gets more. I could never wrap my head around it. I paid for school with student loans, and I felt so guilty when my mom would tuck some cash in my purse for lunch when I was in university.

"I'm sorry. I'll come back soon if I can."

It's just after 9 p.m. The bride and groom arrived late. They pushed dinner before the speeches and performances to feed the hungry guests. That's what happens when you're jamming so much into one day and changing outfits in between every event like an awards show.

He just shakes his head. His disappointment settles into my bones. "Whatever." He stalks off like a petulant child.

Even so, I want to chase after him, and I wrack my brain to think of a way out of this. I hate it when he's unhappy with me, and I want to make things right.

Everyone on the communications and marketing teams rotate weekends to be on-call just in case. It ends up being only a few times a year, and since nothing ever happens, I didn't think much of it when my turn came up this weekend. The only rules are that you have to be in town, and you can't drink.

I could've pretended I had some drinks, and they would call someone else, but it didn't feel right, and besides, this is another chance to prove myself.

"*There* you are." Anjali sashays toward me with a drink in hand. "Can't wait for the dancing to start." She twirls me around, already a little drunk.

The bridesmaids walk through the hall doors in a shimmery swirl of earthy tones, and I steal a look at the ornate crystal vase centrepieces overflowing with lush greenery, gold-painted roses, and cascading orchids that spill over the sides like a flowery waterfall. Twinkling lights are woven throughout the arrangement, and golden rose petals strewn on each table. They cast a romantic glow on the linen-draped tables. It's a lavish display of the world that I'm desperately trying to fit into. *But do I belong here? Is this what I really want? I thought it was, but I'm not sure anymore.*

"I can't stay."

"Why? What's up?" She takes the last sip of her drink.

"There's a crisis at work."

"I get it." She places her glass on an empty side table nearby.

"I should say bye to Auntie Ji and Uncle Ji first, though." I look around frantically as if they'll suddenly materialize. I can already sense Shaan's mom's disapproval, and it's almost too much to bear.

"Good luck finding them in there." She laughs.

I hesitate for a moment and then realize she's right.

"Just go. I'll cover for you."

I squeeze her shoulder and say, "You're amazing, you know that?"

"I know." She winks at me.

I call an Uber, and there's one just a few minutes away. I walk fast, but don't run to avoid attracting any attention from the guests milling about. Sneaking away from the reception might send tongues wagging since Eshaan and I aren't officially engaged. Before you knew it, some crazy story would be circulating that there was trouble in paradise or rumours that I was disrespecting their family by leaving early.

It is exhausting to keep up with. Some family members are open-minded and modern, and others were more traditional, and I've given up trying to keep it all straight. I know enough from witnessing my own family drama from a young age not to say much when someone is nice but nosy.

Today was fun but long. I love weddings, the dressing up and the festivities. I especially love that at family functions like this, Shaan's mom's icy glare turns into a doting mother-in-law look. We both play our parts perfectly—I try my best to be the gracious soon-to-be daughter-in-law, while she pretends to be the proud mother. Sometimes, I wish it wasn't an act, that I could do or say something that would make her love me, but somehow, I always end up saying or doing the wrong thing. She never says anything to me about it, of course, but Shaan always fills me in later for some reason. I wish he would keep her rude remarks about me to himself. In front of others, she would never let her quiet disdain show. No, she cares too much about what people think of her.

The other bright part of my day was Eshaan's Dadi Ji, his dad's mom. She always welcomes me with open arms, and I love just spending time with her. Today, she whispered conspiratorially to me to get her another sweet, and I know she shouldn't have too much sugar, but I couldn't say no to her kind face. We laughed after: It was our little secret.

* * *

It's a long ride from Surrey to the office downtown, but somehow the time flies by and I'm there, ready to face the unknown. I walk to the front doors, swipe my security badge to gain access, and head up the elevator to the twenty-seventh floor.

The doors open, and although I want to get up to speed on everything,

I need to change first. I'm shy about going in wearing my full saree, not to mention it's not the most comfortable to work in.

I stroll down the quiet halls to my office, the dark hallway lighting up with every step. Even though I know I need to get to the boardroom as quickly as possible, I find myself pausing in front of Nick's door. I don't expect him to be there, but he turns as I stop and stares at me. He's turned off the bright overhead lights, and there's only the soft glow of his desk lamp that creates an inviting warm ambience in his office.

Surprise and then intensity simmer in his gaze as he looks at me. I'm catapulted back to the night we first met when he looked at me just like that. He steps forward, closing the distance between us, and I suddenly forget everything else. I can't catch my breath. No one else exists in this abyss, and I don't want to be anywhere else. I take in his black fitted T-shirt and tight jeans, and I can't help but wonder what the emergency called him away from. I'm not sure I want to know.

"Nisha."

He drinks me in, gazing at me from head-to-toe. If my brown skin could blush…

"Wow, you look—" He stops himself mid-sentence and the mandatory sexual harassment training flashes through my head: *Refrain from telling colleagues, especially those of the opposite sex, that they look nice because commenting on appearances is inappropriate.* I want to laugh. Someone saying you look nice isn't the harassment most women in the workplace are worried about.

"You're all dressed up," he says finally.

"I was at a wedding."

"Whose wedding?"

This is when I should say, "My boyfriend's cousin's," but for some reason, I don't.

"A friend's. What's going on?" I quickly change the subject.

"There's been a security breach on our main server, and right now they're trying to determine which data was accessed."

"Shit."

"I know." He runs his hand through his hair, and I can tell he's stressed. A bigger organization could recover from this, but for us, as a start-up, it could be game over. "We're meeting in the boardroom in ten."

"Great. I'm just going to change, and I'll be right there." Except I remember I have about a million pins in my outfit, and it would be nearly impossible to get them out all on my own, especially the biggest one on the back.

He sees me hesitate. "What's up?"

"Oh, um, it's nothing."

I can't ask him to do this, but I also don't want to be in this outfit all night.

"Are you sure?" he presses.

"Actually, I have a pin on the back of my top, and I was wondering if you could take it out for me? I can't reach it myself."

I don't breathe as I wait for his response.

"Of course, no problem."

His words are saying one thing, but his eyes are saying another as they blaze at me. His pupils are inky black pools taking over the waves of blue, or maybe it's just the dim lighting that's making it seem that way.

I turn around, pulling my hair that's flowing down my back to the side. He steps closer so he's right behind me. My breath hitches as his fingers skim my skin.

Breathe, remember to breathe.

"It's where the blouse attaches to this long piece here." I hold the end of my silver saree to show him what I mean. Somehow, my hands don't shake and my voice is steady.

"Got it."

His fingers reach inside my fitted blouse, just barely touching the clasp of my bra and the pin just off to the side of it, and I'm hyper aware of everywhere his fingers stroke my skin. His touch featherlight.

He struggles to undo the large safety pin, and I don't care because it means that he'll have his hands on me for longer. He manages to take the pin out after a couple more attempts. My saree now hangs loosely at my side, the delicate embroidery sparkling with an ombre pastel pink and green shimmer in the dim light. I have to be careful not to let it completely unravel.

I force myself to turn around instead of leaning back into him, and he gently places the pin in my palm, keeping his eyes on mine the entire time. "Here you go," he says. He's so close that his musky pine and sandalwood scent wraps itself around me, calling me closer with every breath.

"Thank you."

I look up at him, and he looks down at me, and I forget why we're here. The soft glow of the lamp makes everything feel surreal, and I don't want to wake up from whatever this is. He slowly drags his teeth over his lower lip, and I watch the movement, mesmerized.

I imagine putting my hands on his chest and then pushing him back against the desk. I imagine him wrapping his arms around me as he softly bites my neck with those teeth, then grazes my ear with his lips. I imagine reaching under his shirt and feeling his sculpted abs and then dragging my hands lower to his fitted jeans, undoing the top button. I imagine things I shouldn't even be thinking about, and he looks at me like he sees my every fantasy. I'm probably imagining that he's feeling something too, but I can't help myself.

Both our phones start beeping at the same time, pulling us out of this reverie. Neither of us checks the notifications.

"I'll meet you in the boardroom," I say hastily. I force my feet to move away from him.

"Sounds good, I'll let them know you're here." His voice is a sensual rasp instead of his usual professional tone.

I walk into my office and hear him walk down the hallway. I slide the door closed and unpin the rest of my saree. It's not like Nick's out there, but my heart races still.

I change into a white satiny button-up blouse with tight black cigarette pants. Then I pull my hair up into a bun and remove my earrings, necklace, bangles, and tikka, placing them carefully on my desk. I have way too much makeup on, but there's nothing I can do about that. I give myself one final look, leaving my saree in a messy bundle on my chair and head to the boardroom, laptop in hand. I try to erase the desire stirring within me.

Stop thinking about him.

Tom nods at me as he sees me walking in, and I take an empty chair in the crowded room. I see there's a rep from almost every department here.

"We don't know what's been accessed, but Nisha, we need you to draft statements for stakeholders, employees, customers, and the media. We'll need to have different variations for the different scenarios."

Adrenaline courses through me with the excitement of everything going on—including my encounter with Nick, which I try to compartmentalize.

"I'm on it." I open my laptop, log in, and start drafting the statements based on templates the communications team has already created for us.

The IT team is trying to determine whether the data breach was external or internal, meaning it could be the result of a hacker from the outside or someone who has violated their access within. Nick has a background in ethical hacking, which is why he was called in to lock down the system and prevent further unauthorized access. Still, there is no way for us to know yet what they were able to take. He'll review my releases, and then they'll be sent for approval. This way, they will be ready to send out as soon as we get confirmation of what's going on.

I dive in, a charge rushing through me—whether it's from the breach or from something else, I don't know.

12. HOTLINE BLING

A few hours later, I've drafted several releases covering every conceivable scenario I can think of. Nick gave me his seal of approval, and I sent them off to the VP of Communications. She had a few edits and then asked me to send the releases to Legal, the CIO, and the CEO.

Legal might take a while, so I make my way to the coffee station where I'm hoping to run into Nick. I make an Americano and lean against the counter, my shoulders slumped, and I close my eyes for just a moment.

"There you are." I startle at the sound of Nick's voice. I must have drifted off. I check the clock: It's 1:30 a.m. Seriously, how did thirty minutes pass?

"Is everything okay?"

"We found out what happened. It was an employee who was fired a couple of weeks ago. He still had access even though his card showed it was deactivated."

"Do they know what he accessed?"

"No data, but he was trying to install malware to affect all the systems."

"And did he?"

"No. Luckily I was able to remove him from our system before he activated it." He leans back against the counter next to me.

"You're amazing." I smile at him.

"It was a team effort," he says, looking away.

"Really, it sounds like it was just you." I laugh.

"No, everyone's been so helpful." He gives me a tired but relieved smile.

"So, what do we do now?"

His expression turns serious. "They're getting the police involved. So, they don't want to send anything out because it would look bad, especially since there's no damage."

"Of course." It makes sense to me, but I'm a little sad we won't get to use my releases.

"But Tom wants us to stay for a couple more hours just in case." He steps away from the counter.

I know he didn't need to fill me in, and I would have found out when I got back to the boardroom, but my heart warms that he came to find me and tell me.

I turn around to grab my Americano.

"Can I make you a coffee?"

"I'm good. I already had two since I got here."

We head back to the boardroom, and the tension is noticeably less as we enter. We chat for a bit, but everyone's tired and waiting for word that they can go home. It's almost 3 a.m. when Zoren, the CEO, finally comes in.

"First off, I want to say thank you for dropping everything you were doing on a Saturday night to come in and help. It means so much to us. Second, the situation is being taken care of. We'll keep the systems locked down until Monday and ask for your discretion as this is now a police matter." He looks around the room and makes eye contact with each of us. We all nod, and there are some murmurs of agreement. "And finally, the best part is you're free to go. Come see Amy for a taxi chit or use the corporate Uber account to get home safely. And you'll get an email from HR next week to cover the extra time you put in. Thank you all and good night."

He gives us one last tired smile and leaves the room.

My shoulders sag with relief. Everyone files out of the room. I save all my releases, thinking they'd be good to have for next time—hopefully nothing like this happens again, but this way I can be prepared.

When I look up, Nick's standing at the door. "How are you getting home?"

"I don't know." I never take Ubers or taxis this late by myself. I know it's fine, but for some reason, it always makes me uncomfortable. I'm usually with friends, family, or Eshaan anyway.

I know I could call Rachel and she would come, but I feel guilty. I've been keeping my distance after our fight.

"I can give you a ride."

"That's okay." I know he lives not too far, and my place is way out of the way.

"I don't mind." He lingers at the door, and the thought of waiting outside for a car at 3 a.m. feels like too much. "I don't know if I can sleep anyway. I'm so wired."

"Thanks. That would be great." I smile at him.

We make our way to the underground car park, and Nick slides into his Polestar and opens the door for me from the inside. I ignore the flutter of butterflies at the thoughtful gesture.

It's pristine inside. I wouldn't expect anything less.

"Any requests?" he asks as he opens the music app.

"Maybe some lo-fi."

"Sure. I like listening to that too."

Nick flicks on the seat heat for me. I lean back, letting it comfort me even though it isn't cold. It's like he wants to make sure I'm comfortable, which is weird, right? I'm just a colleague. For a moment, I allow my mind to drift. What if this isn't just him being polite? I know no good can come of it, but I find myself wishing he wanted to spend more time with me. Maybe in an alternate reality, he does. Or maybe in this one…

We pass a 24/7 diner and I realize I'm starving. I only had a few appetizers at the reception. I watch it until it's out of sight.

"I know it's late, but if you're hungry, there's this great 24/7 diner. We just passed it," he says, knowing just what I need.

"I am," I answer. I really *am* hungry, that's all. It isn't as if I'm purposely extending my time with him.

He turns the car around.

Despite it being almost 4 a.m., the diner isn't empty. We get a booth, and the waitress quickly takes our order. The other people seem drunk, which is usually the case with patrons out at this hour, and I remember the times I have been too, in places like this.

I order a burger and milkshake, realizing too late that I should have ordered something less messy. Nick orders the same, and it makes me like him even more. In a professional context, of course.

My phone buzzes. I thought I put it on silent when I got to the office, but I must have left it on. I glance at it quickly and see a text from Eshaan.

Are you still at work?!

Nick raises his eyebrows.

"You can get that if you need to."

"No, it's fine."

My phone buzzes repeatedly, and I turn it off.

He has a little grin on his face, and heat rushes to my face. Texts this late only really mean one thing, and I don't want Nick to think some guy is messaging me for a hook-up.

"Just my friend checking in to make sure everything's okay," I say, wanting to justify the texts.

His eyes sparkle as if he senses how he makes me feel, but he says nothing.

Our food arrives, and I praise the universe for this tiny miracle.

"I saw you saving those releases you created. Do you mind my asking why?"

I'm grateful for the subject change.

"We don't have a crisis communications plan that covers all these updated scenarios, and I thought I could help create one. That way, if anything happens again, we'll be more prepared."

"That's such a good idea. Most orgs don't plan for anything, and then they're left scrambling," he shares in between bites. "They are lucky to have you, you know."

I brush it off. "I'm sure anyone would have thought of it."

"But they didn't." He takes a sip of his shake, and I do the same.

"Make sure you mention it next week."

"I will," I lie. I want to, but I'm too nervous. His confidence in me gives me a little boost though, and makes me think that maybe I can.

After our meal, the car is warm and the music is low and relaxing. My eyes are so heavy, and I think to myself, *I'll just close them for a second.* The full week, followed by the wedding festivities, and now this all-nighter is finally taking its toll.

* * *

Light shines behind my eyelids. When I open my eyes, the sky is light, and the sun is starting to rise in a medley of soft pink and orange hues like a watercolour painting. It takes another moment for me to realize I'm not in my bed—I'm still in Nick's car.

Shit.

I must have fallen asleep on the way home, and Nick didn't wake me. I look over and he's facing me with his eyes closed. He must have fallen asleep, too, after parking in front of my condo. I take in his gorgeous face: the arched brows, dark eyelashes, stubble forming after a day of not shaving, his hair in disarray but in a way that suited him, almost like he was intentionally going for this sexy, scruffy look. My hand reaches out to touch him, even though I know I shouldn't. I comb his hair back and gently drag my fingers down his face. He suddenly opens his eyes, and my fingers freeze.

My heart starts thumping wildly, but he doesn't seem to notice or react to the fact that I'm touching him like a weirdo.

"Hey, you're up."

I pull my hand back. "I'm so sorry. You should have woken me."

"I couldn't. You were sleeping so peacefully."

He smiles, that luminescent smile that lights up his face and kindles the spark within me that seems to remain dormant until I'm with him.

We stay like that. Bodies turned to one another, eyes locked, and I know I should move, but I can't bring myself to. He brings his hand to the side of my face, his fingertips skimming the soft skin at my temples and then down to my chin. I should turn away, but I don't. Instead, I close my eyes and lean into his touch.

My makeup must be a mess, and I'm not even sure what my hair looks like, but the way he looks at me makes me feel something I shouldn't—like I'm desirable. More than that—like I matter.

Waking up next to him is like a dream I don't want to wake up from.

An abrupt knock at the window interrupts the moment, and I quickly sit up while Nick rolls down the window.

"You're not allowed to park here overnight." It's one of the parking enforcement guys who patrol the area.

"Sorry about that. I'll move." Nick starts the car and moves up a few spaces.

I move to get out, and he says, "Wait, let me get your door." He opens his door and steps out.

"Oh, um, you don't need to," I stammer.

"I don't mind." He walks around to my side and gets my door for me.

How is anyone this nice?

"Thank you for the ride home, and letting me crash in your car, and dinner? Breakfast? I don't even know which one."

"Don't worry about it." He walks me up to the front door of my building.

Even though we've spent all night together, I don't want our time to end. I hold my fob in my hand instead of swiping it and turn to him.

He lingers next to me too.

"It was nice hanging out outside of work," he says with a sweet smile, the one that feels like it's just for me.

I swallow hard. "Yeah, it was." I'm not sure what he's getting at, but my delusional heart starts to hope.

"Maybe we can do it again sometime."

I nod a little too enthusiastically.

"That would be nice," I say, and when I can't think of anything else: "Well, I better go."

He nods, still smiling at me.

I go through the front door and wave at him. He watches me to make sure I get in okay before he turns away.

I feel light and happy despite only sleeping for a couple of hours.

I turn my phone back on in the elevator. Five missed calls and ten texts from Eshaan fill my screen.

My heart pounds as I read them.

I thought you were at work, but it shows you're at some diner? WTF

Call me RN.

I swear to god if you're lying to me...

I completely forgot about location tracking. I didn't think he would even be checking it. Immediately, I feel guilty. The messages dropped off thirty minutes ago, and heavy panic replaces the light joy of spending time with Nick.

I'll tell him some of us went to eat after—but then why would we go so far from the building? My mind comes up with all the questions that I don't know how to answer. I send off a quick text anyway to help placate him. Then I turn my phone off. I can't deal with his response right now.

It's fine. I didn't do anything wrong. I can hear Rachel's voice in my head.

Eshaan's reaction isn't normal.

He's just pissed because I left the wedding. Weddings are such a big deal, and I left when I was being introduced to the family. It reflects badly on him and us, and I know his mom won't let me forget it either.

I'm such an idiot. I should have just booked the weekend off. I go down the path of overthinking, wishing I could change things.

I quietly put my key in the door, not wanting to wake Rachel. She won't be expecting me because I told her I was staying at Shaan's.

I go to my room, change into my PJs and wipe my makeup off. I still feel panicked and guilty, but there's something else, too. Something else that feels like irritation.

I don't have family money to rely on. In fact, if I lost this job, it might take me months to find another one. I have some savings, but with the cost of living so high, they would be gone in no time. Eshaan, who's had everything handed to him, wouldn't understand. I'm jealous that he doesn't have to worry like I do.

After my dad died, my mom started working full-time, and then when I started university, she took a second job on weekends. To help lessen the load, I took out student loans, worked part-time, and lived at home. Adding to the pressure during that time, my sister's wedding was coming up. My mom worried we wouldn't have enough to cover everything.

It breaks my heart to think about.

Sometimes, I would take the bus home from university late at night and see South Asian men and women, my grandma and grandpa's age, going home after cleaning office buildings. I never wanted that to be my mom. That's why I worked so hard.

I press my fingertips into my closed eyelids to stop the tears.

Eshaan said he could cover everything, that after the engagement I would move in with him—if he ever got rid of his roommate—but I can already see his mom's disapproval.

Missing a family wedding for work. Is this the kind of girl you want to marry? No respect for us.

It's almost 7 a.m., and my mind is swirling with anxious thoughts. Finally, the exhaustion catches up with me. These are someone else's worries. Someone else's problems. Fantasy Nisha has it all together, and she will keep it all together.

I'll find a way. I always do. That's my last thought as I fall into a deep, troubled sleep where even in my dreams, I can't find any relief.

13. LOVERS AND FRIENDS

I have no idea what time it is when I wake up, but I'm still tired. I duck my head under the covers. A few more minutes, and then I'll face the day—even though I want to stay in bed forever.

I throw off the sheets and glance at my phone. It's 2:22 p.m. Rachel would say that's a good sign. I hope it is.

I pull on my favourite cozy socks, brush my hair, and head to the kitchen to make some coffee.

Rachel is sitting at the counter and working on her laptop.

"Good morning, or should I say afternoon, sleepyhead." She gives me a warm smile.

"Good morning. Is there any coffee?"

"I'll make you one."

Rachel bought a new fancy espresso machine and I don't know how to use it.

She gets up while I take a spot on the stool at our kitchen island.

"So, how was the wedding?"

"It was so beautiful." I tell her all about the lavish decorations and festivities.

"I thought you were going to stay at Shaan's." She looks at me questioningly.

"There was a work emergency, so I had to go in."

She places a latte in front of me, along with some stevia, and stands across the counter.

I grab the mug and take a little inhale—dark cherry notes with hints of toasty caramel that take me back to last summer, when Rachel and I went fruit picking in the Okanagan. We had smoothies for days on end, made tarts with recipes we found on YouTube, and froze the berries and cherries. Even then they lasted for months. I miss those slow mornings we used to have before I spent most of my weekends with Eshaan.

"Oh, that's right, you were on call this weekend." I don't know how Rachel keeps track of both of our busy schedules.

"I know, I should have changed it, but I had no idea something would actually come up." I add a few drops of stevia and then take a sip. It's glorious. Soft, subtly sweet, and decadent. My mind instantly drifts to Nick's fingers gently touching my face. I pull myself back into this moment.

"Give yourself a break. You couldn't have known." She gives me a knowing look. "Is Shaan upset?"

"Yes." I don't elaborate because I already know that Rachel isn't Shaan's biggest fan.

"It's just that weddings are such a big deal, culturally, and this was the first big family event I've been invited to. It was a chance for me to make a good first impression and I think I might have screwed it up." I take another sip as worry replaces the momentary comfort from the coffee.

"You didn't. I'm sure of it." She looks me in the eyes.

"How do you know?"

"Because, seriously, Nish, you're one of the kindest people I know."

I want to say that she's the only person who sees me that way.

"I know you probably don't want to hear this…"

I take another sip and brace myself.

"But you need to be able to talk to Shaan openly and honestly about what matters to you." She pauses and then gives me a thoughtful look. "I know, I don't have the best track record, but I've learned so much and I care about you. I don't want you to make the same mistakes I did. It's uncomfortable and awkward at times, but it's important to talk."

I let her words land.

She's right. I've spent most of my life avoiding conflict, being the good girl, and doing as I'm told, but over time, that's only made me angry and resentful.

"You're right, Rachel. I wanted to say I'm sorry about everything at the café last week." I look at her and hope she can see how sorry I am.

"I'm sorry, too. I don't want to push you. We're all on our own journey, but we're also here to learn from each other."

I smile. Rachel, the online coach and creator, can turn anything into a teachable moment.

"Why are you smirking like that?"

"Oh, I'm so lucky that I have an amazing friend who cares so much."

She gives me a curious look.

"I'd better call Shaan."

I head back to my bedroom with my coffee in hand. He picks up on the first ring. "Glad you finally had a chance to call. Let me guess, you're still working?"

I take a deep breath. I want to learn how to communicate and have a healthy relationship, and I know this will require patience.

"I'm home now, and I wanted to say I'm so sorry about last night. Nothing has ever come up when I've been on-call before, so I didn't even think to change my shift. I will next time because you, us, that's my priority."

"Nish…"

"What is it?" My shoulders rise and tense at his tone.

"I have to be honest with you. You're wasting your time with this job."

"What do you mean?"

"I mean, you're running yourself ragged and for what? You wouldn't even be able to pay rent if Rachel wasn't giving you a steep discount."

"I know, but they've given me more responsibility and I'm taking on this huge project for their next big launch." I clutch the phone tightly.

He laughs. "You know what they're doing right? Giving you more responsibility without more pay is just a way to work you to the bone.

They're trying to get more out of you instead of hiring someone else. It's just for their bottom line. That's how business works."

"I know it seems like that, but there's this lead position coming up and I really think I'm being primed for it." My voice grows smaller and unsteady.

"You're kidding yourself." I can almost see him shaking his head.

Anger rushes through me, but another part of me wonders, What if it's true? What if he's right? What if this is all for nothing? I shove the thoughts from my mind. I know I'm making real progress at work, even if he can't see it.

"I mean, you know my cousin Anjali? She earns six figures. I get that she makes her career a priority." He pauses briefly and then continues. "You know I can take care of everything, right? After the engagement, you can move in with me, and down the road, we will buy a house—my parents can help."

Shame and anger intertwine. Why can't I be happy with everything Shaan is offering? Any girl would jump at this chance, but it feels like he is trying to snuff out my light instead of kindling it.

He continues, oblivious to my rising emotions. "If you really want to work, you can help out at the shop."

I pull the phone away from my ear for a moment.

He can't be serious. I can already imagine his mom's frosty glares and cutting words if I got something wrong. I love fashion and getting dressed up, but I sure as hell don't want to work retail alongside his parents.

"Anyway, it's cute that you're working so hard, and it's fine for now. Let's just focus on the engagement, and we can figure out the rest later." What he isn't saying is that I should be at home with him, where I belong, but I know it's what he's thinking

"Okay," I mumble, demoralized. I wish I could make him understand.

"I have to get to my parents' place. We're having a little family dinner before everyone leaves."

"Oh, have fun." Sadness washes over me that I wasn't invited. I mean, it's fine. After last night, they probably think I don't want to come. That's how these things work. I know from the drama in my own family that one thing can be repeatedly thrown back in your face for years.

"Could you tell your parents I'm sorry?" I add, hoping to further defuse the situation.

"I don't think it will make a difference. They weren't exactly impressed that you left." Dev calls his name in the background. "Anyways, I have to go. I'll text you later."

I chug the last bit of coffee. I can't face Rachel, not right now. I think about everything Shaan said. Maybe I am kidding myself. I worked so hard to get here, and I still can't help but hope it will turn into something. But maybe I'm wrong.

My phone vibrates in my hand even before I have the chance to put it down, and Mom flashes on the screen. I place my other hand on my heart and take a deep breath. I could call back later, or I could just deal with whatever else the universe wants to throw at me now.

"Hi Mom." I try to keep the sadness from my voice.

"Putt, tu theek aa?" says Mom, asking if I'm okay. It's amazing how she just seems to know when something is up.

"I'm fine. Just Shaan and I had an argument." I know I shouldn't say anything, because I don't want to worry her, but it's too fresh, and I can't keep my emotions hidden like I normally do.

"Ki hoya?" I should have known she'd want the details.

I brace myself and deliberate on how much I should say. Too little and my mom will know I'm holding back, too much and I open myself up to criticism.

"He just thinks I work too much." I don't tell her I left his cousin's wedding for a work emergency.

"You *do* work too much, Nisha. For what? Not much money."

My insides churn. I didn't expect her to side with me, but I also didn't expect this.

"If he wants to take care of you, why not let him? Your father took care of us all."

I dig my nails into my thigh and shake my head.

Yes, and it killed him. The stress of working two jobs for years with the only reprieve he found at the end of a bottle.

"Mom, it's 2026. I want to be able to take care of myself," I manage to say even as my heart races.

"He's going to be your husband. You have to listen to him, not just do what you want all the time." Her voice rises.

"You've been doing what you want for years, and what did it get you, huh? Don't ruin this, too."

"Mom, I—"

I hear her doorbell in the background.

"Preeti's here to drop off Aman. I have to go."

"Okay, bye, Mom."

I let the phone drop into my lap. How would Fantasy Nisha handle this? Because I sure as hell don't know what to do anymore.

14. MY DIL GOES MMMM

I take the SkyTrain early and get a seat, which is a small comfort after the exhausting weekend. I pull out my phone, having forgotten my book on the counter, when I see a notification pop up.

Eshaan tagged you in a post.

There I am. A candid shot of me at the wedding. A soft smile on my lips. A glow of light around me. My silver shimmery saree blends in perfectly with the stunning decor.

My heavy heart grows lighter.

No caption, just a heart.

He posted it last night, and it already has almost a hundred likes.

The post has tons of comments, but the one that catches my eye is from his cousin, Anjali.

She's perfect.

My photo is pinned to the top of Shaan's feed, and my heart melts a bit.

I know we have our issues, but is any relationship perfect? Truthfully, I don't even know what a perfect relationship would look or feel like.

Everything will be okay. I don't know how, but I feel it.

Eshaan is my happy ending, and I have to keep reminding myself of that.

* * *

"Well?" Nick leans on my door frame, looking like heartbreak.

"Well, what?" I say casually, even though my heart races every time he's remotely near me.

"Did you send over the templates and your recommendations to help with the crisis communications plan?" He folds his arms over his broad chest.

"No." I look away.

"Why not?"

He takes a few steps inside.

"Oh, I don't want to step on any toes. I mean I'm sure the VP has everything under control." I look over at him.

"You're making excuses," he says, challenging me.

"Am not," I say childishly.

"You are." He matches my tone.

He settles himself on one of the chairs across from the desk. "I'm going to sit here until you send them." He gives me one of his smirks.

"I'm sure you have more important things to do than sit in my office all day."

"I can clear the afternoon," he says, leaning back and resting his hands behind his head. My stomach flips and it's a struggle not to smile at him. *He's taunting me.*

"Fine. I'll send it in a bit," I lie.

"I don't know if I can trust you."

He has no idea the game I'm playing, and I don't know if I can trust myself either.

"I just want to look them over one more time."

"Show me the email and I'll help look it over."

"Fine," I relent. "But it's just because I don't want you sitting in my office all day." I give him an over-exaggerated glare.

"You're right. I'm too much of a distraction."

My hands pause on the keyboard mid-strike. *Now he's flirting with me.*

"I don't get distracted easily." I look over and allow a soft smile.

Be professional.

He moves closer. So close, I can smell his sandalwood and pine cologne.

I try not to inhale it in desperate gasps.

"Oh, no? Let me see the email."

I pull it up and turn the screen his way.

He takes the wireless keyboard from me, lightly brushing my fingers in the process, and I tingle all over.

He reads it over, and before I can stop him, he hits send.

"I can't believe you just did that." I look at him, feeling both petrified and excited.

"I like to keep you on your toes." He puts the keyboard back in front of me and turns the screen back to face me.

"We'll go celebrate when you hear back." He gives me a wink as I watch him leave.

They'd *better* email back—because I need to know exactly what he has in mind.

15. #EMPOWEREDWOMEN

On Wednesday evening in Minneapolis, Nick and I wander into the large conference hall and the familiar unease of being in large, crowded spaces starts rushing through me. This time, though, I'm excited too. I finally have a chance to prove myself, and despite my nerves, I pull myself together and get ready to make small talk.

I'm waiting for Nick to leave my side any second, as he mentioned he knows a lot of people here, but he doesn't. He stays by my side and points out the hosts of the seminars we'll be attending tomorrow, the keynote speaker for the event, and even our competitors who'll be pitching to investors alongside us tomorrow afternoon.

"Well, if it isn't my favourite IT consultant." A beautiful woman with curly black hair and dark brown flawless skin comes up to us. I clench my jaw.

"I bet you say that to all the tech bros," he replies, and I want to exit this conversation.

She laughs, and it sounds like silk. "You're in the top five for sure. Who's this you have with you?"

"Nisha, I'd love for you to meet Wanda. She's going to be on the Women in Tech panel tomorrow, and she runs her own headhunting firm."

"So lovely to meet you, Nisha." She holds out her hand, and I take it, not liking that I like her already.

"I only take on female clients, but if I ever decide to take on men, Nick will be at the top of my list." She winks at me, and I'm not sure why it makes me envious. "I hope the panel can go ahead, actually. We just had a last-minute cancellation from one of the panelists."

"I'm sorry to hear that." Nick looks at her and then at me, and I can see a thought forming in his head.

"Nisha here is so passionate about empowering women in the workplace. She even did a podcast recently about women in tech. If you need someone, I'm sure she'd be happy to help."

First of all, I had no idea he knew about that. And second, is this really happening to me again? At least this time, it's something I actually want to do. Well played, universe.

Wanda turns to me, and her gaze assesses me in a different way than before. "Is that something you'd be interested in?"

I hesitate. I have no experience, and I don't want to screw up, but I also can't miss this chance.

"Actually, I would love to help, but I'll be honest, I've never done anything like this, so I understand if you want someone with more experience."

She eyes me kindly. "I'm looking for passion more than experience, and I get a sense you have it."

She smiles at me, and light, bubbly hope froths in my chest. "If Nick recommends you, then I don't need to hear anything else."

I fight down the jealousy that she trusts Nick that much and instead feel the joy that he would do this for me.

"The panel starts at ten a.m., and if you give me your email, I'll send you the questions in advance so you can prep."

"That would be so amazing, thank you," I gush.

"No, thank *you*. You saved me from potentially having to cancel."

I give her my details and she heads toward someone else she recognizes across the hall. I can't help but radiate happiness, and I know who to thank for that. I want to throw myself into his arms, but I know that would be wildly inappropriate. Instead, I touch his arm and look up at him.

"Nick, thank you. This is just so incredible. I can't tell you how much this means to me."

He looks at me and my heart skips a beat. "You don't need to thank me."

"I do."

He gives me his most radiant smile, and I can't help but be enamoured with him.

My phone vibrates, and I quickly scan the screen and see that it's an email from Wanda. "Wanda just sent me the details."

"Great. Why don't you go prep, and I'll take care of the networking for this evening."

"Oh my gosh, really? That would be so amazing." I squeeze his forearm that I'm still holding on to.

"I'll walk you out."

When we reach the lobby, I can't help myself: For once, I don't overthink, and just wrap him in a hug. He puts his arms around me, and I can't think of anything else. We hold on too long and I should pull away, but his body is so solid and comforting and I want to just stay here forever. I can feel his breath on my neck, and his heart seems to be beating just as fast as mine. Suddenly, I get conscious of the fact that we're not the only ones here, and I pull back.

"I better go prep."

He bites his lip as he looks at me, and I feel unsteady on my feet. "I'll see you later."

He watches as I get in the elevator and the doors close, and all I want is more reasons to have his arms around me, even though I know that's the last thing I should want.

16. IN DA CLUB

After the panel the next day, I'm floating on air. Wanda and her colleague Mei, who just launched a woman-owned and run AI app, were incredible. I still can't believe I was up there with such incredible women—it was standing-room only. The conversation centred on creating spaces and opportunities for women to thrive in male-dominated industries, supported by other women and, of course, with men as allies. Since I've wanted to do something like this forever, and because Wanda sent me the questions beforehand, I was able to speak up and confidently share my thoughts. Nick even took a few clips of me speaking and sent them to our team chat. My phone was buzzing with encouraging messages and praise from Tom, Zoren the CEO, and even the VP of Communications. I also sent the clips to Rachel and Eshaan. Rachel literally blew up my phone with congratulations, while Shaan just replied with a thumbs-up. I didn't let his reaction disappoint me.

Then I did my first pitch ever, and although I was nervous, Nick gave me a pep talk and by some miracle, we're going through to the next round, and I'm so thrilled we made it through when the leadership team didn't.

I even got an email this morning from the VPs who loved my crisis communications templates. I forwarded it to Nick with a smiley face, and he had this cheeky reply:

You're welcome 😉

It's been a whirlwind, and I'm soaking it all in as we make our way to the spacious hotel lobby after our last seminar of the day, before the cocktail reception tonight. My heels make a soft tapping sound on the marble floor as we walk.

"I know there's that reception tonight, but why don't we just go out and celebrate?" Nick asks. He looks almost nervous, but I can't imagine why he would be, especially around me.

I instantly want to say yes. I would love to get out of here and go anywhere with him.

I shift on my feet and twist the Tiffany promise ring I wear on my right hand that Eshaan gave me on our six-month anniversary.

He catches my hesitation and his eyes turn distant. "It's okay if you'd rather stay here, I just thought it would be nice to have a break." He shrugs.

"I would love to, but I was planning on going out with my friend this evening. We grew up together in Toronto, and he moved here a few years ago, so I don't get to see him that much."

"For sure. Have fun." He starts to turn away, but I place a hand gently on his shoulder.

"You could join us if you'd like." My heart starts hammering, wishing that he'll say yes.

"I don't want to intrude," he says, looking at me with those piercing eyes.

"You wouldn't. He's bringing his partner, so I know he won't mind."

"Okay, sounds fun."

"There's just one thing, though."

"What's that?"

"We're going to a gay bar and it's eighties night." Amusement flashes in his eyes.

"I'm sure I can find something to wear."

"Okay, great. Meet you down here in about an hour?"

"Sure."

I must have imagined his nerves because he's back to his self-assured, confident self as we take the elevator up to our rooms.

* * *

I launch myself at Sunny as soon as I see him on the crowded sidewalk, and he picks me up and gives me a big hug. He looks just like I remember, except this time, happier. His dark hair is expertly styled back from his face, and he's wearing a dark tee with a letter jacket and fitted jeans.

We haven't seen each other since I moved out west, and I realize I've missed him so much. He puts me down, and I turn to Kin, his partner, who I'm meeting for the first time. His vibrant blue, half-sleeve button-up contrasts with his fair clear skin and silky jet-black hair. He looks like a K-pop superstar.

"It's so great to meet you finally, Kin," I say and wrap him in a hug, too, even though we just met. If Sunny loves him, I know I will, too.

"I've heard so many things about you," Kin says warmly.

"Uh-oh, now I'm worried." I laugh.

"Oh, and this is Nick. We work together."

"This is the slave driver you were telling me about," Sunny says and winks at him.

I look over at Nick, worried he might feel slighted, but he just gives me a playful smile.

"Please, tell me we don't have to wait in that long line," I say. The bar is super busy for a Thursday night.

"Kin has an in with the bouncer," Sunny shares.

"Thank god."

"I know your bougie tastes and how much you hate waiting for anything. Plus, we know you have an early morning, so we won't keep you out too late."

"It's so good to see you, my friend," I say to Sunny, and give his shoulder a squeeze. With him, I don't need to pretend, and with me, he doesn't need to either.

Thanks to Kin we skip the line and walk right in. Sunny and Kin wander off to talk with some friends while Nick and I line up at the bar.

"Do you go out to clubs often?" He looks at me with those eyes, and I try to remain steady under his gaze, although it's like he unravels me with every glance.

"Not really."

Maybe turning thirty is getting to me, but I just can't stand the sticky floors and insanely loud music, and everyone smashed out of their minds. You have to go with the right people to have fun. Eshaan and his friends are definitely not fun to be around when drunk, and Rachel and I much prefer cozy lounges. Plus, she doesn't drink anymore.

"Oh?"

I adjust my tight black mini skirt as I search for the right words, wishing I had worn something else, but it's the eighties getup I planned before I invited Nick: mini skirt, high-top sneakers, cropped fuchsia halter top, and oversized jean jacket. I pulled my hair half up with a scrunchie. Nick is wearing tight jeans, sneakers, and a white shirt, and I force myself not to stare. Even in basic clothes he looks devastating, and in this bar, I'm not the only one who notices.

"I really only go with Sunny. We have this tradition of at least going once a year, but it's always a gay bar."

"Why?" He looks at me questioningly as we move up in line.

"He's spent most of his life trying to fit into places he doesn't feel like he belongs, and he just wants to be somewhere where it's not a big deal."

"I get that." He gives me a warm smile.

"It's more fun for me because I can just go out and have fun without worrying about…actually never mind." I forget what I'm saying around him.

"Worry about what?"

I decide to be honest.

"Oh, you know, getting hit on by random guys. Some of them just don't get the hint."

His eyes turn dark as we shuffle up the queue, and he's silent for a moment. Shit. I didn't mean him. I get anxious, worrying he might be thinking that I was saying this about him, about that night I don't know if he remembers, but I can't forget.

"Was I one of those guys?"

I look at him. "What?" I try not to gasp.

"You know, when we first met. I wondered if you remembered me. Do you?"

My breath catches, and I try to tame my out-of-control pounding heart at his confession.

He remembers me.

Suddenly, I'm back there again. Another dark, crowded room, another bar, and this time I can't help but imagine what would have happened if, instead of walking away, I had stayed.

It's our turn to order.

Nick looks over at me. "What are you having?"

"Double gin and tonic, please."

I need the buzz to get rid of the discomfort building inside of me.

"I'll have the same," he says to the bartender. Nick pays for our drinks, and we make our way to a table.

"You didn't answer my question." He looks at me as we both take a sip. This is important to him, and I somehow feel that my answer will change everything.

"You're not a creeper if that's what you're wondering." I laugh, trying to diffuse the intensity.

"Just a guy that couldn't get the hint?" he answers, deadpan.

"Not that either. I enjoyed our conversation."

He leans in, and my pulse skyrockets with his proximity. "What did you enjoy exactly?"

"It just felt natural, not forced or some sort of pick-up line."

Are we actually talking about this? A rush of giddiness hits me. After all this time wondering, I now know for sure that he remembers me. I sag with relief but quickly recover knowing full well I'm walking right into dangerous territory.

Will this change things between us now? Do I want it to?

I refuse to hear the answer my heart pings back at me.

"Good feedback." He smirks at me, and I'm enchanted.

"I can share it in your next performance review." I can't help flirting. He smiles back at me and for a second, I can't breathe. It's that smile that haunted me for months after we met, but I could never tell him that. That I searched for him on the streets, in bars, and at coffee shops, and did a double-take every time I saw someone with his build and hair. I tried creeping him on the internet but couldn't find anything. I even went back to the bar where I first met him, only to find that it had closed down. Worse yet, the reason I walked away was that I was too insecure to take things further. All I could think of were my faults and how he might see all of them.

I finish my drink in record time and need to escape from the intensity of all this, of him.

"I'm going to freshen up."

"I'll get another round."

Inside the bathroom, I want to splash my face with cold water, but I can't risk ruining my makeup. I force myself to look in the mirror and breathe, but already I'm feeling the effects of the alcohol. With the busy day and excitement, I didn't get a chance to eat much, and the double shots are already making me buzzed.

Okay, so Nick remembers, but that doesn't change anything now. I don't know why it feels like it does.

I walk back to the bar and see a handsome man with perfectly coiffed hair and tight pants talking to Nick. I know flirting when I see it. I stop and just watch for a moment. Nick has both of our drinks in his hands, and I can tell he's being polite but doesn't know how to exit the conversation. I watch him struggle for a moment more and decide to come to his rescue.

I walk up to him and wrap my arms around him. "Oh, hey, babe. Thanks for getting our drinks." I smile at him knowingly.

"Darling, you're back. I was just talking about you."

I shoot them both a smile.

"He was just telling me you wouldn't be interested in having company tonight." The handsome stranger looks at me suggestively, and I laugh.

"Thanks, but I'm not good at sharing." I want Nick all to myself. I tighten my grip on his arm.

He leans in. "I wouldn't want to share him either," he says and walks away. I beam, feeling like I've won a prize.

Nick sets the drinks down. "You enjoyed that, didn't you."

"That was the most fun I've had in Such. A. Long. Time." I laugh, and it resounds throughout my body.

"Glad I can be this evening's entertainment." He steps back and hands me my drink, and we both take a few sips.

"What was he suggesting?" I ask innocently.

He takes a long drink before he responds. "You don't want to know."

I elbow him gently. "Oh, but I do."

"I'll let you use your imagination."

I pout at him. "You're no fun."

He smirks at me. "If you want fun, let me show you how fun I can be."

I swig back the rest of my drink as he takes my hand and leads me outside to the rooftop patio. He entwines my fingers in his, looking back at me with a sly grin on his lips. He walks me to a secluded place away from the noise, but where we're not completely alone.

It's dark, and the music is thumping in my ears in rhythm to my racing heartbeat as he leans in. "What kind of fun would you like to have?" he whispers in my ear. Our bodies are almost touching. If either of us even moved an inch, our lips would touch, too.

"You tell me what you have in mind," I whisper back seductively, even though I know I shouldn't let this carry on.

"Why don't I show you instead?"

I wet my lips in anticipation.

He pulls me closer so our hips are touching. He runs his hand slowly and softly up and down my bare thigh, leaving a wake of goosebumps, while he takes his other hand and slips the tip of his finger into my mouth, dragging it across the inside of my bottom lip. I get a taste of him, and I shiver as I close my eyes. I place my hands on his chest to steady myself. The feel of his touch on my skin causes me to stumble slightly more than the alcohol buzzing through my system.

"How's this for fun?" He speaks softly into my ear.

"Not bad," I whisper.

"Not bad?" A challenge he's more than up for.

He replaces his finger with his lips, and I can't pull away. I don't want to. He kisses me gently at first, a lover's caress. Raindrops on an infinite ocean. An amuse-bouche before a scrumptious dinner. Then, like he wants to devour me right there, like I'm air, and without me he can't breathe.

His hand moves up my jacket and onto my bare back under my halter top, and I arch into his touch.

Closer, I want him closer.

I wrap a leg around him, pushing him into me. I'm vaguely aware I shouldn't be doing this, but my thoughts slip away until there is only sensation. His tongue doing tantalizing sensual sweeps of my mouth. His strong hands on my back and hips. Soft at first and then gripping me tighter. My arms wrapped around his broad shoulders. Our bodies pressed up against each other. His warmth seeping into my dry, brittle soul, bringing out emotions, feelings, and passion I didn't think I would ever experience.

I lose myself in the feel of him, barely registering an incessant buzzing in my jacket pocket, until I realize it's my phone. I pull back, and it's such an intrusion, drawing me out of the world of sensation. Our breaths are ragged, and I immediately miss the touch of his lips on mine. It takes me time to register where we are, but then, slowly, the music comes flooding back in, along with the voices all around us.

If his smell was intoxicating, his touch is pure rapture, leaving me shaking with need.

He steps back, and I walk toward him as my phone keeps buzzing. I pull it out and silence it, and in a moment, his lips are on mine again, incessant, hungry, desperate.

My phone buzzes again, and I reluctantly pull away from Nick. It's a message from Sunny.

"So, Sunny and Kin are outside waiting for us." The words feel strange, like a completely different language.

Nick tucks a strand of hair behind my ear, and his gaze drops to my lips before he takes my hand again. He brings my inner wrist to his lips, planting a barely-there kiss that has me weak with longing.

"To be continued." He winks.

As he leads me out of the club, all I feel is his phantom touch heating up my body all over. We step outside, and Sunny and Kin are waiting a few metres down the street, their arms around each other. It makes me so happy looking at them, because I know how much Sunny deserves this.

I don't realize that I'm still holding hands with Nick until we reach them. I let go, immediately wishing I hadn't. I know Sunny would never judge, having been judged and shamed all his life for who he is, but still, it's an automatic response, because I shouldn't be doing any of this.

Nick and Sunny fall in step with one another, and I drop back to walk alongside Kin.

I don't know how much Sunny's told him about me, and I suddenly feel self-conscious, but Kin looks over at me with nothing but kindness shining in his eyes, and it's refreshing.

"You and Sunny are so great together."

"He's incredible." He smiles and looks at Sunny's back adoringly. "I'm lucky to have found him."

"I bet he would say the same about you." I smile as I look over at him.

"What about you?" he asks.

"What about me?"

"It seems like you have a lot of good things going on in your life, too."

I want to laugh and then cry. "Looks can be deceiving," I manage.

It *looks* like I have everything I ever wanted: I finally feel like I'm closer to getting that promotion, I'm getting engaged soon, and I have amazing friends, but somehow, I feel so empty.

"Pizza okay?" Sunny turns around and asks.

"Yes," Kin and I both say at the same time. We look at each other and laugh.

"I can see why you like her so much," Kin says, and I'm not sure if he's talking to Sunny or Nick.

We walk into a cozy little pizza place, which is busy even at this late hour. Sunny snags us a booth in the corner. I sit next to him, leaving Nick and Kin to sit on the other side.

The waitress takes our orders, and Kin takes Nick to the old-fashioned jukebox they have in the corner. A few minutes later she drops off our drinks.

"Remember that time we played truth or dare and you dared me to eat like ten gulab jamuns?"

"I didn't think you would actually do it." I laugh.

"I still can't look at them without my stomach revolting."

His dark eyes pierce into mine, sparkling as the smile leaves his lips, usurped by a mischievous grin I know so well. One that got us into trouble so many times.

"It's payback time." He leans closer. "Truth or dare."

I take a sip from my milkshake as I ponder.

"Truth. There's no way you're making me eat ten of anything that sweet."

"What's really going on with you and pretty boy over there?" He nods his head toward the other end of the room.

I glance over at Nick and our eyes meet. The sky blue, now a midnight abyss, tempting me with a single look. He gives me a soft smile before turning back to Kin.

"Nothing, we just work together," I lie, as I lick my lips and savour the lingering memory of his lips pressed against mine. I ignore the butterflies that float through my abdomen and the desire that stirs elsewhere.

"Give me a break, Nish. He's been glancing over here every few seconds with fuck-me eyes."

"He's probably just looking at..." I look around. "The guy in the booth next to us."

He rolls his eyes and lets out an exaggerated sigh. "Yeah, I'm sure he has a thing for Buzz Cut over there."

"Stop. Sunny, you're the worst." But I'm laughing.

"Come on, and don't even pretend like I didn't see you hand-in-hand leaving the club. Spill."

I shift in my seat and swirl my milkshake absentmindedly.

"You're both hot for each other, obvs."

I bite my lip.

"I can't go there, Sunny. You know I can't."

I won't let myself. I ignore the pang in my chest that reminds me the only time I feel like me anymore is when I'm with Nick, that I felt this instant connection with him and it's a constant effort to hold back. And after that kiss tonight, I'm not sure I want to.

"Because of Eshaan?"

"Yeah, it's a done deal."

He presses his lips together and then looks at me.

"Apne dil di gall suno. Isn't that what your dad used to say to you?"

I nod as tears prick my eyes. "But it's not as simple as listening to my heart now."

"Believe me, I know. You know the shit I've been through."

I grab his hand. I know it too well.

"Remember when Palwinder Auntie busted me making out with that foreign exchange student?"

"The look on her face. She was scandalized. Especially since everyone thought you and me were a thing."

"Looking back at it now, we probably shouldn't have all gone to the local burger place."

"We were nineteen, Sunny. Just kids."

"Yeah, and you had no problem sticking up for me. You could have walked away, but you didn't."

"You should get to be with whoever you want," I say as I shrug. It was the only time I had spoken up about anything and it didn't go over well. Some members of his family still don't talk to him, and well, my mom has never let me forget the disgrace she suffered because of me. I'm grateful to be past that now, but a flutter of nerves rises in my gut that I promptly push down. I have nothing to worry about anymore.

"You deserve that too, Nish."

"I don't know," I deflect. I can't give myself any more reasons to hope for more with Nick. We're not a thing. We likely never will be. Besides, my life is perfectly on track. I just have to keep it that way.

"What about you and Kin? Is it getting serious?" I mash my straw into my milkshake before taking another sip.

"I think he's the one."

My heart leaps.

"Oh my gosh, that's amazing, Sunny!"

His face breaks into a smile.

"Yeah, we're thinking sooner than later."

"Like how soon?" I lean over the table.

"Sometime this year."

"No way. You're getting married before me even?"

"We all knew it would happen." He leans back as a smile spreads across his face.

I turn to him and pull him into a hug.

I squeal. I'm so excited.

"Shhh, keep it down." He glances at Kin and Nick. "I haven't popped the question yet."

"Oh, sorry." I try to put on a neutral expression, but I can't stop from smiling as Nick and Kin return to the table.

"What are you two squealing about?" Kin eyes us curiously.

"Oh, you know, reminiscing about old times." I give Sunny a knowing look. "It was me before you, you know?"

"Right, I forgot you two were a thing."

Nick gives us an intrigued look.

"Sit, we'll fill you in."

* * *

It all feels so easy with Nick. Too easy. That's what I'm thinking when I slide into the backseat next to him when we head back to the hotel. I place my legs to dangle over his right thigh, and he brings one arm around my shoulders and his other around my hips. My skirt hitches too high, but I can't bring myself to care. The buzz of alcohol is leaving my system, but the intoxication of him is still flooding it.

My heart feels light and free after the wins at work, Nick's revelation, and spending the evening with Sunny and Kin, making me act recklessly now. For the first time in a long time, I'm more than just the demands, pressures, and expectations of being a woman; I'm a girl who wants to follow her heart and experience some joy, even if it's fleeting.

Nick lowers his left hand to my leg, grasping it. His fingers and thumb are making enticing strokes along my inner thigh, moving higher each time.

"Did you have fun tonight?" he asks, his breath hot against my neck.

"So much fun." I lean back to look up at him, my eyes shining with a light only for him.

The corner of his mouth lifts in a smile.

He's moving his lips toward mine, and I close my eyes, anticipating his kiss, but the car abruptly stops. I open my eyes to see we're right outside the hotel, and I slowly slide off Nick and out the door. I hear him thanking the driver, and then he's behind me, and we're walking into the lobby and then the elevator. Both are deserted at this hour, and I'm grateful for the privacy. The elevator doors close, and he's hitting his floor button and then in another moment, he's in front of me.

"Nightcap?"

His hand comes up to gently stroke my cheek like he can't help but touch me, and the simple touch sends my heart racing. Being alone with him in a room is a bad idea for so many reasons, but right now, I can't remember any of them.

"We could just hang out."

I breathe a little easier knowing he's not expecting anything, but it's not him I'm worried about. "The seminars start at 9 a.m.," I say.

"That's what coffee is for," he says, looking at me with so much intensity, I can't look away. His gaze heats me up everywhere it lands.

His touch, his presence, and his attention are waking up parts of me that I didn't even know existed. Parts that feel whole, complete, and enough, and it's terrifying when all I've known is the opposite.

"Just one drink."

I freeze in place, my mind refusing to let me cooperate while my heart beats without restraint, encouraging me to free-fall.

"I can't." I look away.

"Okay."

He doesn't push. If he did, I don't think I could trust myself to say no.

"Sleep well," he says, leaning in, his lips brushing against my cheek.

I can't even respond or think when he's this close to me, so I say nothing.

He presses my floor and leaves. I find myself staring at the closed doors. The elevator takes me a few more levels up, and I head to my room in a daze.

17. #FML

I'm staring out the airplane window at the tarmac, desperately trying to regulate my breathing and to get last night out of my head. It never should have happened, but it did, and now I don't know what to do about it. The unease is building, knowing I crossed a line I never should have, but I also can't ignore the intrigue and desire stirring within me.

I was distracted this morning when we divided up to attend different seminars and networking events to maximize exposure for the organization. I couldn't focus on what I was there to do, no matter how hard I tried. I managed to at least make a few connections and exchange business cards, but I know I didn't make the most of this opportunity. I need to get my head back in the game, but it's not going to happen today.

"Mind if we switch seats? I'd love to sit with my friend." I hear Nick's voice speaking to the man next to me.

Luckily for my tortured heart, the man is kind and doesn't mind moving. He gets up and gives us a knowing wink, like he's well aware I'm not just his friend.

"That's better." Nick buckles up and looks over at me, and I lose my focus even more.

The flight attendants go over the usual safety precautions, and I use the time to try to gather my resolve. I need to keep things professional and avoid straying into forbidden territory—like last night—especially if we're going to attend more conferences and events. Still, I don't know how to vocalize it.

Nick turns over to me. "How are you feeling?"

I'm not sure what he's asking. About last night, about him, about what happened? I play it safe.

"A little drained."

"We've got a few hours. Rest for a bit."

I exhale. I don't have to talk or figure things out now. I can just relax and let things be. I try to put my seat back and get comfortable, and Nick looks at me struggling.

"Here." He pulls me toward him, and I nestle into his shoulder. Immediately, I know I shouldn't, but it's so comfortable.

I will allow myself this. His hand finds mine, and we stay like this for most of the flight. I can't actually sleep, but I also can't bring myself to pull away.

He makes me feel something.

Believe in something.

Believe in myself.

I want to run from him and from that feeling, too, but mostly it's like I'm running away from myself.

He seems to see into my soul, and his touch energizes my desire for things that I shouldn't dare to want.

I know I can't let myself have him the way I want, the way I crave, the way my body insists on and my soul wishes for, but I can let myself have this. This moment where my heart feels light and free. I tuck it away in the deepest parts of my mind, knowing I can draw it out when I need it the most.

* * *

It's almost 9 p.m. when we walk through baggage claim with our carry-ons in hand. My eyes land on Shaan leaning against a pillar, looking down at his phone. He looks up, and our eyes meet. *Fuck.*

"Babe, I missed you." He pulls me into a hug and leans in for a kiss. I flinch, but he doesn't seem to notice.

"I had no idea you would be here." I try to keep the panic out of my voice.

"I wanted to surprise you." He grabs my carry-on from me and turns to Nick, who stops behind me.

"Nick, this is Eshaan," I manage.

"Hi, I'm Nisha's boyfriend." Of course, Shaan won't miss the chance to make that obvious.

I can hear Nick's breath catch behind me.

"Good to meet you." They shake hands, and I question every choice that led me to this moment. I try to take a steady breath as my chest tightens.

I catch a glimpse of hurt before Nick's expression turns unreadable and it kills me. I wish I could explain, but what would I say? *This is my boyfriend and soon-to-be fiancé, and I should have told you, but I didn't, and I never should have let you kiss me, but I'm glad I did. I don't know what any of this means, but I want it to mean something.*

"I'd better go. I have an Uber waiting outside. Enjoy your weekend." Nick leaves without even a glance back, his voice flat and distant.

Everything felt so close, so intimate, and now the air is frigid.

The mortification sets in, and then the guilt as I look at Shaan's doting eyes on me. We walk out to the parking lot, and he puts my suitcase in the trunk while I hop into his plush Maserati and try to stop freaking out. It was nothing. Nothing happened. Not really.

He jumps into the driver's seat and turns to me. "Dinner?" I want to go straight home, but I don't want to disappoint him.

"Sure."

"Any place you want to go to?"

"Wherever is fine."

I just have to breathe through one moment at a time.

"How about that sushi place you love?"

"Sounds great," I answer as nausea builds in my stomach. I don't know how I'll be able to eat anything.

As I buckle the seatbelt, I catch a whiff of pine and sandalwood and become acutely aware that I am drenched in Nick's scent that I love so much, but now it's closing in on me, until my breaths are rapid gasps. I wonder if Shaan notices.

Normal, I have to act normal.

I nervously rub my thighs and take a few deep breaths, just like Rachel taught me to do when the anxiety is too much. Box breathing. Breathe in for four, hold for four, exhale for four, hold again for four.

My uneasy heart starts settling back into a gentle rhythm just as we reach the restaurant.

It's not too busy, so we're able to get a table right away. We order, and Eshaan fills me in on what's been going on in his world. I pepper him with questions, so he doesn't ask me anything. It works mostly until we're finishing up.

"How was the conference? You did such a great job speaking." His eyes shine as he looks at me, and my heart softens.

"It was really great. We made good connections and I met a lot of inspiring women."

"It was just the two of you?" I know of Eshaan's jealous tendencies, so instantly, my guard is up with his words. I know where this is heading.

"The leadership team had conferences in New Orleans and Denver, so for this one, we repped," I say calmly even as my heart beats rapidly.

"Do you want to go look at rings this weekend?" I try to redirect him.

"I already found something that I know you'll love."

"Oh." I hide my disappointment. I'm already letting his family pick everything, but I did want a say in the ring that I would be wearing forever.

"Trust me." He looks at me confidently, and I nod and concede like I always do.

We usually spend at least one night a week together, but today, I make up an excuse and ask him to take me home.

Wrongness floods my system, one circuit at a time. I need time to recalibrate before I mess up everything.

* * *

Nick Tremblay started following you.

I lie in bed scrolling through my phone and try to suppress a thrill when this Instagram notification pops up, even though I know I shouldn't care. Then I think of the photos I have up there of me with Eshaan and the most recent one from the fashion show, a selfie of me smiling at the camera, and Shaan kissing my cheek, and I immediately cringe. I'm tempted to delete those, but I know that would look suspect. It's fine, I convince myself. It's better that he knows.

I try to creep his profile, except it's private. I won't hit the follow-back button even as my fingers inch toward it. I have to dig myself out of the hole I find myself in, rather than throw myself deeper into it.

18. THE DOUCHEBAG

I'm sitting in the bar on my own, and I feel lame, but I don't want to leave just yet. Jess just left to head out on a date after our usual monthly drinks night, and I stayed behind to nurse the last few sips of my drink.

"Would you like another?" The waiter comes by, reading my thoughts.

"Sure, that would be great."

The place is full of the after-work crowd, and the mix of office types and hipsters gives the place a cool vibe. I feel bad taking up a booth just for myself, but I tell myself it's okay. *I can take up space.* I repeat Rachel's words in my head, and treat this as a test from the universe to embrace the discomfort.

Nick and I have been keeping it professional. I should be relieved, but instead I'm deflated and more conflicted than ever. I thought keeping my distance would make me feel different, but it's only as if my feelings have intensified. I find myself looking forward to our meetings, rereading our messages, and thinking of him more than normal.

The waiter drops off my drink, and a moment later, Nick appears with a drink in hand as if summoned by my thoughts. I know people from the office frequent this place because it's close by.

"Do you have a moment?"

I should say I don't, down my drink, and get the heck out of here.

That's what a good girlfriend would do, but my voice disobeys me, and already my body is comforted and lit up by his presence.

"Yes."

His hair is tousled, like he's been running his hands through it.

"Everything okay?" I ask him.

"Not really."

"What's up?" My skin prickles with worry.

"I wanted to apologize," he says, looking at me thoughtfully.

"For what?" My heart races, and panic rises in my chest, thinking for a moment that maybe he told Shaan about us. It's ridiculous, but still, I can't stop it. Then something else: the easing of guilt, and a bit of relief? I don't even know.

"For kissing you. I shouldn't have done that. It was unprofessional."

I get the feeling that this has been really bothering him.

I swallow, looking away from him. The words dry up in my throat. My emotions are all over the place.

"I'm sorry. I don't want to mess anything up for you." He takes another sip of his drink as mine arrives.

I'm already doing a good job of that myself, I want to tell him, but I don't.

"I don't want to make you uncomfortable. Say the word and I can recommend another consultant to take my place."

Nothing can happen between us, but the thought of him disappearing brings up this empty feeling in the pit of my stomach.

"You don't need to do that."

I see relief wash over him. I'm sure it's because he probably doesn't want to lose this lucrative contract, but a part of me wishes saying goodbye would be just as hard for him as it would be for me.

I massage my temples. The frustration, anger, and sadness are piling up and I feel like at any moment, I'll collapse with the weight of everything I can't handle but I'm being forced to deal with.

I scan the room for the waiter, suddenly wanting to leave, and wishing

I could escape these feelings. I'm about to thank him for apologizing and tell him he can go now, when he looks over at me with concern.

"Your head hurts?"

"A little, it's fine."

"Here, give me your hand."

I hold my hand out and he takes it, turns it over, and starts massaging the area between my thumb and forefinger.

"There's a pressure point in here that can help to relieve headaches."

My body responds to his touch like I'm straddling him in the booth, and a sigh escapes my lips. I turn more fully toward him and we lock eyes. His hand freezes, but he doesn't let go. I need to know what he's thinking.

"Nick." I look into his eyes. "Why did you kiss me?"

"Because that's all I've wanted to do since I first met you, that night at the bar." He pauses before continuing. "I know circumstances are different now."

His hand feels like it's imprinting onto my skin, and I don't know how I'm going to exist without this touch. Even now, I'm drifting off into whatever this is between us.

He then brings his fingers to the underside of my wrist.

"It's acupressure. There's this one too, for stress relief."

I close my eyes for a moment and sink into the sensation of his strong fingers on my delicate skin.

This touch.

His touch.

I want it to consume me.

I remember how his hands felt on my thigh, my back, and under my top, sacred yet electrifying. How they were at first light and gentle, and then more desperate, clinging to my skin and pulling me closer. I remember how delicious his lips felt on mine as he alternated between soft caresses and sensual strokes of his tongue, like he wouldn't be satisfied until he tasted and touched every part of me. Then, how his body felt pressed into me at the club. Strong, solid, unyielding.

He's pulling away from me, and I'm desperate to keep him close, because if he's going to be my downfall, then I will be his.

I pull his hand into my lap, and his fingers pause. I gaze up at him. I put my fingers on the pressure point on his hand, softly massaging it, while my long nails scrape just slightly across his skin. He leans back like I'm touching him somewhere else entirely.

"Is this how you do it?" My voice is soft and laced with desire.

He takes a deep breath before responding with fire in his eyes.

"Yes," he whispers.

Satisfied that my touch is getting to him, I get braver. I unbutton his cuffed sleeve, and pull it up to expose his wrist, and place my fingers on the pressure point there, circling it gently just like he did for me.

He brings his other hand to tug at his collar, even though there's a cool breeze coming through the front windows.

I let my fingertips linger on his pulse, feeling the beat grow stronger and fiercer with every second that passes.

I wet my lips and reach further up his arm, in a barely-there caress, and he watches my every move. There's so much more that I want to do to him as he watches, but I won't, I can't—but I want to. So desperately.

He regains his composure just slightly as he looks at me, but then his eyes rove over my mouth, my neck, my collarbone, before lifting to meet my eyes again. He inches closer, and I hold my breath.

I notice a few office types walk by from the corner of my eye, and suddenly I'm self-conscious about what this may look like. I remember that this bar isn't far from work, and anyone could see us.

Still, I button up his cuff slowly and place his hand in the little bit of empty space on the seat between us. Too caught up in whatever is happening to stop just yet.

I wish we were alone somewhere private, where I didn't have to worry about anyone seeing us. Where I didn't have to hold back. I'm losing control fast, and I force myself to work through the fog of longing and the buzz of alcohol.

I have to stop this.

"Thank you for showing me that. My head feels better," I say softly. He continues to look at me, and I force myself to look away.

I won't think about dragging my manicured nails down his chest, and I won't look at my wrist and imagine how his fingers just felt on it and how they would feel elsewhere. I won't inhale his scent even as it presses in on me, calling me into dark, forbidden waters. I won't do this to myself, not anymore, but I won't let him forget me that easily either.

He stares at me like he wants to say something more, but he doesn't.

I feel eyes on me and scan the room, zeroing in on a guy blatantly staring at me from the bar. It takes only a moment for me to register who it is.

It's Dev, Shaan's friend and aggravating roommate.

Shit.

My fake calm and cool composure fly out the window, and panic bursts into my chest.

He smiles and lifts his glass to toast to me, and I try not to let my expression show my escalating panic.

Too far, I had almost taken things too far in a public place.

But I didn't, did I?

No doubt he'll be reporting to Shaan about this, if he hasn't already texted him. I should leave immediately, but I'm not going to let him run me out of here, and I'm not doing anything wrong. I don't know why I feel like I am.

The waiter comes by.

"Anything else I can get for you?"

"Just the bill, please."

He comes back in a second, and I pay for my drinks.

"I should go," I tell Nick.

"Is everything okay between us?" He looks at me tentatively, a question in his eyes. There's something dark and tempting beneath the surface that I won't even let myself contemplate.

"Yes, all good."

I walk slowly and casually, even though I want to bolt out of there. I wish I could run away from my feelings for him just as easily, and from the panic boiling deep inside me.

* * *

Hey babe. Can you come over for a bit tonight to my parents' house?

It's almost 7:30 p.m. when I leave the bar and make my way to the station, and the thought of going anywhere except home is daunting. My brain is racing to process everything, and I just want to shut it all off. Plus, I'm worried. Did Dev say something already?

No, he couldn't have.

Why? What's up?

. . .

Just my mom wants to go over some engagement logistics with you, and I want to see you

I take a deep breath. I don't want to disappoint his parents any more than I already have.

I'll be right over.

* * *

I knock and wait outside their sprawling home. I'm nervous, and I wish I'd been able to come up with an excuse not to be here.

"Hi, Auntie Ji."

Her eyebrows lift with surprise when she sees me.

"What are you doing here? Everything okay?"

"Fine. Shaan just mentioned you wanted to go over some engagement stuff?" She looks at me quizzically for a moment but then she opens the door wide.

"Come in, come in."

Shaan saunters into the foyer, looking hunky even in sweatpants and a tee.

"Mom, I told Nisha to come by for a bit so we could show her what you had planned for the centrepieces and menu."

I take off my shoes and follow them into the kitchen, where his mom proceeds to show me what they already ordered. My opinion doesn't even matter to her, and anger and fatigue bubble up inside me.

Obviously, his mom doesn't need my involvement with anything. Why would she? It's *my* engagement, but I'm just expected to show up and look pretty.

The phone starts ringing, and his mom answers it and wanders upstairs, leaving us alone.

"You know I'm okay with whatever your parents decide," I say, hoping to get out of there as quickly as possible. I'm not, but I don't want to make a fuss.

"I know. I just wanted to see you. Let's go hang out for a bit." He grabs my hand, but I pull back.

"I'm going to go say hi to your Dadi Ji first."

He nods. "She's just in the den, watching her dramas."

"I know, I can hear them from here." I walk over and smile. She's wrapped up in the show but notices me as soon as I enter.

"Nisha, aaja, mere naal beh ja," she says, patting the sofa cushion beside her.

"Okay, sure." I sit down, give her a hug, nestle close to her, and start watching.

"What's happening?" I ask as I take in the over-dramatic pause after a woman faints.

"It's too complicated to get into it all." She waves me off, but then continues. "See that woman? She's jealous because she likes the groom too, but she shouldn't want to be with him."

Sounds familiar.

My phone vibrates with a text and I can't help but grin as I see a lopsided photo of my nephew in a pink kurta pajama, my mom's attempt at taking a photo. For the engagement ceremony, my family is wearing pink and Eshaan's is wearing gold. They must have got his outfit today.

Excited for Massi's party!

I react with a pink heart, then put my phone away as a smile blossoms on my lips.

Shaan comes in as the show ends, and I realize it's nearly 11 p.m.

I say bye to his Dadi.

"I'll drive you home," says Shaan. He grabs his keys and we head to his car, but something is off. Dev, the douchebag, must have said something.

He's silent as we pull away from the house, and I don't speak either for most of the drive, but my heart is beating frantically in my chest until I almost can't take it anymore. "Is everything alright?"

"You tell me."

I lean back in my seat. I don't have the time or energy for these games.

"Shaan, please. Tell you what, exactly?"

"Why don't you start with where you were this evening?" He looks over at me, his eyes unimpressed.

"Oh, Jess and I went for drinks after work. You know that."

"That's the only person you had drinks with?" He glances over at me, his tone charged.

I shake my head. "Let me guess, Dev messaged you with some bullshit as per usual."

"So, there wasn't a guy all over you?"

I curse under my breath. "Give me a break."

"So, he's lying and made this shit up?"

"Jess left, and I had a drink with a colleague, that's all."

"I didn't realize colleagues normally touch each other," he adds sarcastically.

"He didn't. I don't know what Dev's talking about." I'm not sure how to explain the headache and the acupressure, but I know Shaan would turn it into something more anyway. He always does.

"Cut the crap. He sent me a photo."

I want to scream. Of course he did.

"That's the guy you went to the conference with." He swerves into a parking spot in front of my building, stopping too aggressively.

"Are you going to tell me what's going on between you and this asshole?"

"There's nothing going on, Eshaan." I look straight ahead, resignation and outrage fuelling me in equal measure.

"Bullshit. You're mad because of a few innocent texts with my ex, but god only knows what you're up to while you're away for *work*."

"Shaan, stop. There's nothing going on between us. I had a headache, and he was just showing me an acupressure point to help." I was right to think this would sound pathetic and stupid—it does, and I immediately regret saying it.

"Fuck. You're unbelievable, you know that, and so naive. Guys will say all sorts of shit."

"He didn't, he wouldn't," I stammer, even though I know he did and he would. My heart races thinking about that kiss, that night.

"Tell me the truth, now."

"Shaan, stop. There's nothing to tell." I finally turn to him and notice that he's about to lose it in a way that I haven't seen before.

"I'll give you this one chance to come clean, but later, if I ever find out you've been messing around on me, we're done. I don't give a shit if we're engaged. I won't protect you either. If anyone asks why it's over, I'll tell them you were fucking around."

Humiliation and tears sting my eyes. It took me nearly a decade to get over the scandal with Sunny. This would destroy my reputation, and I don't think I would ever recover.

"You can tell your friend to stop spreading shit because he has nothing going on in his own sorry life," I spit out, channelling my anger at Dev.

"Don't take this out on him."

"You're always protecting him. You believe him over me." I'm being petty and childish, but I don't even care.

"When he has evidence, I do."

"Evidence of what, Shaan? Listen to yourself."

"I didn't realize you're okay with other guys touching you, but wow, okay."

"Whatever. I can't do this right now." I open the door, and he grabs my arm, hard.

"This isn't over."

I pull my arm away. "Believe what you want, but I didn't do anything wrong." The words are shaky. I'm horrible, and now I'm lying, and this could mess everything up. But I know that with Shaan's jealousy, coming clean isn't an option. If he's this crazed over a guy touching my hand, I can't tell him that he kissed me, too. I get out and slam the door of his precious fucking car, knowing how much it will irritate him.

He speeds away, and I use the last bit of strength I have left to head up to the condo.

My life is a fucking mess and I'm the creator of it all. Is this what Rachel meant when she talked about taking charge of our destiny? I doubt it and myself more than ever.

19. HOT IN HERE

Nick glances at his watch while I pull out my phone and scan the display for the time.

"We can't go." I look up at him, unsteady on my feet, maybe from my too-high heels, or maybe from my proximity to him.

"Oh, we have to go." He gives me a smirk and runs a hand through his lush golden locks. His navy half sleeve collared shirt is tight across his chest and his hair glistens in the noon sunlight as we stand on the sidewalk on Davie Street. We just finished our meeting with Henrik, an investor from Europe. He was so impressed with our pitch he signed on the spot and then gave us passes to the brand-new Nordic spa he's also part owner of.

"Another hour won't make a difference, especially not now since we roped him in," he says casually as he glances over at me like it wouldn't make a difference if I said yes or no, but his eyes tell a different story. He pops on his aviators as I shield my eyes with my hand and turn to look at him.

"Okay, fine, but if we get busted, it's totally your fault."

"I'll take the fall." He pulls off his shades just enough to shoot me a wink. Damn him and his sexy face that I can't say no to.

Little does he know I'd let him take me beyond the atmosphere if it meant I had more time alone with him.

It's blistering hot even though it's not yet summer and the streets are crowded. He takes my hand and I hold on tighter than I should. We're out together in broad daylight, but I don't think about that now. I won't let myself.

English Bay Beach is just a block away, and the ocean sparkles in the distance. A sequinned turquoise chunni swaying in the wind.

"It's just right here."

He leads me through the door of a sophisticated glass storefront with a fancy stylized logo. Immediately a sense of calm washes over me as notes of lavender and patchouli float toward us from a nearby diffuser. I wander over to the main desk, with Nick close behind. A woman with straight long chestnut hair and a broad smile greets us.

"Welcome to the Atlas Nordic Spa. You two are among our first customers, we just opened last week." Her name tag says Samantha.

"We heard. Henrik sent us over with these." He hands over the passes.

"You're guests of Henrik." Her eyes light up. "Right this way." She steps out from behind the desk.

"Actually, we need bathing suits."

She looks up and bites her lip.

"Oh, we're still waiting for our women's stock." She squints her eyes and looks at me. "But I think I have something that should fit you. I'll be right back."

I look over at Nick as he grins at me.

"Oh my gosh, I hope she doesn't come back with something hideous."

"Doubt it." He turns around and places his elbow on the ledge of the reception desk. "Besides, you'd look good in a paper bag."

I mock roll my eyes, but I store his compliment away to replay later.

"I found this. It should just fit you."

Samantha puts a red bikini on the counter in front of me. I press my lips together and look at it, testing the fabric with my fingers. It's so revealing, it would make my skimpiest lingerie look like a nineteen-fifties nightgown in comparison.

"Will this work?" She looks at me with doe eyes.

"Sure, it's great. Thank you."

"Great! Luckily for you," she says, gesturing at Nick, "we have lots of men's suits in stock. She points to the abundantly stocked shelf behind him.

Of course, he gets his pick, and I'm stuck with whatever *this* is. I push down my nerves of wearing the bikini in front of him.

He chooses a pair.

"I'll get these, please."

"You're guests of Henrik, so these are on the house."

She gets out from behind the desk and leads us to the change rooms.

"The men's changeroom is over there and women's is just here." She smiles. "For now, it looks like you'll have the place to yourselves. Enjoy."

I take a sharp inhale as my heart rate rises.

She returns to the front desk.

"See you inside," Nick calls after me.

In the change room, I take in the granite grey floor, wooden bench, and black mini lockers. I head over to them and start changing slowly, letting my erratic breathing calm.

She was right, the bikini does fit perfectly. I turn to glance at the mirror hanging from the ceiling and bring my hands to my hips.

Damn. I look good.

I grab my purse to freshen up my lip gloss, powder my nose and I pull my hair into a high bun.

I check my phone for something other than the usual barrage of work emails. Not a word from Eshaan since our fight last week. I ignore the anger that flares in my chest at him, at Dev, and at myself. He was overreacting as usual, but I won't give him the satisfaction of apologizing either. It would make me look guilty and I can't risk that—because I am. We're supposed to meet tomorrow for engagement shopping, and he hasn't cancelled so there's that. I push him from my mind. For once, I'm going to let myself have fun. I stuff my belongings in a locker and close the door.

I steal a final glance in the mirror before heading into the spa area, where Nick is waiting in the cozy lounge.

"Hey." I walk over to him as he gets up, his eyes roving my body, before he abruptly looks away.

"Thanks for waiting for me."

"Yeah, no problem." He rubs a hand over his face and hair.

"You okay?" I say nonchalantly, knowing very well he's not okay. He can't be, not after seeing me in this.

"Fine, good. Great, actually."

He smiles and his usual confident demeanour returns.

"Where should we start?"

He reads aloud our options from signage on doors. "Hot tub, sauna, or cold plunge?"

"I think someone needs to cool off, so maybe the cold plunge?" I open the door and walk into a room with stone walls that make it look like it's carved into the side of a mountain.

"It is pretty hot outside," he says as he walks through the door I'm holding open for him.

"Right, outside." I can't stop the smile forming on my face as I look up at him through my lashes. "Good thing it's cool in here."

I dip my toes into the cold water and shriek. "It's fucking freezing!"

I turn around but Nick's right behind me and I ram right into his hard chest. It's the first time I let myself actually look at him, the hard ridges, the tanned skin, his flexed forearms on either side of me. I'm gawking.

"You dipped like one toe in."

I come back to earth from whatever orbit he sends me into.

"It was like my full foot, okay?" I glance back at the icy waters. "Not happening."

He moves in front of me and holds out his hands.

"You can do this"

I don't budge.

"You're way more capable than you realize, Nish. Of this...of everything."

Now, I know we're not talking about the cold plunge.

My shoulders sag as I relent.

"Okay, but if I die of hypothermia while we're playing hooky, that's also on you."

He smirks. "That won't happen on my watch."

I place my hands in his and he slowly guides me down until we are submerged up to our shoulders. My breaths are short and quick. It's uncomfortably cold, but I feel the warmth of his words. The safety they invite me into.

He won't let anything bad happen and I believe him.

Eventually it feels more manageable.

"See? It's not that bad."

I smile up at him. There's so much that's wrong about this, but as I do when I'm with him, I let myself enjoy the moment. It might not last, but it feels more real to me than anything in my life right now.

Our eyes don't leave each others' and he's only inches away. My hands are still in his. It's dark and still freezing and the only place I want to be.

He holds my hand tighter almost as if he senses that this fleeting moment is all we'll ever have.

The arctic chill paired with the intensity of him is too much. I pull back and lift myself onto the edge of the pool, my feet dangling.

"I think I'm ready for the sauna."

"Sure."

"But you can use the hot tub if you'd like." It's a test and an invitation. What I'm inviting him into, I'm not sure.

"So, hot tub alone or the sauna with you." He purses his lips and places his thumb and index finger on his chin. "Hmmm, let's see..."

I make my way to the sauna before looking back.

"I won't be offended if you choose the hot tub."

"There is no reality where I'd choose a room that didn't have you in it."

I let his words pour over me like maple syrup, covering me in sticky sweetness that I want to lick off my fingers and maybe his.

This room emanates warmth, not just because of the hot coals steaming in the centre, but from the cedar wood panel benches and the backlit orange wall. It's so comforting, it's like walking into a warm hug, but with Nick next to me, it feels like a blazing hot inferno. I sit on the top bench in the corner of the room and Nick sits right beside me. So close that our thighs are touching even though the room is empty except for us.

I close my eyes and let the heat soothe me. The constant tension that lives in my shoulders unspools. My neck loosens and I stretch it side to side.

We sit in silence for a few minutes, and I feel no need to fill it. With him there's no need to constantly justify myself or watch everything I say or do.

"Can I ask you something?" he says.

I open my eyes as he shifts to face me. He brings his thumb to my forehead, wiping away a bead of sweat. My body that was so relaxed a moment ago is suddenly on high alert. His touch an electric current.

"Do you ever think about the night we met and wonder…" He watches my face for my reaction. "What if?"

His eyes drop to my mouth and then up to my eyes again.

My heart thumps wildly and sweat drips down my chest. I bring my fingers to my throat and down in a caress as I ponder his words. He watches me as he waits for me to speak, like he can't help but soak up the sight of me.

I swallow hard as I watch sweat trickle down his face, his shoulders, his chest, and lower. I need to know how he feels before I tell him how I do. "Do you?"

He takes my hand and brings it to his heart. It's beating as fast as mine. "All the time." He looks down at my hand on his chest and continues. "I think about what it would be like to be with you, to touch you, to…" he says slowly as if he's testing the words on his tongue and relishing the sound of them.

There's no echo, but every syllable resounds in my chest.

"To hold you." He brings my fingers to his mouth. "To do so many things to you."

My breath catches at his admission, but I'm starving for more than words. He lets go of my hand and reaches for my chin, pulling it toward him and I can't stop the magnetic pull. His lips are on mine and the taste of him is salty, sweet, distinctly masculine, divinely him. Like all the most tantalizing things I've never let myself experience. His tongue finds mine and each stroke melts me down until I'm nothing but putty in his arms. He pulls me across his lap and I move without thinking. Only the thin layer of my bikini bottom and his swim shorts separate us. I press my chest into his as he lets out a soft growl, my softness meeting his hard ridges. All I want is to feel his solid strength holding me, like this, forever.

It's too hot—from the heat of the sauna or him, I can't tell—but I can't pull away. I don't want to. I want to stay suspended in this vortex—the only place where I don't have to pretend to be someone I'm not, or that I want something I don't.

"I brought you both some tea refreshments."

Samantha is at the door with two tumblers filled with ice and an amber liquid.

I move off Nick, slowly. My head dizzy and my breath ragged. He wipes the sweat from his brow.

She looks at us and then quickly looks away.

"I'll just leave this here for you." She places the tray on the lower bench near the door and rushes out.

Nick gets up, walks toward the lower bench, and takes the glasses from the tray.

He walks back to where I am, hands me one, softly clinking his glass against mine.

I gulp the tea down in one go as he takes a few sips and then places it down.

"I don't even know what time it is. We should probably head back," I say, trying to pull myself back to reality even though I don't want to.

"We should."

But neither of us move. I bring the cool, empty glass to my cheeks trying to cool down all the conflicting emotions burning within me.

I slowly get up, wobbly on my feet. Nick steadies me with a hand on my shoulder. I smile at him, and he takes my glass from me, setting them both down on the bench.

I walk backwards to the door, not wanting to take my eyes off him, until my back is pressed up against it.

"Let me help you cool down." He takes out an ice cube and stalks toward me like a lion approaching its helpless prey, but I'm not afraid. I already know I'd let him devour me.

He outlines my lips with the ice cube and I close my eyes to fall deeper into the sensation. Then he brings it down to my neck, following its cool trail with his lips. I shiver despite the high temperature in here. He brings the melting ice cube down in between my breasts and then he kneels before me, like he wants to worship every part of me. He brings the ice cube to my stomach and it disappears into nothingness, melting into the sweat on my skin. He licks me and kisses my stomach, going lower, until I grab him by the shoulders to pull him up. He brings his lips to my neck, biting and sucking as I wrap my arms around his broad bare shoulders, writhing against him.

Someone nudges the door behind us to open it and I shift forward, almost falling into Nick. He catches me as two ladies enter. I know they're staring at us, but I can't bring myself to look at them. I only have eyes for him.

He takes my hand and leads me out the door. The cool air feels refreshing and my skin tingles with goosebumps. The real world comes rushing at me, but I wish I could stay in this one, with him.

He leads me to the lounge where he wraps me in one of the robes that are laid out for us, and then gets me a glass of cucumber water.

"You good?" He sits on the next lounge chair and brushes my hair out of my face.

"Yeah."

I down the water and then turn the glass in my hands. I have to say it. I look at his face, wondering when it became so familiar, so comforting. There are still a few drops of sweat on his brow.

"Nick."

"Yes." He looks at me like no one else exists.

"I think about that night, too."

He swallows and I watch the Adam's apple in his throat, wanting to touch him there and everywhere.

"I used to think about what it would have been like to be with you, to touch you…"

To love you.

Then I get up slowly and head to the change room. Because after confessing that, I'm afraid I'll confess something I'm not ready to.

* * *

When I head to the reception area, Nick's already there. He looks fresh and rejuvenated, but I feel like a hot mess. Washing my hair would have taken forever, so I just rinsed off and quickly changed. My insides churn with the pressure of everything I won't let myself feel for him.

"I hope you enjoyed your visit," says Samantha. She shoots us a knowing smile.

I lower my eyes.

"Thank you. It was great."

Nick walks toward me. "It really was."

Then a wave of panic washes over me. What if she tells Henrik what Nick and I were up to in the sauna?

I shove it down and shoot her a grateful look. I follow Nick out the door.

The sun is too bright. I squint to look at Nick.

He's appraising me and his eyebrows draw in as he brings a hand to his mouth.

"Shit, Nisha, your neck."

I instinctively put my hand on my neck. Another wave of panic hits. "What is it?"

He pulls out his phone and puts it in selfie mode and that's when I see the massive hickey forming. With my smudged makeup and frizzy hair, I look like we were doing way more than kissing in there.

"I can't go back to the office like this."

"I'm so sorry, Nish. I'll drop you off at home." He shifts on his feet. "I can tell Tom you're not feeling well."

The waves of panic turn into a tsunami of agitation as I walk beside Nick. The crowds from earlier are gone and the buildings are a blur.

Eshaan's taking me jewellery shopping with his mom tomorrow. She wants me to pick out my own gifts for the ceremony. At least that was the plan, before the fight. I haven't heard anything different, so I assume it still is.

My head is spinning worse than when I was in the heat of the sauna. How am I going to try on any necklaces that she'll expect me to?

"Nish, talk to me," Nick says as we approach his car.

"I'm just a little dehydrated."

"I can go grab you something."

"I'd feel better if we were on our way."

He opens the passenger door for me, concern flashing across his face.

I muster a small smile even as my heartbeat thunders in my ears. I settle myself into my seat as he walks around and gets in. He starts the car but we don't go anywhere. Instead, he rests his hand on the steering wheel and looks over at me.

"I didn't intend for *that* to happen."

Newsflash, neither did I.

I give him the briefest of glances and then stare straight ahead. "Can we just pretend it didn't?"

He angles his body toward me. "Is that what you want?"

"Yes," I lie.

Only then does he shift gears and start driving.

What the fuck am I doing? Eshaan is giving me everything on a silver platter, and I am one wrong move from destroying it all. I need to put an end to this.

This needs to stop. I'm getting engaged. I try to get the words out, but they get stuck in my throat.

I don't want to end this. I only want more of him and I know he wants me too, and that makes this fucking impossible.

20. GOLDEN

I take a seat at my desk and pull out my compact to peek at my reflection. My long hair is up in a sleek high ponytail and I'm wearing a flowy chiffon blouse with a high neck and long ruffly sleeves. I've tucked it into grey high-waisted dress pants. It's fancier than what I would normally wear to the office, but it's the only thing I have that covers the hickey. It was bad yesterday, but it's even more noticeable today.

I tuck my compact away back in my drawer and take a deep cleansing breath just as Rachel taught me.

I have to push yesterday from my mind, and more importantly I have to stay away from *him*. It will be a challenge considering he's sitting only a few metres away from me in his office next door. There's also the fact that I have to see him for forty-plus hours a week, but it has to be done. Anything is possible, right?

This must be what the motivational speakers are talking about: not doing illicit things with sexy-AF men you work with because if anyone finds it out it will destroy your relationship and quite possibly your career.

Shortly after I log in and start checking the emails that I never got around to last night, there's a light knock at my open door.

"Hey."

Nick is standing there in a light taupe cashmere sweater with off-white pants. His sleeves are rolled up just enough to show off his tanned forearms and expensive watch.

I try to slow down my racing heart.

Be professional.

"Did you see that email from Henrik?" he asks.

My heart rate accelerates and immediately my thoughts drift to yesterday. Did Henrik find out? It's ridiculous, but of course my mind goes there.

"Just logged in."

He steps inside my office. "He emailed Tom singing our praises."

"That's great," I manage, genuinely pleased and of course relieved. This is about the pitch, not what followed.

"Tom responded back and he's already looking into more opportunities for us."

Right. Us. Together, alone, pitching.

"Wonderful." I plaster a smile on my face.

"Just wanted to let you know, and to ask if you want to get coffee." His eyes flick to my neck and I ignore the sensation that comes up as I think about his mouth there.

I tug at the top of my neckline and then smooth my hand over my ponytail.

"I'm taking a longer lunch today so I'd better not." I should add that I'm meeting my boyfriend and soon-to-be mother-in-law, but I don't.

"I can grab you something," he offers.

I know I have to limit interactions with him, even though I don't want to. And I obviously really want an extra-sweet matcha latte, but I need to stop giving in to temptation.

"I'm good actually."

He nods, but is that a flash of disappointment? I need to stop overanalyzing his every move.

"I better get back to it, but thanks."

He shoots me a smile and leaves, and only then do I get up, slide my office door closed, and sink back into my chair.

Trying to be professional around Nick feels like work, but everything else with him? It comes so naturally.

* * *

We wait outside the jeweller's door and I'm about to hit the buzzer when Eshaan stops me.

He takes my hand and kisses it, and the beard he just started growing for the ceremony scratches my skin.

"I'm sorry for going off on you last week. I know you would never mess around on me."

My neck itches and I avert my gaze from his.

"It's just, I don't trust other guys around you," he continues.

I squeeze his hand, even as my chest constricts.

"Everyone at the office knows we're together," I say in a rush.

Today is warm, but not hot like yesterday. Still, I can feel beads of sweat forming on my forehead, and I'm grateful for the soft breeze.

"Sure, but you know what guys are like. You've experienced it."

I inwardly cringe as he brings up Raj, my only other relationship—well, I thought it was a relationship, but it wasn't. It was just a hook-up for him.

"You know how serious I am about you. That's why I get a little crazed at times."

I nod. He wants to build a life with me, and that's what I want too. A real partnership that I can count on.

He gestures to the store behind us. "That's why I'm doing all of this for you."

"I know and I'm so grateful."

He gives me a big smile, and I try to muster one as my mouth goes dry.

I don't deserve any of this.

"We better go in," he says. I nod as he hits the buzzer and we walk through the secure double doors. Eshaan's mom is already waiting for us. She's dressed impeccably as always in a traditional salwar kameez with a muted floral print and embroidered fuchsia edges. She walks with an air of grace and elegance I have yet to master.

"Hey, Mom." Eshaan gives her a quick hug.

"Hi Auntie Ji." I hug her too and notice she even slightly squeezes back.

"You can start calling me Mom," she says to me.

I nod, but I don't think I'm ready for that quite yet.

I'm not sure what to say to express my gratitude, so I say, "Thank you for this."

She waves me off, like spending thousands of dollars on gold jewellery isn't a big deal. For them, I'm sure it isn't.

"Anyone want a mango lassi? There's a good place nearby," says Eshaan.

"That would be great," I say, ignoring the tightness in my chest. I'm grateful for a little more breathing room.

He gives my hand a squeeze and leaves.

The jeweller comes over to us. "What are we looking for today?"

"Gifts for the Kurmai and sets for the wedding," says Eshaan's mom.

"Oh, very good."

He clasps his hands in front of him and does the head waggle that I can never quite get the hang of.

"Let's start with bangles," she adds.

He brings out gorgeous bracelets and bangles, some simple, others more elaborate, all nicer than anything I've ever owned.

Eshaan's mom directs him as she points out others she likes.

I stand there awkwardly.

"What about something like this?" She picks up a gold one inlaid with crystals, and hands it to me to try.

"Swarovski crystals. Best quality. Number one."

It fits perfectly, the gold complementing my brown skin and the crystals glittering in the bright overhead lights. The bangle is gorgeous but lavish.

"Maybe something simple like those?" I point to the simple gold bangles.

"Nonsense." She shakes her head. "We'll go with these."

The jeweller sets the lavish bangles aside for us as I remove the one I tried on and hand it to him.

"Show us sets for the wedding."

A knot forms in my stomach.

The wedding.

We move over to the corner of the shop and look through the spotless glass displays.

"Perhaps something you would wear after the wedding too," Eshaan's mom says.

"Something simpler then?" I venture.

"How about this?"

She points to a set with the same pattern of crystals, but with gold tear drops. It's stunning, with matching earrings and a tikka. I gasp. "It's beautiful."

Eshaan's mom pauses as she looks at my top, finally registering it.

"You girls these days with your fashion." She shakes her head. "How are you supposed to try the necklace on?"

I bring a hand to my neck, unconsciously covering the mark even though I know she can't see it.

The jeweller steps in, not wanting to derail the sale. "She can try over the blouse."

He hands me the necklace and I place it on my chest. It's breathtaking, but it feels like it's getting heavier with every passing moment.

I place it back carefully and the jeweller adds it to our growing stash.

A few other customers come in and a lady comes out of the back to help them.

We look at anklets which Eshaan's mom insists on getting me as well, and a fancy gold chain. I've always wanted one, but it all feels like too much.

"Now you can take off that necklace you usually wear and wear this."

"Oh." She's referring to the white gold chain I wear almost every day from my dad.

"The gold suits you so much better."

"Yes, of course," I say as a lump forms in my throat. I don't want to seem ungrateful.

I rarely take my dad's necklace off. I know it's cheesy, but it's the last thing he bought for me before he passed—a gift for my sixteenth birthday. He wanted to go to the South Asian jewellers, but I insisted yellow gold was too gaudy, so he took me to the mall and let me choose a two-hundred-dollar white gold chain. I still love it. I know it isn't worth much, but it means everything to me. It feels like I'm carrying a part of him with me wherever I go.

Shaan's mom moves to the cash to settle up and I stand back awkwardly, not knowing what to do with myself. She hands me the box with the necklace, but she saves everything else for the ceremony. His family is always sending me nice outfits to wear to events, and now all of this. A part of me wonders if they just want to make sure I look good enough to meet their standards. I shove the thought away.

I know gifts are a part of the ceremony, but it feels like a lot—too much.

Outside the shop I take her hands.

"Auntie Ji, thank you so much. Everything is so beautiful."

"Theek aa," she says, waving off my gratitude. "I have a few more things to take care of for the ceremony.

She walks off without another word.

I wait outside, and Shaan strolls up a few minutes later. It's much warmer now and the hot sun beats down on me. He hands me my mango lassi.

"Thanks."

I take a sip, letting the refreshing sweet and tangy flavour cool me down as well as the emotions burning inside of me.

"Find something you like?

"Yes, your mom went all out and got me the most gorgeous stuff."

"Of course she did. You're going to be my wife."

I choke on some lassi and I start spluttering.

"You okay, babe?"

"Yeah, fine." I pull out my phone and realize it's already time to get back to work. "We should probably head back."

In the car Eshaan shares all the little touches his parents are adding for the ceremony. They're going all out and I'm going to hell. That I know for sure. He parks in the loading zone in front of my building. Normally he would rush off, but today he gets out and opens my door and when I step out, he pulls me into a hug. There are a few guys approaching us on the sidewalk and I pray that Nick is not one of them.

He leans in for a kiss. I give him a little peck.

"I don't know how to thank you for all of this."

"I can think of some ways." He gives me a sly grin and then leans in for another kiss. The guys that were down the street a few moments ago are now right behind us.

Shit.

Nick's eyes meet mine and I quickly look away. Of course he chooses *this* moment to return from lunch. From the corner of my eye, I see him heading through the front entrance.

"Stay over this week?"

"For sure," I say with so much enthusiasm that I'm worried he'll know it's fake.

I wait a few moments so I don't have to take the elevator up with Nick, and then head through the door, giving Eshaan a quick wave. I go the long way, so I don't have to walk past Nick's office, and slide my office door closed behind me before collapsing into my chair and putting my head on my cool desk.

Every day is bringing me closer to locking in my life with Eshaan. The life I thought I wanted, that I dreamed about from the first time I saw Shah Rukh Khan and Kajol on the big screen with my dad at the local theatre in Brampton that played throwback Bollywood movies.

But my life isn't a Bollywood movie no matter how much I want it to be. Things with Eshaan aren't perfect, but we both want the same things. It's a future I can count on—the future my family wants for me.

Things with Nick are reckless, crazy, and have the potential to be disastrous. I lift my head up and bring a hand to my neck. Desire stirs within every part of me as I think of him. He isn't offering me anything beyond the physical, yet I can't stay away from him.

Worse yet, I don't want to. This is beyond messed up. I am beyond messed up. But one thing I know for sure: I can't mess up what I have with Eshaan.

No. Matter. What.

21. TREE THERAPY

"Aren't you glad I dragged you out here?" Rachel gestures to the canopy of towering trees that surrounds us.

"It's beautiful, Rach, and exactly what I needed."

I fill my lungs with cool, humid air and place my hand on a nearby tree trunk, already feeling more relaxed. The worries from the week are still there, but they don't feel as prominent anymore after our long walk.

"We used to do things like this all the time, before…" Rachel says.

Before Eshaan.

"I miss it."

"Me too." I link my arm in hers as we continue on the trail, our steps soft on the lush carpet of the forest.

"We haven't had a proper catch-up in a while. Tell me everything." Her emerald eyes sparkle, matching the vibrant greenery around us.

"You first. You've been so busy. It looks like business is really picking up."

"It is and I love it. It's such a dream come true to build something from scratch and see it flourish."

"I can imagine."

I think about my recent success, and going for what I really want at work, and smile to myself.

"How's the investor pitching going?"

"Great, actually. We nailed a pitch with an investor from Europe. Tom was thrilled."

"We, as in you and Nick?"

I nod.

She gives me a half smile.

She points to a log just off the trail.

"Should we stop here and have our snack?"

"Sure."

She pulls out a thermos of Genmaicha tea and some cucumber sandwiches. She hands me one and I carefully unwrap it and then take a bite. She does the same.

"That's great about the pitch."

"It is. I feel like I'm really making headway."

"Of course you are, Nish. You're a superstar." I don't know about that, but I don't say anything. "How are things with Nick anyways?"

"What do you mean?" I deflect with another bite of my sandwich.

"You know what I mean." Rachel gives me a sidelong glance. She'll know if I'm keeping something from her, but I can't tell her the full truth either.

"I, um, we kissed." I scratch at my neck and avoid her gaze.

"What?"

She gets up, knocking over the thermos in the process. I move it back upright and then stand up too.

"I know, obviously, it never should have happened—"

"How was it?"

"How was what?"

"Come on, Nish, the kiss." She's gesturing wildly with her hands on either side of her.

I get hot just thinking about kissing Nick, and the warm forest air suddenly feels more stifling.

"It was…"*Explosive, earth-shattering, mind-blowing, like fireworks lighting up the sky on the darkest of nights.* "Incredible," I say quietly as I stare at the forest floor.

She brings a hand to my shoulder.

"What are you going to do?" she asks.

"Nothing. Forget about it."

"Is that really what you want?"

What I want? I don't know what I want anymore. It all seemed simple before—a done deal—and now it feels like a thousand-piece jigsaw puzzle, where all the pieces don't fit. I'm running out of time to make sense of it all.

"The ceremony is booked, and I even went shopping with Eshaan's mom for the wedding jewellery."

"Nish, who cares? This is your *life* we're talking about."

"It's not that simple, Rach. This isn't about just us anymore. It's about our families too."

I hold the last piece of sandwich in my hand, no longer feeling like eating it, but I finish it anyway.

"I can't just walk away from that because of a kiss." Or whatever that was in the sauna, which I won't mention to her or to anyone.

"Is it really just a kiss, or are there feelings there too?"

I sigh audibly. Maybe for me there are, but for him? I can't say for certain. Sure, he is kind and generous and thoughtful—but he's like that with everyone. Okay, maybe just a tad more with me.

"Rachel, please. Nothing can happen with me and Nick. Can we just change the subject?"

She opens her mouth as if to say more but stops herself and then packs everything up.

"Have you ever heard of forest bathing? You walk through the forest and pay close attention to all your senses, watching as the sunshine hits the forest floor, listening to the scurrying of the animals and the birds serenading you, taking a deep inhale of the refreshing pine scent, and touching a tree or leaves. It's basically immersing yourself in nature to relieve stress."

"I've heard of it," I say, with a little too much of an edge in my voice.

"Why don't you just take some time now, to sit and reflect? I'll meet you back in the car." She glances at her phone. "Maybe in an hour?"

"Okay," I relent. Maybe I do need some time to process this all. I sit back down on the log as she leaves.

I know where I stand with Eshaan, but with Nick, I have no idea what he wants. A relationship? Casual dating? A fling? The truth is a guy like him isn't single unless he wants to be, but my delusional heart wonders if he's waiting to meet someone like me. Before Minneapolis and the sauna, I thought I was imaging this all, but now? I know it isn't just me.

I get up and head deeper into the forest, lost in thought. What would Fantasy Nisha do? The answer is instant: She definitely wouldn't sit here and ruminate on her own.

I pull out my phone and scroll to his number, hitting dial before I have a chance to overthink this.

"Nisha, hey," he answers on the third ring.

"Hi," I say as my hands shake.

"What's up?"

We never speak on the phone and I sure as hell don't call him outside work hours on a Saturday afternoon.

"I, um…" I stumble. It sounded so easy a moment ago, but now that he's on the line, my courage flees.

"Is this about the email I sent this morning about getting a copy of the updated investor plan for Henrik? I didn't expect you to get back to me today."

"Oh, yeah. I just wanted to make sure you didn't need it right away," I lie.

"All good, I don't."

I hear a woman's flirty laughter in the background and then a muffled, "Just one sec," from him.

"Anything else up?"

"No," I say too quickly as my heart instantly deflates like a punctured ballon. "I'll let you go."

"See you Monday."

"Yeah, see you then," I grumble into the phone, wishing I never called. I pull it away from my ear and stare at the black screen in my hands.

Am I really willing to give up everything with Eshaan for this? To be just another girl among the many Nick is likely dating?

No fucking way. That's something Fantasy Nisha wouldn't budge on either. She knows her worth, even if I'm still figuring it out.

22. GIRLS' NIGHT OUT

So, home?" I turn to look over at Anjali as I put on my seatbelt in Rachel's car I borrowed for the night. We just finished dinner at Vij's on Cambie after shopping at Metrotown all afternoon.

"Nish, it's nine p.m. on a Saturday and you seriously want to call it a night?"

My stomach flips and I tighten my grip on the steering wheel.

"Let's go out somewhere fun."

Eshaan doesn't like me going to clubs or bars without him since our huge fight about the photo in the restaurant a few months back, but I can't tell her that. I know how it sounds.

"Or we could go get dessert or something?"

She gives me a glare. "Dessert? Really, Nisha? I rarely get a weekend off and you know I'm never in town for long."

She pouts her perfect lips at me and I cave.

"Okay, yeah."

Eshaan is out having fun at some Bhangra competition—why should I head home and twiddle my thumbs waiting for him?

"Amazing, let's go back to yours and change." We'd both picked out hot new dresses at the mall.

I nod and start to drive. I guess we're doing this. A lightness spreads through my chest and my head is in a cloud of anticipation. Work's been crazy the last couple of weeks, Rachel's busy most weekends with her business stuff, and Eshaan just asks me to tag along to whatever he already has planned, which is rarely anything I want to do.

"My bedroom is just through there," I say when we get back to my condo. "I'll use Rachel's to get ready." I quickly change into my sparkly nude sequinned dress. It has a low-cut halter top and hits mid-thigh. It's something Eshaan would hate me wearing. I pair it with dangling crystal earrings. I go into the bathroom to touch up my makeup, adding eyeshadow, a swipe of highlighter on each cheek and I redo my eyeliner so my eyes pop.

"Nish, you look fucking incredible," Anjali says as she joins me in the bathroom.

I meet her eyes in the mirror.

"Anj, you look stunning yourself."

She sashays next to me showing off her curve-hugging burgundy dress that has a cut-out under her chest that shows off her tiny waist.

"Bathroom selfie!" she says.

We do our sexiest pouts as she snaps a few photos of us and then starts clicking away on her phone. I glance at the screen over her shoulder.

"Can you not post that?" I manage.

"What? Why?" She looks at me puzzled.

"Shaan doesn't like me wearing stuff like this."

She places her phone on the counter face down.

"Are you serious?"

I nod, as my chest tightens.

"It's not the nineteenth century." She shakes her head. "I won't post it, but I am going to talk to him about telling his girlfriend what she can and can't wear."

"Where should we go?" I say quickly, trying to change the subject. He won't like that I shared that with her, but if I didn't and he saw the picture it would be an issue, and I just can't deal with any issues right now.

I apply nude lip gloss.

"You must know all the latest hotspots. With all the travelling I do for work, I barely go out here anymore."

I wrack my brain as I redo my soft waves with a curling wand. I have literally no social life and feel so lame, but then I remember overhearing Nick talking with some of the tech guys about this fancy new club that's super luxurious. They even host celebrities. They were planning on checking it out this weekend.

Anjali tousles her hair in the mirror next to me. "It has to be luxe though; I'm not spending the night in some grunge bar with nineteen-year-olds."

"Give me a second, okay?" I finish curling my hair, unplug the wand, and head into the living room. I can't go to the place Nick mentioned, can I? What if I see him? What if he's with someone else? He probably is, but maybe that would help me move on and get my mind off him. It would be soul crushing, but necessary.

My phone buzzes with a new notification. Eshaan just posted something. The first clip is of Dev's bhangra group who are all wearing rainbow turbans with white kurtas and dhotis. They're dancing to Diljit Dosanjh and I smile to myself. I kind of wish I was there with him, even if it is for Dev's event.

The next post is a picture of Eshaan surrounded by the women's Giddha team.

Of course.

Irritation flashes through my chest as I scan the faces and then I freeze. The woman right next to him is Sonia, his ex. What the actual fuck? I had no idea she would be there tonight and of course Eshaan didn't mention it. Maybe that's why he didn't push me to go with him like he usually does.

"So, did you find a place?"

I look up from my phone to see Anjali sauntering in like the queen she is.

"I know just the one."

* * *

The place is booked solid when we arrive, but Anjali manages to sweet-talk our way in.

"This place is straight fire," she says when we get inside.

We look around taking it all in. Teal spotlights shine on the small round cocktail tables and the cozy armchairs surrounding them. The ceiling is lit in geometric patterns of the same bright teal colour and the dance floor is full of gyrating bodies. Here, our outfits are perfect as everyone's dressed to the nines. The bar takes up the entire back of the place, an amber glow backlighting the most expensive selection of liquor I've ever seen.

"Let's get bottle service," says Anjali. There's no way I can afford bottle service, but before I can respond she jumps in. "I'm treating."

She snags a table just as a couple gets up and we sit side by side, perusing the drink menu.

"Anything you want?"

"I'm good with anything."

I scan the crowd, but there are so many people that there's no way to tell if Nick is here, and maybe that's for the best.

Anjali orders a bottle of Grey Goose Altius vodka, which I've never heard of but if she's ordering, I know it's premium.

A waiter comes back shortly and mixes us vodka sodas.

I take a sip and it's strong, but also silky, refreshing, and easy to down.

"Easy there. Eshaan will be pissed if I bring you home wasted," she says as she scans the crowd and our waiter hands me another. He will be more than pissed if he finds out I'm in a place like this without him, but I don't mention that.

"Any hot guys here? For me obvs. You're off limits," she says as she shifts her dress down on either side and then takes another sip of her drink.

"Wouldn't know."

"Such a good girlfriend."

I look away and shift in my seat.

"Oh, there's a fucking hot dude that keeps glancing over here," she says into my ear. "How do I look?"

"You look amazing, but you already know that."

"I do." She gives me a sly wink. "Shit, he's coming over here."

I turn and my heart leaps in my chest. It's Nick wearing a fitted black dress shirt that's unbuttoned down to his chest with tight grey pants. A few ladies turn to look him up and down as he passes and I wonder what it's like to have women constantly throwing themselves at you. Am *I* one of those girls? I push the thought away and turn to Anjali, trying to remain unaffected.

"Mind if I join you?"

"Of course." Anjali tosses her hair back as he takes the seat in front of us.

Do I pretend not to know him? I try to look anywhere but at him.

"Just wanted to say hi, Nisha." He draws out my name like he knows me intimately and Anjali immediately stiffens and turns to me.

"You two know each other?"

"No, I mean, yes." I'm already floundering. "We work together."

Nick smiles broadly as he takes a long sip of his drink.

"Yeah, we're just colleagues," he says in a way that suggests we aren't.

I don't know whether to feel elated or stressed. What if this gets back to Eshaan?

Anjali's sultry demeanour returns as she brings a hand to her collarbone.

"So, you're here alone?" She raises her eyebrows suggestively and takes a sip of her drink and this is my literal worst nightmare.

My mind starts spinning as I think about her and Nick together.

I pull my hair back and stare at my drink, wanting more of a buzz, but not feeling like drinking anything. My insides coil tighter.

"I'm waiting for someone," Nick says. He glances over at me and gives me a smirk, sitting back and draping his arms over the chair. I'm just starting to realize he's a little drunk. I've never seen him anything but cool and collected, even the night we first met. *Fuck it.* I down my drink and grab the bottle, pouring myself a straight shot.

"My friend over there, though, wanted to come say hi to you, but he's a little shy."

He gestures to a guy I don't recognize. He has dark wavy hair that's just above his chin and he's wearing a navy blazer, white shirt, and khaki trousers. He looks like a European footballer.

"Shit. He's hot. Ronaldo vibes," Anjali says in my ear. Relief floods my system.

She gets up as he approaches our table and they immediately start chatting. Nick takes the empty seat next to me. I don't know how she's still single—she hits it off with guys so effortlessly.

They wander to the bar together, leaving Nick and me alone.

I down my vodka and it burns my throat. I quickly pour myself another. I look at him and he gives me his dazzling fucking smile.

"Can't believe I get to see you on a Saturday," he says as he runs his fingers through my hair.

I grip my glass tighter.

"Don't let me keep you from your evening," I say tersely. He's waiting for someone who isn't me and I can't hide my irritation at that.

He laughs and moves closer, placing his hand on my thigh. My pulse quickens and I know I should move it, but I don't. I glance around. I can't see Anj anywhere.

"You're waiting for someone, right?"

"I just said that in front of your friend." He gives me a flirtatious half smile. "But if you want, I can tell her you're the one I'm waiting for."

He starts to get up and I panic, grabbing his arm.

"Nick, stop. She's Eshaan's cousin." He freezes for a moment, his mouth drawing into a thin line, before he flops back into his chair.

"Right, your boyfriend. You're still seeing him?" He raises an eyebrow. I'm not sure if it's a question or a challenge.

"Yeah."

He leans in really close. "Okay, but…does he make you feel like I do?" His hand returns to my thigh, and he inches it up slowly as his eyes drift from my legs to my chest and then to my lips.

I open and close my mouth before placing my hand on his and moving it away slowly.

"Someone might see us," I say instead of answering his question.

He leans in as the music gets louder. "Come with me." He gets up and offers me his hand. I look around again and then take it as he effortlessly helps me up.

I pull down my dress with one hand as he leads me through the throng of people.

The buzz from the shots quells my usual anxiety. I shouldn't be letting Nick hold my hand, not with Anjali here, but the thought drifts away as Nick leads me up the stairs, down two hallways and past a velvet rope holding a sign that says VIP Only.

He opens an unlabelled door and leads me inside, closing and locking it immediately.

The lights are dim but I catch our reflection in the silver gilded mirror to the side. I vaguely register that we're in some kind of luxury bathroom before Nick's hands grip my waist and he brings his mouth an inch from mine.

"You didn't answer me earlier."

My heart rate escalates as he stares at me, his eyes dark and intense like the ocean on a stormy night, and I'm riding a strong wave directly toward him.

"You know the answer," I say softly, not willing to admit the truth to him or myself.

That's all the invitation he needs to put his lips on mine. He takes my tongue in his mouth and sucks it as he grinds up against me. Every thought leaves my mind. All I can feel is him, his warmth, his solid body pressed up against mine.

He moves my dress up until it's at my waist, kissing down my neck and shoulders as my core shakes with need. Him, this, us—I want him so bad.

I grind back against him too until he's hard against me. My tongue caresses his in desperate strokes. I bring my hands to his belt buckle and rest them there for a second, not sure I can go any further, even though I want to. I move my hands away and wrap my arms around him instead.

"I want you so fucking bad. You have no idea," he says as he lifts my leg up under the knee, pushing me against the wall.

The buzz starts to wear off and my mind starts to clock in, even as my body ramps into overdrive.

I shove him back, leaving my hand on his chest.

"Is this all you want?" My eyes search his face for a hint that there's more he's feeling for me.

He takes a micro step back and runs a hand through his hair. "What else do you think this is?"

My heart crushes into a million different pieces.

He steps forward and places his palms on either side of me.

"You have a boyfriend, remember?"

"Yeah, thanks for the reminder," I say under my breath as outrage explodes through me.

"I don't have a problem with whatever this is," he says as he brings a hand to my chest, cupping my breast.

I shove it away. "I do." I pull my dress down as my face burns.

"What do you want from me, Nisha?"

"Forget it."

I unlock the door but my hand rests on the knob. I turn back to him as he stands there looking so dumbfounded I almost feel sorry for him.

"I'm not some girl you just fuck in a bathroom."

Then I open the door and walk into the hallway. I don't look back.

* * *

"How was Ronaldo?" I ask. My insides tremble, but I don my armour.

"A fucking bore, but a totally hot kisser."

I turn to her as we walk down the street, the loud music fading behind us with every step.

"You kissed him?"

"Yeah, dude. A single girl's got to have some fun, right?"

I give her a little smile, as we continue to walk along in silence.

"Do your parents ever pressure you about marriage?" I ask as she stops next to me and ruffles through her purse for her foldable flats.

"Honestly, they were really supportive of my career in the beginning." She steps out of her high heels one foot at a time and pulls on the flats. She picks up the heels with one hand as we continue down the street.

"But now?" I ask. My feet ache and so does my heart.

"Now that I'm thirty-two it's like they bring it up a lot more. They're getting worried I'll miss the window and they might not get grandkids."

"How do you deal with it?"

"Most of the time I shrug it off, because I like my single life. But if I met the right guy, maybe…" Her eyes get a faraway look.

"You met someone."

"Maybe." She smiles as she tucks her hair behind her ear and looks down. "I met him in the UK, on a business trip actually."

"You never told me."

"There's nothing to tell," she says. We stand on the curb waiting for the crosswalk signal.

"We just stayed late talking after a few meetings and have been kind of messaging the last little while." She transfers the heels to her other hand before continuing. "We just gel, and he gets me and my ambition. He doesn't expect me to be home with a dinner plate."

"Like Eshaan," I say quietly. The light changes and we cross.

"Eshaan's parents were always working when we were growing up. I think he just wants things to be different for his kids, you know?"

I nod. That makes sense. My dad worked all the time, but my mom was always home taking care of us. We ate homemade lunches and dinners of fresh rotis, dahl, and sabji every day. She took us to Girl Guides, Bollywood dance classes, and the library every week—insisting we only read school-related books. I'm glad she was around, especially since my dad mostly wasn't.

"Anj, I'm so happy for you."

"Who knows, maybe we'll just be friends. I'm just going with the flow."

I don't know how she does that. I can't flow with anything, and trying to control every outcome isn't working for me either.

"What's his name?"

"Inderjit, but he just goes by Inder."

"I need to see a picture."

She smiles and pulls out her phone and then proudly hands it to me.

"Holy shit. He looks like Hrithik Roshan."

She swoons. "I know, right. Total hottie."

"You need to lock that down."

She gives me a wink. "I like you, Nish, a lot. I'm glad Eshaan found such a babe like you—not to mention you're one of the kindest and most loyal girls I know."

I swallow back the lump in my throat.

"We should get an Uber," she says, and we pull out our phones to order our cars. "You're staying at Eshaan's, right?"

"Yeah. It was so good to see you, Anj." I wrap her in a hug.

"You too, Nish. Can't wait for your engagement."

"You should bring Inder."

She bites her lip. "We'll see. There's my Uber. Is yours nearby?"

"Just two minutes away."

"I'll wait with you." And she does. Suddenly I don't feel so alone with the weight of everything. Maybe not everyone gets my ambitions and goals, but she does, and that's something.

23. CHA TIME

In Eshaan's kitchen the next morning, I make my cup of cha like a ritual, crushing the cardamom, cloves, and ginger with a mortar and pestle. I take a stainless-steel pot from the cupboard, fill it with water, and then set it on the stove. I add the spices and wait for the water to boil. I try not to think about Nick and last night, but he's always right there and I can't help replaying it all. It's like he knows exactly what to say, exactly how to touch me, exactly what I want most.

I add the tea bags and let everything simmer. The sweet, earthy aroma fills the air and reminds me of the comfort of home, and my heart softens. Back in Toronto, I craved freedom, and now that I have it, I love the independence—but I wonder if that's all Nick is. A chance to escape the pressure and expectations. Maybe I should just let myself. Guys do it all the time, but I already know I can't separate the physical from the feelings. I'm already too hung up on him. There's a good chance I'm just entertaining these thoughts after seeing the picture of Sonia, and the fact that Eshaan didn't come home until nearly 3 a.m.

I run my fingers along the gleaming granite countertop, and then walk over to the stainless-steel fridge to get the milk. I add some to the simmering water and raise the heat to high. As soon as it rises, I take it off the heat, remove the tea bags, and strain it into two cups. I hold mine in my hands and lean against the counter just as Eshaan comes in, wearing a grey tee and basketball shorts.

"Hey babe."

He gives me a peck on the cheek, and I resist the urge to turn my face away.

"I made cha." I point to the cup sitting on the counter in front of me.

"You're the best." He gives me his most charming smile, but it does nothing for me.

He stands across from me and takes a sip.

"How was last night?" I ask casually.

"Great. Dev's team was awesome."

"Yeah, I saw the clip you posted of them." I stare down at my cup. "And the one with Sonia's Giddha team."

"Nish, come on. I didn't know she would be there."

He takes his cup in one hand and goes to the other side of the counter, taking a seat on the barstool.

I clench my teeth so hard, my jaw hurts. "You just had to take a picture of her."

"Yeah, I actually did. The outfits they were wearing are from the shop," he says, his tone razor sharp.

I stare down at the floor, but I can't let this go yet. Even though he has a reason for everything. "Dev was home just after one a.m. Why were you out so late?" I glare at him but keep my voice calm.

He shifts back in his seat. "Nish, he had rehearsals every night this week for the performance. He was baked. He left early."

"And you stayed out until three a.m.?"

"Yeah, I ran into some guys I went to high school with," he says as he takes another sip of his steaming cha. "Seriously, stop it with this shit."

His words are like a slap in the face. I feel tired and hollowed out, and I need to stop creating drama where there isn't any. I was the one in a bathroom with Nick last night, and here I am questioning Eshaan.

I wander over to him and sit beside him.

"Sorry, I just got anxious when I saw the picture."

"It's cool. But watch what you say next time." He takes the last swig of his cha and gets up to put his cup in the sink.

Frustration bubbles in my chest. I already watch everything I say around him.

"Hey, I got you something. Be right back." His harsh tone from earlier is gone and I sag into my stool. I watch as he retreats to his room and returns a moment later with a tan shoebox. He hands it to me and I read "Christian Louboutin, Paris" on the top of the box.

There's no fucking way.

I place the box on the counter and lift the top open. The interior is a bright red. I carefully unwrap the shoes and then lift one out and gasp.

It has two clear straps and it's encrusted with gorgeous blue, yellow, and pink pastel jewels.

"Eshaan, these are stunning."

"I thought they would go with your engagement lehenga perfectly."

I hold it like I'm holding Cinderella's slipper, turning it this way and that in the light.

"Try them on."

I lift out the other one and slip them on my feet and do a model walk in the kitchen. They fit like a dream.

"These must have cost more than my outfit." I stop in front of him. With the heels I come up to just above his shoulders.

He wraps his arms around my waist.

"Only the best for you, babe." He gives me a sweet smile. "Oh, I've been meaning to give you my credit card for anything else you need for the engagement." He reaches for his wallet on the kitchen counter, slips out his card, and hands it to me. "Here."

"I already have almost everything," I say in a rush.

He leans in for a kiss.

"Keep it just in case."

As his lips touch mine, my stomach sinks. "Let's go get some chole bhature." For all his faults, the man knows what I like.

"I'd love that."

He goes to get ready, leaving me standing there, thinking of last night and feeling cheap in five-thousand-dollar shoes.

24. OVER IT

I'm putting a lid on my extra-sweet matcha latte on Tuesday morning when someone comes up too close beside me. I'm still raging and exhausted from the weekend and now I'm irritated. Why can't this person just fucking wait two seconds?

"Nisha," Nick says, his voice deep and low.

I drop my shoulders and inhale deeply without turning to look at him.

"I have to get back to the office," I say curtly.

"Please. I just need two minutes."

I'm not falling for him or whatever this isn't anymore.

"No, just no." I turn to him finally, looking him directly in the eyes. He has the good sense to look away.

"Please," he whispers.

His eyes are soft and his forehead is creased with worry. A small part of me wants to hear what he has to say. Maybe he'll tell me what I so desperately want to hear from him, but then what? I can't just ride off into the sunset with him.

"Two minutes," I spit out. We sit down at a nearby table.

"I know I said I would keep it professional because of work and other considerations…" He trails off. "I'm trying, but it's so hard, Nisha."

I shake my head.

"I'm sorry it's so *hard* for you," I say not bothering to keep the sarcasm from my voice.

"I didn't mean it like that." He brings his hand to his forehead and then places it on the table in between us.

"Listen, on Saturday I was drunk and behaved like a complete idiot. I want to apologize." He glances away, but only briefly. "It's just that when I saw you, I couldn't stay away." He takes a sip of his steaming hot coffee and winces. "You're smart and amazing and so insanely attractive."

I eat up his words like a starving woman, but he's not saying what I want him to.

"And unavailable, unless..."

My heart jumps out of my chest.

"Unless what?"

"Unless, you want to be, for me."

He scans my face for my reaction, but I don a cool mask. I don't know exactly what he's asking me but he's definitely not confessing his love and devotion.

I don't know why that kills me so much.

"Available for what, Nick?" I lean back into the booth, my eyes assessing him in a new way. If he's messing with me, I'm going to mess with him too.

There's no one nearby, so I move to join him on his side of the booth. I bring my hand to his knee and then move my fingers slowly up the inseam of his pants. He stops me just before I reach too high.

"You didn't answer me," I whisper as I lean into him.

His blue eyes hold my gaze as he bites his lip, and his thumb caresses my wrist.

"Whatever you want."

I harden my heart and build my resolve, ignoring the temptation of what he's offering me.

"I could get us a room tonight," he whispers.

I bite the inside of my cheek so hard it hurts, before I lean in even closer to him. "You know what I want?" I move my hand from his and bring my fingers to his abs, stroking him softly up and down.

"What?" he says, his words barely a whisper as his eyes watch my hands and his breaths go shallow.

"Outside of work, I want you to…" I move my hands to his face to turn his head so he's looking directly at me. "Stay the fuck away from me."

I ignore the flash of hurt in his eyes and hastily get up, nearly knocking down my drink in the process. I grab it just before it does. He gets up too.

"Nisha, wait," he calls after me too loudly. I round the corner behind the booth, stopping a moment before I collide into Jess.

My heart pounds as I wonder how much she overheard and what she might have seen.

She shoots a curious look over my shoulder.

"You went for coffee without me," she says as her eyes bounce from me to Nick and back again.

"I stopped by your desk, but you weren't there," I say.

"Sorry, I had to do a quick debrief with Tom."

"Hey Nick," she says over my shoulder.

"Hi Jess. How are you?"

"Great actually."

I turn slightly to include him and make my face as pleasant as possible, but tension has my nerves strung so tight they're about to snap.

"Good to hear. I have to make a call, but I'll see you ladies back at the office." He walks to a booth on the other side of the room and only then do my shoulders soften.

"What was that?" She glances over at me.

"What was what?" I say as I take a sip of my latte.

"Things seem kind of tense between you two."

"Sorry, just some crazy work shit came up as always. It's been stressful."

She rests a hand on my shoulder. "Sorry, Nish. You really do work too hard."

"I better get back for my nine-thirty."

"See you for lunch tomorrow?"

"Absolutely." I give her my most convincing smile, even as the tightness grows in my chest.

I walk slowly. My body wants to turn back and rush into Nick's arms, and the rest of me wants to throw my latte at him.

25. BECAUSE THE NIGHT

I'm still in my office at 7 p.m. on Friday, staring at my computer screen. I'm not registering anything in front of me, but unable to leave my desk. I somehow made it through the week by drowning myself in work and a drink or two after. It doesn't help that I have to see Nick multiple times a day for work stuff or that he's always so kind when I do: jumping in when Tom asked me something about Henrik's investment I wasn't sure about, and even updating our pitch deck when the new template they wanted us to use screwed up our formatting—a task way below his pay grade. Even now, even still, all I want is to be around him.

Eshaan's out with his cousins and Rachel is going out with some friends from the studio. She invited me along, but I don't feel like making small talk.

My phone buzzes with a notification. I don't bother looking, but then it buzzes again.

I unlock it to find texts from Eshaan and immediately my anxious heart races into overdrive.

> **When were you going to tell me you went out with Anjali???**

Here we go. I take a deep breath and do what I always do. Smooth things over. I reply that I told him we were going out for dinner after shopping.

And the club afterwards? You know how I feel about that.

I quickly let him know it was Anjali's idea. I know she won't mind that I share that part, but still, I feel shitty putting it on her even though it's true.

I don't give a shit whose idea it was.

My thoughts scramble as I try to think of a way to defuse the situation, but I don't know what to say or do that won't make him more upset.

Dressed like a slut.

My hands shake and I suddenly feel lightheaded. Anjali must have said something to him. I place my phone down, but I know I have to think of something fast before Eshaan completely loses it. But I can't bring myself to respond. He always thinks the worst of me, and maybe he's right. I bring my face to my hands as I think about what happened that night and the fallout this week at the coffee shop.

My phone buzzes with more texts but I can't bring myself to look at them. Tears slip down my face and my shoulders shake with sobs. Everything I do is wrong, no matter how much I try to do things right.

I shouldn't have gone out with Anjali, especially knowing Nick would be there. And now everything is a mess. But I still don't regret anything that's happened with him even though I know I should.

"Nisha."

I startle at the sound of Nick's voice, but I don't remove my hands from my face. I didn't think anyone was here and I don't want him to see me like this. I try to take some deep steady breaths, but I can't calm myself down enough to even pretend I'm fine.

I hear movement and then a comforting hand on my shoulder. I know I should push it away, but I can't. The simple touch is a balm for my aching heart.

He pulls me up toward him and I let him. My face rests on his chest as he wraps his arms around me. His scent is comforting, inviting, calming. The rhythmic beating of his heart, my own private symphony. I can't help but wish it was beating only for me.

He smooths my hair and rubs my back and makes me feel like I'm someone special, when most of the time I feel like I'm the opposite. For once, I let myself feel that I am.

That for this moment, I don't need to be perfect or have it all together or even get it right. I can fall apart and that's okay. I know he won't judge me for it, even though I'll judge myself later for all of this.

The office lights turn off and only the light from the setting sun fills the office.

He holds me closer and I don't think I ever want to leave his embrace.

My phone starts ringing Eshaan's ringtone and it breaks the spell. I move away slowly to silence it and then take some tissues to wipe my face.

Nick stays right next to me, concern stamped on his face. He steps closer, running the tips of his fingers along the side of my face, leaving a wake of sparks I feel everywhere. It's then that I fully take in the sight of him. He changed from the casual Friday jeans and tee he was wearing earlier today to a crisp white dress shirt, rolled up to his elbows with tight khaki trouser pants and sneakers. He's obviously ready for a night out and I can't even deny how much that bothers me. He has a life outside of work that has nothing to do with me and that makes me so unbelievably sad. Another tear escapes and he wipes it away softly with his thumb. I can't bring myself to move away. His blue eyes hold my gaze.

"What's wrong?"

Everything.

I shake my head. "I'd rather not talk about it."

He nods in understanding and doesn't push.

This is the part where I should move away or he should, but we stay rooted to the spot. His gaze holding mine, his eyes searching my face for the words I won't share with him.

I swallow hard, mustering the courage to walk away from him, from this.

"Do you have plans for tonight?"

Does sitting at home alone and contemplating the disaster that is my life count?

"No." I shake my head. "Why?"

"I'm going to Symphony at Sunset. My friend plays bass in the orchestra and I promised him I would come watch." He takes my hands. "Come with me."

Spending time together during the workday is one thing, but to go out with him on a Friday evening? I can't do that, can I? My mind is telling me to turn him down and go home, but my body is already sizzling with the anticipation of being near him, even after the club bathroom fiasco.

"I don't know if that's a good idea."

He gazes out the window behind me.

"I heard you loud and clear at the coffee shop, so you don't have to worry about anything like that," he says sincerely as he meets my eyes. "Think of it like a team-building event." He shoots me his dazzling fucking smile, and all my reservations melt away. "And I'll take you home right away if it's not your vibe."

I need to escape everything with Eshaan—even if it's just for tonight—and I know I shouldn't, but I can't help myself.

I nod.

Just for tonight.

* * *

I'm sitting on the blanket Nick's laid out for us, with a glass of white wine in a tumbler he brought along, standing out in my black tank and blazer that I paired with jeans for work today. At my request, we're in a secluded area away from the crowd.

He lounges next to me, propped on one elbow, one leg sprawled in front of him, and the other drawn up as he rests his hand on it. A *GQ* model photoshoot pose, and I appreciate the sight of him. The arch of his brows, the fading sunlight glinting off his perfectly coiffed hair. His dress shirt and pants outlining his trim silhouette.

I take another sip of wine and let myself relax. My phone is on silent and location tracking off, even though Shaan would be enraged if he found out.

I will worry about that later. For now, I push the fear and discomfort down.

"Are you comfortable?" Nick looks over at me, his eyes glittering like the ocean next to us.

I nod. "Want some?"

"Sure."

I hand him his wine tumbler and watch his throat as he takes a sip.

The soft notes of Bach drift through the crowd and I savour their power, emotion, and beauty.

He pours more wine into the tumbler and then hands it to me, our fingers softly touching. I take another sip, letting the cool, crisp notes of rose, ginger, and lychee linger on my tongue.

The sun dips below the horizon as we sit next to each other, sharing the wine and soft touches. Even doing nothing with him feels like something. As it gets darker, he lies down and I lie next to him, and we stare at the stars.

He rolls onto his side and I do the same.

He plays with my hair absentmindedly and strokes my face, like he did back in the office.

"I hated seeing you that upset."

I look away and then back at him

His body goes tense and his eyes tight. "Is it him? Did he do something to hurt you?"

I don't want to lie to him, so I say nothing.

He knows and I know, but I can't say it and he knows that too.

"Nick?"

"Yeah?"

I don't know what I want anymore, but there's one thing I know for sure. "I didn't mean what I said before. I don't want you to stay away from me."

He gets up slowly and leans against a tree. I follow him and he pulls me toward him and holds me close and I surrender to this moment. I can't help it.

He holds my hand and kisses it, then he kisses the inside of my wrist, then the top of my head as I sink deeper into him. He's my shield and I want him to protect me from everything. Because as soon as I leave here, I'll have to face everything out there that I don't want to.

We stay like this as the symphony ends and until long after everyone leaves. Until it's just us and the sound of the waves in the distance.

It's dark and chilly, but with him, I've never felt warmer.

Tomorrow I will deal with reality, but tonight I'll let myself have this.

26. THE FALL

I have to at least try to be professional. It doesn't really matter that we are already at another conference in Seattle, and it's just us. Nick knows about Eshaan, and Eshaan knows about Nick. Shaan barely talks to me, and it makes my unease grow with every passing day, but I know he will come around eventually. I didn't tell him I was away with Nick. I can't, not now.

The day has been a blur of sessions, meetings, and networking opportunities, and it seems like my bad luck is seeping into work too. One investor has already said no, and another—Charles— said he's on the fence, after questioning us like he's some kind of detective. I should have spent more time preparing instead of getting wrapped up in the drama of my life. His rapid-fire questions about potential competitors and staying relevant in a growing market are on repeat in my head as I sit in the hotel lounge, working on my third drink. Even Nick, who has way more experience than I do, was frazzled by Charles.

I swirl my drink, realizing I have to get it together, otherwise I'll be at risk of losing more than my relationship.

"Hey."

I look up to see Nick looking over at me. "We'll get them next time."

"I don't know if there will be a next time," I say, not even bothering to hide my disappointment. "At least for me."

He sits down across from me. "These things happen, and trust me, it's more common for investors to say no than to say yes." He gives me a reassuring smile, but I can't even force myself to fake optimism.

He places his hand over mine.

"Tell you what, why don't we debrief while it's still fresh, and that way we'll be ready to field everyone's questions when we get back to the office tomorrow?"

I know he's right, even though all I want to do is drown in a pool of gin. "Okay."

He gets up. "I'll see if I can find a meeting room for us. I'll text you with the details." He doesn't find a meeting room for us though, and that's how we end up in his room. The last place I should be.

27. SMOOTH OPERATOR

I glance around the office supply closet, my pulse slowing, and my breathing returning to normal after a frantic day full of endless emails, back-to-back meetings, and urgent requests. Eshaan's finally no longer mad at me, which is a relief, but that ongoing stress, along with the usual grind, has been way too much. So here I am, in my calming place. The shelves are neatly lined with notebooks, pens, pencils, and Post-its. I browse through the stash for any new arrivals I can add to my office, much like a chef searching for the finest ingredients in a gourmet kitchen.

A smile spreads across my face when I think about how, when I was a little girl, I'd obsessively pick out the best stationery from the big-box office supply store each summer and arrange everything meticulously on my desk once I was back in school. Organizing always calmed my frayed nerves no matter what was going on at home. It has the same effect now.

I settle on a slick new gel pen that conforms to my thumb and index finger like it was made just for me. I step back to see if there's anything else I want to add, when I hear voices in the distance, coming closer and eventually stopping outside the closet door. I don't recognize the first voice.

"I can't believe you get to work with *her* every day. I wouldn't be able to get anything done at all."

I quickly realize that whoever's outside doesn't know I'm here. I think about using the printer to make my presence known, but I hesitate, my interest piqued by who this stranger is talking about. I love juicy office gossip as much as anyone. Just then, I hear Nick's voice.

"Who are we talking about?" he asks casually.

"That babe whose office is right next to yours."

The only office next to Nick's is mine, but this guy must be thinking about someone else. Even still, my heart starts beating erratically.

"Long dark brown hair, sexy pouty lips, body like fire in a fitted blazer."

Shit. Is he talking about me? He can't be. I've never heard anyone describe me like that.

"Oh, Nisha?"

My heart skips a beat.

"Yeah, Nisha. What's going on between you two?"

A long, drawn-out pause unfolds, and just when I think I can't take it anymore, he replies.

"Nothing. We're colleagues. I don't think of her like *that*." His voice is flippant and dismissive.

Heat starts rising to my cheeks when I think back to us in his hotel room just this past weekend. How Nick looked at me with those piercing eyes that made me forget everything. Even the day etched with disappointment from the failed investor pitches and my persistent self-doubt faded away into oblivion. All that was left was pure desire and desperate longing. For a moment, all my rational excuses of why I shouldn't want this, want him, slipped away. Once we were alone in his room, he leaned in, his body just inches from mine, and I moved closer as if we were drawn together by an invisible force. I held my breath as he brought his fingertips to my face and then his thumb to my lower lip in one fluid motion, caressing it softly. Barely a touch, but I shivered like he was exploring the most sensual parts of me. My arm seemed to move of its own accord, my hand reaching up and my manicured nails brushing through his soft, golden blonde hair and then landing on his shoulder, needing to feel his solid form, an anchor to ground me before I floated away.

The stranger's voice cuts through my swirling thoughts.

"Bullshit. I see the way you look at her."

"Seriously, she's not my type at all."

I freeze in place, my fingers clutched around my pen, with dread pooling in my gut as I remember how he leaned back into the cushions and pulled my hand down over his heart. It was beating wildly. I fell into him, resting my head on his broad chest. We stayed there suspended in time, neither of us wanting to break the spell or ruin the moment. It could have been minutes, or hours that passed, it didn't matter. My body longed for more, but at the same time, this was enough. Having Nick's arms around me should have felt awkward, foreign even, but it felt like the most natural thing in the world. Too intimate for what we weren't to each other but not intimate enough for my rebellious heart. *If I had him with me in the storage closet just for a few moments…*

I remember desperately trying to build my resolve to pull away, to leave his room. *Just for a moment,* I told myself instead as I nestled deeper into his chest and took a strong whiff of his fresh, enticing pine scent. The one that captivated me so many months ago, and that I've wanted to douse myself in so many times since then. It was late and silent except for the rapid beat of his heart and mine. I took one final deep inhale and then untangled myself from his embrace. I got up from the couch, looking away as I said, "I should go."

I heard him rustle behind me, and I urged my feet to move. I took one step toward the door before he grabbed my hand and pulled me back toward him.

"Stay." His eyes were hungry, wild and unravelled, in a way I hadn't seen before, and I felt this uninhibited urge to unravel him more.

He pulled me down into his lap, his hands moving up and down my thighs and his mouth just inches from mine. I was one moment away from making a very bad decision.

I continued to run my nails through his hair, and he closed his eyes and bit his bottom lip.

Just for a moment.

He opened his eyes, his gaze penetrating me. As I looked into the endless blue, moving away was not an option I could even fathom.

He wrapped my long ponytail around his hand, gently pulling it back as his lips skated down my neck. He kissed the soft spot between my collarbone before he moved up again, grazing the sensitive skin behind my ear.

"This is a bad idea," I whispered slowly, even as I arched into him.

"Such a bad idea," he whispered back as he pulled me closer toward him.

A second later, his mouth claimed mine, making me want to be his, if only for this moment. His kiss was deep and relentless, asking for more with every moment that passed. I gave him what he wanted too willingly because of what I was too afraid to admit: I wanted him too. Scarier still, I wanted this to mean something.

We eventually pulled away, breathless. Foreheads touching, bodies intertwined. He put his hands under my shirt and his fingertips brushed over my bare skin.

"You're so fucking hot." His voice was husky with desire.

He moved to the side and lay back, pulling me on top of him. I felt him hard beneath me and it was getting tougher each time, to walk away, to say no to this.

He's chipped away at my defences bit by bit, and I've let him.

He rocked my hips against his and I knew I had to leave.

I scampered off him and rushed out the door, while he called after me. I slipped out without turning back to him and soon found myself alone, back in my room.

* * *

My fingers are wrapped so tightly around the pen that they're starting to sweat. It all makes sense now. He didn't say I was beautiful or stunning, just hot. An object to lust after. To desire. To conquer.

"Right," the mystery voice continues. "I forgot your type is someone you only have to see for one night." Laughter. "So, you won't mind if I ask her out once my contract's over?"

I don't want to hear another word, but I'm on a collision course and all I can do is watch as every word of Nick's confirms what I always feared. I'm not good enough. Not for someone like him, and the way things are going with Eshaan, maybe not for anyone.

"She's seeing someone," Nick says in a low voice, I can barely make out, even though I know they're just outside.

Guilt courses through me as I think back to his fingertips lingering on my face, how he pulled me back into his embrace. It was so smooth, so seamless, and that's because it had to be a practiced move. I fell for it, fell for him and his act.

I'm Such. An. Idiot.

"Damn. Oh, well. Had to ask."

I should feel flattered at the man's words, but instead, I feel ill.

The pen slips from my grasp and clatters to the floor. The sound echoes too loudly. I stay pinned to the spot by the printer, holding my breath and praying to every god I've ever heard of that they don't come in here.

"Can we not talk about this here?" A barely audible whisper dripping with discomfort.

"Sure, man. What do you need my help with anyway? Seems like you have a good handle on things here already."

I hear soft steps on the padded carpet. They start talking about work and their voices start fading in the distance.

I try to regulate my breathing. Breathe in—slowly, deeply—count to four. Now let it go. Exhale to six. I can hear Rachel's calming voice in my ear, but the breathing technique doesn't help to quell the nauseating feeling in my stomach.

That must be the new consultant that Nick brought in to help after the recent security incident. From the sounds of it, he's a friend who knows Nick well, much better than I do.

I stand there stunned, trying to process everything I heard, but my mind wants to shut it all out. I bring my hand to my heart, trying to calm its frantic beating, until my phone buzzes inside my pocket. I slip it out on autopilot and click on the message notification.

Can't wait to see you tonight babe. xx

The sickening feeling grows, and I place my arm on the wall to steady myself. The solid feel of it helps release some of the tension building in my shoulders and the tightening around my chest.

I peek outside the supply room, making sure there's no one around, and walk briskly back to my office. I glance at the clock hanging from the wall. It's almost 7 p.m. Thankfully, the desks are empty this late, and I don't run into anyone.

I close my office door and drop into my chair, resting my elbows on the desk and sinking my head into my hands.

What the fuck am I doing?

Shame settles on me like a cloud of dust, coating the most vulnerable parts of me I so foolishly exposed.

No one could ever love you, not the way I do. Eshaan's voice echoes in my ear. Words I don't want to believe or even acknowledge after our last heated argument, but now they're the only things preventing me from completely falling apart. He's right. No one else would want me, not in a serious way.

I know I'm playing a dangerous game that could cost me everything, but I don't know how I'm ever going to escape from it.

28. #POSSESSIVEAF

I linger at the corner of the bar, ordering another gin and tonic to avoid going back to the table. I can only take Eshaan's friends in small doses, and I have as much in common with the other girlfriends as I do with a houseplant. Maybe even less. One keeps droning on about how tired she is because her dad is making her actually work at their family business a couple of days a week instead of just depositing money into her account each month. The other has spent the whole time so far swiping through lipstick colours to best match her saree for her cousin's upcoming wedding, settling on nothing, and boring us with the reasons why every option won't work. And then there is Dev, the birthday boy, who welcomed me by looking me up and down with so much scrutiny that I wanted to slap the beard right off his face.

I gulp down my drink, imploring the alcohol to kick in as fast as possible, and when it doesn't, I go get another.

"Here you go." The bartender slides the drink over casually with a wink. "I made it a double for you."

"Thank you." I could hug him. I know I should go back to the table soon, but I can't get my body to move.

There's a light touch on my shoulder and I turn around to see a tall man with soft brown eyes staring back at me. He has closely cropped hair and a lopsided smile.

"Nisha, right?"

I bristle, instantly remembering the resonant voice from earlier this evening.

"I'm sorry, have we met?" My voice comes out colder than usual, but he doesn't seem to notice.

"Oh, right. Silly me. I'm the new consultant who will be working with Nick. I saw you at the meeting this morning but didn't get a chance to introduce myself. I'm Matt."

He holds out his hand and I shake it warily.

"Nick mentioned you've been working together."

"Yes, well, we were assigned to the same project," I say with a nonchalance I don't quite feel.

"He tells me you've been doing an incredible job." I try not to roll my eyes even as my traitorous heart beats faster at the mention of Nick's praise.

"That's nice." I take a sip to avoid talking further.

"I'm excited to come on board. It's been a while since I've worked at a start-up."

I want to stay annoyed at him, but his friendly demeanour draws me in and I smile and say, "Oh, you'll love it. It's the best place I've ever worked. Where were you before?"

Someone jostles him from behind before he can answer, and he abruptly leans forward, pushing into me and sloshing my drink all over my hand.

"So sorry about that," he says, his eyes wide. He genuinely looks so distraught that I warm to him even more.

"Don't even worry about it."

"Let me get that for you." As he reaches behind me to get a napkin from the counter, someone yanks his shoulder back.

"What do you think you're doing?" It's Eshaan, and he looks at Matt with such venom that I immediately tense up.

"This is Matt." I step in between them even though I want to shrink back. "He just started working with us today. Matt, this is Eshaan." I try to keep my voice smooth and composed, but it comes out shaky.

Eshaan continues his icy stare, ignoring me completely. People at nearby tables turn to gawk and sweat starts forming on my brow.

"Matt just came by to say hello."

"That's right. Nisha and I are going to be working together for the next little while," he says unconvincingly, even though it's true.

"You've said enough of a hello, you can fuck off now."

"Let's go, please." I try to pull Eshaan away and lead him back to the table, but he stands rooted to the spot.

"Of course, enjoy your evening." Matt backs away gingerly. A ghost of an expression I can't quite decipher lingers on his face.

People turn back to their conversations as if nothing happened. Eshaan's eyes land on me and he shakes his head.

"I can't even leave you alone for a second without you flirting with some rando."

I stiffen, the words landing like a blow. "That's not what was happening. We're going to be working together."

He laughs but there's no humour in his voice. "Just like that other work guy who was all over you."

I clamp my mouth shut knowing full well that I can't even deny that anymore. "Let's not do this, Shaan, please," I finally manage.

"Are you serious? You're off talking to guys at the bar on my friend's fucking birthday and I should just let this go?"

He gives me a look of disgust. "No one else would put up with your shit, you know."

His words slice through me, and my breathing turns ragged as I think back to what happened earlier this evening. I reach out and touch Shaan's cheek, immediately wanting to defuse the tension between us. "You're everything to me."

His eyes soften a fraction, but the jealousy shimmers like hot flames behind them.

"How can I prove it to you?" I hate myself for being so weak and needing to please him.

"Stop wearing shit like this out anymore for starters." He looks down at my dress, and I instinctively wrap my arms around myself, suddenly feeling too bare.

He stalks back toward the table.

I stand there and watch him retreat before I take a few quick steps to catch up to him, like the pathetic woman I am.

* * *

I lie staring at the ceiling after a restless night's sleep, letting my swarming thoughts take over.

Starting today, I won't just have to worry about awkwardness with Nick but with Matt, too. I cringe as I think of how Shaan acted like a total psychopath around him. I pick up my pillow and put it over my face. Maybe I'll call in sick today and just hide under the covers. Hide from the world and run away from my problems. It's what I'm best at—according to my family, anyway.

The worst part is that Shaan's right. I was angry at him for a few texts with his ex, when I'm out of control when I'm alone with Nick. It's like my sense of right and wrong have gone out the window.

Suddenly the words I overheard him say to Matt take over my thoughts.

I don't think of her like that.

His voice plays on repeat in my mind, my own personal torture chamber. It feels so real, what we have, like the most real thing in my life right now. The way he looks at me, like he really sees me. The things he says that make me feel like I matter. The small thoughtful details he always remembers.

My extra-sweet matcha latte.

How he can sense my nerves before every pitch and says just the right thing to calm me.

His arms, a personal haven.

His soft lips…

I have to stop this. Suddenly I'm twenty-one again, vulnerable, naïve, and taken advantage of.

We're just having fun, right? Nothing serious. From what I've heard about you, I thought this is all you'd be into.

Nick's been nothing but himself, and I've been pretending to be someone I'm not. Someone who's okay messing around behind her boyfriend's back. The rumours about me don't feel like rumours anymore. They are a reality I recreated when I had the chance to start over and start fresh. Now, years later, I'm in the same situation I spent so long running away from.

Matt confirmed what I already knew from the first night I met Nick. He was only interested in casual, and I would never want to be just that. Maybe in another lifetime we could be together, one where he wanted more or I wanted less, but in this one, it isn't meant to be. At least this time no one knows. I have to keep it that way and keep myself away from Nick, no matter how fucking mesmerizing he is.

I have a chance at happiness with Eshaan, a real chance, but I'm starting to wonder if I'll ever be happy with him. After last night, I'm not sure about anything anymore. But one thing is clear: He's my only option.

29. BEHIND CLOSED DOORS

I'm debating getting a third coffee to get me through the rest of the afternoon when Matt pops his head in.

"Do you have a minute?" A nervous look flashes on his face.

"Sure." He slides the door closed behind him but doesn't step any closer. "I just wanted to say I'm sorry about Friday. I wasn't trying anything. I wanted you to know that."

The knot buried all day in my stomach loosens a little as he looks at me sheepishly.

"I mean, Nick mentioned you were seeing someone, so I—"

I cut him off, not wanting to be reminded of the conversation I overheard between them.

"It's me who should apologize. My boyfriend shouldn't have behaved like that."

"No, it's fine. I mean, I get it. I'd be the same way."

"Would you really?"

A laugh escapes my mouth, imagining Matt with his kind teddy-bear demeanour trying to be menacing.

"Okay, maybe not that intense." He grins back at me. "I hope this doesn't affect us working together."

"It won't." I get up from my desk. "I appreciate you coming by."

He smiles and slides the office door open to leave, just as Nick comes to a halt in front of my door.

His eyes go from me to Matt and back again.

"Matt came by to introduce himself." I don't know why I feel the need to explain myself, but I do. Should I be worried about this impulse I have to lie?

"Sorry, I should have done that." His voice is steady, but there's an edge to it that only I seem to notice.

"No worries, man." Matt claps a hand on his back. "Well, I'd better finish off a few things."

He leaves Nick and me alone. Nick shifts on his feet.

"Since I'm here, can I check out that new remote-work app for you? Some people have been having trouble."

"Sure, I guess."

He comes up right behind me and kneels next to me as I nudge the keyboard to the side so he can take over. A stronger, more principled woman who values herself would have offered him her chair and swiftly moved away. But I'm not strong, and I'm not principled when it comes to him.

I'm an addict, and he's my drug of choice, and every single day, I'm chasing another hit.

If I turn my head, my face will be entirely too close to his, so I stare straight ahead, watching as he expertly navigates the screen.

I can do this. Be professional. My calm composure lasts all of two seconds.

"Matt said you told him I was seeing someone," I blurt out.

He freezes. "It just came up," he fumbles.

His arm brushes mine, and he doesn't move it away. I turn to face him for a moment, even though I know he's close, too close, and anybody could walk by and see us.

"How?" I challenge.

His blue eyes stare at me intensely before answering. "He thinks you're gorgeous and was wondering when he should ask you out."

And because I love to punish myself, I say, "Even if I wasn't seeing someone, he's not really my type, and I don't think of him *that* way," echoing his words back to him.

Realization dawns on his face as he gets up. "It was *you* in the supply room on Friday."

I don't answer. I stand up and brush past him to slide the office door closed, and then I lean against the wall with my arms crossed. My heart is in tatters.

"Does it matter?" I give him a cold stare, letting my embarrassment, humiliation, and feeling of being used fuel my fury.

He hesitates for a moment before he closes the distance between us and wraps his arms around me, gently pushing me back against the wall. His eyes search my face, while his hands clutch my hips like he's holding on for dear life.

"I'm so sorry. I never wanted you to hear that."

I want to shove him away, but I don't move. "Why, so you could just keep messing with me for the thrill of it? You're like a cat with a bird, Nick. It's pathetic."

His hand reaches for my face, his thumb moving back and forth, caressing my cheek. "I would never mess with you like that." He sounds sincere, but I'm not playing the part of love fool anymore. "Matt's going to be working here for a while. I couldn't risk him letting anything slip," he adds.

I roll my eyes and pull his hand away from my face. "For your reputation or mine?"

"For us. You're forgetting that we're a team, Nisha." He holds my gaze, unflinching.

My anger slips away and my desperate heart wants to believe his every word, even though I know they can't possibly be true. I know what I heard, the dismissive tone, the thoughtless words he uttered when he thought no one else was listening.

I trace my fingernail down the side of his face, then neck, watching as his pulse quickens, not being able to help myself. "You're a liar."

"Then why are you still standing here?"

Because I can't control myself around you.

I find myself falling into his trap again, and he knows it.

I watch as his eyes drop to my mouth, and in less than a moment, his lips are skimming mine and his body is pressing into me. I lose my focus, lose my breath, and lose control just as a knock at the door sends him flying back, and I stand there stunned for a moment before I regain my composure and remember where we are.

Tom comes in with a notebook in hand as I quickly step behind my desk, flustered, but I pull myself together while Nick plants himself hastily in the chair across from me.

"Great, you're both here. I need you both in Seattle tonight. Charles changed his mind, and he's willing to give us another shot," he says, oblivious to what he almost walked in on.

Nick and I look at each other. "We're on it," he says with a confidence only someone like him could muster in a moment like this.

"Good. I need you both on your A-game." He levels a stare at us both that says, *Don't fuck this up.*

"Nisha, whatever you said in your last email made him reconsider. Amp that up in the pitch."

His praise gratifies me in a way I'm not used to. "You got it," I say shakily, still flustered, but now with warmth spreading through my chest too.

"Get yourselves on the next flight out. The meeting is at their HQ at ten a.m. Amy will take care of the bookings for you."

He leaves, and dread fills me as I think about Tom almost walking in on us. It's no secret I'm with Eshaan, so this wouldn't just look bad, it would risk everything I've worked so hard for, especially since Nick's been hyping me up since he started here. I don't want anyone to think it's because there's something going on between us. Much to my family's disappointment I upped and left everything I knew to come out west and prove myself, and I'm so close to that promotion and the next step toward my dream career. I can't have another scandal after I barely survived the last one.

Careful, I have to be more careful.

Nick turns to me. "We should go talk to Amy about those bookings."

I follow him out the door, knowing full well I should sprint in the opposite direction.

30. IT'S COMPLICATED

There are no available flights to Seattle until tomorrow afternoon, which means the only way to make it on time for the meeting is to drive. I would say it's just a coincidence that we're forced together like this, but Rachel would say it's synchronicity. That's what I'm thinking about when I look over at Nick's profile and see his jaw tense. I've never seen him upset, but the thought that he is with me is almost unbearable.

"Can I ask you something?" Nick finally breaks the silence.

"Sure, what is it?"

"What was Matt doing in your office earlier?"

"Nick, obviously he was hitting on me," I tease, needing something to break the tension between us.

His grip tightens on the steering wheel. I guess he's not in the mood for joking.

"He came to say hi. I told you already." This is the last thing I want to talk about. I angle my body toward the window and sink into the seat a little more as if I could sink out of this conversation.

"I know him. He was antsy all day, but after he spoke with you, he was relaxed, calm, his usual self."

"I have that effect." I laugh, trying to lighten the mood.

He looks over at me as I adjust my body forward again. "It's okay if you don't want to talk about it, it's just I hope he didn't make you uncomfortable, that's all. He can come on pretty strong."

"It was nothing like that."

I debate whether to tell Nick the whole story or let it go, but like always, I can't hide from him.

I take a deep breath. "Matt and I ran into each other on Friday night. Well, he came up to me at the bar I was at and introduced himself. We talked for a bit. It was nice."

"Did anything else happen between you two?"

If anyone else said that I'd be offended, but Nick seems almost worried and protective of me.

"No, of course not. It's just that Eshaan saw us talking and got the wrong idea and was pretty pissed about it. Matt just came by today to apologize and to let me know he wasn't trying anything."

"Oh."

"It was sweet."

I see Nick's shoulders relax. "Thanks for telling me." He looks over at me with an easy smile.

"Anything else you want to know?" I smile back as I say the words, even though he can't see me.

"About you? Everything."

My heart thaws, and a warm glow surrounds me. With Nick, I feel like I can just be me. Imperfect, anxious at times, and even completely messed up. We could be just friends—but knowing how my body reacts to his makes that feel impossible—or we could be whatever this is. Somehow, this will have to be enough.

* * *

It's nearly 10 p.m. when we stride into the hotel lobby.

I'm exhausted. The events of the weekend and everything that happened today have left me depleted, and I'm fading fast.

Nick takes one look at me as we approach the check-in desk and says, "You go first."

"Thanks." Gratitude seeps into my bones as I give him a tired smile. I walk forward as the receptionist greets me.

"Welcome to the Lotte Hotel. What name is your reservation under for this evening?"

"Nisha Dhaliwal."

Her fingers move quickly on the keyboard, and a flash of confusion passes along her face. "I don't see a Nisha here. Is there another name?"

"Maybe, Nick Tremblay?"

"There's nothing under that, either."

"Give me one second." I pull out my phone and look through my emails to find the one from Amy that has the name and details of the hotel. She booked the hotel for next Monday evening.

"Shit," I mutter. "Sorry, it looks like our reservations were booked for next Monday. Do you have any rooms available tonight?"

"The hotel is almost fully booked, as there are so many events downtown this week. Let me see what we can do."

Nick comes up behind me. "Everything okay?"

"Amy booked our reservations for next Monday, and they might not have any availability for tonight."

"We'll figure it out," he says reassuringly as I hide my panic. I need to have things mapped out. Anything else makes me anxious.

She keeps tapping away. "We have one room left. It's a high-floor two-bedroom suite with a balcony. Would that work for you?"

I hesitate, and Nick catches it. "You stay here. I'll find somewhere else."

The receptionist looks over at him. "The other hotels are likely full or close to fully booked as well," she says matter-of-factly.

"We'll take it," I say before I can think better of it.

"Are you sure?" asks Nick.

"Yes."

I don't want Nick wandering downtown Seattle all night before our big pitch. I wouldn't want any colleague doing that, that's all. I try to convince myself there isn't anything more to it.

"I'll just need a credit card for incidentals."

Nick hands her his card and takes care of the rest of the check-in. He turns back to me with the hotel keys in hand.

"Let's go."

We make our way through the lobby and up to our room on the twentieth floor. Nick pushes the door open, and the room is stunning with a mid-century modern feel. There's a funky white couch in the centre, with bright orange lamps resting on minimalist side tables. Behind the large TV in the centre of the room is a mirror. I take in our reflection, and I can't help but like how we look together, except that we aren't together, and we never will be. I look away and focus on the carpet that has an abstract design, and then the simple white curtains. A perfect combination that makes the room warm and inviting even at this hour. There are two bedrooms, one on either side of the sitting room.

Separate rooms. I can do this. I exhale.

"Are you hungry? We could order room service," he says.

"I'm good. I think all I need is a shower and a bed."

"Me too," he says, and there's a moment where we just look at each other. "Okay, sleep well."

He heads in one direction and I go in the other.

I close the bedroom door and lean against it, fighting the urge to join him in his room.

I lock myself in the bathroom to shower, acutely aware as I'm undressing that he's just a few feet away, and that makes me flush all over.

Get it together.

I shower quickly and jump into my PJs: a lacy tank top and matching silk pajama shorts. Rachel said I needed to stop wearing old, ripped T-shirts to bed as that was bad energy, but now I feel too exposed and wish I had packed one. It's not like Nick is going to barge in here, although I'm not sure if I'd mind if he did... *Stop, Nisha!*

I lie in bed. My body is so tired, but my mind is wide awake. I replay the events of the past few days in my head. Questioning, doubting, and second-guessing everything.

I shouldn't have lingered at the bar on Friday. I could have avoided everything with Matt.

I should have told Nick I didn't need his help and avoided almost getting busted by Tom.

I should have apologized more profusely to Eshaan, especially with our engagement ceremony only a month away. I can't stand it when he's upset with me, and this time he's thoroughly pissed.

Then my thoughts drift to tomorrow and the pitch. Nick and I practiced our presentation in the car, but I'm nervous. There is still a chance we could lose, and my promotion depends on this. I've been so focused on all the drama in my life that I'm losing sight of what I want—to be successful and finally show everyone that I'm not wasting my time on my career. I'm making something of myself, instead of just being a fuck-up.

I toss and turn for what feels like forever, and then finally look at the clock. It's almost midnight. I remember the balcony, and suddenly, the need for fresh air overwhelms me.

I throw on a robe just in case and quietly open my door. The sitting room is dark, and Nick's door is closed.

Good.

I tiptoe to the balcony and find the curtain pushed back and the sliding door already open. I look outside to see Nick lounging on a loveseat. His body splayed out. One arm behind his head and one leg hanging over the side. His eyes are closed, and he looks so breathtaking I can't help but stare. I drink in the sight of his tight white tee hugging his slim, muscular body and his black lounge pants accentuating his strong thighs. I never get to check him out in this much detail, and I'm not going to miss this chance.

"Come join me," he says, sensing my presence.

"Oh, I didn't know you were out here."

His mouth rises into a smirk as if he knows I'm ravaging him with my eyes.

"Couldn't sleep. You?"

"Me neither."

I come outside and move to the railing to take in the view of the city lights, buildings, and ocean around us. It's stunning. I love imagining people in their homes and what their lives are like. Kids tucked soundly into bed surrounded by their stuffies. Couples binge-watching Netflix together. Artists working on their creations late into the night, driven by something beyond comprehension. Late-night workers hustling to take care of the city and their families.

"Seattle is beautiful, isn't it?" I whisper to him as he comes and stands next to me.

"It is." He's looking at me and not the view.

If this is an act, then I want to be a part of the whole damn play.

I unconsciously start rubbing my neck, not even realizing I'm doing it until Nick looks at me with concern. "Is your neck hurting?"

"It's a little tense. Too many long days at the office." I play it off even though it aches with stiffness.

"I could give you a little massage if you like," he says innocently, but I know we're on dangerous ground.

"That would be great." The need for release and my exhaustion win over.

I step away from the railing and join him on the loveseat, and he moves to sit behind me. He brings up one leg to rest beside me, so I'm in between his legs.

He starts kneading my shoulders through the robe.

"Here." I slide down the robe to my elbows to give him easier access and pull my hair to the side, needing to have his bare hands on me.

His cool hands touch my hot skin, applying the exact right amount of pressure to work out the knots.

A soft moan escapes my lips.

"That good, huh?"

I don't even try to deny it. "So good."

I melt into his touch even more, each stroke releasing the tension, the fear, and the worry.

We stay like that. His strong hands move deftly, and my body relaxes more with every delicious movement.

It's bliss, it's wonderful, it's not enough.

He shuffles closer and presses his lips close to my ear. "I'd love to show you what else I can do with my hands," he whispers as if reading my mind.

I shiver.

He pulls down the strap of my tank top and drags his lips down my neck as he guides me back into him. I succumb all too easily. Everything is so effortless with him, and I can't fight it anymore. Fight him, fight this, fight whatever is happening between us.

I feel his hardness against my back, and I know I should move, get away from here, but my body doesn't budge an inch.

He grips my chin and guides my head to turn toward his, and then his lips move across mine lightly. My lips part, an invitation. He doesn't waste a moment before he's kissing me thoroughly while moving his hand down my neck, then my chest, before lifting my tank top and making gentle teasing circles on my stomach. His fingers start moving downward, and my breath hitches as he reaches my shorts. He slips his hands underneath them, pausing right at the spot on my lacy underwear that's drenched right through.

"You're so wet for me," he whispers into my ear.

My body confesses things I never intended to. He pushes my underwear to the side, gliding his fingers along my clit as I lean back into him and hold my breath.

I stifle a moan and bite my bottom lip. It feels good, too good, and my restraint loosens with every stroke.

I don't want him to stop, but I grab his wrist before he can continue.

"Let me make you feel good." His finger lingers on me, right there, waiting for my permission.

I don't respond. My mind is having trouble forming coherent thoughts.

He waits patiently before adding. "You don't know how long I've wanted to do this."

My grip loosens slightly of its own accord.

He pulls his hand away and shifts out from under me, repositioning himself between my legs and then hovering over me.

He brings his fingers, still wet with my desire, to my lips.

"I could just get you off, that's it, with my fingers…"

He brings his tongue to my mouth so I'm tasting both him and me.

"With my tongue."

Then he's licking a path from my mouth, down my chin, and in between my breasts.

"With both."

He pulls my tank top down entirely, taking my nipple into his mouth, teasing and sucking while dragging his other hand down my stomach. My breath hitches, and I dig my nails into his back. He starts to tug down my shorts.

"Wait," escapes my lips, some sort of sense slowly coming back to me.

"This doesn't have to count," he adds. His breathing is shallow and rapid.

Count against what? My hazy brain tries to comprehend. His one-night rule? Me cheating? The thought has me inwardly cringing, even as my body sizzles with his touch. My pulse skyrockets as he peers up at me from between my legs.

He knows he has me on the cusp and doesn't waste the chance. "It doesn't have to be anything more than this," he confirms, trying to entice me.

Instead, I stiffen at his words. I know for him, this is nothing, a bit of fun, but for me, it could be catastrophic.

A drunken kiss, the sauna, the club, his hotel room, and even what happened in the office earlier today were all bad enough, but this is crossing a line I'm not sure I would ever be okay with. How could I ever look Eshaan in the eyes again?

If we continue, there is no coming back from this.

You're so desperate for attention. It's sad, really. Eshaan's words float back to me right on cue, making me instantly ashamed.

What am I doing? Nick isn't making me any promises. He's honest about what this is, and here I am, still letting him put his hands all over me.

I get up and shove him away, my body protesting the movement. He quickly moves back and stands up. I avert my eyes, so he doesn't see them glazed over—desperate desire mixed with shame. I pull up my tank top.

"I can't do this," I say breathily.

He doesn't say anything. Instead, he bends over to cover me up with my robe.

Finally, he says, "I get it."

The breeze blows my hair in front of my face, and he tucks it behind my ear. His hand lingers there. He looks at me like he wants to say more, but he doesn't utter another word.

I want to ask him what this means. What I mean to him, but he doesn't give me the chance. Instead, he strides back inside without even a glance back, adding confusion and hurt to the equation.

Regret mixes with the tears streaming down my face. I'm nothing to him, and here I am, so willing, so ready to give up everything.

I stifle a sob and somehow manage to make it back to my room, where I close the door and drop in a heap on my bed. I wrap my arms tightly around myself and cry.

Eshaan's voice resounds in my head.

It's so lame that you feel like you need to dress like that to get attention.

No one would even notice you if you weren't with me.

You're dropping everything for this job, but let's face it, it's getting you nowhere. You wouldn't even be able to pay rent if Rachel wasn't giving you a steep discount.

And then my mom's too.

Why can't you be more like your sister? She doesn't bring shame to our family.

Who's going to put up with someone like you?

Your dad would be so disappointed in you. His little girl, doing things like this?

I let myself drown in their disapproval and judgment.

I deserve it. In fact, I deserve much worse. I let the hurt, the pain, and the guilt ravage me, wanting to punish every inch of myself for being so damn stupid.

31. NEVER ENOUGH

"We look forward to working with you."

That's it. We did it. The elation of this win breaks through my bubble of anguish. After everything we've been through for this account, it's finally working out.

I try not to seem too eager as we get up.

Charles, a top gun angel investor, is going to give us even more than we asked for. He reaches out to shake my hand, and he holds it and my gaze for longer than appropriate with a sly grin playing on his lips. "You're one to watch, Nisha." He looks me up and down slowly like he's perusing the dessert menu of a Michelin-starred restaurant.

I hold his gaze confidently. "Thank you."

He must be at least twenty years my senior, but he's handsome, clean-cut, fit, and entitled, like most white men who've accumulated his level of wealth. Discomfort starts to mount, but I don't pull my hand away. He's offering up millions—I can pay this little price. Women do this every day with every unwanted glance and touch they have no choice but to endure.

Nick comes to my rescue. "We'll send over the contracts later today." He holds out his hand.

"All business, this one." Charles laughs and finally lets go of my hand, giving Nick a brief but firm handshake.

With that, we file out of the room and say our goodbyes. I practically skip to the elevator, and as the doors close, Nick hits me with his thousand-watt smile.

"You were incredible in there."

"Thanks," I say curtly.

I barely slept and woke up with a pounding headache. My eyes were puffy from crying, so I drenched a towel in cold water and placed it over my eyes for fifteen minutes before meticulously applying my makeup, hiding my shame under layers of concealer.

I tamped down all the guilt, rage, and frustration and donned the mask I started wearing as soon as I moved here, becoming Fantasy Nisha—the empowered woman with no fucks to give, who can make it in a man's world.

I will fall apart later, but for now, I have my armour and I'm not letting anyone get through again. Not even Nick.

We step out of the elevator and Nick points to a seat in the lobby. "I'll email Amy to send the contracts over. Why don't you tell Tom we got the deal?"

Of course, he wants *me* to get the spotlight by telling me to email the boss with the good news. Before, I would have thought that was sweet, and now I see it for what it is: Just another gimmick to help weaken my defences.

"Okay, I'll do that."

We sit down and type quietly on our phones. I finish up just as Nick does.

"Ready?" he asks, standing up.

"For the drive back? Not really," I respond without thinking. I love being in new places, and I hate going on any trip, even a work one, without checking out some of the local vibe.

"Let's go out and celebrate then."

Is he fucking kidding me? I did want to see some of the city, but not with him. Not now. I spent all night mentally berating myself for letting my guard down repeatedly over these last few months. He's not into me in any meaningful way. A hot rush of shame fills me again. Of course he isn't. I'm nothing special. If it wasn't for Eshaan, I'd be completely alone like I was before.

I push off the seat and start heading out the door as he follows behind.

"We should get back," I reply, my heart heavy.

"They're not even expecting us back until late this afternoon," he counters. He shoots me a look that normally would have me eating out of his hand, but now all I want is to get away from him. He's just another man that I can add to my long list of mistakes.

"What's wrong?"

"Nothing."

He doesn't push, but a part of me wants him to.

We keep walking down the street toward his car.

"Why don't we just check out Pike Place Market? We can get coffee and then head back."

"Fine." I don't have the energy to play this game with him. The one where he makes me think he gives a shit and then I realize he doesn't, but only after I embarrass and humiliate myself.

I buckle up as Nick easily manoeuvres us through the streets of Seattle.

I check my phone, and a smile breaks out on my face when I see that Tom has already emailed back. I scan the email and brim with joy. He's thrilled we got the deal. Then I read the rest, and my heart plummets.

> **You're a dream team. Nick, we're going to have to talk about an extension.**

There's nothing else about me or that promotion I've been promised, but Nick, who's probably already making more than double what I am? They want to keep him longer, even though they love to talk about how we need to cut costs.

Of course, they do.

I'm not anyone worth noticing at work or otherwise. No matter how hard I've been working for this. How much I've put into this role and given to this company. I bite my lip to hold back the tears prickling my eyes.

Nick looks over at me, a hint of worry creasing his forehead like he senses the shift in my mood. "What happened?"

"It's nothing."

I turn up the music volume, so he gets the hint that I don't want to talk about it. In fact, I don't want to talk to him at all, especially after what happened last night. The truth I don't want to admit is that I want to mean something to Nick, even if nothing can ever come of it. To know that there's even a small part of me that's lovable, worthy, and deserving of someone like him. But all of this is confirming what I've known all along: I'm not good enough, not for a promotion, and not for him.

I smooth my skirt down with my hands, trying to get my emotions under control. I can break down later.

We make it to the market and spend some time wandering through the stalls, stopping here and there to check out the shops and the trinkets. We stand out because we're grossly overdressed—Nick's in his suit, and I'm in my pencil skirt, crisp red blouse, and pumps—but it makes for fun conversation with the vendors. That, along with the vibe and the ocean air, helps to settle my mood.

I remind myself that later I can rage and cry. For now, I can pretend. I'm so used to it. Pretending my mom's harsh comments don't bother me, that Eshaan's jealousy and possessiveness are normal. Pretend that I'm a decent human who deserves good things, that my dad wasn't an alcoholic who succumbed to his addiction even before he got diagnosed with cancer, and that Nick is nothing to me. That's what we do in my family. It's what I can do now.

Nick gently takes my hand on the boardwalk and interrupts my dark thoughts. "You haven't said much since we left the meeting."

I pull away even though I want to keep holding on—to him, to us—even when there's nothing to hold on to. "Just a lot on my mind, I guess."

He steps closer, and this time, I step back, not willing to let him get to me. Not again.

"Listen." He looks up at the sky as if he's trying to find his thoughts, but now it's like he's coming up with another practiced, calculated move. "I'm so sorry about last night. I feel awful about how I acted."

"Why? It's fine."

You messing with me and then running out? It's all fucking okay. Guys get to do whatever they want after all, and women are left picking up the pieces of our shattered dreams and broken hearts.

"It's not. It was too forward of me, and I'm sorry. I took advantage of the situation, and of you. I would never want to be like Charles this morning, thinking he could do whatever he wants because he has money and power."

I laugh. "No, you're fucking worse because you don't even realize it." I can't help myself.

He staggers back like I slapped him. Good. Let me mess with him for a moment. He even has the audacity to look hurt. "Look, I don't chase after women who are already in relationships or pretend that I'm available for something that I'm not. They know it's casual."

"Thanks for the memo. Could have used it…" I count on my fingers for dramatic effect. "Three months ago, dude." The words are like acid on my tongue.

He's silent, and it's even more enraging.

"I guess I'm the lucky exception that you just happened to rope in and then release when you realize you won't get what you wanted."

He moves closer, but I hold my ground. "Is that what you think?" I sense anger in his voice, and this time, I don't even care. I'm sick of constantly having to placate the men in my life. "That I just want to fuck you?" His words hit me like a sucker punch, even though I should have been ready.

Tears sting my eyes, but I don't want him to see me cry. "I don't know what you think. I've never known." I shrug, the fight leaving my body. It's the truth. "Anyway, it doesn't matter."

What's the use in arguing with Nick? What, for this messed-up fairy tale that doesn't even exist? Where I already have my prince charming but keep falling for the evil villain who doesn't want me? I mean, *not really*.

"I care about you, Nisha. A lot. I just can't do anything more than this."

"You care about me? What does that even mean?" I shout at him, and I don't even give a shit that people are turning around to look at us.

"It means I'm sorry, okay? I shouldn't have let things carry on like this for so long."

"But you did. Why?"

"Fuck, I don't know okay. You're different from anyone I've ever met before." He brings his hand to his forehead and drags it slowly through his hair. "But that doesn't change anything for me."

Of course it doesn't.

"Go to hell, Nick." I sigh and take a step back, looking out at the ocean.

The thought of spending hours in the car with him makes me want to vomit. I make a split-second decision as I realize I don't have to keep putting myself through this.

"I have to get back. I'll find my own way." I rush off as fast as my impractical pumps take me.

"Wait." He easily catches up to me. "Nisha, let me explain." He approaches me cautiously like I'm a frightened animal.

I can't take it anymore. "You've said enough. Please." Tears stream freely down my cheeks, and I can barely make out his fuzzy form.

He offers a tissue. How does he always fucking have everything I could possibly need at his disposal?

"If that's what you want." He holds the tissue out. An offering.

"It is." I don't take it. Instead, I wipe the tears from my eyes with my hand.

He takes the same hand and gives me his car keys and the tissue. "You take the car."

He leaves. The moment he's gone, all I want is for him to come back because still, I'm a desperate fool, but I stand silently and watch him leave.

No one would want to be with you. Not how you are.

You're right, Mom, you were always right. I believe you now.

32. FLOWERS AND BANQUET HALLS

I walk through the doors of the condo, looking like a hot mess. My mascara is all over my cheeks, running through my caked-on foundation, and I'm lugging my carry-on behind me, along with Nick's laptop and mine.

"You're back!" Rachel's voice comes toward me before I see her. She freezes when she sees my face.

"What the fuck happened?" Shock takes over her expression.

I drop everything to the ground and just fall to the entryway floor as the door closes behind me.

She rushes over and puts her arms around me. "Breathe."

The panic takes over, and I can only take shallow gulps as Rachel rubs my back and smooths back my hair. "It's okay. It's going to be okay."

She holds me and rocks me as I cry, even though I cried non-stop on the three-hour drive back to Vancouver. The tears are a river leading to a never-ending ocean of despair. I wish I could tell her everything—that I'm in love with Nick but he doesn't want anything more with me, and it doesn't matter because I'm with Eshaan. That a part of me thought that maybe, just maybe, we could figure it out, and that's what I was

wishing for all along, and why I didn't stop things between us even though I know I should have.

Rachel holds me until my breathing finally returns to normal. Her thumbs wipe the tears from my eyes. "As much as I like hanging out with our expensive shoes, let's go inside."

I can't even force a laugh.

She pulls me up and walks me inside like I'm something precious, and tears come flooding back when I remember I'm not. I'm nothing. No one.

She sits me on our revolving cozy chair, wrapping me in a blanket. "I'll make us some tea."

I don't want her to leave my side, but I nod, staring into nothingness until she returns with a steaming, fragrant cup and places it on the coffee table in front of me.

"Tell me what happened," she says, pulling up one of the suede pink ottomans to sit next to me. She takes my hand, and her touch immediately makes me feel safe. "Did you break up with Eshaan?"

"What? No, that's not happening." Not now. Not ever.

I tell her everything that's been going on with Nick, and I don't hold back this time. I tell her about the sauna, the club, the hotel rooms and even the night out at the symphony. I tell her everything I overheard with Matt, even though it's embarrassing to share, and even how Tom almost walked in on us. I let it all out, all the shame, humiliation, and guilt, knowing that other than Sunny, she's the only person I know who won't judge me.

The worst part is that this time I have no excuses. I am no longer young, naïve, and inexperienced with men. I know the warning signs. I can tell when a relationship is headed nowhere, when it's meaningless, but somehow, I still can't stop myself from falling for Nick. He makes me feel seen and understood in a way that I haven't before, but it's my fault entirely for thinking that this could ever be something more. This time I'm damaging more than myself. I'm also setting fire to my one chance at happiness and for what? For nothing.

I wipe tears from my eyes. "I was so upset that Shaan exchanged a few texts with his ex, and here I am doing all of this behind his back."

Her eyes narrow in on me. "What texts?" I remember that I didn't tell her because I know she has reservations about Eshaan, so I stopped sharing things that paint him in a bad light.

"It was a while ago now, and it doesn't matter. They were harmless, and he told me nothing was going on."

The look of suspicion and doubt only deepens in Rachel's eyes. "Nish." She hesitates. "There's something I've been meaning to bring up with you, and I know you've been through a lot, but I think we need to talk about this."

I take a sip of my tea. I'm not ready for Rachel's truths. Not yet. "What time is it?" I ask, hoping to delay this conversation she wants us to have.

"Five-thirty."

"Thank god." I relax back in my chair.

"Why?"

"You know, we're finalizing everything for the engagement party today, remember?"

"Oh, that's tonight?"

I swat her gently, knowing she remembers.

"I'm kidding. I've had it blocked off in my calendar for like two months."

"We should get ready." I take a few more sips of tea.

"I guess we should." I can tell she's struggling and wanting to tell me what's on her mind. I plead with her silently, *Please not tonight*. "Promise we'll talk later, though."

"I promise."

Rachel helps me up. At least I have one person I can count on and who respects my wishes.

We get all dolled up and put on almost-matching salwar kameez outfits. Mine is gold and hers is pink, the engagement ceremony colours. We don't need to dress up for this as it's just a routine visit to see the hall, but I always feel better when I look my best.

Rachel does my makeup and by some crazy miracle makes me look like I haven't been crying all day.

I give her a hug. "Rachel, thank you."

"For what?"

"For everything."

"I'm here for you always. You know that, right? You don't have to wait until things get crazy to tell me things."

"It's just that work is so busy, and then all the engagement planning. I've been in over my head."

"I know. Now you know for next time." She gives my shoulders a squeeze.

I hope there's never a next time when it comes to the shit I've been through.

"Come on, let's take a snap for the 'gram." Rachel starts posing us in the full-length mirror she installed precisely for this purpose.

"I'll tag you." She starts clicking away. As she's doing that, I remember Nick started following me a few weeks ago.

"Should I block Nick, the asshole?"

"No way. Let him see that you're not affected by him and his shitty bad-boy moves."

She's right, and I feel better already. I will find the strength to move on from all of this and put it behind me. I follow her to our front door as my phone vibrates in my purse. I pull it out and glance at the screen.

"Rach, it's my mom. I'm going to take this. I'll meet you downstairs."

"Sure. Sounds good. I'll bring the car out front."

I give her a quick smile before swiping the green call button. "Hi Mom."

"Tu ki kardi aa?" she asks, wondering what I'm up to.

"Just heading to the hall to meet Eshaan and his parents."

"Today?"

"Yes. We're going to finalize everything. I'll send you photos." I hover in the entryway.

"Do you have time now?"

"What is it, Mom?"

"You ordered your engagement lehenga, but did you get your set yet?"

"Not yet, but I still have time to pick something out. Don't worry." I open the door and step out into the hall. I'm not sure what this is about, but I know better than to rush my mom.

"Why don't you wear my wedding set? I know it's old-fashioned now, but you've loved it since you were a little girl."

I lean back against the door and bring my hand to my neck, imagining what it would be like to wear that gorgeous piece of jewellery. The gold necklace and earrings my dad's family had given to her so many years ago. So different from the fashion sets everyone wears now.

"Mom, really?"

"Yes. It would look so nice with your lehenga and I want you to have it. Your father always said he would give it to you on your wedding."

I laugh even as a tear slips down my face. He's thinking of me even now.

"Thank you, Mom. I would love to."

"We've been waiting for this day for so long and now it will be even more special."

I nod even though she can't see me.

"Okay, you better go. Best not to keep Eshaan and his family waiting."

"Mom?"

"Yes, putt?"

"I love you."

"I love you too, Nisha. Now go," she says, her voice soft and tender like my own.

* * *

We walk through the hall doors where my Bhua Ji is already waiting for us. "You girls look beautiful," she says in her British English lilt that reminds me so much of my dad.

"Thank you, Bhua Ji." She wraps me in a hug, and then Rachel, too.

"Hi, Auntie Ji."

My Bhua gives Rachel an approving once-over. "See, you girls should wear more of this stuff, instead of the modern clothes." She teases us with a smile. I know this is a special moment for her too, especially since she introduced me to Eshaan in the first place.

I see Eshaan in the distance, and my heavy heart lights up. He comes over, looking dashing in a kurta top and gives me a peck on the cheek, keeping the PDA in check in front of my Bhua before giving Rachel a quick side hug.

"I had a photoshoot just before." He looks down at his clothes.

"You look so good," I whisper in his ear.

"You look amazing, too." His eyes roam over my body. "I love you in traditional clothes."

"I know, that's why I wore this, duh." I playfully touch his arm.

"Okay, you love birds, let's go check out the hall," Rachel interjects after dramatically rolling her eyes.

His parents are already inside.

"Hi, Auntie Ji and Uncle Ji." They give me a quick hug, and even his mom's smile toward me is genuine.

"It's stunning," Rachel whispers.

The entire hall is transformed into a mystical, magical place, where chandeliers hang from the ceiling, and silver and gold banners glitter like stars in the dim lighting. The tables are precisely decorated with gorgeous centrepieces that have candles, crystals, and flowers somehow effortlessly woven together, while the dim lighting and soft Hindi music make it feel like I'm on a Bollywood film set. They have an event this weekend with a couple who chose the same package as us, but Eshaan's mom wanted to see everything before the big day. I knew she would make over-the-top adjustments, wanting her son's engagement party to be the talk of the town. Seeing this, I don't care what her reasons are. It's breathtaking.

Eshaan takes me by the hand and walks me up to the stage. "Well, what do you think?"

"It's so beautiful," I say, my voice breaking as I turn to him. Nothing could ruin this moment.

"Oh, babe, I'm so glad you love it."

We continue to walk around arm in arm while his parents are in a corner talking with the owners, and Rachel and my Bhua are chatting away.

I can't believe I was willing to risk this. My heart flutters and then slams against my chest as I think about how I almost fucked everything up.

My eyes land on the roses on each table.

"What is it?" Eshaan follows my gaze.

"It's nothing."

He tilts my chin up to look at him. "Tell me. We're about to get engaged. No secrets."

If he only knew.

"It's just that my dad's favourite flowers were peonies. He would get them for us every birthday."

"We'll get them changed."

"Oh, no, that's okay."

His parents are already covering all the expenses. I don't want to add another one.

"Anything for you." His lips graze my ear, and I shiver.

He steps closer. "Stay over tonight?"

I wrap my arms around his waist, although I know I shouldn't in front of our family. He does the same.

"Dev's out for a couple of days." He answers my question before I even ask, knowing I hate staying over when he's there.

"Yes." *A full body fuck-yes,* I say in my head as Rachel would.

Eshaan tells the decorators to change the flowers, and we have one final look around. Rachel takes a few photos of us together and sends them to Eshaan to post. Then we walk out together and say our goodbyes.

"Shaan's going to drive me home," I say casually to Rachel with his parents in earshot, even though we're both almost thirty years old. It's so comical. It makes me laugh, but—I play the charade.

"Okay, I'll see you at home then." She winks at me.

We jump into Eshaan's Maserati, and I sink back, letting the luxurious leather engulf me as he flicks on the seat warmers. He knows how much I love them any time of year. He knows me.

He looks over at me with hunger in his eyes and places his hand on my thigh as he revs the engine and we pull out onto the street. "You're so fucking beautiful, you know that?"

I don't feel beautiful, not now, after everything I've done, but for a moment, I forget the guilt and shame, and remember why I fell for him.

* * *

My alarm goes off at 6 a.m. I turn it off and snuggle into Eshaan. His arm is resting over me, and I don't want to leave and face everything, but I have to. I start to get up.

"Stay," he whispers groggily. "Call in sick."

I'm tempted. It's been non-stop at work for weeks, but after winning this big pitch, we'll need to debrief and see if we can replicate the strategy to approach new investors and those who bailed before.

"I have to go. I landed that big deal for them, remember?"

"And are they even giving you a raise?"

"They better be," I joke, trying to avoid the question.

"Nish." He starts getting up, looking at me with sleepy, sexy eyes. "Did you think about what I've said to you? You're wasting your time there."

Here we go again.

"They aren't going to give you a raise, no matter how hard you work for them."

"Shaan, please, not today."

"Fine. After we're engaged, we'll figure things out. You don't need to work anyway."

He brushes it off like my whole career is a bit of dust on his shoulder, not something I've been working so hard for, for years. I ignore it, like I always do.

"I'm sorry about last night," I say as I look down at my hands. I pretended I had a headache, but the truth is I just couldn't let him touch me like that. Nick has ruined me for anyone else. I can't even think of sleeping with my soon-to-be fiancé. And the worst part: I don't want to.

He kisses my forehead.

"Don't even worry about it."

He throws the sheets off and gets up.

"Besides, I booked a week at the Empress for us in Victoria. You can make it up to me then." He gives me a wink then leaves the room to use the main bathroom like he always does when I'm here. I brush my teeth in the ensuite and jump in the shower. My neck is stiff, and my chest is tight even though I should feel relieved. Things with Nick are over and Eshaan doesn't have to know about any of it.

I start getting dressed, grateful I keep some of my work clothes at his place, when Eshaan's phone pings with a couple of texts. Without thinking I grab it from where it's lying on his nightstand.

When do I get to see your sexy face?

You've been keeping me waiting too long already...

What the actual fuck?

I can't see who it's from, but I know already.

I thought he stopped texting his ex, but apparently not. I try to get into his phone, but he changed his password, and my mind tingles with suspicion.

Shaan comes out wearing nothing but a towel and looks at me sitting half-dressed on his bed.

"What are you doing with my phone?" He takes it from me.

"Why is Sonia still texting you?"

He opens his phone and reads the text, his eyes widening for a moment before his expression returns to neutral

"She doesn't get the hint," he says too casually.

"Didn't you guys break up like two years ago?"

"She's trying to start shit up. She knows we're getting engaged soon," he says as he uses another, smaller, towel to dry his hair.

"Block her."

"What?"

"I said block her, now." I get up and fold my arms across my chest, trying to look stern while wearing nothing but a shirt.

"Fine. She'll probably just message me with a different number. That's why I didn't before."

"Right," I mutter under my breath.

I watch over his shoulder as he hits block and then chucks his phone on the bed.

He grabs me and gives me a kiss. "You're the only one I want. You know that, right?"

And despite the warning bells sounding in my head, I kiss him back.

33. ASSHOLES AND EXES

"Love you, babe."

"Love you, too."

I lean over to kiss Eshaan before hopping out of his car and onto the sidewalk in front of my office building.

I hear a low whistle and look over to see Matt staring at the car as it speeds off.

"Boyfriend has a nice car."

"Thanks."

"I hear congrats are in order. You killed the pitch." His words help to lighten the heaviness cloaking me.

"Thanks. I'm stoked about it." We walk side by side to the elevators.

"You'll have to tell me your secrets to getting investors to spend millions."

"I just pout my lips at them."

He looks over at me as the elevator doors open and laughs nervously. "How's this?" he says, adding his finest pout.

I squint my eyes in mock judgment. "Work on it, bro. Anyways, we're doing a debrief this week. I'll send you an invite."

"That would be great."

The elevator hits our floor, and we walk out.

"I'll see you at nine-thirty."

I look at Matt, confused.

"Nick's not coming in today or maybe this whole week. He got called in on a big project for another client. He asked me to step in."

I feel a flicker of disappointment even though I don't want to see him. "Oh, I'll see you in a bit then."

He smiles and walks away, and I head to my office. I drop my bag on my desk before sitting on my chair and pulling out my phone.

First, I check a message from Rachel.

Nick came by last night to get his car and stuff.
So don't stress.

I reply:

Thanks, Rach. You're the best.

Eshaan tagged me in a few Stories. I swipe through them and look through my list of viewers, looking for only one name. Nick saw a couple. The one with Rachel and me, and then the one with Eshaan that was captioned: "Countdown's on until I put a ring on it." He has his arms around me, and we're both smiling and looking at the camera. It doesn't feel like me. It's someone else whose life I'm living in an alternate reality where I don't have to worry about gorgeous assholes and clingy exes. Then I look up Sonia and see that she's still following Eshaan and liking all his posts, including the ones with me. I look at her grid and scroll through, seeing that she has kept pictures of herself and Eshaan up there.

Why the fuck would she do that?

Something doesn't sit right. I sit there ruminating. What if there's more going on between them than he's telling me? So many nights I've been away for work, and it would have been easy for him to do anything, and for me not to even find out about it—just like it was easy for me to end up in Nick's arms. The difference is that I would never cross that line.

You almost did.

I push away the thought, not wanting to go there. Before I can fall deeper into this black hole of worry, Matt slides up to my door.

"Ready?"

"Ready." I follow him into the hallway and down to the meeting room. My fucked-up life can wait.

34. #AWKWARD

Nick's been MIA for a week, and I ignore the familiar pang I feel whenever I walk by his office. Instead, I focus on the day ahead.

I look forward to my meetings with Matt. He's fun and goofy, and Nick was right, he doesn't always watch what comes out of his mouth, which is refreshing when everyone is so buttoned up at the office, trying to get an edge and get ahead.

I get there early and sit in the same spot as I always do, in the middle of the large boardroom with the glass walls. I start setting up my laptop and pulling up the meme I can't wait to show Matt when I hear him enter.

"Matt, you're going to love this cat meme I found." I smile at my screen and look up, but it's not Matt standing there, it's Nick. He hovers hesitantly at the door.

"Matt's going to be a little late. He's just finishing up a call."

He walks in and finds a spot across from me, and suddenly, the large boardroom is too small. I can't get a breath. I remind myself that the walls are glass, and if I just take a few strides, I can be out the door. It helps with the anxiety. Then I take a calming breath. I'm not going to let Nick upset me anymore.

Nick logs in to his computer, and I pretend there's something fascinating on my screen, waiting for the awkward moment to pass.

He breaks the silence. "Just so you know, I'm not taking the extension."

I don't know what to say, so I blurt the first thing that comes out of my mouth with more coldness than I intended. "Oh…why's that exactly?"

I give him a level look and, for the first time, take in his dishevelled appearance. Every day since he started here, he's been dressed like he just walked out of *GQ*, but today, dark lines surround his bright eyes, and his hair is out of place instead of expertly styled. Even his shirt looks rumpled, as if he couldn't be bothered.

I worry if everything is okay, even though he's not mine to worry over.

"I just feel like it's for the best, I guess." The unsaid words linger in the air: *So you don't have to stress about me anymore.*

Matt comes waltzing in and sits next to Nick. "Hey, nice of you to make an appearance," he jokes as he looks over at Nick.

"Nish." He tips an invisible hat to me.

I smile despite everything.

"Hey, Matt."

He looks over at Nick. "Dude, you look like hell," he says, not one to mince his words.

"You always know how to make a guy feel great." Nick's voice is filled with irritation, and I'm not used to it.

"They must have put you through the wringer over there."

"Something like that," he says. "Anyways, bring me up to speed on what I missed."

We somehow manage to get through the meeting with Matt helping to defuse the mood. I can do this. It will just be for a few more weeks, and then I'll never have to worry about seeing Nick again. I don't know why I'm not more relieved by that.

We walk out of the boardroom just as Jess comes careening down the hallway with the biggest flowers I've ever seen: peonies.

"Nisha, these are from your boyfriend, or, should I say, soon-to-be fiancé." She gives me a little grin. The flowers are a lovely, soft pink that resembles freshly spun cotton candy set in an intricately decorated porcelain vase wrapped with a golden ribbon. They smell like heaven.

She glances at the laptop in my hand. "Here, I'll help you take them to your office since your hands are full."

"Thanks, Jess."

"Wow, a nice car *and* flowers. This guy's the full meal deal," Matt says, making me wish I could turn myself invisible.

"Coffee?" Nick says to Matt in a gruff tone. I don't look over as I don't want to see the expression on his face.

"Sure. See you ladies later." They walk off.

Jess is gushing all the way to my office, and her normally infectious enthusiasm isn't doing anything to lighten my mood.

"Where would you like these?"

"By the windows would be great, thank you."

I plug in my laptop at my desk, walk to the window, and then brush my fingers over the soft petals before opening the card.

I know it's not your birthday, but I wanted to make you as happy as you make me. Love, Eshaan.

"You're so lucky, Nish. You don't know how hard it is to find someone half decent." I place the card back in the envelope. I should be happy, but that's the last thing I feel right now.

"The dating scene not going well?"

"Remember Daniel, I told you about? We went out on a few dates, and it was going great. And this weekend, I stayed over, and the next morning, he was scrolling on his phone for two hours." She lets out an exasperated sigh. "I mean, what could be that compelling when you have a naked babe in your bed?" She shakes her head.

"Oh, Jess. You deserve so much better than that." I mean it. Jess is kind, sweet, and so pretty—even more so because she doesn't realize it.

"I know." She shrugs. "Anyways, he's out."

"What about Matt?" I throw his name in the ring.

"Oh, he doesn't even notice me."

"Maybe I can help?" The two of them would be so wonderful together.

"Really?" Her eyes light up."

"Let's talk about it over lunch sometime this week."

"You're the best." She looks over at me with excitement, and some of the tension surrounding me dissipates. I smile at her warmly as she walks out of my office.

When she's gone, I turn to look at Eshaan's peonies and my smile slips away. I will find a way through all this.

35. FILLERS AND FEELINGS

The week passes in a flurry, so I don't even have time to ruminate too much. With Nick leaving, he spends most of his time training the IT guys, and with my successful pitches, I get to hand-pick my team to help with future ones, almost like I'm in management—but without the salary perks. It's still exciting, but I feel the wind being taken out of my sails. Increasingly, I'm thinking Eshaan is right; they're not going to promote me. I debate whether I should just ask Tom for a raise, having brought in so many funds for the company, but I don't know if I have the confidence to do that just yet.

Matt is in all our meetings now as he's staying to help with the transition once Nick's gone, so we're never alone together. It's for the best, but my heart is heavier by the day.

In the evenings, I help Rachel with marketing for her online business to take my mind off things, or else I'm with Eshaan, finalizing the details of the ceremony. I'm even spending time with his parents, who are warming up to me more as things are about to get official.

I've almost forgotten about the texts, but I can't deny that there is a lingering nervousness. I want to bring it up, but everything is going so well that I just can't convince myself to. It's probably nothing. I was wrong about Nick, and I'm probably just paranoid now about other things, too.

It's 2 p.m. when a message from Jess flashes on my screen.

We haven't even had lunch yet to talk about cuteee M.

With a bear holding a heart GIF.

I instantly reply with an apology, then peek at my calendar. It's full every day for the next week. I text back and suggest drinks after work tonight instead at a swanky bar that just opened nearby.

Really? Yes, I'm in. Come grab me at 5:30.

* * *

"So, how was the rest of your day?" Jess asks as she leans back into the booth, perusing the happy hour drinks menu.

"Busy. Now I'm going through resumes to find the perfect team to build."

"You're so lucky." She sets the menu down.

"How do you mean?"

My brain is too tired to go through options, so I opt for my usual gin and tonic.

"Going to all these conferences, pitching to billionaires, working on these big projects. All of it." She looks at me, impressed.

"You could do it too, you know." I smile at her encouragingly.

"Not really, I don't have the qualifications."

"That doesn't matter as much anymore. Experience is just as important."

She looks at me, unconvinced.

"You could always ask to work on a few other things. That's what I did. I'm also happy to ask on your behalf if that's something you'd be interested in."

An idea starts forming in my head that I know Jess would love, but I'll have to check first to see if I can make it happen.

"I'm not sure."

"Just think about it."

The waitress comes by and takes our orders.

"Is everything okay?" Jess looks at me curiously once we're alone again.

"Yes, so great." I lie so effortlessly now. It must be a latent gift. Some people develop allergies as they approach thirty—I seemed to develop a knack for taking liberties with the truth.

"You seem preoccupied lately."

"Oh, it's just been a lot, you know, work plus engagement stuff."

"Such a hard life, getting engaged to the man of your dreams, making waves at the office. Poor you," she says with a dramatic emphasis that helps me instantly lighten up.

"I know, first-world problems, right?" We giggle like schoolgirls, and it's nice to laugh.

The waitress brings our drinks.

"Cheers." Jess brings her glass to mine.

"To new opportunities," I say, giving her a knowing look.

She sets her drink down and stares off into the distance, something catching her eye.

"Guess who just showed up." Her eyes twinkle.

"Who? You know I can't keep up with your online dating guys."

"Not that. It's Nick with a hot brunette. I mean, she's like holy shit, gorgeous."

I bristle, but my masochistic tendencies make me look over. There he is, back to his immaculate self, standing next to a woman who looks like she walked out of an Instagram Reel. She's all done up, with a top so tight and low I wonder how she can breathe. Her lips are unnaturally full, and so is her bust.

My heart constricts, and the familiar humiliation—that I spent the last week trying to bury—resurfaces. I can tell by the way she's looking at him that this is a date. It hasn't even been that long since the fiasco in Seattle, but clearly, he has already moved on.

Of course he has.

"Oh," I say nonchalantly, even as my heart plummets to the ground. I've been such a fucking fool for him.

"Interesting, right? I've always wondered what kind of women he's into."

I don't respond, lost in my self-imposed anguish. He can do whatever he wants with whomever. He is single after all, unlike me.

"So, anyways, tell me more about Matt and how you're going to set us up." She's thankfully oblivious to how distracted I am. "Talk to Maintenance and trap us in the elevator?" I force myself to laugh. "Or—I know!—you set up a meeting for the three of us and then don't show."

I gulp down the last bit of my drink and order another.

"Actually, I was just thinking we could all go for drinks sometime, and then you could get to know each other better."

"That works too, even though I was really hoping for the elevator." Her light energy makes me smile even as my dignity shatters.

"Great. I'll plan something for us soon."

"Yay. In the meantime, I'll shoot come-hither vibes his way." She winks at me.

"You're too much, you know." I manage to make my voice sound normal even though I'm reeling inside. Red-hot rage mixing with shame. Both are threatening to consume me.

"You love it," she chides. Then, switching tone, she says, "OMG, she's moving closer to him." I just can't take the play-by-play anymore as the familiar feeling of anxiety returns to my chest. I have to get out of here.

"I need to get going," I say in a rush, trying to keep my voice cool.

"Oh, come on. Already? We've only had two drinks."

"I'm meeting Shaan in a bit," I lie, again.

"Another round?" The waitress comes by, answering my silent plea.

"Just the bill, please."

She wanders away and comes back in a moment.

"This one's on me," I say.

"Thanks, Nish, and thanks for the encouragement."

We get up, and she hugs me just as I see Nick's head turn this way. He's seated with his back to us, but he must have seen me when he turned to speak with the waitress.

"I might just hang out for a bit and finish my drink," she says mischievously.

I avoid his gaze, although I know his eyes are on me.

"Please don't tell me you're spying on him."

"Oh, I'm not, obviously. But don't worry, I'll report back on anything scandalous." She winks.

Scandal? She has no idea.

I leave as quickly as possible, hoping to keep at least a little bit of my dignity intact.

I walk out through the front door into the cool spring air. It provides an ounce of relief. I can't understand why this bothers me so much. How does he have this much power over me?

It hurt to see those texts on Shaan's phone, but seeing Nick with someone else feels even more devastating.

It's fucked up.

I'm fucked up.

I know I should rush to the SkyTrain station, but I'm paralyzed. I stand there, waiting for my breathing not to be so shallow and my emotions not to be so intense. The air is warm and sticky, even though it's not yet summer. I lean against the cool smooth marble beside the door, as if its solid strength could give me some of my own, when I hear steps behind me and feel a touch on my shoulder.

"Hey, I was hoping you were still out here." I turn around to see Nick looking at me, his eyes frantic and uneasy.

I'm not sure what to say, so I say nothing. We're nothing but professionals placed together in what feels like a cruel cosmic joke.

"That—" he gestures inside "—isn't what it looks like."

I'm petty and angry, even though I have no right to be. I cross my arms over my chest.

"So, you're *not* on a date?" I spit out.

He exhales. "I am. I've cancelled on her a few times, but this time she insisted I show up, and I thought maybe I should because—" he stumbles.

"Because what?" I pin him with my gaze.

"I didn't realize things were so serious between you and him. So, you're clearly not available, Nisha." He gives me a look as if that settles it.

I shake my head. "You're right. I'm not, and you don't owe me anything." I start to walk off, but he blocks my way.

"We're nothing to each other," I say as I glare at him.

He leans in and whispers, "You're something to me."

He's so close that I can smell his intoxicating cologne, and it reels me in. I scream at my body to move, to push him out of the way but it disobeys me.

He steps closer and puts his arms on either side of me as I move back, realizing there's nowhere for me to go, only the smooth wall behind me, just as the door swings open.

"What the fuck?" His date stands staring at us. "You're a real piece of work, you know."

My body goes rigid as adrenaline surges through me. No one has ever seen us together, not like this, and fear grips me.

He doesn't step away from me or even respond but gives her the briefest glance before turning back to me.

"Whatever, asshole." She huffs down the street, leaving us alone again.

"I want this, I want you. So badly." I can see the longing, the fire, the desire in his eyes. They mirror my own. He brings his knuckles to my cheek, touching me tenderly as his eyes unravel my defences. I swallow hard, knowing I need to turn away, but I can't move. Desire replaces the panic. I place a hand on his solid chest, and I close my eyes as he brushes my lips with his.

Run, I need to run. To stop this from happening again.

His lips meet mine. Softly at first and then with a desperate hunger that I easily match. His tongue slips inside my mouth, and he takes my wrist and holds it on the wall next to me gently, pinning me in place as if he's afraid I'll run away again, from him, from this.

The door opens again and a large group exits. He pulls away, but he doesn't stop looking at me with his eyes full of lust as their loud voices try to pull us out of this vortex. He has no intention of letting me escape that easily. He grazes my bottom lip with his teeth, rousing desire where I've been desperately trying to extinguish it. My body takes over, and I tingle as I think about him biting and teasing every part of me.

"Come home with me." His grip is still soft, but now possessive, as if I'm his and his alone, or at least he wants me to be. "No one has to know."

I want to smack my palm into his face at his suggestion. A moment ago, he's talking up someone else, and now he's saying this.

I don't get the chance.

The door swings open and I see Jess from the corner of my eye. Her eyes widening as she sees Nick's hands on me and mine on him. I shove him away more forcefully than intended, and I turn to her, trying to look calm and collected.

I smooth down my hair as the panic returns. We're being too careless, and now his date isn't the only one who's seen us together.

"Oh, hey. I thought you had left already." She looks at me with a cloud of confusion.

I take a rapid inhale of breath and bring my hands together to stop them from shaking. "I had to make a quick call, and Nick came out to ask me something." My voice quivers, and this time, even I can't make this lie sound real.

"Oh." She looks at us questioningly, her mind filling in the blanks. My heart races, worried that she'll figure it all out.

"Sorry, I shouldn't have taken up your time outside the office. We can catch up on things tomorrow." He sounds composed but runs his hands through his hair and his eyes shift from me to Jess like he's rattled. "I'll see you both tomorrow." He gives me one last glance and walks across the street. We both watch him go.

"I'd better go try to catch the next train." I give Jess an easy smile even though my heart's hammering, my lips are tingling, and my cheeks are inflamed.

She looks perplexed, but she says nothing. I hope she'll never figure it out, but at the same time, I wish she knew everything. Maybe she could make sense of this because I sure as hell can't wrap my head around it.

36. WHAT JUST HAPPENED?

I walk by Jess's desk in the morning and I'm relieved to find it empty. I spent the evening stressing about how much she had seen.

I breathe a little easier as I arrive at my desk, check emails and create my to-do list for the day, prioritizing tasks in order, when a message flashes on the screen from Jess.

Coffee in 15?

I quickly reply, wanting to avoid discussing last night with her. I let her know that I'm swamped and suggest tomorrow instead.

It's important.

I tell her I just have to finish an email, hoping to buy myself some time to calm down.

I'll go now and order for us.

There are no emojis or GIFs—none of the Jess-isms I've gotten so used to—making worry claw itself back into my chest. Something's wrong. I walk to the coffee shop, lost in thought. There's no way she knows anything. I haven't told anyone what's been going on and I know Nick wouldn't either. I find Jess seated in our usual booth around the corner with our drinks.

"Hey, Jess. What's up?" I hold my breath as I take a seat.

"I know what's going on with you and Nick."

Fuck. I'm fucked. But I can't let her know that. "What do you mean? There's nothing going on."

"Don't." She looks at me with irritation. "I saw you two together, and I just figured it out, and I just wonder why you didn't come to me."

"Figured out what exactly," I say cautiously.

She puts her hand on mine and looks at me. "You can trust me, Nish. If he's making you uncomfortable, we'll figure out what to do."

I'm more confused than ever, and it must show.

"Look, last night, I saw how close he was standing to you. If he's harassing you—"

"What? No, he's not. Why would you even think that?" Nervous energy courses through me.

"I wasn't going to say anything, but I saw him chase after you at the coffee shop a few weeks ago." She pauses and I try to process her words. "It seemed like you handled it, so I didn't ask you about it and obviously you're with Eshaan, and he knows that, right?"

"He does."

"And then yesterday, it didn't make sense. Why would he abandon his date to follow you outside?"

"We had an urgent client request come up, and he wanted to fill me in on it." The lie is thick on my tongue.

"Nish, stop protecting him. I saw his hand pinning you against the wall."

Anxiety rises up, and I don't know how to stop it or control it or what to say next. I could tell her the truth, or I could let her believe that Nick's some kind of sleaze bag forcing himself on me. Either option is horrible, but the latter is the worst.

She continues. "I know he's been coaching you and even helped you get on that panel. Is he making you feel like you owe him anything?"

"No, he wouldn't, he didn't," I stammer. A mouse, cornered.

"Jess, where is this coming from?"

"I had a close friend who was dating a narcissist, and it was crazy because if you met him, he was the most charismatic guy you ever met. We all loved him, and he turned out to be an asshole."

Her words hit me in the chest, and I go cold, but not because they describe Nick.

Is it Eshaan? Everyone except Rachel keeps telling me how perfect he is for me. Even my mom is constantly pushing my concerns aside and convincing me to cater to him, but no one's ever seen Eshaan lash out at me like he does in private.

I toy with my cup sleeve and look at Jess, agitation rising in my chest. I can't go there now. I have to deal with this first.

"You haven't shared this with anyone else, have you?" My mind races, and I can't help but worry that she might say something that would hurt Nick or cost him his job.

"Of course not," she says. "I wanted to ask you about it first." My mind whirls, trying to come up with a plausible half-truth that would throw Jess off. "We'll figure this out," she continues, "but I need the details."

I take a deep breath and continue to spin my web of lies. "When Nick first started working here, he didn't know I was seeing someone, and we were spending a lot of time together, at conferences, in meetings, and even late at night during the crisis situation."

She nods and looks at me with kindness in her eyes, urging me to continue.

"One night, after a long day at the conference in Minneapolis, I was heading out to meet up with a friend, and I ran into Nick on my way out and asked him to join us. We were drinking and having fun, and he might have taken it as something more because later that night, he kissed me."

I don't tell her I kissed him back or have been chasing his touch ever since.

"I told him then I was seeing Shaan, and he's been keeping it professional. Yesterday though, he said he has feelings for me, and I told him nothing could happen. I tried to walk away, but he wanted to talk more, and that's when he grabbed my wrist." I make it sound innocent when it was anything but. "It got heated, but he wasn't hurting me," I quickly add.

"Still. What a jerk." I see her thoughts churning, and I know I need to throw her off even more.

"I feel bad because maybe I was giving off mixed signals." That part, at least, is true.

"Nisha, no. Everyone at the office can tell you're loved up. Don't give him a get-out-of-jail-free card and blame yourself for giving the wrong impression. That's what these kinds of guys want. They tell us it's what we're wearing, or else they take kindness as a sign that we want to screw them."

That wasn't Nick, but I couldn't tell Jess the truth and risk anyone else finding out.

"Look, he's done in a few weeks, and we barely work together now. He also messaged me last night and apologized." I try to defuse the situation.

She looks at me with doubt swirling in her eyes. "Okay. Well, if anything else comes up, let me know. I'm good friends with Cathy in HR. She can help with this."

"No, Jess, please, I don't want to do that." I'm acting too desperate, and she can sense it, making her even more wary. She thinks I'm protecting him, but she has no idea that I'm only protecting myself like the shit person I am.

"Okay," she relents. Her eyes say what her words don't. *I'll let this go...for now.*

* * *

We head back to the office, and although I'm pretty sure that Jess won't say anything, the unease sits with me. Although I'm shit, I still have to tell Nick. Maybe he has a better way for us to deal with this.

He's not in his office, so I go to mine in hopes of getting some work done, but my mind replays everything in my head.

What have I done?

I wanted to hurt Nick a little, but something like this could destroy his reputation or at least maim it, and the thought makes me feel sick to my stomach. By lunch he still hasn't shown up and at four, I just can't take it anymore. I message him.

I need to see you. Please.

I hit send on the text before I can second-guess myself.

His reply is instantaneous. It's an address. I assume it's his and then this.

I'll be home all evening.

I absently scroll on my computer until 5 p.m., and then I fling myself out of my desk chair and out the door like there's a fire in the building.

* * *

The Uber drops me off outside of his expensive-looking high-rise, and I freeze. What the hell am I going to say to him?

Jess thinks you're a predator and wants to report you to HR, and I'm too scared to tell her the truth because I'm afraid this will get back to Eshaan somehow, and he'll destroy me, so I let her believe these lies about you. So, I basically threw you under the bus. Okay, byeee.

Or what if he thought I was coming by to sleep with him? I wasn't even sure that wouldn't happen either. Self-sabotage as Rachel would call it. I'm masterful at it.

I could still leave and just hope that things would blow over, but somehow my feet start moving toward the door, and before I know it, he's buzzing me in, and I'm in the posh elevator.

I walk to his door in a daze, and he opens it before I even have a chance to knock.

"Come in."

I walk past him to enter and take in his stunning place. He has modern white furniture, including a stylish daybed in the far corner, a glass coffee table sprinkled with tech mags in front of the sectional leather couch, and a massive TV mounted on the wall.

I continue to look around in awe.

Gorgeous paintings by digital and modern artists are tastefully placed on the walls. The galley kitchen is situated off to the side, featuring a marble island adorned with an ornate silver bowl at its centre. I instantly think of his sister. She's studying design, and although I only met her once, I can see her influence everywhere.

But the most breathtaking feature is the floor-to-ceiling wall of windows overlooking the ocean. How much exactly is Nick getting paid? I feel a crush of disappointment again, thinking about my promotion or lack thereof, but I push those thoughts away. I'm not here to admire his HGTV condo or lament my salary.

"Can I get you a drink?" he asks, like I'm a proper guest.

"I'm fine, thanks." Even still, I eye up his liquor cabinet filled to the brim with high-end bottles, along with a crystal decanter and glasses at the ready like he's a Las Vegas baller.

"Are you sure?"

"Yes."

I stand behind the kitchen island, and he moves to the other side of it, both of us knowing we need to put some distance between us.

"What's up? It sounded urgent."

"Jess had questions about last night," I say calmly.

"What did you tell her?"

I take a seat on the stool in front of me, suddenly feeling the crushing weight of everything.

"She thinks you're harassing me," I say as I bring my hands to the sides of my face to ease the tension in my throbbing temples.

He leans back against the counter as his face turns grim. "Shit."

"I know. I just told her we kissed on a drunken night out while we were at a conference because you didn't know I was seeing someone." It's mostly true. Now the hard part. "Then I told her you came out yesterday to confess your feelings, even though we both know nothing can happen between us."

He steps a little closer to me, but the island is still between us.

He looks like something is eating at him. "Nisha, I have to ask you something."

"What is it?" I feel a prickle of apprehension as I drop my hands on the smooth granite counter.

"Am I harassing you? I mean, you've never stopped me, and I guess I thought you were attracted to me too, but after everything in Seattle, and now with Jess—"

"Nick, no." I get off the stool and wander over to him.

"It's a messed-up situation, but no. I've never felt like that. Ever."

He sighs in relief, takes my hand, and kisses my fingers gently. "I'm sorry for everything."

"Me too." His touch, his words, relieve some of the overwhelming pressure I've been struggling under all day.

He lets go of my hand but holds my gaze. "It's just that every time I'm near you, I can't help myself. I want to touch you everywhere you'll let me, and when we're not together all I'm thinking about is being around you again and it's fucking insane."

He backs away. "I know you're not mine…" He rubs his hand over his face. "Even when I was on that date, I couldn't even focus or care because she wasn't you." He looks at me with tired and sad eyes.

My breath catches in my throat at his confession, and my heart starts beating rapidly with hope. Maybe there is something more between us and it's not just me being delusional.

"I don't want to mess up everything you have going for you, and now with this shit at work and the other day when Tom almost walked in. Fuck." He drags his hand through his hair and then puts his hands on the counter behind him, as if he's stopping himself from coming closer or touching me.

Little does he know I'm willing to walk into the inferno with him and set my whole life on fire.

I close the distance between us and take his head in my hands, his arms still resting on the counter on either side of him. Air barely fills my lungs, and then in a moment, my lips are crushing his, my hands are in his hair, and he's wrapping his arms around me and lifting me onto the counter behind us. His hands rapidly push my skirt up to my waist so I can straddle him easier. I feel his hardness, and I can't even deny how much I want him anymore. I put my hands under his shirt and lift it easily over his shoulders as he starts working the buttons on my top, kissing me down my neck. His hands are frantic, clumsy, like he's barely maintaining control. He fumbles with the buttons for a while before my shirt is open, and he's tugging it free from the waistband of my skirt and launching it behind me. He brings his hands to my underwear, swiftly pulling it down so I feel both the coolness of the granite under me and his hot fingers pushing their way inside of me. Each thrust causes me to almost come undone, and I lose focus as I try to undo the top button of his jeans and start to unzip his pants.

His bare chest is close, but it's not enough. I push his hands away and perch on the end of the counter, guiding him closer to me. He grabs my hands.

"We should stop," he gasps, barely audible. He's breathless, and so am I.

"Why?" I pull my hands free and caress the length of him as I see him struggle to hold it together.

"I have nothing to offer you, and you deserve way more than a quick fuck."

He backs away and bends down to grab his shirt, and then zips up his pants, leaving me on the counter mostly undressed.

"I don't care if this is all this is." I would take breadcrumbs from him if that's all he's willing to give me.

He shakes his head and picks me up from the counter like I weigh nothing at all. He pulls my skirt back into place and then walks behind me to pick my shirt off the ground with trembling hands.

"This isn't who you are, and I know it's not what you want." He looks like he's fighting a battle inside himself that I know nothing about, and I start to think I'm wrong about him. So very wrong.

"You deserve everything good and right and beautiful in this world." Something cracks inside of me as he looks away and then back at me with his soul in his eyes. "And I…I don't deserve even an inch of you."

His eyes are so full of misery that I know he isn't lying, but it would be so much easier to walk away from him if he was.

37. SWEET SURRENDER

I leave Nick's place before we make a decision we can't walk away from, but my body has never felt so heavy, my heart so lost.

I get home and crawl into bed even though it's only 8 p.m. When Rachel comes in to check on me, I tell her I'm not feeling well. I'm not ready to let this go, to let him go, but I have no choice now. I have to.

He has reasons I know nothing about why he can't commit to us, and it's not something I can work through for him. Only he can do that.

I fall into a fitful sleep, waking up in a cold sweat, wondering how my life went from wanting a fresh start to this.

At 5 a.m., I head to the office. The SkyTrain is mostly empty, and when I arrive only the security guard is there. I walk through the dark and empty halls and stop outside Nick's office. For the first time, I see everything. I see him.

I think of the time he told me he was taking care of his mom and paying for his sister's university education because his dad left them with nothing. I think of how he's been encouraging me to speak up more and ask for what I want, and how he even went out of his way to get me on a speaker's panel, pulling strings when I had no experience and it would be a risk for his contact to take me on. I think about how he never accepts accolades and instead sends them in my direction, no matter how high that person is on the corporate ladder.

I think of how he dropped his car keys in my hand without even a second thought, and of the time he was willing to wander the night to find another hotel to make me more comfortable. I think of the way he looked at me when he first met me, and he asked me what lit me up. And then how he really listened when I answered. I think of all those months I spent searching for him, doing a double take every time I saw blue eyes that weren't his, and once even reaching up and touching the shoulder of a man with his hair and build.

And for reasons I don't know, he doesn't think he deserves goodness even though he's so good inside. A bright light guiding my heart in infinite darkness

I am a fool, yes, but I want to be his fool, even if it costs me everything.

* * *

The week goes by, and Nick and I still barely see each other, but instead of awkwardness and anger when we do, there's this softness between us—we've laid down our swords and bared our hearts.

I silently communicate with him as we pass each other in the halls and when I sit across from him in meetings.

I see you, all of you.

He silently communicates back.

I want you, all of you. Not just your body, your heart and soul too. But I don't deserve it. I don't deserve you.

And that's how we speak now.

Words whispered in our hearts and communicated with our eyes and through gentle touches. I brush his arm, he caresses my fingers, we share a glance. All above board, but more intimate than ever.

I don't know how to figure it all out with Nick or Eshaan, but I surrender to a universe I'm starting to think has a plan for me after all.

38. THE GODDESS

Eshaan opens the door, looking wrecked. His shoulders are slumped, his hair is in disarray, and his clothes are rumpled like he hasn't changed them in some time.

"Shaan, is everything okay?" I step closer to him and put a steady hand on his shoulder.

"Not really." He stands there looking off into the distance and not saying anything more. I don't want to pry, so I stand there patiently outside his parents' house.

"Come inside and have some cha," Shaan's mom says in the background.

I follow Shaan inside and see his mom sitting at their kitchen table with cha at the ready. He sits down but looks dazed, like I've never seen him. My heart starts beating furiously as Auntie Ji pours me a steaming glass of cha in a bone china cup—the ones my family also had but never used and instead displayed in the dining room hutch.

"Sugar?"

"Yes, thank you."

She adds a spoonful and gives it a stir before handing me the cup.

I graciously accept it, used to the comfort of cha any time of day to soothe my worries at home with my family, and now with his.

She takes a sip of hers with a weary look. Her beautiful short black hair rests softly at her shoulders. She's wearing a simple pink suit with an intricate rose pattern, paired with golden bangles on each arm and gold hoop earrings. She looks both traditional and modern and pulls off the no-makeup look with such grace and beauty. Normally, she looks young for her age, but this evening she looks so much older.

We drink quietly. The only sound is that of the ticking clock in the living room.

Shaan finally speaks. "My Dadi Ji isn't well."

"Oh, Shaan, I'm so sorry." I think of the sweet old lady who always pulls me into a hug and tells me to gain more weight, saying I'm way too skinny. I often sit with her and watch South Asian TV dramas at high volume. At Shaan's cousin's wedding, I snuck her an extra jalebi because she insisted.

I find myself tearing up. Not her, not now.

And I know how much she means to Eshaan. She practically raised him while his parents were busy running the shop.

"They're not sure how much time she has left, and she's fading fast," says his mom.

"Oh, gosh. Is there anything I can do? Can I see her?"

"She's resting now, putt." She gives me a tired, half-hearted smile, and I'm grateful for the term of endearment from her.

I nod, not wanting to disturb this precious, beautiful lady, but my throat constricts with worry that I won't get another chance.

"Shaan, tell her about the engagement," his mom adds.

I look over at him, and my heart goes haywire.

"We want to move up the engagement to next Saturday. The hall called us, and there was a cancellation, and I just really want her to be there…" He chokes back a sob.

"Of course." I move closer and wrap my arms around him as his mom gets up to rinse her cup at the sink.

"I called your mom and told her already," she shares. "They'll change flights so they can be here, and anyone who can't make it next week will be at the wedding."

"Thank you, Auntie Ji."

I remember I missed two calls from my mom, and I haven't had a chance to call her back. I should have.

I finish my cha and lead Shaan over to the couch where I sit with him, reassuring him with my presence. Stroking his back and then settling in next to him with my head resting on his shoulder for as long as he needs.

* * *

It's 11:11 p.m. as I step into the elevator up to Nick's condo. I messaged him after leaving Eshaan's house, wanting him to hear the news from me first. It's more than that though. I need to end this chapter before I start the next one. I asked to come over, and he said yes without hesitation, even though it's late for a weeknight.

And now I'm at his door, and he already has it open and is waiting for me.

"Come in."

"Do you just stand there holding the door open, or have you timed it perfectly from buzzer to when I come up?"

"You'll never know." He winks at me, and I smile a sad smile. I guess I never will.

This time I wander around his living room like I have all the time in the world. I don't.

"Tell me about this." I point to a floral painting, but if you look just closely enough, you can see a curvy, feminine figure hidden within.

"You don't want to know."

"I want to know everything about you," I say, repeating the words he said to me in Seattle.

"My sister, Lucy, got it for me. She said it would help me attract 'the one' who's supposed to be a divine feminine goddess, but she placed it strategically here to ward off the wrong ones. She said that they wouldn't be able to make it any further than a first date," he laughs.

"Is it working?" I wonder out loud.

"Well, I haven't had many second dates, so yes, I guess."

I smile.

"What's the story about the daybed? "

"Oh, Lucy wanted that for when she stays here. Said my place was too 'bachelor pad.' She also figured this mythical goddess in human form would like having it around."

"I love Lucy already."

"She likes you, too." I remember our brief meeting when Rachel and I bumped into them at brunch. She has his same piercing blue eyes and golden blonde locks.

I drift around his living room, wanting to cherish every last detail of this night. I run my fingers along the couch and the wall, and even flip through the magazines neatly piled on the coffee table. I laugh when I see *GQ*.

"What?"

"Nothing."

I guess I'll always have *GQ*.

He fills me in on every single piece I ask about, just watching me as I wander and touch the intimate parts of his life. I came to say goodbye, but now that I'm here I want to delay that part and get to know him in a way that I never had the chance to before.

The silver bowl is from Granville Island, made by a local artisan; he bought it when he went with his mom a few years ago. The liquor cabinet is something he's been stocking every time he goes through Duty-Free, which is why the selection is so impressive. I ask him about an Indigenous wooden carving sitting in his kitchen next to the coffee machine. He tells me he received it while visiting sacred lands in the interior of British Columbia from an elder who helped him ground and connect to the land and himself.

I wander to his living room and pick up the ornate Ek Onkar that's displayed on Nick's mantel. Crystals are inlaid on top of the sacred words. The symbol is found in every Punjabi home I know in Surrey and Brampton.

"Where did you get this?"

"Oh, my mom went on a yoga retreat in India. She got one as a housewarming gift for me. Said it represents our interconnectedness." He looks at me with his bright eyes sparkling in the low light. "I'd love to learn more about what it means."

I'd love to teach you.

Too bad I'll never get the chance.

My eyes drift to the hallway where the door to his room must be, but I don't dare go in there, not trusting myself still.

I stand behind the same stools I did when I first visited here.

"Drink?" he asks.

"Yes, please."

"Gin and tonic?"

"You always get my order right." I smile softly.

He grins.

I watch as he expertly adds the gin, bitters, ice cubes, tonic water, and fresh berries to the shakers before pouring two drinks. He brings them over to where I'm standing by the stools.

"What are we celebrating?" he asks.

"This moment."

We clink glasses, and I take only a small sip, not wanting to dull my senses as much as I normally do.

I walk over to the sectional and set the drink down carefully on the glass coffee table. He does the same, and then we sit down next to each other. Our thighs touch, just barely.

He looks at me like I'm something to him, and now I believe I am.

I move my fingers along his face as he closes his eyes with my touch, caressing his eyebrows, strong jaw, soft lips, then running my fingers through his golden locks and down his neck. I don't go lower, not anymore.

"What are you doing?" he asks gently as he opens his eyes. "Not that I mind."

A tear rolls down my face. "Memorizing every inch of your beautiful face."

"Can I do the same?"

"Yes."

"Close your eyes."

He brings his thumb softly to my lips, then moves his knuckles across my cheeks, presses the pads of his fingers gently to my eyelashes, and brushes his fingers through my hair, taking care to place my long hair back out of my face. Another tear escapes. He leans in and kisses it away, and when he's done, I press my lips to his. I will allow myself this.

"What is it? What's wrong?" he whispers.

I take a deep breath, not wanting anything to disturb this moment I built for us.

"I'm getting engaged."

"I know."

"It's next week."

"What? I thought it was next month."

"We had to move it up."

His eyes widen with surprise and then flicker with sorrow.

"I just wanted you to hear it from me first."

He nods, looking away as he tries and fails to compose himself.

"Nisha," he says my name like a prayer. "You deserve every happiness and to have someone who loves you so much and is ready to commit to you in every way you want and need." He brushes his fingers across mine, pausing for a few moments like he's trying to find the right words to say before he continues. "I don't know if I could ever be that person for you." He looks away, but I take his chin and turn his head toward me.

I can't stop the question that slips from my mouth. "Why?" I hate how desperate my voice sounds.

"I don't know if I could play the part." His ocean blue eyes turn icy.

"Would anything change your mind?"

Would anyone?

"It's just that my parents had a difficult relationship, and it was hard on my mom. So hard for her and for all of us."

"You're not your dad," I venture. My voice small.

He shakes his head as he replies, "This way I never will be."

His face is grim, resolute, and I can't bring myself to push him more on this, to open myself up in this way when he's already made up his mind.

I nod this time, looking into his eyes as his words shatter my heart.

"Nick." I take his hand. "Thank you for picking me up when I was at my lowest and struggling to believe in myself, and for encouraging me to go for what I want when I was terrified to."

I tighten my grip.

What I want is you.

"I'll never forget your kindness and everything you've done for me." My voice cracks and I look up to stop the tears.

I'll never forget you.

I slowly get up, knowing I've done what I came here to do, and now it's time to leave and start my new life—the life I always wanted.

Our drinks sit untouched, and I think it's a shame we didn't finish them, and now we'll never get to. I walk to the front door and Nick holds it open for me.

"Nick," I say as he turns to me. His face is stamped with sadness, and I wonder if it's always been there.

"Yes?"

"I hope you find your goddess."

I wish I was her.

He looks at me with such tenderness.

You are.

I walk out the door and then look back as I approach the elevators.

He's still standing at the door and holding it open even though I'll never walk through it again, and that's how I want to remember him. The man who opened all the doors for me, especially the door back to myself and my heart.

39. COLD HEART

Eshaan and I sit on a park bench watching the sunset with our ice cream cups in our hands—mine is filled with mint chocolate chip, topped with sprinkles, and Eshaan has salted caramel—as people mill around us.

It's warm out as summer is quickly approaching, and the ice cream shop is busy even at 8 p.m. I dip my spoon in his cup and take as much as I can.

"Hey, not so fast."

He takes my spoon and feeds me, and I take a spoonful of my mint chip and do the same.

"You wanted a big scoop of mint chip, so now you have to stick with it," he says as he bumps my shoulder.

"I wanted salted caramel, too." If only life were that easy, and you could always get every single thing you wanted.

We finish our ice cream and discard the cups in the compostables bin.

He grabs my hand. "Want to walk for a bit?"

"I'd love to."

He's lighter now that his Dadi Ji is doing a little better. She's excited about the engagement and, for once, is listening to the doctor's orders. I'm so happy because I know how hard it is to lose someone. The grief never truly goes away, but the good memories become even stronger.

I think of Dad and how he would always bring home Neapolitan ice cream, even though I only liked the chocolate—Mom liked vanilla, and Preeti loved the strawberry, so it was perfect for our little family.

We walk along the beach, close to Stanley Park, and my mind drifts to Nick. I always imagined running into him on the Seawall after our first meeting at the bar, more than a year ago now, before he showed up at the office. My heart still pangs at the thought of our missed opportunity, even though it wasn't meant to be.

I have to trust that the universe has big plans for me, as Rachel often reminds me, and for once, I'm starting to believe in the universe and in myself. But I have to take the first step and take charge of my life.

We stop and gaze out at the ocean as the sun dips lower on the horizon, and I muster up the courage to ask something I should have asked a long time ago.

"Shaan, before Saturday, I need to ask you something."

He turns to me with curiosity in his eyes. "No, you can't drive the Maserati," he laughs.

"It's not that." I look down at my sneakers, now covered in sand. I let the ground beneath me support me as I brace myself to say what's coming next.

"What, then?"

"Did anything ever happen between you and Sonia since we've been together?" I hold my breath as I hazard a glance up.

His eyes turn cold. He takes a few steps away. "I can't believe you. My Dadi Ji is practically on her deathbed, and my family is spending a small fortune on our engagement party, and you ask me *this* three days before our engagement?"

He shakes his head and turns away.

I'm rattled, but I realize he didn't answer the question, and I need to know for certain before I devote my life to him.

I walk up to him and place a hand on his shoulder. "Shaan, please, I need to know the truth."

He turns to face me. "No. Never. I swear to you on my life." He looks me straight in the eyes as he says every word without blinking.

I sigh with relief and the pent-up tension I've been holding for weeks finally releases, even as guilt consumes me, knowing I can't say the same.

40. #BOSS

I sleep well that night for the first time in a long time. Being brave with Eshaan gives me the courage to tackle the other things in my life I should have addressed a long time ago, too.

I take a deep breath as I knock on Tom's office door.

"Nisha, sit. I'm just finishing up an email, and I'll be with you in a moment."

I sit down, trying to settle my racing heart and push down the doubts in my mind. I have to do this for me.

He pushes away from his screen and turns toward me. "Our quarterly is not until next month, but it's nice to see my top performer in here." He gives me a wide smile.

"What can I do for you?"

I hesitate, and then it rushes out.

"Thank you for noticing that, Tom, that I'm a top performer, that means a lot to me, and I'm having a lot of fun building my team. There's just one thing that's been bothering me. I'm not going to lie."

He leans back in his chair. "I'm sure we can take care of that easily for you, whatever it is."

"When I took on this dual role, you mentioned a promotion if things went well, and it looks like things are going pretty darn well." I smile.

"They are for the time being, but you know how it is with start-up life. One moment you're on top of the world, the next you're scrambling."

I try to quell the rising apprehension. I have to keep going.

"I hear you, but I think it's important to reward those who come along on the up-and-down journey. What do you think?"

"I would agree with you." He smiles and lights up. "What would fit the bill?"

"I'd love to talk about stepping into a team-lead position, seeing as I'm doing the work already." Now the tough part. "With a possible boost in salary."

He steeples his hands, with his index fingers resting on his mouth, and for a moment, I think I've screwed it all up and shouldn't have said a thing, but then he exhales.

"Tell you what. I'll do you one better. How does director sound?" A big smile breaks out on his face.

"That sounds incredible," I say, visibly shaken.

"Your ambition hasn't gone unnoticed, you know. I've been trying to figure out how to place you to best maximize your skill set. Now I have it. Director of Digital Marketing and Investor Relations with two teams under you and you as their ringleader." He leans back, satisfied with himself.

I almost can't believe what I'm hearing.

"Wow, that would be great."

"I'll get Amy to send over the new contract later this week."

"Thank you so much."

"You deserve it, and I appreciate your initiative in having this conversation."

I get up to leave.

"Oh, and Nisha?

"Yes?" I turn back.

"You'll get the salary to match."

"Thank you. Thank you so much." I practically dance all the way back to my office, and there's only one person I want to tell, but I won't say a word to him. Not anymore.

41. HARD TRUTHS

"I can't believe you were going to get engaged without getting a fresh manicure." Rachel looks at me, feigning disbelief as we settle onto the couch in our living room. I admire my new nails as I realize I haven't felt this relaxed in a really long time.

"I know, right? Thanks for always coming to my rescue. How did you get us a booking on such short notice?" The spa we went to today was uber posh, and the nail tech we saw is usually booked out weeks in advance. It had been a perfect morning.

"Perks of being an online influencer." She shoots me her beautiful smile, and I'm so grateful I have her through everything.

"I'll sneak a pic of your hand with the ring tomorrow for her if that's okay."

"Of course. If it can help her get more business, you know I'm all for it."

We're sipping Hojicha tea in our satin kimonos that Rachel got for us on her last trip to visit family in Japan, and I feel like a movie star. I even took the day off work, and now our faces are glowing, our nails are polished, and every inch of us is waxed. Rachel insisted we also do a soak in the spa whirlpool and then sauna first to purify, renew, and relax.

"I can't believe tomorrow is the big day." I lean back into the cushions and take a sip of tea. It's been a whirlwind of everything coming together so beautifully, and I'm still brimming with joy as I think about how it's all working out. Knowing that I don't have to worry about Eshaan's ex and thinking of my promotion have me glowing inside and out.

Rachel sets down her tea as something flits across her face. "Nisha, there's something I wanted to talk to you about."

I know that look, and I'm not sure if I'm ready for it. "Rachel, I…" I set my cup down and examine my newly polished nails as if they're the most fascinating thing I've seen in the world.

"Nisha, I need to say this. I couldn't call myself your friend if I didn't."

I glance up at her and tighten my robe around myself. "Okay." Whatever it is, I can handle it. I'm getting braver by the day.

She takes a deep breath. "When Nick came by to get his car, we talked for a long time."

My stomach churns. I don't want to hear any more.

"He was so rattled by everything that happened, I could see it all over his face, and I invited him inside to have tea. He didn't want to impose, but I insisted."

She sees me getting flustered.

"Relax, it's nothing like that." She looks away. "It's just that, Nisha… Nick's in love with you. I could see it written on his face and in his aura."

I suck in a breath.

"I know all this craziness happened between you two, and well, he told me that he got his heart broken many years ago and never really got over it. He didn't go into details, but I could tell it was bad. Now he's terrified of that happening again. Then there's the trauma of his deadbeat dad. He just figured it would be easier not to have to deal with any of it."

I should be surprised at Rachel's words, but I'm not, and the sadness I've felt since I left Nick's condo becomes full-fledged sorrow.

"Rachel, I appreciate you telling me this, but it doesn't make a difference. Nick and I've been talking already, and he told me he can't commit to anything with me, so it doesn't matter."

Rachel gets up and starts pacing the room, and I get anxious just watching her. "Regardless of his situation, do you think it's normal to have such strong feelings for someone else?"

The words hit me like a bowling ball to the head. I rub my temples, a dull ache already forming as I take in her words.

"I mean, you and Eshaan have only been together for barely a year—why the rush? Maybe all of this is a sign to slow down and just figure out what you want."

I stand up and press my nails into my palms. "Rachel, you just don't get it. Nick basically told me he doesn't think he could ever commit to anything more than casual—not with me, and maybe not with anyone, and I'm not going to throw away everything with Eshaan for that. I need someone solid I can count on who's in it with me, through everything."

Rachel stops pacing and turns to face me. "And is Eshaan in it with you? Really?" she challenges.

"I know you don't see it, how incredible he is. The things he's done for me." I look at the ceiling, exasperated.

Rachel steps closer and takes both of my hands. "Nisha, it's *you* that's so caught up in getting engaged and married before you're thirty. You're so preoccupied that you can't see that this isn't some race to the finish line. Or another thing to check off your to-do list."

I pull my hands away. "I thought you knew me, Rach. I really did. You always talk about going for your deepest desires, and those are mine. My whole life, I've dreamed of getting married, and someday I want to have kids too. Those things matter to me."

"I know they do, but is this the way to get there?"

"What, so I should just be like you? Swear off guys to work on myself and just watch as the clock ticks by?"

"I know it seems counterintuitive, but you have to love yourself before you can be in a loving relationship."

"So now I don't love myself," I huff out.

"Nish, you put everyone before yourself and your needs. Your mom, Eshaan, his family, and even your colleagues. And I know you stay up late overthinking and worrying you're not enough."

Anger simmers within me at her words, even though I know they're accurate. I look outside, summoning strength before turning around. The sun is setting in a magnificent medley of pink, orange, and red hues.

"Rach, you know I didn't grow up with parents who had a magical fairy-tale love story like yours. You know the shit I went through. My parents could barely stand each other, and most of the time my dad was either at home drunk or at work, and then he passed away, and my whole life went to shit—even worse than I thought it could. So, I'm sorry if I have baggage." I drag out the last few words to make my argument stronger. "Eshaan gets that and accepts me as I am."

Her voice rises an octave as she speaks. "I can't do this anymore, so I'm just going to come out and say it." She throws up her hands in frustration. "He uses your insecurities to manipulate you."

"Un-fucking-believable." I shake my head. "That's bullshit."

"Is it? The way he tells you what to wear and goes apeshit when another guy even looks at you?"

"It's not like that. He just gets a little jealous at times."

"A little jealous? He's so possessive of you, like you're a prize and not a person."

And now both of our voices are raised.

I look into her emerald eyes, flecked with gold under her perfectly shaped brows. The eyes that have shown me such love and kindness, that helped me through the hardest days of my life, that gave me a chance to start fresh. Now, they're reflecting things I don't want to see.

I look down at my shiny toenails, painted pink and coated with golden glitter.

"I can't with this, Rachel, and I can't believe you wait until the day before I'm getting engaged to throw this at me."

"Nisha, seriously, don't do that." She brings her voice back to normal. "You know I've tried to bring this up multiple times before, and I know you've held back a lot from me. Not just what happened with Nick, but what's happening with Eshaan too. You know I have a good read on people."

I'm so sick of hearing about this spiritual shit. If that's all it took, we'd all be living our best lives with a crystal in our pocket and an oracle deck to turn to for every decision.

"Maybe you can stop *reading* Eshaan and just focus on your own fucking life. Use your intuition and shit to find yourself someone instead of doling out relationship advice when you're not even in one."

I instantly regret the words as they leave my mouth, and I catch the deep hurt in Rachel's eyes before she shakes her head and retreats to her bedroom, while I'm left with my head spinning with her honest words and my thoughtless ones.

I hate myself for hurting the one person who's always been in my corner. She's been my anchor through everything. I wouldn't even be here if it wasn't for her. I would be stuck in Toronto, making excuses to get out of meeting guys my mom wanted to set me up with. I'd be at the same monotonous government job that paid well but drained my soul, hanging out with friends who couldn't care less about me—the same friends that didn't warn me about Raj, the first guy I had ever been with, even though I found out later that they knew he was never serious about me.

Rachel was more than a friend. She was a lifeline, and I've been so horrible to her. Not just tonight but for weeks, keeping things from her when I should have been more open. Even now, I know I should at least try to listen and see things from her perspective, but I can't go there. I won't. I'm too close to having it all.

I head to her door, and I'm about to knock, but I hesitate. Mentally, I'm not in the right space to apologize properly. I need to get my shit together before tomorrow and before I screw everything up. I go into my bedroom and throw on some lounge pants and a sweater. I need to go outside.

* * *

The next morning, I'm up early to make us both avocado toast before I head over to my Bhua Ji's place to get ready.

I have the plates waiting, along with some steaming hot coffee with cream and sugar for me and a sugar-free cacao for her, but she doesn't come out of her room.

I knock gently but there's no response. I wait a few more seconds and then push the door open. My eyes dart around the room but she's not here. The scent of the incense she normally burns on her altar every morning lingers in the air so I know she couldn't have left that long ago.

Still, my fingers tingle and my toes go numb as I wait. I don't know if I can make it through today without her, and I'm a few moments away from full panic mode when the front door opens. I rush to it and sigh with relief as Rachel steps inside, in her workout clothes, looking tired.

"Rach, I'm so sorry. You've done so much for me, and I never should have said what I did."

"Yeah, you shouldn't have. That wasn't cool, Nish."

"I know and I'm so sorry. It's just that without you, I don't know if I can do this, any of it, and I know I might have screwed everything up between us—" My voice breaks.

She holds her arms out and I fall against her.

"Nish, stop. I'm not going to abandon you on your special day. Whatever you decide, I'm in it with you, now and forever."

Relief washes over me at her words. "I love you."

"I love you, too." She takes me by the arm, and I relax. Somehow, everything will be okay.

42. HAPPILY EVER AFTER

I stare at myself in the floor-length mirror in the bathroom of the event hall, and I almost can't believe it's me. Rachel expertly applied my makeup to create a flawless look with shimmering gold eyeshadow, winged tip eyeliner, perfectly filled-in brows, a light bronzer to accent my cheekbones and finally a dusty rose lipstick on my full lips. My hair is pulled to the side in long, smooth, cascading waves, while my neck is adorned with my mom's gold necklace from her wedding, with matching dangling earrings.

My arms have shimmering gold bangles, and I have a bindi and tikka placed on my forehead to complete the look. It's the lehenga that gets me most. It's light pink with delicate gold embroidery that shines like a sunset. The top is short and fitted, revealing a bit of my midriff, with a scooping neckline on both the front and back, where the flowers resemble peonies. It's a two-piece with a matching flowy floor-length skirt. All of it Eshaan had custom-made for me in India, and I feel like a fucking princess. I'm finally getting my Bollywood happy ending after all.

I can't help feeling, though, that at any moment, something catastrophic will happen, that will ruin all of this. Ruin me. Like when I was with Raj all those years ago. He said and did everything right, but something always felt a little off. I ignored my intuition and regretted it. Is that what I'm doing now? Bypassing my body's signals and wisdom? Or am I just afraid because of what happened before? Time is rapidly running out to make sense of things, and I have to hope this is the right move. Eshaan isn't Raj—he's committing to me in the most meaningful way. I don't know why that doesn't give me more comfort.

Rachel is wiping her eyes behind me. "Oh, Nisha, you look so stunning. I just can't."

"Oh my gosh, stop crying. You're going to make me cry." I turn to her.

"Your dad would be proud of you."

I lose it, and tears fall down my face. "You think so?"

"I know so."

We hold each other and I bask in the warmth of this special moment.

"Okay, now let's fix your makeup. Guests are already starting to arrive."

She pulls out her makeup case, which she brought along for moments like this, and expertly touches me up. I take one final look in the mirror before we head to the waiting area. My heart vibrates with an undercurrent of anxiety even though there's nothing to worry about, not anymore.

We're walking down the corridor when her phone starts beeping with texts.

"Rach, who's blowing up your phone?"

"Shoot, just give me one sec. I told my clients I was off duty for tonight."

Her eyes widen, and she brings her palm to her mouth as we both come to a stop.

"What is it? You're stressing me out…you know how anxious I get."

"Nisha, why don't we get some fresh air? It's going to be a while until everyone is settled."

She leads me by the hand in the opposite direction, down a corridor I've never been down before, one that looks like it's just for staff. She stops at a fork and then checks her phone again as if she's looking for directions.

"Rachel, where are we going, seriously? I don't think we should be in here." I'm already a little jittery, and this detour is not helping.

"Trust me." She leads me to the end of the hall and out to a side exit. Rachel pushes the bar and the door swings open. A wave of ease washes over me with the fresh evening air. "Okay, this is nice actually." I sigh.

"Nish, don't be mad." She says as she holds the door for me.

"Why would I be mad? This is exactly what I need—"

My heart moves up to my throat when I see Nick standing there on the empty concrete path that runs beside the building. He looks dishevelled yet achingly handsome in a fitted grey suit with no tie and his collar undone. The fading light glints off his immaculate shoes.

I look at her, bewildered. I can't find words. Rachel holds me steady with one arm while holding the door open with the other as Nick comes closer.

I suddenly wish I had eaten more today. I've had nothing since breakfast and just knocked back a double gin and tonic before coming here.

"I'll be right inside the door, just knock if you need me." Rachel leaves me alone with him and closes the door behind her. There's no handle and there's no escape, and strangely, instead of being anxious, a wave of calm washes over me.

"Nish." Nick looks at me like nothing exists except us.

He swallows as he continues to walk toward me slowly.

My body betrays me just when I need it the most, and I find myself walking toward him too.

Those irises.

The sharp cut of his jaw.

The way he runs his hand through his thick, golden locks.

I have no chance.

All noises fade into the background and the smell of samosas drifts away as I inhale the delicious scent of his sandalwood and pine cologne. A vortex has opened, and the world slips into nothingness.

It's only him and me. Us. His arms wrap around me, and I lean my heavy head and heart against his body. I could drown in this embrace. God, let me drown.

He tries to say something.

"Shhh, please." I don't want him to say another word, to break this spell, this magic between us. It may be the last time I ever experience it. Experience him.

I nestle deeper into him, and fleeting thoughts race through my mind. Thoughts I shouldn't even dare to think. I could leave right now with him. Slip through the darkness and out of my dutiful reality into a dream world.

My mind flashes to the lavishly decorated hall waiting for me inside. The disco ball hovering in the centre of the dance floor. The pearl-coloured satin seat covers on chairs surrounding evenly spaced tables, topped with freshly cut peonies, just how I wanted. The room bathed in pink and gold lights like the endless cosmos in a distant galaxy. The hundreds gathered, including a long list of everyone I've known since childhood. The embarrassment, the ridicule if I gamble, listening to my soul.

"You're breathtaking."

He doesn't move to kiss me, and I almost can't stand it. Then my mind comes back to reality.

"Nick, what are you doing here?"

"I don't know." He looks so lost and confused. "I just had to see you again and tell you this before it's too late."

"Is everything okay?" My body tingles with anxious anticipation.

"No, it's not. Not even fucking close, Nisha." He holds me tighter, bringing his lips down my neck and then back up again in the softest caress that's like the touch of a feather. He pulls back and moves away from me, and the distance feels too far, even though it's just a step.

"My whole life is a dumpster fire right now, and I had only one chance to make it right and I'm afraid I fucked that up too."

I brush his cheek with my thumb. "Nick, let me help. You've done so much for me, it's my turn now."

"I don't know if you can."

"I can try." I look into his sad, fearful eyes and can't fathom what has him like this.

"Nisha." He looks on the verge of tears. "I've been such a fucking fool. I'll never forgive myself for watching you walk out the door and not racing after you and telling you this."

"Telling me what?" My heart beats with irrational hope.

"I'm in love with you and I have been since the first moment I saw you. I spent months searching for you, and when I saw you at the office again, it felt like it was the first time I could finally breathe again."

I snap back like I've been hit in the face.

"You touched my soul in a way I never even thought was possible, and the crazy thing is, you don't even realize the impact you have on me, on everyone."

"Nick." I stand there stunned, like I'm on some stupid TV show and someone's going to come out and say that I've been punked. He can't mean this. Not after everything. Not now.

"You're such a stunning light in the world, and without you in my life, it's like I'm in perpetual darkness. The sun doesn't seem to shine as bright, nothing tastes good, and everything is so mediocre. It's life in black and white after glimpsing a few seconds of 4K television."

Only he would use tech to describe his feelings.

"What are you saying, Nick?" My mind still won't let me believe what I'm hearing.

"I love you, Nisha. I always have and I always will. And I want you, but not just for a night."

His intense gaze cuts through me, and he moves closer to clutch my hands like he'll never be able to let them go.

He brings his lips close to mine, and they hover there as he whispers, "I want us to be together, to figure this all out."

I pull back as my heart beats out of control in my chest. "Nick, why are you doing this?" I shake my head, and suddenly my outfit is too tight, and I can't catch my breath. It's too much. I've waited for these words for so long, and now, I don't want to hear them as reality hits me full on in the face.

"You had a million chances to share this—the conference trips, in Seattle, even at your condo this week, and you didn't say a word."

"Nisha, I'm so sorry. It took me too long to realize I deserve this chance at happiness. That I could be someone worthy of you."

"This chance? And what? If it doesn't work out, you're just going to go back to your old ways?" I challenge.

"No, that's not what I meant."

"I can't build my life—my future—on a whim, Nick, with someone who let me walk away so many times. Who let me believe I didn't even matter."

"Nisha, please, I'm so sorry. I've been a mess, not just now, for weeks. I'm not sleeping, I don't eat. I can't even focus on work. I know I should have done something sooner, but please tell me it's not too late."

He comes closer, and I move away, my body trembling.

"I can't do this, Nick. I need someone solid in my life. Someone who wants me and isn't afraid to claim me, instead of only taking action when they think they'll lose their chance at a shot they didn't even want to take."

I turn my back and start walking away, like he's done so many times, and then I turn my head around again.

"I'm not a piece of clothing you just try on and discard, I'm the whole fucking department store." Rage flows through my body like waves, racking me.

"Nish, please. Wait." He catches up and moves in front of me. I try and fail to push him out of the way, my strength fleeing me.

"I get it, I fucked up, royally." He sighs. "I'm a fuck-up."

I have tried so hard for months to move on from him, and he's selfishly pulling me in again when he already made his decision and now he's trying to change the choice I never got to make.

"Forgive me. For this, for everything. I want you to be happy, even if you're not with me. So promise me this one thing, okay?"

I just shake my head. I choke out, "I can't promise you anything."

The ground shakes beneath me, and I pray that it opens up and takes me. Takes me away from the crippling anxiety, the pent-up pain, the anger consuming me, the exhaustion of always trying to get it right and epically failing anyway.

He puts his hands on my arms and looks me in the eyes, with those damn piercing blue beauties that I've spent so long trying to forget and now it's like they'll just haunt me forever.

His grip steadies me before it leaves me untethered and floating away into a dark abyss I'll never find my way back from.

"Be happy. Every single day of your life." With that he turns away and, for the last time, he walks out of my life.

I fall onto the steps. Ignoring the persistent vibrating of my phone and the calls coming through one after the other.

Rachel peeks her head out the door. "Nisha."

I don't even have the energy to respond. "Nisha?" She looks down at me on the steps. "Are you okay?" Her voice sounds desperate.

"I don't think I'll ever be okay again, Rachel." My voice doesn't sound like my own, and my whole body goes cold.

I feel so betrayed and angry at myself, at Nick, and at Rachel. I feel guilty that I have a decent guy waiting for me inside, and for months I've been messing around with someone else. I'm confused, wondering if Nick meant those words he said or if it was just a last-ditch thing to do because he wouldn't have another 'chance' as he called it. And my body betrays me because all it can remember is him—his lips, his touch, his eyes, his solid strength—and without him, I feel like I can't even exist.

I look up at the only person I felt like I could ever count on—the one who threw me into the flames.

Now all I want to do is burn.

* * *

I follow Rachel out to the now almost empty hall lobby where my mom sits on an armchair that's tucked away in the corner, with Preeti bringing her some water. My sister shoots me an intense glare, her jaw tight and eyes narrowed. A heavy knot forms in my gut as I realize I must have given my mom quite a scare.

I look away just as my Bhua approaches me.

"There you are, darling. We were all so worried." Her kohl-lined eyes glint with kindness.

"I just needed some fresh air," I lie.

She nods and grabs me gently by the elbow and walks me closer to the hall entrance. I glance at the pink-and-gold glittery sign: "Welcome to Eshaan & Nisha's Engagement Ceremony." It all feels surreal, a mock-up, a trial run. This can't really be happening.

I peek inside the hall to see the tables filled with hundreds, and my pulse thunders in my ears. I recognize a few of the faces of my aunts, uncles and cousins, but there are so many people I'm not sure I've ever seen before.

"Everyone's already inside. We'll head in now, and Aman will walk you in."

"I'm ready, Massi Ji. I've been practicing a lot at home with Mom and my stuffies watching." Aman grins with pride. His large, innocent brown eyes shine at me, and I smile softly just for him. I don't need to be walked in, but Aman insisted after seeing it in a Bollywood movie, and all of us thought it was adorable.

My mom approaches. Her eyes drawn, yet relieved.

"Tu bahut sohni lagdi aa." She's never told me I look beautiful, so I take it.

"Thanks, Mom," I say as she adjusts my necklace—her wedding necklace—and I take her fingers and give them a squeeze.

I can do this for her.

This is the right thing to do. I don't know why this sense of wrongness is short-circuiting my system and constricting the air flow in my chest.

"We need to go in now." Preeti grabs my mom by the shoulder and leads her inside, while my Bhua follows closely behind. Rachel gives my shoulders a squeeze and goes in, glancing back. She mouths, "I'm sorry." Her eyes look sad, and I know she means it. I'm sorry too. For this whole crazy mess of my life.

"Let's go, Massi." Aman tugs at my hand, but I glimpse movement on the engagement sign and turn to see a monarch butterfly that's somehow made its way inside. It lands on the corner and then suddenly it flies away toward the front door, a sign that I could still run away from all of this, that maybe it isn't too late. I fight the urge to follow it outside and instead grip Aman's tiny fingers in my own as he walks me inside.

The first line of my dad's favourite song floats in: *Ek ladki ko dekha…* It's the song I chose to walk in to, and a tear escapes my eye. I wish he was here with me now so I wasn't so alone in all of this, in these intense waves of emotions I can't make sense of.

I pass through a floral archway bursting with peonies, cascading orchids, and pink roses. It's so ornate and lavish, it's like we're exchanging vows and not just a ring. My family is clothed in extravagant outfits in varying shades of pink, while Eshaan's is in gold. The two colours blur together as tears coat my eyes, and I desperately try to hold them in.

The crowd turns toward me, with loud whispers of how adorable my nephew is and how stunning I look. I feel nothing for a moment, and the numbness is a welcome reprieve from the torturous emotions running through me.

If this were anyone else's ceremony I would be gushing over the exorbitant yet tasteful touches, but now, all I see is excess. Too much care for the things that don't matter and too little for what does.

Every step is heavy like I'm slogging through mud, not walking on a plush carpet in the Louboutins Eshaan bought me just for today. I stare straight ahead. Eshaan stands near the beautiful gilt-edged loveseat at the front of the hall, but all I see are Nick's eyes. All I sense is his anguish and my own, all I hear is his voice saying, "I love you."

I swallow the lump in my throat and fight back the tears as Aman tugs me forward. I must have slowed down as I look up to see Eshaan's brow furrowed with concern, followed by a flash of annoyance. I force my feet to move.

I have to do this.

I've been going to parties like this for two decades. When I was a child, I loved every moment of it. The dimmed, romantic atmosphere. The gorgeous traditional clothes and bold, glamorous makeup. The centrepieces and tables. The speeches and laughter. A simple hall transformed into a magical fairytale.

All I ever dreamed of was a happily ever after for myself.

I loved the beauty of the ceremonies, but more than anything, I just wondered what it felt like to be that loved. To have someone look at me as if I were the most beautiful woman in the world. Now I feel like I finally found it.

The elusive, fairy-tale love.

What all the Bollywood songs are about.

What Rumi wrote endless poems about.

Except it isn't the man I'm gracefully stepping toward, who's grinning at me like I'm a prized possession rather than a partner. No, it's the man I brashly sent away when he confessed his love for me.

I didn't say it, but I wish I had.

I say it now in the depths of my heart, wishing he could hear me.

I love you too, Nick, so much. You're everything I've ever wanted.

Even if it wasn't meant to be, I want him to know how I feel, and now I will never get the chance to tell him.

I sealed my fate and his by walking away.

We're at the front of the hall too quickly, and Aman is placing my hand in Eshaan's.

"Awww," the crowd says in unison.

Shaan intertwines our fingers, and I resist the urge to pull away. His hand feels foreign, cold, like a death grip.

I look up to see my mom smiling at me from her table in the front and wiping a tear from her eye. I hope I smile back, that I'm still capable of it.

Pretending got me here, and pretending will get me through this. Just a few more hours, then I can break down, I promise myself.

My uncles, guy-cousins and Aman come up to do Eshaan's shagun. I pull my hand away from his so he can receive their blessing, as they drape a red scarf onto his shoulders and into his lap. I look down but I can't ignore the significance of what's happening and what this all means. My eldest Mama Ji takes the role of my dad, placing a gold kara on Eshaan's wrist and feeding him a sweet, as is tradition, while I try to ease my rising panic.

His mom, aunts, girl-cousins—including Anjali—and Dadi Ji come up behind us shortly after. I sit there and numbness fills me, even as his mom gives me her blessing with pride and hugs me close, like I'm the daughter-in-law she's always dreamed of, instead of the opposite. She covers my head with the red bridal chunni, my official welcome and acceptance into their family, and then feeds me a sweet too.

His mom hands Eshaan some brilliant red sindoor and he turns to me, applying the powder to my forehead and into the part in my hair, marking me as his bride and soon-to-be wife. This can't be happening, but it is.

The only time I'm comforted is when Eshaan's Dadi Ji is pushed up to us in her wheelchair. She's so weak and frail now, but she still lifts her hands up to touch our heads in blessing, and we get up to touch her feet to show our respect.

I look in her kind eyes, and they say everything I need to hear. "Putt, sab theek ho jayega." She tells me everything will be okay.

I'm not sure how anything will ever be okay again. Even so, I cling to her words as Eshaan is before me on one knee. I should be looking at his face, but I'm scanning the room, looking for the only face I want to see: Nick's. Wishing that he could do what I would never be able to—stand up for our love—but only the eyes of the endless crowd stare back. My left hand trembles as Eshaan takes it, so he tightens his hold to stop the movement. It looks gentle and caring, but it's like a vise grip. I try to pull my hand away, but he holds it too strongly in place. I can barely move it.

"What the hell is wrong with you?" he whispers before he starts sliding the ring on my finger. It inches closer to my knuckle, but it doesn't feel like a ring at all—it's a noose around my neck. He pulls it over my knuckle and turns to smile at the crowd, finally releasing my hand. I bring my other hand to my mouth and let out a sob as I stare at it. The ring is over-the-top, like everything else this evening, and something I never would have chosen for myself. A two-carat diamond surrounded by a smaller ring of diamonds, and then two thin bands of diamonds.

It's a dead weight that's already dragging me down. I sense the envious glares of other women, but it doesn't bring me even an ounce of pride or satisfaction. I got what I wanted, but it's so shallow and empty. A beautiful cover to an empty existence. A mirage, when I got to experience the real thing, even if it was just for a fleeting moment.

Everyone must think I'm just emotional rather than a hot mess, questioning my life decisions.

Eshaan pulls me up from the seat as the guests erupt in applause, and then he brings my hand to his mouth and kisses it.

We're swarmed by people and lost in a sea of congratulations until Anjali pulls me aside.

"Welcome to the fam, Nish." She puts her arm around my shoulder and gives me a knowing look. "You have no idea what you just signed up for."

"I think I have a pretty good idea," I say as I look around at the opulence and Eshaan eating up all the attention like it's his ceremony and not ours.

"Come on, let's get a drink." She leads me to the bar where I intend to drink my way to salvation. The first sip is bitter and tastes like regret.

* * *

The rest of the evening is a blur, where I simply do what I'm told. It's what I imagine a near-death experience to be like. I know what's happening around me, but it's not me experiencing it.

Smile for photos.

Hug others when they come up to me.

Take selfies when approached.

Dance when I'm dragged onto the floor.

Perform like a circus monkey.

Rachel hovers next to me from time to time, her face taut with worry, but I ignore it and her for the rest of the evening.

In between each act, I slam back drink after drink, until the music and the voices fade away and the only sound I hear is the piercing shattering of my heart breaking. It's the last thing I hear before I faint into the arms of the man I'm now engaged to, and who I'm not even sure I want to be with.

43. DRIVE

The next afternoon, my mom and Bhua Ji insist we all go out for lunch after Rachel told them I fainted because I hadn't eaten all day. They also insist I down two cups of cha to help settle my stomach before we're allowed to leave the house.

It should feel nice to be so taken care of, but even without the hangover I feel nauseous as I replay the conversation with Nick repeatedly in my head.

I try and fail to put it out of my mind as we arrive at the restaurant, seat ourselves, and order steaming bowls of chole with deep-fried bhature. The smell alone has me salivating. I immediately down two glasses of water, and both my mom and my aunt continue to ignore the fact that I'm completely hungover.

"Just like her dad." I heard my mom whispering to my aunt in the morning when I woke up in my little cousin's bed. "Doesn't know when to stop and embarrassed us all." I can't even feel shame anymore, just deep pain in every part of my aching soul. Their words are weapons but I'm used to it, so it slices but not as deep.

I glance around the restaurant. I see young couples and families, and I smile as I see an older Sikh couple who look very much in love. I wonder how they found each other and managed to stay happy over the years.

Eshaan, who was at first concerned about me, later ripped into me for drinking too much and not eating enough, like I was a little girl who spoiled his big event and not his fiancée.

What the fuck do you think my family's going to think? His words echo in my head, but for once, I'm beyond caring what he or his family thinks—more words, more weapons. I will lay down my own and just let them hurt me. It's what I do and all I know.

The food arrives in red plastic trays. I start topping my chole with red onion and white vinegar when my aunt points behind me. "Nisha, is that your friend over there? She's waving at us."

I look back after stuffing my face with a big bite and stop mid-chew. It's someone who looks familiar, but I can't place her. She starts walking toward us.

"Auntie Jis, hi. I'm Nisha's friend, Sonia. Do you mind if I talk to her for a bit? We haven't seen each other for so long."

Sonia? Here? Now?

"Right, Nisha?"

I try not to choke on my food. *What the fuck is she doing?*

"Right." The word tumbles out of my mouth.

I get up as she says, "We'll be right back." She smiles at them like we're old friends when we've never met, or even spoken, once.

We step outside and walk to the corner of the plaza where it's less busy. She turns and levels me with an edgy stare.

"Look, I know we don't know each other, and I was debating if I should even do this." She crosses her arms over chest. "But I keep thinking that if it were me, I'd want to know."

Icy dread spreads through me. I want to turn and run, but I stay rooted to the spot, unable to move away from something I always knew was coming.

"Eshaan and I have been seeing each other on and off for months."

I didn't think it was this.

"What does that mean?" My voice trembles.

She looks away and takes a breath. "We've been sleeping together." She doesn't meet my eyes. "I tried to stop it, and I know it's a shit move."

I stare at her, and I know she's not lying. I'm the only one lying to myself.

"I would never want to interfere, and you seem like an amazing woman. I just, I never got over him, and he would just reel me in, and I would say it was just this one time, and then it continued like that."

My legs start to shake and the world feels like it's spinning. I place a steadying hand out, but my fingers only find air.

"He said it was *you*, that you wouldn't leave him alone," I say quietly, needing to know the whole truth.

"Of course he did. He's never going to admit to being an asshole. Besides, I have proof." She pulls out her phone from her purse.

I don't want to see it, but I have to know.

She hands it to me and shows me all the texts, along with photos. Some of them are explicit.

"I'm sorry for telling you now. I wasn't planning to. I just saw you there, and I know you just got engaged. At least you know now before the wedding."

She looks at me tentatively before adding, "I know he loves you, so maybe you can work this out. And you don't have to worry about me anymore. I told him it's over."

I hand back her phone, unable to read another word.

"I know you probably won't believe it," she adds, "but all this has been eating me up inside."

"Thank you for telling me."

"I'm so sorry." She shoots me a look of deep regret.

I swear on my life. Eshaan's face flashes before me, uttering his lies.

I had the prince and the villain mixed up in my story all along, and now it's too late for either.

I walk back to the restaurant slowly. I pass a sewer drain and want to throw my ring into it.

I think of all the times he humiliated me and said I was flirting with other guys, when he's been fucking his ex for months. All those times I felt so guilty for even letting Nick touch me, while Shaan and Sonia were doing god only knows what.

This is a cruel galactic joke, and I can't even believe the disaster that's my life. I'm not even sure I care anymore.

The bell on the door jingles when I walk back in and sit on the stiff red seat that's feeling more like an electric chair.

"Who was that, darling? I don't remember seeing her at the engagement," my Bhua Ji says.

I eat a spoonful of the chole.

"Shaan's girlfriend." My mom and Bhua look at each other, shocked.

"Who?"

"His girlfriend." I keep chowing down the food even as I want to throw it all up. I'm beyond pain. I'm beyond dignity. I'm beyond caring.

"She told me Shaan has been cheating on me for months with her."

My mom looks around. "Chup kar!"

Sure, Mom, I can be quiet for now. Keeping my mouth shut is what got me here, but it's not going to help me escape this. I continue shovelling food into my mouth until my dish is wiped clean.

My Bhua takes a deep breath.

"Putt, these things happen. It was before the engagement?"

I want to scream that of course it was—we haven't even been engaged for a day. Unless he fucked her last night while I was passed out. I wouldn't put it past him.

I don't say anything, though, knowing I'm seconds away from losing it. Instead, I just nod.

"No need to do anything rash. Let things settle," my Bhua continues, placing her hand on mine.

My insides are quaking. I just told them he's been cheating on me, and they tell me to be quiet and forget it even happened? What the fuck kind of reality is this?

I want to topple the tables and take a bat to the room and destroy every fucking thing in here.

I had to deal with all this shit for so long, and I thought it was because I was the problem. I wasn't good enough, and that's why my mom's love was so conditional. I did something wrong just by being born a girl and was constantly reminded of my shortcomings.

It wasn't enough to watch my dad die and know that no one intervened to help stop his alcoholism. They simply watched in silence and did nothing. And after he passed, no one stepped in to help us, even though I was only in high school, and Preeti was in university. My mom only ever worked part-time. Then, I watched as Sunny was put through the ringer after everyone found out he was gay, and then they put me through the same for pretending to date him.

I was made to believe I was bad for wanting to chase my dreams and not a guy. For not being married with kids by now. After all, that was the only goal worth having. And it couldn't just be a good, decent guy, no, it had to be a South Asian guy from a 'good' family.

And now, they say this.

I'm done. I just want the pain and fucked-up situation to end.

I get up from the table. "I'm going home."

"Putt, there's still family here. Your sister is at the house waiting to see you." My mom softens, not wanting to unleash her full venom in front of anyone else.

"Tell them I'm not feeling well."

She wants me to live a lie? Surely, she'll have no problem telling this one. I leave the restaurant and don't even bother to look back.

* * *

I don't go home. I go straight to Shaan's house and wait outside on the driveway as I text him to come the fuck outside. Now.

Nish?

I reply to let him know I'm outside in the driveway.

Then come in.

I reply with all caps this time:

OUT. NOW.

He comes out. "Hey, we were just having a late lunch. Want to join?" Without a care in the world.

"Fuck you."

"Nish, what the heck has come over you?" He tries to appease me, knowing that many of his family members are still hovering inside and outside the house, and some of his younger cousins are playing on the expansive front lawn.

"Let's go for a drive, asshole." I walk over to him with a fake smile as his cousins continue to look.

He can sense I'm pissed.

"Okay, okay."

He pulls out his keys, and I grab them. "This time I'm driving."

I walk to the driver's seat just as his little cousins wave at us. I wave back. I'm glad they're there because I know he won't make a scene in front of them.

We buckle up, and I don't care that I've never driven his car before or that it's worth more than a hundred thousand dollars. I drive carelessly, zig-zagging through the streets way too fast before taking the ramp to the highway. I don't even care if we get pulled over.

Thankfully, since it's Sunday, it's not too busy.

"Shit. Slow down."

I'm reckless but I'm tired, so very tired, of everyone's shit—especially his.

"What's going on?" he asks gently. I'm sure he's more concerned that I'll total his precious car than he is about why I'm upset. I continue speeding.

"Why don't we call Sonia and find out what's going on? Maybe she's up for a threesome seeing as you've been fucking her for so long and she's probably bored out of her mind."

"What are you talking about? I told you we didn't do anything."

"Stop the shit, Shaan. I ran into her at lunch today with my mom and Bhua, and guess what? She hauled me outside and showed me your texts and photos."

I take an exit onto a quiet farm road and drive even faster.

"Nish, pull over. Let's talk about this calmly."

I want to drive into a telephone pole, but I know that's the rage talking, not me, and I try to get a handle on myself.

I stop the car in a field in the middle of nowhere and we both step outside. He walks over to me, and for once, he has nothing to say. No lies to spew. He's quiet as he looks at me.

"I just can't believe this. All those times you made me feel like shit if a guy even looked at me."

He shakes his head and gives me a cold stare that would have me apologizing profusely before. The nerve of that look when he knows he's in the wrong.

"What did you expect? You're off every other weekend at some conference or working late most nights. And don't even lie that those guys never tried any shit with you."

I can't believe what I'm hearing. He's trying to put this on me.

"I didn't fuck anyone, Shaan, ever, but guess what, you did and not just once, but multiple times. For months."

He gives me a cocky stare, and I just can't stop the rage that's coming up.

I slap him and he grabs my arm so hard it throbs, and then he releases me like I'm a rag doll and I almost fall backwards into the car.

I stand there motionless.

"Nisha, shit. I'm so sorry. I shouldn't have done that." His face softens as I look at him incredulously.

He comes closer.

"Stay the fuck away from me." I hold my aching arm. "We're so done."

"Look, let's calm down and talk about this."

"I'm done talking. I'm done with you." I enunciate every word as if he's a toddler.

"So that's it then? We just walk away from all of this?"

"What did you think would happen, Eshaan, really?"

He looks at me as if he's weighing everything I've said. He's quiet for a while, and I am too. The fight goes out of him. "What are we going to tell our families?"

I hate that question. He's been cheating on me for months, and all he cares about is what mommy precious and daddy dearest are going to think. "Why don't we do a slide show, and we can just do a run-through of your texts and pictures?" I smirk at him. "Or better yet, I'll send it to the fam group chat." I cross my arms. "What is it that they say?" I look at the sky with my pointer finger tapping on my chin. "A picture is worth a thousand words?"

"You wouldn't." He gives me a pointed stare.

"She already sent them all to me," I lie. "Every last one. And I would."

"What do you want me to do then?" He caves, my erratic behavior probably showing him that I'm not beyond this.

"You leave me the fuck alone and say it was all *your* shit. Otherwise, your family finally gets to learn what a dickhead you really are."

I get back in his car. He doesn't even try to get in, and for that I'm thankful. I drive away, leaving him in the middle of nowhere. It's one of my finer moments.

I drive the car back to his place, leaving the ring in the car and the keys in the mailbox.

I don't want to see his family.

I don't want to see my family.

I don't even want to see Rachel.

I take an Uber downtown, walk into a liquor store, grab a bottle of gin, check myself into a nearby hotel, and down nearly half of it.

My phone is dead, and I feel like I'm dying too.

44. MIA

I wake up with a throbbing headache and my mouth completely parched. I'm so exhausted that I don't want to get out of bed, but my thirst drives me to grab the too-expensive hotel water bottle sitting on the coffee table a few steps away from me.

I finish the bottle before staggering back to bed and lying there. Light streams through the curtains I only half-closed last night, and I look over at the clock to see it's 9 a.m. Check-out is in a couple of hours, and I have to pull myself together, but I can't move.

After a night of drinking, my anxiety is heightened, and my nervous system is on high alert. I feel everything I didn't on the night of the engagement: the despair, hurt, embarrassment, humiliation, and white-hot rage all make their presence known and I punch my pillows and then scream into them before huddling in on myself and just crying.

Rachel tried to warn me, not just on Friday, but so many times before, and I shut her out. I can't deny that the red flags were everywhere. One moment, Shaan was telling me how much he loved me, and the next, he would cut me down with his words, using the things I shared with him against me. I just didn't want to see it or believe it.

I think about how he would often leave me at events and tell me he needed to 'work the room,' and how he would barely even check on me all night, except when he saw a guy talking to me. How when I asked him about Sonia, when I first saw his texts, he said I was being ridiculous and insecure. How he put down my aspirations and didn't even try to understand how hard it's been financially, because his parents paid for everything, and he would always rub in how much they were doing for us. How he would side with Dev instead of me during arguments and didn't understand why I didn't want to stay over when he was there. The cheap shots he took at what I wore. The list and signs were endless, and I wonder why I didn't see them.

Because I didn't want to.

When I met Eshaan, he checked so many boxes that my family had ingrained in me, and I let myself get caught up in all of that. It felt good, for once, to have my mom's approval instead of her disappointment in everything I did. So, I forced myself to look the other way. To stop noticing, and this is where betraying myself left me.

I tormented myself for my feelings for Nick, when at the same time Shaan was with Sonia and lied to my face about it with ease. Then my mom's and Bhua's reaction confirmed that I never wanted that life. One where I was expected to look the other way and ignore destructive and unhealthy behaviours, silently putting up with them the way they did. The way they felt they had to.

I get it. They didn't have the financial stability to walk away, especially with kids. But I don't have to worry about that, especially now.

My promotion officially starts in a week, and with it, a steep increase in pay. I can walk away from all of this and be okay. They never got that choice, and I thank the universe for my career and my situation that gave me one.

Life is shit, but I don't have to keep sitting in it.

At ten a.m. I take a quick shower and try—for the moment—to take control of my life. My phone's dead, and I'm not ready to deal with everything that's waiting for me. Most of my family flew out this morning, and I feel a pang at not seeing them.

It's okay to focus on me after everything I've been through.

This time it isn't Rachel's voice in my head, but my own.

I wrack my brain wondering what I should do and then finally remember that Eshaan and I were supposed to be leaving for Victoria this afternoon on the one o'clock ferry. My bag is already packed and if I leave now to pick it up from our condo, I can just make it.

After everything, I deserve this. I'm going to take this fucking trip.

* * *

The Uber drops me off at the Empress Hotel in downtown Victoria, and I take it all in. The hotel and nearby legislative building look historic and almost European. Nature is in full bloom around me with vibrant red, yellow, and purple flowers bursting through the nearly fluorescent green shrubs and trees surrounding the majestic hotel. I walk through the grand entrance and the lobby is equally magnificent. Sunlight streams through the windows that make up most of the walls. A spiral staircase with a golden railing leads upstairs, and statuesque pillars stand tall throughout the lobby. I head to the front desk and enter the small queue, taking a deep breath and letting my shoulders soften. Maybe this will be the start of my fairy tale.

"Checking in today, Miss?"

"Yes, the reservation should be under Eshaan Johal."

She taps away for a few seconds.

"I have it right here. Paid in full. We'll just need your ID and a credit card for incidentals."

I hand over my ID and his credit card that he gave me a few weeks ago to pick up anything else I needed for the ceremony.

She clicks away again on her computer and then hands me over two key cards.

"Enjoy your stay."

"Oh, I will." I give her my best smile and head to the elevators.

It's the Harbour View Suite. Eshaan showed me the pictures online, but when I enter the suite, it's breathtaking. There's a small circular dining table off to the side with fresh flowers sitting on top, surrounded by cozy beige chairs. The living room is right next to it, with a couch, and cushy armchair. Both are tastefully decorated with violet pillows.

I leave my bag at the front and slip off my shoes as I wander around, heading into the bedroom off to the side. It has a massive king-size bed, with ornate lamps and a gorgeous floral painting on the wall, but what gets me the most is the view from the room. It's the Inner Harbour. The gleaming white boats softly rock in the water, like they're dancing to music only they can hear. Only a small knot keeps them moored. I dream of unmooring, slipping off my restraints and finding freedom. Maybe this is my chance to free myself from all that no longer serves me and embrace what does.

I collapse on the bed and close my eyes and for once, feel like I might actually be okay. I lie there for a while until hunger gnaws at me and I wander back to the living room and find the room service menu. I order honey garlic chicken wings, buttermilk fried calamari, truffle fries and the ten-layer chocolate cake, because why not. It's time to let myself indulge in all my desires.

After my private feast, I soak in the tub, letting the water wash away all the hurt, discomfort, and pain of everything. It's still there after I do, but the torment of emotions softens a little, giving me a slight reprieve.

I haven't charged my phone and don't want to just yet.

I will give myself today and maybe tomorrow too, before dealing with everything. I fall into a deep sleep and awake in the night after dreaming about a different ending for me the night of the engagement. One that includes Nick. But he's not here and I cry softly into my pillow wishing that he was.

45. ME TIME

After breakfast in bed, I doll myself up, even though I still feel like a disaster wearing a cute short floral dress with sneakers and a jean jacket. I don't wear as much makeup as I normally do—it's time to let some of the real me shine through. No more masks or pretending, just the real Nisha Dhaliwal.

When I finally head outside, it's a sunny day, and the streets are busy with traffic and tourists. It's nice to melt into the hubbub around me.

I wander the grounds around the hotel and find a hidden garden. I sit down on a bench for I don't know how long, letting nature soothe me the way it always does. The flourishing greenery brings a small part of me back online as I do.

I explore the area until I find a cute coffee shop tucked out of the way. It's unassuming and further away from the city centre, but it's busy. I walk in and order my extra-sweet matcha latte and then wander back to the downtown core where I see a huge Lululemon storefront just across from my hotel. Retail therapy seems enticing. It's been so long since I bought anything other than work clothes, so I take a final sip of my latte to energize me, discard the cup, and walk in.

I start piling yoga pants, tanks, and lightweight jackets on my arm when a saleswoman approaches me.

"Can I get a room started for you?" I turn around to see a tall, slim, beautiful blonde standing next to me with a smile, and I just stare. Those eyes. Nick's eyes.

She looks closely at me too, and surprisingly, she remembers me—though I'm not sure if I want her to.

"Oh, hi. Nisha, right? We met a few months ago at brunch. Wait, what was the place called…" She starts tapping her foot, trying to think of it. "Patisserie something."

I almost want to deny it and leave, but I'm done hiding and lying.

"Yes. It was L'Atelier Patisserie. Hi Lucy. It's good to see you again."

"You too." She beams at me.

"Here, let me take that." She takes the pile. "Are you ready to try these on, or would you like to look around more?"

"I'm ready." I follow her to the change room as she hangs my clothes up nicely and writes 'Nisha' outside of the change room door.

"I'll check on you in a moment, but holler if you need anything."

"Thanks." I slip inside the room and try on the pants first, and even though it's my usual size, they're a little loose. I know I haven't been eating well with everything going on.

There's a knock at the door. "Nisha, how's everything fitting in there?"

"Actually, could I get a smaller size in these pants? I open the door and give her the other two and point to the ones I'm wearing.

"Sure thing."

I'm debating on what to try next, looking through the tops, and then finally settle on the racerback; I've always wanted one. I slip it on before Lucy's back at the door.

"I have those pants here for you."

I quickly open the door, before I have the chance to look at my reflection, and step outside.

"Oh, that looks so nice on you." I can tell her praise is genuine, and I smile, but then something flashes in her eyes as she looks at my arm and bites her bottom lip. I follow her gaze and realize there's a dark bruise forming where Shaan grabbed me. I put my other hand over it, self-consciously, and she looks away.

"Let me know how the other tops fit," she says with an extra bit of kindness. I want to cry.

I try everything on and settle on black leggings, the racerback tank I've always wanted, and a lightweight jacket. I bring it to the till where Lucy's waiting for me.

She rings up my purchase and is about to hand me my bag when I see her hesitating.

"Nisha, I hope this isn't weird, but Nick's said so many amazing things about you, and well, I'm finishing my shift in a few minutes, and I was wondering if you wanted to grab a late lunch or early supper? I'd love to pick your brain about being a woman in tech."

I can't resist supporting another woman and don't even hesitate. "Oh, of course. That would be lovely. It's my first time in Victoria and I'm not sure where to even go."

"Really?" Her eyes bug out for a second. "Okay, I know where we have to go then." She smiles, and it lights up her whole beautiful face. I try to ignore the resemblance that stares back at me.

"Just give me a few to finish up here."

"You got it."

I head over and peruse the bag selection, then I look back through my purchase. It's nice to buy something and not stress about how much I spent.

Lucy comes up behind me. "Okay, I'm ready."

I follow her out the door as people mill about, and I catch a sight of a double-decker tourist bus. It makes me smile.

"Where are we off to?" I ask, curious.

"Oh, it's a surprise."

I follow her across the street, and we stroll on the sidewalk that overlooks the marina in the harbour. I don't see any restaurants just yet, but I take in the view. There are mosaic whales and dolphin statues, and even a large Canada sign where people are posing.

Lucy sees me eyeing the dolphin. "I can take your picture if you like."

"Oh, no worries. My phone's battery is dead."

"I'll use mine and send it to you." She smiles.

"Okay, sure." I pose next to the dolphin just as someone walks by and offers to take our picture together.

"Thank you." Lucy gives the man her phone, and we take a few fun and silly poses. It's like we're already friends, even though we've only met twice. *I deserve a family who loves me. I wish there was a reality where she could be my family.*

The man hands the phone back and Lucy shows me the pictures. I look happier than I have in months, even without much makeup. "Make sure to give me your number, or I can send them to Nick, and he'll get them to you."

I freeze at her words. "Oh, actually, here's my number." The heat rises in my cheeks—I don't want her to send anything to him. I turned him down to get engaged to a man who's been cheating on me for months.

We reach a set of concrete steps and I follow her down the walkway, when I finally see it. A shack with two fish on it, one red and one blue.

"Is this it?"

"This is it." She turns to me. "I hope you like fish and chips!"

"I love fish and chips."

"Thank goodness because it's like a big deal around here."

We make our way to the stand, and luckily it's not too busy at this hour. We both order the halibut and take our lunch to a counter built into a fence that overlooks the water.

We sit on the stools, and I only wait a moment before taking a bite. The deep-fried goodness is exactly what my hungover body and broken heart need.

"So delish, right?"

"It's amazing," I reply between bites. I look over at Lucy. "Thanks for bringing me here."

"I should be thanking *you* for joining me. I'm so excited to learn more about you. Nick raves about you all the time."

I swallow hard and try to choke back the emotion that comes up at her words. "What do you want to know?"

"Well, I still have a couple of years before I finish my degree, but I don't know where I want to work after. What industry."

"With design, you're lucky because you can pick and choose." I dab my malt vinegar–coated fries in ketchup and take a bite.

"Do you like working in tech?"

I finish my bite before continuing as she watches me, waiting for me to respond. "I love it, but it can be a lot at times, especially at start-ups. There are a lot of extra hours you have to put in, which is great when you're single, but might be harder later on."

"Oh, is there someone special in your life right now?" The question comes out of left field, and I can tell that she's fishing. When I look over at her, she seems nervous.

"Not anymore."

"Oh, I'm sorry." She places her hand gently on my forearm. "I know it's none of my business, and we barely know each other, but did he do that to you? To your arm?" Worry creases her forehead.

"Yes." I don't know why I'm telling her, but she's kind and easy to talk to, and it's nice not to lie and just get it off my chest.

"He's never done anything like that before, but it was the final straw."

She nods. "I'm so sorry you had to go through that." She pauses before continuing. "My dad was abusive toward my mom, so I just, it's—"

"That must have been so hard." Nick never mentioned that.

"It was, but I'm lucky. Nick sheltered me from a lot of what was happening." She looks away.

"You have an amazing brother, you know."

"I do." She gives me a sweet smile, and I find myself liking her even more, even though I know we can't be friends. I can, however, just enjoy this. That's what life is after all, just moments. I wish I had enjoyed more moments instead of stressing about the future and overthinking the past.

"Nick showed me the art you gave him with the goddess," I say, hoping to lighten the mood.

"Oh, that." She looks shy as she adds, "I made it."

"Oh, my gosh, wow. I had no idea. It's brilliant. At first, it looks like flowers, and then you look closely and see a beautiful silhouette."

"Thank you." She beams with pride.

"I gave it to Nick because either he's not dating at all or he's out with women who totally don't deserve him, and if I'm honest, most aren't up to my high standards." She pretends to scoff. She pauses and then adds, "I want someone who's good to him and I can hang out with, you know?" She gives me a lingering look.

I don't want to hear the details of Nick's dating life, but I swallow my discomfort.

"Well, I'm sure the painting will help send out the right vibes."

She holds eye contact while she says, "I think it already has. I only gave it to him last Christmas."

I laugh. "Then it's only a matter of time," I say as I add another crack to my already splintered heart.

When we're done, we grab our empty boxes and throw them out.

"Where are you staying?"

"The Empress, actually."

"That's amazing."

I don't tell her it was the trip I was supposed to take with my fiancé. "It really is."

"Want to walk a bit more?"

"I'd love that."

We pass a massive, ship-like structure with wood panelling and lush greenery outside.

"What's that?" I ask, genuinely curious.

"That's this incredible ship that's been repurposed into a Nordic spa. You have to go there before you leave." I think of the last Nordic spa I was in with Nick and my cheeks burn.

She pauses as if she's pondering something. "You usually have to book in advance." Her face lights up. "But my friend works there. I'm going to call her and see if she can fit you in. Is this evening okay?"

"That would be great."

She steps away and makes the call as I stare at the sea and pretend not to listen. She comes back a moment later.

"Okay, you're so lucky." I feel anything but. "They just had a cancellation for six p.m., so we can head on over right now if you like."

"Thank you."

She smiles at me sweetly. "You're so welcome."

"I would join you, but I have to get to the university."

It's June, and it's getting late, so I look at her curiously.

"Oh, I take evening classes during the summer so I can finish my degree sooner. Nick hates it and says I should just have fun, but he's been helping me so much and I want to be able to take care of myself, you know?"

"I do know," I tell her.

We hug and I'm sad.

I add her to the list of people who are leaving my life that I'm going to miss.

Shaan's Dadi.

Nick.

Lucy.

And I head up to the sauna with my sad and heavy heart.

46. BETTER NOW

I spend two hours using the sauna, and my body starts to detox. Not just all the alcohol, but my thoughts are lighter too, and that tight feeling that always seems to be lingering in my chest loosens.

Lucy's friend is so welcoming, it fills my heart. She even gives me her employee discount, and I want to cry thinking of the kindness I've been shown today. It helps me believe in the universe and myself again.

My child, everything will be okay. I hear Shaan's Dadi's voice in my head.

Maybe she's right.

I finally charge my phone when I get back to the hotel but decide to wait until tomorrow to go through my messages. I order more room service, watch HGTV, and stay away from the liquor menu, even though I could really use a drink. I fall asleep with the TV on and wake up at 5 a.m. to turn it off and snuggle back into bed, falling asleep again until just after nine.

Rachel's right. It's nice to spend time with myself, and for the first time, I'm able to enjoy my own company without being constantly distracted by work, my phone, or men—no matter how captivating they are, or one is in particular.

I sit up in bed and start checking my messages after taking a few long, deep calming breaths.

I have five missed calls from my mom, so many pictures from the family group chat from the engagement party, only one message from Shaan, and several frantic texts from Rachel, apologizing.

I disable notifications from the family group chat, as I can't bring myself to look at any of those photos. A reminder of the lie I have been living for so long. Then, I mentally prepare myself for Shaan's text.

My Dadi is getting weaker by the day. I can't tell my fam we broke things off. Not yet.

I feel a flicker of frustration, but mostly there's sadness and understanding.

I would never want to hurt that sweet old lady who reminds me so much of my own grandma, who passed away when I was just ten years old.

I understand. Let me know how she's doing.

I brace myself for a call with my mom. She spends most of it telling me off for disappearing and not spending time with my family that came for the engagement, and then finally asks how things are with Eshaan. I know full well that she's more worried about our reputation than me, so I tell her everything's fine. His Dadi is sick, and we'll figure things out later. I want to tell her we broke things off, but I just can't deal with her reaction just yet. She's leaving tonight, and even with everything and how strained our relationship is, I'm sad I didn't get to see her and say bye.

Then, I take another deep breath and call Rachel.

She picks up on the first ring.

"Nisha, I've been so worried, and I feel so horrible. I should have never let Nick ambush you like that, and on your engagement. It's just that—"

"Rach, it's okay," I interrupt her.

"It's not. I knew how much the engagement meant to you, and I messed up. Big time."

"Rach, listen please. Shaan and I are calling it off."

For a moment, the silence is deafening.

"What? What happened?"

"He's been seeing someone else for months." I hear her gasp on the other end, although I'm sure she's probably not that shocked. She warned me after all. "Sonia, his ex, came up to me and confessed everything when I was out with my family on Sunday, even showing me the texts and photos."

"Nisha. I'm so sorry. I really am." Her compassion threatens to dissolve the calm and peace I cultivated since getting here.

"I know," I say quietly.

"Did you talk to him about it?"

"I confronted him, and it got ugly."

"Shit. I'm so sorry. I should have been there."

"No, Rach. You've been there so much, but this I had to do myself. We're waiting to see how things are with his grandma, and then we'll break the news to everyone."

"Oh, babe. Where are you now?"

"In Victoria, like Eshaan and I had planned, but I just came here alone to take some time to really think about everything. I might just stay here for the rest of the week. Let things settle and find myself again."

"Nisha, I'm so proud of you, you know that."

"I'm proud of me too," I manage.

47. SHE RISES

I spend the rest of the week exploring the city, and it's fun. I've travelled for work and for a little while when I took that semester off and met Rachel, but nothing on my own for a long time.

I visit the Butchart Gardens and spend a whole day wandering around, letting the greenery revive me.

I go to Fisherman's Wharf and indulge in mini donuts without guilt as I wander the docks and take in the whimsical, colourful houses built right onto the water.

I go to the Dallas Road Pavilion, which has an incredible stairway that I take right down to the ocean. I stand on the last step and just stare out at the sea, trying to forget what the ocean blue reminds me of.

It's my last day in Victoria, and there's only one place I want to be. Growing up in Toronto I always dreamed of living close to the water, and now that I do, I barely go to the beach—but that will change, starting now. I go to Willows Beach and settle in on the sand. It's not pristine, but the rocks, driftwood and tangled seaweed make it more real, and that's what I need. I tug off my sneakers and pull off my socks. Then I dig my feet into the warm sand until I hit the damp, cool grains underneath the surface. I stare at the expansive ocean and watch as the sun glitters over it, reminding me of my engagement outfit that did the same. Varying shades of pink and gold, sprinkled with delicate embroidery that looked stunning on the outside, but on the inside, I could feel every stitch. Just as I can feel everything now. The anguish, the relief, the fear, the devastating heartache, and the emotions too big to name.

I lose myself watching the rhythmic waves and let the tension around my heart unspool until the sun rises higher in the sky. I eventually take my new journal out of my bag and run my hands over the lovely pink leather cover, which is embroidered with shiny gold moons. I picked it up earlier from a local maker's shop, and I love it. It's been years since I wrote in a journal, even though I always had a diary as a child.

It's time to process everything that happened and try to make sense of it all. The hardest part is being honest with myself.

It's my need for constant approval and validation from my mom and Eshaan that made me disregard my emotions and distrust my intuitive nudges. Gaining everyone else's approval isn't worth it, even though I thought it would be. I have to live with myself, and I can't live with this. Being with someone who doesn't understand or support my dreams and career, and who lies so effortlessly and puts me down so easily. I hate being single again, after dreaming of a solid partnership for as long as I can remember, but it's already better than whatever I had with Eshaan.

I write non-stop for I don't know how long and realize that it's okay for me to be incredibly ambitious and passionate about my career, even if others don't understand, and it's okay to not follow the status quo and instead do things on my own timeline. To live in a way that makes me happy without having to constantly explain my choices to others or convince them to see things my way. And finally, that it's okay to be almost thirty and not have my life figured out.

Doing what I need, not what everyone else wants, goes against everything I learned growing up. Yet it feels right in a way that I never anticipated. Like a deep knowing that I'm on the right path, even though I'm not yet sure where that path will lead me.

I stare at the waves, letting the realizations sink in, and decide that it's time to officially say goodbye to Fantasy Nisha and embrace the real

Nisha. Maybe she would never be enough for the world, but she's more than enough for me. Although it hurts to even think about now, maybe someday she will be enough for someone else, too. Tears cascade down my cheeks as I wonder if that will ever be possible. If I even wanted it to be anymore. I couldn't imagine a future without Nick, but now I have to, and it's more than I can bear. After everything, my heart still longs for him even though it's too little, too late for us.

Just call him.

I brush the thought aside. I can't put myself through any more heartbreak.

The man that will be the hardest to get over is the one I'm not even in a relationship with. It'd be comical if it weren't so sad. I wipe my tears away as an eagle swoops up and glides across the crashing ocean waves. It flies higher until it's barely visible against the soft, pillowy clouds. A toddler who's spent the last five minutes staring at the ocean suddenly breaks free from her mom's grasp and splashes her little feet at the shoreline. I smile as I watch her stomp around without a care. I silently wish that I could be as free as that eagle and as unburdened as that little girl. Maybe I'm taking my first step to be.

As tempting as it is to continue to dwell, I know nothing good will come of it. I have already been through so much, and I don't need to put myself through more. The heartache and heartbreak are already all-consuming.

My only regret is how I handled things with Nick. Even being here, away from everything, does nothing to stop the bottomless pit growing in my stomach, knowing that I lost my one real chance at happiness. Still, I do my best to forgive myself for everything, and although I'm not ready yet, somehow, I will find a way to forgive Eshaan, too.

I don't know what the universe has in store for me anymore, but more than ever before, I feel that everything will be okay.

* * *

I told myself to stay away, but Lucy keeps messaging me, and I've been sending her photos of what I'm up to. I stop by and see her at the store before I leave.

She pulls me into a hug and walks me out, where she stands looking at me for a second and then blurts out, "I know you're just getting out of a relationship, and I know it's not my business at all, and I know I shouldn't even be saying this, but my brother really likes you. Like, *like likes* you and he's tried to deny it, but it's so obvious because he's the worst liar. Maybe when you're ready, you could ask him out? Okay bye!" She leaves before I can even reply.

I know I can never pursue anything more with him. He told me he doesn't do relationships, and I obviously don't have a good track record either. If things didn't work out it would destroy me. I can't risk my heart. We missed our chance, and we will never ever get another one.

I take the ferry back to Vancouver on Friday, and even though I'm still sad, I feel like a lighter, happier version of me.

The best part? I like this version of me.

48. PLENTY OF FISH

I can't help but smile as I walk into my new office on Monday. It's spacious and bright with an incredible view, and even a couch in the corner. I wonder how I'll decorate it. I think about asking Lucy, but I'm not sure I should continue talking with her. My phone buzzes with a text.

> **It was so nice to connect last week. Hope I didn't make things awkward. I would love to be friends, and you don't have to date my brother for that (but you should totally consider it...when you're ready 😉)**

I smile despite myself. She has this light, bubbly energy that's infectious. I don't think I would ever not want to be her friend, but the thought of hearing about Nick's exploits makes my heart plummet.

One day at a time. One moment at a time.

I sit in my chair and twirl around, giddy with excitement.

"Whoa, look who's moving up in the world!" Matt pokes his head into my office.

"Come in, sit." I gesture at my guest chair.

"We missed you around here, you have no idea," he says as he sits.

"Fill me in." I lean back in my cushy chair and clasp my hands before me.

"Oh, don't you worry, I'll tell you every last detail, but first, how does it feel to be an engaged woman?"

His eyes flick to my bare ring finger.

I look down at my hand before hiding it under my desk. "It didn't work out."

"Nisha. I'm sorry." He looks sad for me, and I realize I'm still sad too, about it, and about everything.

"It's okay. It's for the best." I know it is. Even though everything still hurts.

"I haven't told anyone else yet, so..."

He straightens up and looks at me with softness in his eyes. "I'll keep it on the down-low."

"Thanks."

"Well, there's plenty more fish in the sea, as they say." He tries to make me smile, and I love him for it.

But I only want one.

I look into his deep brown eyes and manage to give him a little smile.

Matt fills me in on everything I missed, including the marketing team not liking any of his memes—a tragedy, according to him—and then that Nick has already started a new contract and Matt will officially take over starting today.

He's gone.

I have no more reasons to see him, and my heart sinks as I realize I'll never see his gorgeous face in the halls again or see him sitting across from me in meetings, or at the coffee shop down the street, or anywhere else, really.

It's fine, even though it isn't, because I have to move on.

I'm not sure what Nick wants. I'm not sure what I want either, and for the first time, I'm going to take some time to figure it out instead of jumping in, even though I'd leap off a cliff for him, even now.

"Thanks for the update."

"Anytime."

He heads out, and I look at my calendar. My next meeting is with my team. The team that I'm leading and I'm so damn excited about it even with the crushing heartbreak that lingers in my chest. Everyone will be divided into two teams eventually, but we're starting as one for now so I can learn more about their skills and then help place them where they'll shine most.

I head to the boardroom early and see my A-players file in. They are all women, but there's one woman at the back who I want to see the most.

Jess comes in looking timid and uncertain, but I'm glad she's here. I spoke with management to see if I could have her come on board, and they were happy to give it a shot on a trial basis to see if it is a good fit for her and the company. I know it will be. She isn't confident, and I know that feeling because that was me, but I know it's only a matter of time until she finds her groove. It's so wonderful to create this opportunity for her.

"Welcome, everyone! I can't tell you how excited I am to have you on board."

Expectant faces look up at me, and it finally starts to sink in. It's me leading the charge.

"Let's dive in, shall we?"

I'm making a difference, and this time, I believe it.

* * *

"Jess, do you have a moment?" I ask as most of the other women are already out the door after the meeting.

"Of course."

I close the meeting room door to give us some privacy as she walks over to me.

"I'm so sorry about everything with Eshaan." She gives me a sad smile and squeezes my upper arm.

"Me too." I filled her in on the weekend with what happened between us, and now it's time to fill her in on everything else too.

"Thank you for offering to discreetly share about the break-up so no one asks me about it."

"I'm here for you, always."

I squeeze her arm back in gratitude.

"Let's sit." I gesture to her chair and take one beside her.

"What's up?"

"I wasn't completely honest with you when you asked about Nick a couple of weeks ago."

Her eyes go wide, and she places her hand on mine. "Please don't tell me he has been harassing you. That on top of everything with Eshaan—"

"No, it's not that." I pause, not sure how to be open about this.

"The thing is, Nick's feelings for me weren't one-sided. I was falling for him as we worked together."

She gives me a knowing look. "I thought that might also be the case, but you didn't say anything."

"I know. I wanted to tell you, but I was scared. If Eshaan ever found out, it would have been bad."

"I get that." She gives me a nod.

"To be honest, I wasn't sure what to make of everything with Nick either." I'm still not sure what we were. I take a breath and continue. "The night you saw us, Nick was trying to deal with the fact that I was getting engaged, and we were both trying to move on. It was just harder than we both thought to stay away from each other."

"Oh, that's so romantic." She beams at me. "But now, things are different, right? You'll figure things out."

I shake my head. "No, I don't think so."

"What, why?" She turns more fully to face me.

"All of this crazy shit happened because I rushed into things with Eshaan. We haven't even told our families yet that things are over and that's going to be a gong show. My mom's going to be so disappointed, and his parents went all out for the party, so they'll be devastated. I don't even want to think about what all the hundreds of guests will be saying about me." My heart starts hammering just thinking about my mom's reaction. "I'm not sure if I can trust myself or my feelings after all this."

"Nish, you're being too hard on yourself. It was a complicated situation, and you did the best you could. Don't give up on your chance at happiness because of what happened. Who gives a shit about what anyone else thinks?"

Tears spring to my eyes. *I'm not sure I deserve a happy ending.*

"Where did you leave things with Nick?"

"We said our goodbyes after the engagement got moved up, but then he showed up to the ceremony."

"OMG, what? You didn't mention that this weekend." Her mouth hangs open as she processes this.

"You're telling *me*. All this time I spent wondering how Nick really felt about me and then as I'm about to get engaged he confesses his love, and it was all so confusing."

"Confusing? It sounds epic! Better than Netflix."

I laugh even as my heart plummets. I obviously didn't make the right choice, but what else could I have done? Ride off into the sunset with him?

Sorry, Mom. I know how much you wanted this for me, but I fell in love with someone else. It wasn't part of my plan or your plan for me, but Mom, I love him.

It was an impossible choice.

She pats my arm. "You've been through a lot. Take the time you need and I'm sure everything will fall into place."

I try to let her reassurance calm me, but truthfully, I'm not sure I believe in happily ever afters anymore. Those were just meant for the movies.

* * *

Eshaan calls me later that afternoon, his voice filled with sadness.

"She doesn't have much time left."

"Can I come see her?" I clutch the phone as I wait for him to reply.

"Yes. She asked to see you. That's why I'm calling."

"I'll be right there."

I leave the office early, telling my team that a family emergency came up and that I'll check in with them tomorrow. They look at me with concern and tell me they'll take care of things here. It's only been a few hours, but I relax, knowing I don't have to juggle all the balls in the air all the time. I have support.

I take an Uber straight to Eshaan's parents' house and rush inside, not even bothering to knock, and I go to his grandma's room on the main floor. I know the way by heart, having been there so many times.

Her face is sagging, and her light is quickly fading, but even so, she perks up as she sees me.

"Nisha, putt, you came."

I nod as tears stream down my face.

"Sat Sri Akal, Dadi Ji."

I sit next to her and take her hands in mine as she asks if I've eaten. She doesn't even wait for me to answer before she's calling Eshaan's mom in and ordering her to make me something. It makes me laugh inside, because only someone like her could order someone like Shaan's mom around.

She's not satisfied until she sees me have tea and sweets, and for the last time, I bring a little sweet to her mouth.

Shaan comes in and sits next to me, and we sit like that for a while as she lies down, tired already from my brief visit. She opens her eyes briefly.

"Raji khushi raho," she says, telling us to be happy together. I almost can't bear it. Then she falls asleep, and I know it's time to leave.

I say bye to Eshaan's mom, and he walks me out. "Thanks for coming."

"Of course. Thank you for letting me see her."

He looks like how I feel—destroyed. He has dark circles are under his eyes, his beard is scruffy instead of perfectly trimmed like it usually is, and his eyes are bloodshot.

"Nisha, I—" He looks remorseful, but I don't want to get into anything now.

"Shaan, focus on your Dadi. Let's not do this now."

I leave and stand in the driveway, crying as I wait for my Uber. It's hard to turn off my emotions, but still I try to turn the tap off on my heart, with him, with Nick and with everyone.

If only I didn't feel so much, this would be so much easier.

49. #NOFILTER

The next day, I leave work earlier than usual so I have time to call my mom before it gets too late. Rachel's still out, so I have the place to myself, but I wish she were here for moral support. We haven't told Eshaan's parents yet, but we will soon, and I want my mom to hear it from me first. I could put this off a little longer, but I know it will only make it harder.

I settle into the loveseat in our condo and hit Mom on my phone, tugging at my dad's necklace I wore today, hoping he'll give me the strength I need for this conversation.

"Nisha! Preeti and I were just looking at your engagement photos," she answers by way of greeting. "That one of you and Aman is so sweet."

I haven't looked at any photos, and I don't know if I ever will, but I play along. "That is a really nice one."

"How's Eshaan's Dadi?."

"She's pretty weak now."

She tuts. "At least she could be there for the Kurmai."

I pause. "Mom, I have something to tell you."

"What is it, putt?"

I hold my breath and grip the arm of the sofa.

"Eshaan and I are calling things off."

"Call it off? What does that mean?"

"We're breaking up." My heart goes up into my throat.

She's silent for so long that I pull my phone away to check that we're still connected before she finally answers.

"Why…why would you do this? So many people came for the ceremony. What will they say now?"

My shoulders stiffen. Her first thought is of strangers and not me. Not my pain or hurt, just the opinions of others. My happiness and well-being are not even an afterthought.

"I know, but I just can't stay with him."

"Is this because of that girl?"

"Yes, he's been seeing her for months, but it's not just that. I don't think we're good for each other."

"You find this out now? Why not before the ceremony? Do you know how bad this makes you look? Makes us look as a family?"

"I was confused, I know I should have stopped it sooner, but I—"

"Who will marry you now, after this beizzati?" She uses the Punjabi word for humiliation, and I wonder exactly whose humiliation she's so worried about.

I let out a long, aggravated sigh. Maybe no one, but I'm not going to carry on this dysfunctional legacy of sacrificing my life for the sake of appearances. Luckily, with my career, I don't have to.

"I'm sorry, Mom. I really am. I never wanted to disappoint you."

"Then work things out with Eshaan. His parents are good people. They're a nice family," she retorts, like it's as simple as that.

"I can't, I just can't." I shake my head vigorously even though I know she can't see me.

"Nisha, think about your future."

"That's what I'm doing, Mom. That's why I'm doing this."

Her voice turns harsh, and she starts launching into more reasons why I need to stay with Shaan, but I pull the phone away so I can't hear them. This is tough enough already.

"Mom. I need to go. I'll call you later this week." I hang up as tears overflow and my breath comes in rapid gasps.

My future?

Being alone has to be better than living a lie. Maybe I can't make her understand, but I can start living in a way that is good for me. For my heart and soul. That's what I will find a way to do, even as my heart throbs with the pain of hurting her, and my body tenses with the frustration that she just doesn't get it.

50. THE STRANGER

The week comes to an end in a blur, and when I look at the clock it's already 6 p.m. As I head out of the office, I don't want to go home and be alone. Rachel will be out late promoting this hip new restaurant she's had her eye on. She asked me if I wanted to tag along, but for the time being, I'm done smiling for the camera.

I think of that cool bar Jess and I went to months ago, and the itch to have a drink takes over. Just one to take the edge off, I tell myself.

It's close by so I walk there, and because it's early, I find a booth for two in the back. I order my usual and lean back in the chair. It's been a lot. My emotions are all over the place, and I take a moment to centre myself.

I finish the drink, and I'm contemplating another when a man comes up to me.

"Mind if I keep you company?" He's handsome in a rugged way with a dark beard and a lumberjack jacket over his muscular frame. For some reason, I find myself saying yes, even though I'm not sure I'm in the mood for company. He takes a seat before me, and we order another round.

We're talking mostly about nothing important, but he's easy to talk to and it's kind of nice to have a guy's attention and not have to worry about Eshaan telling me what a whore I am.

A nice distraction from my fucked-up life.

We keep talking, and suddenly the bar around us gets crowded, and I lose track of how many drinks we've had. When he leans over and asks if I want to go back to his place, I find myself again saying yes.

I think about how principled I've been over the years, and where it's gotten me. Engaged to a guy who's been cheating on me for months, and in love with a guy who couldn't even commit until the last moment, and who knows how long that would have even lasted.

I get up and realize I'm unsteady on my feet. Lumberjack takes my hand in his and leads me out of there, but it's crowded, and I'm stumbling as we move through the crowd and tables.

We're almost out the door when I lose his hand and stumble straight into someone else.

"Nisha?" Piercing sea blue eyes are staring back at me, and I wonder if I've finally lost my mind. "What are you doing here?"

I don't know if I say anything, but we stay like that, staring at each other until Lumberjack appears again.

"She's with me."

"She's wasted, man, seriously," Nick says in a harsh tone.

Lumberjack stands there looking at us and then makes the split decision to leave me with the altruistic stranger. He doesn't take his eyes from mine, and I forget who I was even talking to before or what I'm doing here.

"How much did you have to drink?"

"Not much," I say, but the words slur.

I finally realize that I should leave, and I try to move toward the door, but before I know it, Nick is in front of me.

"How are you getting home?"

"I'll take an Uber."

"Let me drop you off."

"No." I try to shove him away, but I realize I can't balance without him, and I end up leaning into him instead. He puts his arms around me to steady me and leads me out the door, onto the cold street, and then into his car, which is parked nearby.

I'm so tired.

"Where's your bag?"

"I don't know, I think I left it at the office."

"Is Rachel home?"

I don't why he's asking me all these questions.

"She's out dealing with a client thing until midnight."

I can barely form coherent sentences, and Nick reaches over to do my seat belt.

* * *

I wake up and we're in a parkade, but it doesn't look familiar. Nick's next to me. I realize I must have passed out while he was driving here, wherever this is.

"Where are we?"

"My place. You can sober up here, and I'll drop you off when Rachel's home."

I want to protest, but my head's spinning. He comes over to the passenger side and helps me out, walking me to the elevator on my swaying legs. I'm tipsy on my heels as we step into the building and he pulls me closer to steady me. I rest my head on his shoulder.

This is nice. I don't know why this feels so nice.

He walks me to his front door, holding me close with one arm while unlocking his door with the other and then leads me down the hall.

"You can lie down for a bit if you want."

I murmur something that sounds like, "Sure."

He practically carries me to his room and lays me on the bed. The room I wanted to visit for so long.

"I'll get you some water."

I peel off my blazer and then my stiff, uncomfortable work pants and lie down under the covers in a haze, too drunk to be self-conscious.

He comes back and stands next to me with a glass in his hand.

"Drink this."

I sit up and take a few sips of water before handing it back to him.

"I'll let you get some rest."

I reach over and grab his wrist, almost tumbling off the bed in the process.

"Lie down with me?" Now that he's here, I realize how much I missed seeing him, and I don't want him to leave.

He hesitates.

"Please."

He softens, and I shift over as he lies stiffly next to me.

"Under the covers." I don't wait for him to respond but pull the duvet around him too.

He lies back, and I wrap my legs around him, desperate to feel his warmth and his body next to mine. He holds me close. I look up at him, tracing his lips, and I see his breathing quicken.

I can't resist and push my lips onto his. He relents for a second before gently pushing me away.

"Nisha, no. You're drunk."

I run my hands down his chest and brush my fingers over the front of his pants.

"Does it matter?"

"It matters to me." He pulls my hand away, but then brings it to his lips. "Get some rest."

He makes to leave, but I hold on to him.

"Stay."

He squeezes me back.

"I'm not going anywhere."

* * *

I wake up to the smell of coffee and bacon, and for a second, I wonder where I am. My brain is foggy, and it takes a minute.

A hotel? Can't be. Home? No, Rachel doesn't eat bacon or any meat for that matter.

I rise and lean on my elbows as my mind flashes back to Lumberjack from last night, and fear grips me thinking of what might have happened, but then I remember running into Nick and him bringing me back to his place. I sag back into the bed with relief.

I'm hungover, but I want to look around the room that I've wanted to see for so long. This isn't what I had in mind when I'd imagined finally seeing it, but the universe works in mysterious ways.

It's minimal yet cozy, featuring a neutral beige chair in the corner, a king-size bed, and a dresser off to one side. The windows have the same incredible view as the living room, I assume, but the blinds are drawn closed. A crack lets the bright sunlight in, so I know it must be late.

I glance at my phone and it's almost 11 a.m. I get out of bed and see the clothes that I discarded so quickly last night lying nicely folded on the beige chair.

I get myself to the adjoining bathroom on wobbly legs, and there's a towel, T-shirt, and pants laid out for me. They must be his sister's, and I smile just thinking of her.

I slowly step into the steam shower, still woozy. I let myself linger as the hot water pours over me, washing away everything from last night, last week, and even the last month. I love being back here, even though I'm not sure what's waiting for me on the other side of the door. Maybe I could just stay in this shower forever and not worry about anything again?

I quietly walk into the hallway and linger at the kitchen doorway, taking in the sight of Nick in joggers and a tight white shirt, with a tea towel thrown over his shoulder, as he makes breakfast. Making *me* breakfast. I want to engrave this memory in my mind.

"Hey, you're up," he says, giving me a soft smile. "I'm glad the clothes fit. Lucy mentioned you were the same size."

I come and sit down at the counter stools, and I wonder what else Lucy has told him, but I don't stress as much as I usually do. I'm not hiding anything anymore, even if it's difficult.

"Breakfast smells amazing."

He hands me a freshly squeezed orange juice and coffee with cream and sugar on the side, just how I like it.

I gulp down the juice.

"Thank you for this." It doesn't feel weird being here and eating breakfast with him even now, and I can't seem to wrap my head around the fact that he always feels like exactly where I'm meant to be.

"Let's go to the table."

He moves the plates over while I take our coffees. We sit across from each other, and although I'm hungry, all I want to do is wrap my arms around him and never let him go. Instead, I bite into the salty bacon and eat the eggs in what's probably world-record time. We sit in silence as we eat, and it's fine. It's more than fine.

I help him clear up, and I know it's probably time for me to leave, but I can't move away from him. I never could.

"Can you stay for a bit? Or if you need to leave, I can drop you off somewhere," he says, much to my relief.

"I don't have anywhere to be." Breaking off an engagement and disappointing my entire family suddenly left my social calendar open all the time. Go figure.

"Come sit on the couch."

He tops up my coffee, and we take our cups over there.

"Thank you for…"

"I just wanted to…"

We speak at the same time.

"You go first," I tell him and take a sip of coffee.

He sets his cup down.

"Lucy messaged me on Wednesday morning saying she spent the day with you to try to make me jealous."

I laugh.

"I just had to get away from everything here."

"She said you were going through a bad breakup."

Two actually.

"I guess I am." I stare down at my cup, wishing it held the answers I needed within it.

He turns to face me, folding one leg up under him. "Did Eshaan hit you?" He can't keep the outrage from his voice as his eyes go dark.

"Nick, I don't want to talk about it. Please. Things with Shaan are over."

He gets up and paces the room. "I can't believe he laid a hand on you."

"It doesn't matter." I get up, too. Placing my cup next to his on the table.

"It does. No one should ever do that."

I forget that this is something he had to watch his mom endure.

"I'm okay, really, and Shaan knows he messed up."

He walks over and pulls me into a hug. "I'm so glad you're okay." I rest my head on his chest and hear his heartbeat, letting its gentle rhythm calm me.

"I missed you so much."

"I missed you too, Nick."

"What happens now?" I ask, hating myself for opening myself up to be hurt again.

He looks at me. "I'll go wherever you want, Nish. As long as we're together." He runs his thumb over my cheek. "But only if that's what you want."

I move closer. "It's the only thing I want."

It's that easy, and with him, I realize it always was.

51. US

When Shaan's Dadi Ji passes away, Shaan and I go to the funeral. It breaks my heart that I'll never again see the beautiful woman who gave me so much comfort and joy over the last year. I'm grateful to be a part of this moment, as hard as it is.

Later that week, we sit down with Eshaan's parents and break the news. His dad thinks we should try to work things out and not be so rash, and his mom lays into me, assuming of course, the breakup is my fault, and shockingly, Eshaan tells her the truth about what happened with Sonia. She stares at me with her mouth gaping open, trying to comprehend how her perfect son could do something like that. Neither of his parents have much to say after that. On my way out, Eshaan hands me my things and tells me how sorry he is about everything that happened. I believe him.

My mom is still unhappy with me, but that's not new. I decide I have to live my life for me now and not for others, even if it causes a rift between us. I hope she'll come around, but I'm not sure if she ever will. I will just have to make peace with it.

Then there's Nick. He's the brightest light in my life, and I'm so grateful we gave our relationship a chance. I'm spending most nights in his condo, and sometimes I can't believe after everything that I get to have this. To have him and to be happy.

We're not talking about the future, and that's okay because I'm enjoying every moment of the now. I know he's committed to me, and he doesn't need a ring or a fancy ceremony to prove it.

We visit Lucy often, and she comes and sees us in Vancouver too. I feel like I'm a part of his little family. His mom adores me and keeps telling Nick to lock it down, and we both just laugh. I love that she's traditional like my mom. They have that in common, and if one day they ever meet, maybe they'll discover they have so much more in common too.

I'm doing a great job leading my team, and it's quietly growing. We have even more women joining us, and when I'm not working, I'm speaking. I even landed a few gigs in Toronto, Seattle, and Minneapolis about diversity and inclusion in the workplace, but not just that, I've also shared insights on how to be a top-performing team, which is unbelievable. I never thought I could ever do anything like this or that people would want to hire me for more than just to cover the diversity angle.

Everything I've ever dreamed of is all happening, and it's even better than I imagined and I'm so grateful I leaped into the unknown.

It's where I found love.

It's where I found success.

But most importantly, it's where I found myself.

EPILOGUE

2 YEARS LATER...

I don't have a ring on my finger, but Nick and I are officially living together now, and it's glorious.

I've never felt so completely loved as I do with Nick. There were some challenges early on as I healed my heart from everything that happened, but he supported me every step of the way. Truthfully, I didn't know how to even have an adult relationship, but I've learned how to communicate my needs and share what's on my mind instead of holding back or letting my anxiety get the best of me. He did the same and shared what was coming up for him as he dealt with the trauma of his past with his dad.

He's patient and kind, and the best part? I finally know what those Bollywood movies are really about—the real reason they run singing through fields and are ready to give everything up for the one they love. It isn't because of lavish parties or celebrations, although those are fun too. It's about finding someone who loves you for you and supports you no matter what, through everything. I've learned to trust myself, to trust Nick, and to trust the universe. I know it will all work out, and it's okay if it's not on my timeline. And update—it turns out that Nick loves Bollywood too!

I stopped drinking because I realized I was using alcohol to distract myself instead of dealing with what's coming up for me. Instead, I've been working with a healer to process, and now I don't feel anxious all the time over everything. It's an easier transition than I thought it would be, with so many great zero-proof options that Nick quietly added to the liquor cabinet. He got rid of everything else.

Mom was shocked at first when I told her about Nick, but when she met him all her objections slowly melted away. On our last visit, she gave me a stern talking to. "You'll never find anyone better than him." She's right. He's perfect for me.

My mind slips back to the here and now as Nick comes to a stop in Stanley Park.

"Are you sure we have enough time for a walk before dinner?"

"Relax, it's such a beautiful evening and you're the guest of honour, so what if we keep them waiting a little?"

Sunny's in town with Kin and we arranged a get-together with all of us including Rachel, Lucy, Jess, and Matt, and I'm excited to spend time with my favourite people all in one place. Jess and Matt are officially a thing too, thanks to my office matchmaking skills. They never did get trapped in an elevator together, but I did see them coming out of the office supply closet with ruffled clothes and cheeky smiles on their faces.

Nick walks over to my side of the car and opens the door. "I told them we'll be a little late."

He always thinks of everything. I'm relieved because I hate keeping people waiting.

He holds out his hand and I take it. I adjust my sky-blue lehenga with silver embroidery that Nick encouraged me to wear tonight.

"I can't believe I'm going to be a VP," I say in awe as we start walking along the beautiful pathway right next to the ocean.

He looks at me sincerely. "I can. You deserve it."

I smile and relish his words and this achievement. My career is flourishing, and I'm even doing some consulting on the side with Rachel. It's just a side hustle for now, but maybe it could be more someday.

We walk for fifteen minutes before we sit on a bench to gaze at the ocean. I look over at him in his grey suit, his shirt the same light blue as my outfit. We complement each other perfectly.

"It's so beautiful."

He's staring at me as he says, "It is."

He reaches down to pick something up from the ground, and when I turn to see what it is, he's on one knee before me, and he takes my hand as my heart flutters uncontrollably.

"Nisha, you are the most incredible woman I have ever met, and I want nothing more than to spend the rest of my life with you and if I'm lucky enough, every one that comes after, until it's just you and me forever."

I gasp—it's finally really happening—and I break into the biggest smile as I think we're probably spending too much time with Rachel and Lucy if those are the words he's so carefully chosen for this moment. They're always going on about synchronicity, destiny, and magic. I used to laugh before, but I know in my heart now that there's a much bigger light guiding all of us.

I'm about to pull him up and say, "Yes" or "I do," or whatever you're meant to say, but he reaches into his pocket to pull out a ring and slips it on my finger. A perfect round solitaire, the one I had dreamed of all my life. Elegant, simple, beautiful.

I bring my hand to my mouth. "Oh, Nick. It's so stunning."

"Is that a yes?" He laughs.

I pull him up. "A thousand times, yes!"

He picks me up and kisses me, and I'm lost in him and the beauty of this moment when applause and warm laughter erupt behind us.

At first, I think it's some kind strangers who witnessed our special moment, but when I turn around to say thank you, Rachel, Sunny, Kin, Lucy, and Jess are rushing toward us along with Matt. He has a tripod and a camera in hand.

"Caught the whole thing!"

They wrap us in a hug, and I've never felt so fulfilled and loved.

A moment later, a ray of sunshine lands on the group of us so perfectly, and I know in my heart it's my dad, celebrating with me from wherever he is.

"Apne dil di gall suno."

His reminder to listen to my heart lands in my ears with the ocean breeze. The words he whispered to me so many times over the years.

I'm finally listening to my heart, Dad, just like you always told me to.

We stay like that for too long, and we probably look like a bunch of weirdos, group-hugging on a Wednesday evening, but for once, I don't care what anyone else thinks.

I'm alive.

I'm loved.

And I finally have everything I ever wanted.

Can't get enough of Nisha?

Access bonus content including the *Everything She Wanted* playlist when you sign up for Rosey's Love List at roseykaurhwang.com.

ACKNOWLEDGEMENTS

To my incredible husband, Michael, my real-life Prince Charming. Thank you for encouraging me to write from day one. I'll never forget the custom Starbucks card you made me nearly twenty years ago, with the title "Author" next to my name. It's because of you all I want to write about is love.

To my darling daughters, who inspire me endlessly to pursue my dreams. You're the reason I believe anything is possible. I wrote this book to show you the magic that unfolds when you follow your heart and live your purpose. May you listen to its quiet nudges always.

To my beautiful mom. You showed me from a very young age what it means to be a strong, independent woman, and that left a lasting impression on me. Thank you for teaching me that pyaar naal sab kuch mil janda. You're right, love does give you everything. I feel so blessed to have you as my mom. Thank you for supporting me even now from where you are.

Chloee Teng, thank you for asking to pre-order eleven copies before I had even written a single word, beta reading my manuscript even though you've never read romance, and flying in to support me not once, but multiple times. You didn't doubt me for even one second, and your faith in me gave me so much faith in myself. You're the best friend I've ever had, Chloee, and I'm so grateful for your presence in my life.

Sarah Woods, my dearest mentor and cherished friend, thank you for being there for me through the laughter and the tears, and saying, "Rosey, you got this," when I needed to hear it most. I'm beyond grateful for your support in helping me *be* the love that I came here to be. Here's to letting our beautiful hearts shine brightly.

Shelley Mahon, my dear sweet friend, thank you for being the first person to read *Everything She Wanted* and then reading it again multiple times after each iteration. I deeply appreciate your thoughtful feedback and the care you took in looking over my manuscript. I adore you, Shelley, and I'll always cherish our friendship.

Thank you to the incredible team at Sugar Shack Books: Genevieve Loughlin, Mo Duffy, Alison Strumberger, Ashley Macdonald, and Jordan Beaulieu for seeing the magic of this story. With your support, I've been able to share it with the world better than I ever imagined.

With so much gratitude to Erin Craig, my amazing cover designer. I had a vision that the book cover would be pink, but what you created is beyond anything I envisioned. Thank you for capturing the heart of my story and the essence of my characters so beautifully.

To my global clients, including the most remarkable heart-led founders, conscious entrepreneurs, and soulful visionaries: Thank you for supporting every version of me. I'm so grateful that I got to be a part of your dream and now you're a part of mine.

Thank you, Bebe Ji, Nikka Mama Ji, and Vaddi Mami Ji, for supporting me from heaven. Everything I adore about you made its way into this book so that you may live forever among its pages.

To my Messy First Draft writing group at the Alexandra Writers' Centre Society: Thank you for being my biggest cheerleaders from my very first draft to today. I'll never forget how you broke out into applause when I shared that I finished my manuscript and celebrated each milestone with me as if it were your own. MFD forever!

To my online community who've encouraged me through every shift—of which there have been many, lol—thank you. Your likes, comments, messages, and emails, as I embrace my full expression and my deepest purpose, are everything. May witnessing my journey inspire you on yours.

With infinite gratitude to you, my beautiful reader. I dreamed of you holding this book in your hands and imagined you reading every word. Whatever season of life this story finds you in, may it help you remember that you are deserving, worthy, and meant for all that you desire.

Xo,
Rosey

P.S. Universe, you were right: This is beyond my wildest dreams. I'm so grateful for every single moment.

ABOUT THE AUTHOR

Rosey Kaur Hwang writes binge-worthy contemporary romance novels that are all heart yet unconventional, taking women deeper into the places within themselves that prevent them from living their own fairy tale. Off the page, she guides writers to bring their stories to life and into the world through her Acceleration Coaching and intentional digital marketing. When she isn't writing or supporting her global clients, you'll find her tucked inside a local coffee shop sipping a chai latte, curating dreamy playlists for her books, or savouring time with her husband and daughters. *Everything She Wanted* is her debut novel.

For inspiration on following your heart and living your dreams, connect with Rosey on Instagram @xoroseyhwang or visit roseykaurhwang.com to learn more.